I0676541

M'tak Ka'fek

Doug L. Hoffman

ISBN 978-0-9884588-7-1

Published by
The Resilient Earth Press
http://resilientearthpress.com

Books By Doug L. Hoffman

The T'aafhal Inheritance Trilogy
Parker's Folly
Peggy Sue
M'tak Ka'fek

Non-fiction (with Allen Simmons)
The Resilient Earth
The Energy Gap

Preface

This is the third book in my promised trilogy about Earthlings finding their place in the galaxy. As many people have noticed, the T'aafhal Inheritance contains a number of plot devices that have been used before—the discovery of an ancient space ship full of advanced technology, human development being guided by aliens, mysterious evil alien overlords, etc. Yes, you are exactly right, but then there are only so many story lines in all of literature, let-alone in science fiction. I said from the start that I was going to write traditional science fiction, the type I grew up reading, and I have done just that. I make no apology for stealing plot ideas from previous authors going all the way back to Homer.

More to the point has been criticism of the events at the end of the second book, *Peggy Sue*, where Earth is laid waste by an alien attack. In the preface of the first book in the series, *Parker's Folly*, I expressed my disdain for what I termed dark, gloomy portrayals of post industrial dystopias, yet I went and destroyed the world. Not exactly. This novel is not about mucking about in the ruins of man's civilization, it is about humanity (and some polar bears) rising phoenix like from the ashes—not that there aren't challenges and mortal danger. Look at it this way, at least global warming is no longer a problem.

I would also like to say a word about military ranks. I have heard from a number of readers calling out the abbreviations that I have used for the ranks of various characters. Military ranks vary from country to country and among services within a country. For example, in the Royal Navy a low ranking officer might be a sub-lieutenant, while in the U.S. Navy this rank is called a lieutenant junior grade (JG). The abbreviation for the lowest officer rank, American designation O-1, is 2d Lt, 2LT, 2ndLt or ENS in the U.S. Air Force, Army, Marine Corp or Navy, respectively. I have tried to be faithful to the branch of service of the characters and use the appropriate abbreviation. However, I find that the U.S. Navy use of all capitals in their abbreviations looks disruptive on a printed page so I have used mixed case versions: Lcdr for LCDR, Capt. for CAPT, etc. The other thing to note is that when the Marines refer to Lt. Bear as LT it should be read as "el tee," slang for lieutenant, not an abbreviation.

i

Again, I must thank the multitude of friends and family members who helped me in writing this book. Heartfelt thanks go out to Rik Faith, Bobby Johnson, David Metheny, Clayton Ward, and Jesse Perkins, who provided many corrections and suggestions. Special thanks to Darina Semenova for help with Russian language idioms. The book was much improved by their efforts.

With any such enterprise, it is customary to dragoon one's family into reviewing (or at least listening to readings of) the book in progress. My mother Mary and sister Melinda both offered enthusiastic support which was greatly appreciated. The number of early readers is far too large to list them all here, but I did appreciate every review and word of encouragement.

I would also like to thank Allen Simmons, my coauthor on two previous works of non-fiction: *The Resilient Earth* and *The Energy Gap*. Al got me addicted to writing in the first place so, if you enjoy *M'tak Ka'fek*, at least some of the credit belongs to Al.

Lastly I would like to dedicate this book to my father, Clair J. Hoffman, who passed away while it was being written. It was he who taught me that life was an adventure and to never stop looking for new things to try. His book of autobiographical tales, *Son Of A Coal Miner*, was the first book I ever helped publish, so he was at the root of my foray into publishing and writing.

This, of course, brings us to the obligatory disclaimers: all the characters in this book are fictional, not representations of any real person, living or dead; Any mistakes in the science, cosmology, engineering, etc. are purely my own and not the responsibility any of those thanked above. The book was written using LibreOffice4 and the cover art done using the GIMP. Ebook formatting was done using Calibre. This is the final book of the T'aafhal Inheritance trilogy, following *Parker's Folly* and *Peggy Sue*. I have greatly enjoyed writing these books and I hope that you derive some small pleasure reading them.

Regards,
Doug L. Hoffman
Conway, Arkansas
October 8, 2013

For my father,
Clair John Hoffman

Prologue

Kansas, a week after the sky fell

Clem stood on the back of the tricycle, peering into the drizzling grayness. Around him were the scorched remains of Kansas, charred wheat fields stretching off to the hazy horizon. The trike was his only major worldly possession, built by his own hands out of the engine and rear-end of an old Volkswagen and the front-end of a wrecked chopper. Its wooden body boasted three fiberglass bucket seats and a sign on the rear that read "Jesus is coming, act busy."

He hadn't seen Jesus, but this sure seemed like the end of days to Clem. Seven days ago the world came apart when gigantic meteors fell from the sky all around the globe. At least that is what the radio stations had said before they went silent. Since then there had been no radio, no TV, no word from the outside world except a brief message that Doc Lewis picked up on his short wave that said there was an enclave of survivors somewhere down in Texas.

That was where they were headed, a little band of survivors from a small town in southern Nebraska. Thirteen in all, a baker's dozen of frightened people whose world had been turned upside down in a single day when hell had come to Earth. After the tremors, the sky turned black and fire rained down from the heavens—ejected debris from the major impact in the Great Lakes region reentering the planet's atmosphere. Houses and corn fields were set alight in Nebraska, and evidently here in Kansas as well.

Just when the whole world seemed on fire the rain came—torrents of rain mixed with ash and dust, extinguishing most of the fires and coating everything with gray mud. After three days the deluge eased, replaced by leaden skies and seemingly perpetual drizzle. That was when the survivors decided to head south, seeking shelter and others who may have lived through the great calamity that had befallen their world.

"See 'em back there?" asked Lem, siting in the left side seat, huddled in a poncho against the drizzle. Lemuel Souther was Clem's best friend and riding companion. He had been visiting when the sky fell, having lost his last job as a motorcycle mechanic in Des

1

Moines. Not that Lem was a bad mechanic, but a combination of the bad economy and a fondness for weed led to his dismissal and subsequent trip to visit his old friend Clement Mathews in Nebraska. A fortunate thing too, since Des Moines and every other human habitation within 500 miles of the Great Lakes was wiped out by a primary impact.

"Yeah, I think I see movement back down our trail," replied Clem, climbing down from his perch. "With this ash and mud everywhere it ain't hard for anybody to track us."

"We're about the only people out here," Lem observed, "'cept for those murderin' scumbags that's following us." Two days ago, the Nebraska survivors' caravan—three SUVs, an RV and Clem's trike—came upon what looked like a police roadblock on the state road headed south. As usual, Clem and Lem were riding point and got a better look at what was happening up ahead. There were several cruisers with lights flashing and figures wearing smoky the bear hats motioning to an approaching SUV to stop.

Hopes of finding a vestige of civilization were quickly crushed when they saw a family being dragged from the stopped vehicle by the supposed police officers. As the two refugees watched with growing horror they saw a man, presumably the father, forced to his knees. The kneeling man was then summarily shot in the head while his wife and daughter were dragged, struggling behind the police cars. Another younger man, perhaps a son, got out of the vehicle and tried to intervene. He was also shot by one of the "police."

Clem turned the trike around and sped back to the rest of the survivors' little caravan. Informed of what happened at the roadblock, they decided to give it a wide berth. The survivors quickly backtracked a few miles and headed down a different road, hoping to leave the false police and their hapless victims behind. Unfortunately, a few hours later Margery Lewis, Doc's wife and nurse, noticed that they were being followed.

For a night and half a day they had been running from the pursuing blockaders, whose number also included a clutch of national guardsmen in a pair of Humvees. At least one of the military vehicles had a large machine gun mounted on top with a man sticking up through the roof hanging on to it. Why these former protectors of society had gone rogue, turning on the people they were sworn to protect, was anyone's guess. Now that the thin veneer of civilization had been stripped away, brigandage must have seemed more appealing than trying to protect the helpless and hold back chaos.

The fleeing survivors had hoped to lose their pursuers overnight, careening down darkened roads with their headlights off, pausing only to refill their gas tanks from jerrycans brought from home. Now they were running out of gas and running out of time.

After a quick consultation with the returning trike riders, the caravan members decided to circle their vehicles and make a last stand against their pursuers. Don and Sue Fredrick and their two children got out of their Jeep Grand Caravan and Don handed out weapons—a lever action 30-30 for his wife, and a pair of .22 rifles for their son and daughter, keeping a .300 Winchester hunting rifle for himself. The others in the pathetic little band were similarly armed with a hodgepodge of hunting weapons and small arms.

Clem and Lem were the best armed, each brandishing a Chinese made SKS rifle with after-market 30 round magazines. Both had put in time in the Army, enough time to know that they didn't stand a chance against the big .50 caliber M2 machine gun on the bandits' Humvee. Demonstrating a good grasp of the tactical situation, Sue told her husband, "Don, you use that hunting rifle and take out the man on the machine gun first."

Don grunted in reply and fiddled with the scope adjustments on his rifle.

"Well, buddy, I think we've run outta time," said Clem to his friend. Neither of them considered running out on the others in the caravan.

"It was borrowed time at best, Clem. If there is any justice left in the world we'll take a couple of those bastards with us."

"Yeah, I think we need to be sure that the kids don't fall into their hands either," he said quietly. The two friends' eyes met in silent agreement—they could both still remember the screams of the young girl at the roadblock as they sped away. If, make that when, they were overrun they would kill the children if they were still alive.

3

"What's that?" asked young Don Jr. holding his .22 rifle tightly. There was a low thrumming sound, barely audible above the gusting wind.

"Probably the Humvee," said Doc, hunkering down behind a fender, 12 gauge shotgun in hand.

"No, that," Don Jr. replied, pointing at a dark shape moving through the low clouds a few hundred feet above the sodden gray landscape. Whatever the dark shape was it was moving rapidly and quickly disappeared from sight.

"Get ready everyone," called Sam Jenkins, driver of the fancy Lexus SUV. Sam was the town's lawyer and mayor. He had been made mayor mainly because no one else wanted the job and, as mayor, he provided the town with free legal services. His wife Amy, the town librarian, was huddled next to the side of their truck, almost catatonic.

The thrumming sound returned, growing louder. A large dark shape materialized out of the swirling clouds, descending into the space between the fearful refugees and the pursuing murderers. As the refugees looked on the brigands' column halted and the heavy machine gun on top of the lead Humvee began firing.

"What the hell is that?" Lem asked not really expecting an answer. Several of the survivors shrank down behind their vehicles, but Lem could tell from the angle of the .50 cal's barrel that it was not firing at them. It was firing at the huge dark shape hanging in the air between them.

There was a loud ripping sound, like a gigantic band-saw amplified nearly to the point of pain. A stream of green fire reached out from the dark shape to play across the pursuers' position. The brigands' vehicles disappeared behind a curtain of bright explosions, accompanied by the sound of rolling thunder. When the sound ceased, the pursuers were gone, save for a few pieces of smoking debris falling back to the ground more than a hundred yards away.

"I guess that takes care of that problem," said Clem.

"And maybe swapped it for a bigger one," added Lem

"Don't borrow trouble, boys," said Doc, slowly standing up from cover behind his RV.

"Be careful, Eustis," added Marge, the only one who called Doc by his given name.

"Marge, if that thing wants us dead we're dead," he answered.

The large dark aircraft pivoted, presenting its blunt back-end to the little band of survivors. Mud, water and dirt flew, escaping from beneath the craft as it descended. It settled to the ground on landing legs that extended just before touchdown, sinking at least a foot into the rain soaked field. The thrumming sound ceased, replaced by random popping and creaking noises.

A muted whine heralded the opening of a wide door, folding outward to form a ramp. Even before it touched ground, the first of four dark figures trotted down the ramp. Roughly seven feet tall and wider than any man, the giant figures looked like something out of a video game. Instead of moving toward the refugees, the armored figures fanned out and formed a perimeter, facing outward, cradling what could only be weapons.

"Are those people?" asked Josephine Fredrick, Don's sister.

"Or the aliens who blew up the planet!" responded Don Jr.

A fifth dark shape moved down the ramp, this one larger than the first ones and moving on all fours. It loped down the ramp and continued ten yards toward the huddled survivors. There it stood up on its hind legs, ten feet tall, and surveyed the scene. Evidently satisfied, the creature sat down on its haunches.

"See, they are aliens!" yelled Don Jr., raising his rifle to his shoulder and firing a round at the huge figure sitting in front of them.

"Don!" shouted both his parents in horror, as the bullet glancing off the alien's faceless metallic head, the ricochet whining off into the distance. The entire band of survivors froze in place, awaiting the strangers' retribution.

The large stranger's "head" turned transparent, revealing a furry white profile inside. With a long snout and black nose the creature looked for the world like a polar bear. "Nice shot, Kid," a deep contralto voice said, "now please put your weapons down before you folks hurt yourselves."

As the survivors lowered their weapons, the bear said, "things are secure, you can come out, Lieutenant."

In response to the bear's call a more human sized figure emerged from the ship—a woman wearing a space suit with a transparent bubble helmet. The woman's complexion was dark, her face thin with a long straight nose and high cheekbones. Her head was helmeted by closely clipped, dark curly hair and her smile was dazzlingly white against her ebony skin. When she spoke it was with a noticeable English accent.

"Good afternoon, I am Lieutenant Melaku. It appears that you people could use some assistance."

Part One

We Have Met The Enemy...

Chapter 1

Task Force Alpha, the Kuiper Belt

Quiet tension filled the bridge of the Peggy Sue, Earth's most powerful warship. More significantly, the Peggy Sue was Earth's only starship, a fact not lost on her captain, Commander Gretchen Curtis. Commander Curtis had been the ship's first officer on two previous voyages and had been in command during her last action.

Pursued by aliens of unknown origin, they had to fight their way out of the Sirius system. In doing so, they left behind a number of crewmates and the ship's original captain, Jack Sutton, stranded on a derelict alien space cruiser. Captain Jack and his skeleton crew evidently managed to get the four million year old warship into action as the Peggy Sue ran for home and safety.

Arriving back in the solar system, safety was not what they found. While they had been away, a gigantic alien vessel had entered the system in a sneak attack on Earth. It unleashed a massive bombardment of asteroids, pummeling the planet and killing much of the human race. The planet's ecology was ravaged and its climate plunged into chaos. Scientists from Farside Base said that it was likely that the material ejected into Earth's atmosphere would trigger a new glaciation—what non-scientists would call an ice age.

But the aliens evidently did not think the destruction of humanity's home world complete, for they continued on into the Kuiper Belt to gather more asteroids to hurl at the stricken planet. Many among the crew, and from the moon base as well, wanted the Peggy Sue to immediately pursue the alien vessel, but Captain Curtis knew that was not the proper course of action. To be sure, there were times when a quick reaction was called for, and sometimes a quick reaction could win the day. But Gretchen was sure that this was not one of those times.

Gretchen recalled the words of her mentor and friend, Captain Jack Sutton. Jack had quoted a saying from a 19th century French chemist named Louis Pasteur: "Chance favors the prepared mind." *How was it that Jack rephrase it? "It takes careful preparation to be able to act impulsively."*

With Captain Jack missing and Earth under continued threat there was nothing else that could be done—things at home must be put in order before any impulsive mission of revenge. The wounded members of the crew were transferred to Farside Base, along with members of the science section and all their data. It was that data and those scientists who held the key to Earth's future defense. Also deposited at Farside was NatHanGon, ambassador to Earth from the strange inhabitants of Gliese 581d. The Triads, long lived, highly intelligent, trisexual plants, were the only alien race discovered so far that was not openly hostile to Earth creatures.

Trips were made to the shattered planet below to recruit new personnel among the survivors, and to salvage irreplaceable scientific equipment and genetic samples. Pilots and crewmembers participated as a way to stay active while in port and as a way to help those few who survived. New crewmembers were added and immediately engaged in intensive training—drills to increase their proficiency with Peggy Sue's weapons and internal systems.

Munitions and other supplies were loaded, new armored shuttles were added along with a larger compliment of Marines. Then, satisfied that things at Farside were stabilized, at least to the greatest extent possible under the circumstances, Captain Curtis took the Peggy Sue in pursuit of those trying to kill her planet.

Accompanying the Peggy Sue were four of the six small ships built by Farside shipyard during the former's absence. Not intended for long interstellar voyages, they were the only other combat craft in humanity's arsenal. If the Peggy Sue was the size of a Navy destroyer then the corvettes, as they were officially designated, were more the size of PT boats. That was a moniker their six man crews adopted with pride.

Once it became clear that the moon base powers-that-be would not allow all of them to join the hunt for the alien invader, the PT boat crews drew lots to decide which of them would accompany the Peggy Sue. Those who lost were greatly disappointed—everyone wanted to get some payback for the surprise attack on Earth.

Those titularly in charge of humanity's space defense force consisted of a council of billionaire industrialists, who had backed the construction of the Peggy Sue and Farside Base, and senior scientific advisers, who had signed on to the project when its primary aim was to take mankind into space on a permanent basis. At least that was the publicized mission. Those in the inner circle, led by former Texas oil-man TK Parker, knew the real story behind the construction of the Peggy Sue, her amazingly advanced technology and the real purpose for her initial trip to the Moon.

Decades ago Parker came into possession of an ancient device of alien origin, found in a mountain on the Arabian peninsula. Spending years of effort, and a significant part of his fortune, Parker managed to assemble a team of scientists who discovered how to access the device known as "the artifact." The device turned out to be the long-term memory store for a self-aware alien computer—an Artificial Intelligence or AI. From it they learned many marvelous things, and several shocking things.

Things about the origins of mankind and why certain polar bears can talk. Things about the history of the galaxy and an ancient war fought millions of years ago. Things about the destiny of bears and humans and the mysterious creatures known as the Dark Lords. But there would be time to ponder all those things later. Right now, Peggy Sue's pitifully small armada was closing in on the enemy at hand.

As if on cue, Lt. Billy Ray Vincent called out from the helm "Captain, we have the enemy on targeting sensors and are closing at 14,000 m/sec. We should be able to disable their propulsion systems with the main railguns on the first pass."

They had been observing the alien ship for days with Peggy Sue's two meter optical telescope, using light from the infrared to the ultraviolet. The ship was a monster over five kilometers long with a swollen head where it carried captured asteroids for dropping on its targets. Based on the ship's IR signature, the main propulsion systems were located in the aft portion of the intruder. There were also signs from neutrino emissions that a cache of antimatter was stored just forward of the engines. The plan of attack called for the PT boats to sweep the hull forward while the Peggy Sue disabled the enemy's maneuvering capability.

More problematic was the second phase of the attack, which called for two assault shuttles full of Marines to board the disabled ship and secure its antimatter stores—assuming the invader survived the initial attack. A secondary objective was to try and identify any

11

computer navigation equipment from which the location of the attackers' home system might be ascertained.

A distant third priority was to capture any aliens left alive for interrogation. The Triad ambassador, NatHanGon, was positive that any spacefaring race would know at least one of the ancient trading languages and that communication with any prisoners could be established no matter what their mode of interchange. The Earthlings were not so sanguine.

"Steady on Mr. Vincent, bring the main battery online," the Captain ordered. The main battery consisted of two railguns that ran almost the full length of the ship itself. Because of this arrangement, the railguns were aimed by pointing the entire ship, an action under the control of the helmsmen. Billy Ray, the XO, had more experience piloting the ship than anyone else and would be at the controls during the attack.

"Mr. Medina, make ready all shields and secondary weapon systems; gunnery crews and torpedomen look alive," Curtis ordered. Unlike the main battery, the secondary X-ray laser batteries and the torpedo launchers were targeted independently by their own crews.

"Aye aye, Captain," responded Jo Jo Medina, the ship's chief engineer. Lt. Medina had been with the Peggy Sue from the beginning and was among Earth's most seasoned space war veterans.

"All weapons manned and ready, Captain," announced a subtly feminine voice. It was the voice of the ship's computer, a highly capable but non self-aware quantum device based on alien technology. Interfaced with part of the artifact's memory system, the ship's computer was constantly discovering new information left by its builders—a long dead race known as the T'aafhal.

"Peggy Sue, send a message to Farside: Enemy in sight, maneuvering to engage."

"Yes, Captain."

It was after the last great battle of the long war against the Dark Lords, four million years ago, that a badly damaged T'aafhal battleship took refuge on Earth and set in motion events that would eventually lead to the evolution of a bellicose, intelligent native species—*Homo sapiens*. The aliens' goal was to create a race to succeed themselves as defenders of the Galaxy's warm life. How well the plan succeeded was about to be demonstrated, for the aliens who had attacked Earth were about to find out just how bellicose Earth-creatures could be.

"Task-force Alpha, Peggy Sue," Captain Curtis signaled, "We will be in position to begin our initial attack run in five minutes, on my computer's mark."

Cargo Hold, Peggy Sue

Standing in silent ranks, like graphite statuary, Peggy Sue's Marine contingent observed the developing tactical situation on their suits' heads-up displays. Normally, the ship carried twelve human and two ursine Marines, but this time there were four times that many on board. There would have been more but that was all that could be squeezed into the ship's two large landing shuttles. The task of leading the Marine boarding party fell to Captain Jennifer Rodriguez.

Capt. Rodriguez, newly promoted from the ranks, had been with the Peggy Sue from the beginning and had participated in every major battle fought with aliens so far. She had been the gunnery sergeant of a squad of Marines originally sent to capture the Peggy Sue but ended up leading the ship's Marines on both its interstellar voyages. The only action she missed was the first skirmish beneath Crater Giordano Bruno.

Since she was the senior Marine with the most extensive extraterrestrial combat experience, Rodriguez was commissioned directly as a captain so she could command the boarding assault. She had still not come totally to grips with becoming an officer, but fortunately mustangs—officers promoted from the enlisted ranks— had a long history in the U.S. Marine Corps. One of the newer crew members made the mistake of wondering aloud if Rodriguez deserved such a promotion in front of Senior Chief Zackly.

"Listen, you snot-nosed excuse for a sailor. There ain't many things more aggressive than a Marine Gunnery Sergeant except maybe a Marine Captain," the grizzled Chief replied. "The first is too mean to quit and the second will just as soon shoot you and get

13

it over with. So yous better watch yer mouth in front of Captain Rodriguez."

The boarding party itself was organized into four fourteen member squads, each leavened with a few veterans from the ship's previous engagements. Not that the new Marines were untested in battle—they had come from the SAS, U.S. Army Rangers, Russian Spetsnaz, Australian Commandos, Navy SEALS and U.S. Marines—combat veterans all. Most had been rescued from untenable positions on Earth following the alien bombardment. All were given the choice of being repatriated ground-side or of joining the fight against the marauding aliens that had tried to snuff out humanity. Some chose to try and salvage their lives and their countries back on Earth, but most chose the chance to strike back.

Jennifer would personally lead 1st and 2nd squads in Shuttle One while Shuttle Two would carry 3rd and 4th squads, led by Lieutenant Westfield. Westfield was also a former U.S. Marine, a Lieutenant Colonel, and therein lies a tale...

* * * * *

The mountain passes of the Hindu Kush, an 800 km (500 mi) long mountain range that stretches between central Afghanistan and northern Pakistan, are some of the most desolate and isolated on Earth. The range separates the basins of the Kabul and Helmand rivers from that of the Amu River, known in ancient times as the Oxus. There has been a military presence in the mountains since the time of Darius the Great. Over millennia foreign armies marched into the Kush only to return shattered and defeated. The armies of Alexander the Great, the British Empire, the USSR and, most recently, the United States of America left their blood on the arid slopes of those jagged peaks. Even when the belligerent natives did not attack, the mercurial weather could strike an army down. In 1750, the army of Ahmad Shah, retreating from Persia, is said to have lost 18,000 men from the cold in a single night.

In a remote pass northeast of Kabul the remains of a battalion of U.S. Marines was fighting for its life, fleeing from an impromptu coalition of Taliban, foreign al-Qaeda and opportunistic locals. Being far inland and a good distance from the nearest asteroid impact, the Kush suffered only secondary effects from the space-borne attack—the aliens primarily targeted heavily populated littoral regions. Meteor showers from ejected material reentering Earth's atmosphere were followed by ash and heavy overcast that triggered early snowfalls.

More critical from the Marines' point of view was the total destruction of the chain of command. Contact with the outside world simply ceased, along with air and logistics support. In effect, the battalion was cutoff from the world in a matter of a few hours, left abandoned among a superstitious, hostile population who blamed the presence of foreigners for the frightening, unnatural events unfolding around them.

LtCol Reginald "Dirk" Westfield first attempted to move his Marines southwest, toward Kabul and the larger UN forces stationed around the Afghan capital, but ran into heavy resistance and blinding snow storms. Given little choice, he reversed his march and led his battalion back to the northeast, higher into the mountains. Understrength at only 300 Marines, they fought a running battle as they retreated.

Two days later the battalion was down to fewer than 200 effectives, those bone tired and freezing. In keeping with Marine tradition, they carried their dead and wounded with them, hoping against hope for evacuation or at least safe haven. Running into armed men in front of their line of march, the harassed group of Marines pulled back into a side valley where they faced their pursuers on a narrower front.

Soon they were being pushed back, farther up the narrowing valley. The Colonel ordered his men to dig in, though the frozen ground offered little purchase. It had started snowing again and visibility dropped to a dozen meters. The Colonel called his remaining officers together to plan what was probably their last stand.

Known as Dirk to his colleagues—he never really liked the name Reginald and despised "Reggie"—the Colonel had only recently taken command of the battalion. The rumor was that he had been a fast riser who put a foot wrong back in the States and had been banished to the wilds of Afghanistan as punishment. That story was half true: LtCol Westfield had been in command of the Marines who captured and incarcerated the squad from the Peggy Sue when they returned after the starship's first voyage.

His treatment of the returning Marines had been less than collegial, leading to bad blood between Peggy Sue's Marines and their former comrades in arms. When the squad, led by then GySgt Jennifer Rodriguez, was rescued from under the noses of the Colonel and around 40,000 other Marines stationed at Camp Lejeune, it was decided to put those directly involved with the internment on ice. Westfield and his men were sent to the most remote location possible, hence the Colonel's arrival in the mountains of the Hindu Kush in time for the end of the world.

The reason for his being located in the asshole of the world not withstanding, he was actually a pretty good Marine—his only concern at present was trying to save the lives of his men. Unfortunately, there seemed little hope for escape from their predicament, being surrounded by Afghanistan on three sides and angry Afghans on the other.

"We need to find some cover, ASAP," the Colonel said to his subordinates. "The locals are probably going to try and overrun us as soon as they gather sufficient strength."

"There's not much cover to be had, Sir," replied one of the Lieutenants. Westfield's second in command, a Major, was among the wounded, by now possibly among dead.

"The men can't hardly dig in this frozen shit, Sir," the First Sergeant said. "We can use what little cover nature put here and stack gear to fill in some of the gaps." *It's not going to do any good,* was the Sergeant's unvoiced conclusion.

As the Marine officers conferred sporadic gunfire could be heard —the crack of AK47s and the higher pitched snap of M4s returning fire. The snowfall eased and, as visibility improved a bit, native fighters could be seen working their way up the surrounding ridgeline. Soon the Marines would be totally encircled and enfiladed by their foes. Westfield thought he heard a low thrumming sound over the incessant moaning of the wind. Straining his hearing, he longed to identify the sound of rescuing aircraft, but then dismissed it out of hand as wishful thinking.

"What the hell is that?" demanded the Lieutenant, his extended arm pointing up slope to the detachment's rear.

16

"I don't know," replied the First Sergeant, turning to follow the Lieutenant's gesture, "but it sure wasn't there a few minutes ago."

"Is it some kind of helo?"

"I didn't hear any rotors or engine noise," said Dirk, focusing on the large dark shape 200 meters behind their position. "Sergeant! Get some of the men to cover that thing, but do not fire until we find out if it is a friendly."

"Yes, Sir!"

The Sergeant moved down slope, shouting orders to the nearest Marines, who quickly positioned themselves to cover the strange craft. As they watched a large door opened, dropping down and outward to form a ramp wide enough for a Humvee to drive up. Before the ramp even touched the ground large dark figures descended, looking like something from a video game or Hollywood SciFi movie.

"Holly shit!" said one of the Marines, "are we in Halo 9?"

"Maybe we got bigger problems than the towel-heads," replied another.

"Belay the chatter and keep them things covered," snapped the Sergeant. "Sir, are you seeing this?"

Before the Colonel could reply several muffled thumps were heard, like a door being repeatedly slammed in the distance—the sound of heavy mortars being fired. Someone yelled "Incoming!" and the Marines hugged the ground for all they were worth. From the dark craft behind them came a crackling sound and overhead a number of detonations—the mortar rounds exploding ineffectively in the air.

As mortar fragments rained down on the Marines' positions, their fatal energy already spent, a pair of odd six-wheeled vehicles emerged from the sides of the unidentified intruder. One went to either flank and opened up with what sounded like mini-guns on the locals along the ridge tops. Again the crackling sound could be heard, followed by more aerial mortar shell detonations.

"They seem to be attacking the locals, Sir," said the Lieutenant, stating the obvious. "Does that make 'em friendlies?"

17

"That thing looks like some kind of transport. We need to see if they can get us off this damned mountain. Tell the men to pull back toward the aircraft!"

"What if they are hostile, Sir?"

"If they are they can shoot us," Dirk shouted, *because that is surely what the Taliban will do if we stay here*. He turned and started moving up slope toward the beckoning craft. As the Marines advanced another of the robot like figures descended the ramp and stood as if waiting for their arrival.

As Dirk neared the figure he noticed that it was constructed of a gray-black, graphite colored material. It's limbs and joint areas were banded by strips of varying widths—from half a centimeter to several. Its head was a smooth bubble, seemingly made of the same gray material; covering its chest and around its waist were straps, pouches and pieces of gear. Cradled across its chest was a very large, very nasty looking multi-barreled weapon of some kind.

As the Colonel neared the imposing, seven foot figure he lowered his M4, letting it hang from its carry strap. *I don't think these fellows are from around here*, he thought. Holding up both arms, hands open in what he hoped was a universal sign of non-aggression, he called out, "I am LtCol Dirk Westfield of the United States Marine Corps. I don't know if you can understand me, but we are under attack by indigenous hostiles and need shelter."

The figure stood like a statue, the only sound the wind whistling through the jagged peaks and the crackle of small arms fire in the distance. After several interminable seconds a voice issued from the statue.

"Your name is Dirk?" the dark figure asked.

"Yes." the Marine replied.

"Your mother actually named you Dirk?" the figure reiterated.

"Ah, actually my first name is Reginald," Dirk replied, confused by the cross examination. He was not sure what kind of response to expect but that was not it. *Why would some space alien care what my name is?*

"Well, Reggie, it would seem that balance has been restored to the force," the alien continued. "And I always thought that karma crap was, well, crap."

Now Dirk was totally confused. *This conversation cannot be happening, maybe I'm hallucinating from lack of sleep and altitude sickness.* As the befuddled Colonel stood in front of his towering interlocutor the rest of the battalion's Marines were assembling just down slope from the alien craft. The sound of small arms fire drew nearer.

"I never did catch your name during our previous encounter, Colonel. Of course, you weren't too keen on conversation at the time." As the figure spoke its "head" turned transparent to reveal the head of a woman inside.

"My God," Dirk exclaimed, "you're the gunnery sergeant from that squad of Marines, the ones who came back from the renegade spaceship."

"Right the first time, Reggie," Jennifer Rodriguez replied. "I guess I shouldn't be surprised you never learned my name either. You know, I have had dreams about what I would do to you if our paths ever crossed again."

His mind raced. *This must be some kind of cosmic payback, retribution for my past sins. But I was under orders not to talk with the returnees any more than necessary—and not to let them talk to anyone else. Hell, for all we knew they were aliens made up to look like Marines. Not that it will make any difference to the pissed off woman in front of me.*

The sound of gunfire continued to draw closer, his men continued to fight and die. The Colonel sank to his knees and pleaded, "Do what you want with me, Sergeant, but for God's sake save my Marines."

Jennifer's eyes narrowed and her head tilted to one side, as if she was seeing him in a different light. "That, Colonel, was the correct response," the former gunnery sergeant, now Captain, said. Keying her suit radio, Jennifer gave orders to the rest of her Marines and the shuttle crew: "All right people, let's get these poor refugees on board—and disarm them as they board. I do not want any accidents on the trip back to base."

19

"Aye aye, Ma'am," replied newly promoted GySgt Washington for the rest of the squad, motioning the embattled Marines forward with a wave of his armored arm. The two battle bots and several of the armored space Marines moved down slope along the refugees' flanks, laying down a murderous wave of fire to cover the extraction.

"Thank you," Dirk said, hanging his head and sighing in relief. "Thank you."

* * * * *

The rescued Marine battalion was delivered to Farside Base 12 hours later, where the survivors were fed and bedded down after the welcome luxury of a long hot shower. The penitent LtCol Westfield was debriefed by Commander Curtis and Captain Rodriguez. In the end, Dirk volunteered for duty with the space Marines, even though that meant starting out as a new second lieutenant.

Privately, Capt Rodriguez was happy to gain a battle seasoned field grade officer like the former Lieutenant Colonel. It slowly became clear that he was not the total asshole or mindless martinet that their previous interaction suggested. Jennifer had still not fully forgiven him for how his men had treated her squad, but having him as a subordinate was definitely helping the healing process.

If having to call Jennifer "Ma'am" grated on the ex-colonel he did not show it. Instead, he threw himself into learning the new equipment and tactics required to wage infantry warfare in space. His success in that endeavor was indicated by his promotion to first lieutenant and position leading the second shuttle of boarders in the upcoming action.

Now they were all Peggy Sue's Marines, awaiting the order to board the landing shuttles—56 men, women and polar bears all in space armor and heavily armed. No one knew what to expect when they boarded the alien spacecraft, or even if they would be called on to attempt an assault. For now, all they could do was watch as the Navy engaged the enemy.

Bridge, Destroyer of Worlds

The Captain of the People's ship *Destroyer of Worlds* watched the alien ships approaching. *They are much faster and more maneuverable than we are,* he thought, *no chance of out running them.* Bowing to the inevitable the Captain issued commands to his crew.

"Fire debris into the path of the incoming enemy ships, and mix in a few mines as well," he snapped, *perhaps that will slow them down some.* "Eject a messenger pod to the aliens' blind side and launch the auxiliaries. Have them concentrate on the large enemy."

They had done grievous damage to the third planet's ecosystem, large impactors obliterating all the major inhabited coastal regions. Most of the warm life vermin must have been eradicated. Those that did not die directly from the attack would surely perish from lack of food and exposure as their civilization came crashing down around them.

Strange, he thought, *life struggles to raise itself out of the primordial ooze, eventually creating a technological civilization without ever appreciating how dependent a species becomes on its own machines and gadgets. Technology makes proliferation possible and a species seemingly secure.*

In reality, technology makes those who depend on it vulnerable to any major disruption. Technology, industries and orders of magnitude more individuals than a planet could ever support in a primitive state all woven together in a web of interdependence—a web that is surprisingly fragile and easy to break. And once broken, such civilizations are not just reduced or diminished, they implode. They collapse into ruin, carrying their creators to extinction. Yet these creatures stubbornly refuse to die.

"Captain, the auxiliaries are away and a wave of detritus has been sent toward the incoming enemy ships," confirmed one of his lieutenants.

"Very good, Number Two." It was just luck that the ship now chasing his had been out of the system when they started their attack on the infested planet. Now it would be much more difficult to complete their mission—they might even fail.

21

For the *Destroyer of Worlds'* crew the possibility of surrender did not exist for the Dark Lords did not tolerate failure. Failure might only be grudgingly accepted if every one of the People on board the Destroyer gave their spirits to the void in the attempt. Such a sacrifice might be deemed sufficient for the dark ones to spare the People's home world.

Bridge, Peggy Sue

The anxiety and excitement were palpable on board as time until the assault ticked down. More than half the crew were seasoned veterans of other space battles, but the capabilities of this foe were unknown. What weapons the enemy possessed could only be guessed at based on observation during the chase. The alien vessel was huge, massing several million tons, but it seemed a crude construction. Much of the mass was attributable to the asteroids it carried in its bulbous prow—projectiles used to destroy worlds—the rest appeared almost an afterthought.

"Captain, CIC. The hostile seems to be launching a number of smaller craft."

"Roger, CIC," Gretchen replied. *I guess they know we are coming. Good thing we waited for the corvettes to become operational, or we would be facing the oncoming craft all alone— definitely better to be prepared, to not rush ahead half-assed.* "Go in half-assed and come back with none," was another of Jack's sayings. "Task Force Alpha, re-target on the smaller craft. The Peggy Sue will target the mother ship."

As she received acknowledgment of the change in orders, Gretchen tried to cope with the rapidly evolving tactical situation. *I guess the old saying is true, no plan of attack survives contact with the enemy.* "Helm, full ahead. Concentrate main battery fire on the enemy's engines astern. X-ray batteries in defense mode until we see what they throw at us. Torpedomen ready a spread on my mark..."

Chapter 2

ESS Deloraine, Task Force Alpha

Lt. Elizabeth Melaku was sitting in the command pilot's chair of the corvette *ESS Deloraine*. Known to her friends as Beth, the lieutenant was of Ethiopian descent though born and raised in the UK. Tall and attractive, with a narrow straight nose and prominent cheekbones, she looked every inch the warrior, a worthy representative of her ancient homeland's people. She had been a pilot in the Royal Navy but, like so many others, was caught in the downsizing that plagued the armed forces of all western countries in the early 21st century.

Her ship was officially designated a corvette, a class of small warship that had been present in the world's navies for centuries. During WWII, the first Royal Australian Navy kill of a full-size submarine was attributed to a corvette, the HMAS Deloraine. There was a significant Australian presence at Farside Base and in the shipyard, hence the name of her ship.

The Deloraine was a relatively small, trim vessel, intended for patrolling the solar system, not interstellar missions. Much smaller than the Peggy Sue, each corvette measured 42 m (138 ft) in length with a beam of 8.5 m (28 ft). Eight gravitonic torpedoes mounted in launchers on the hull brought its diameter to 10 m (33 ft). Like pontoons on an outrigger, port and starboard 14 m (46 ft) winglike extensions mounted the X-ray secondary batteries and shield generator pods. Aside from the eight torpedoes the craft's main armament was a center-line mounted railgun 32 meters in length. A secondary 15mm multi-barreled railgun was mounted beneath the keel to provide close in support or to lay down a cloud of "sand" to help thwart plasma bursts.

The ship's complement consisted of six: a command pilot, pilot, engineer, navigator and two gunners mates. Like the crew in a two seat jet fighter, command pilot Melaku sat above and behind the pilot, WO François "Frenchy" Bouchard. Bouchard is a name of Norman extraction that means "brave" or "strong." It is also a French nickname for someone with a big mouth, which described the French-Canadian Warrant Officer to a tee.

"The main railgun is online, Skipper," Frenchy reported, "Now these *salopards étrangers* will find out what it means to mess with a *Québécois!*"

"Steady on, people," Melaku cautioned, "wait for the word."

To either side of the Lieutenant were weapons stations for the gunner's mates. Their job was to do targeting for the torpedoes and oversee the mostly automatic functioning of the X-ray laser counter batteries. Like the pilots, the gunners wore lightweight helmets with curved, face covering visors. The helmets' purpose was not protection but to support the visors, which provided a holographic view of the space surrounding the craft. Driven by the ship's sensors, the visor wearing crew could look outside the ship in any direction, unencumbered by walls, consoles and even their own bodies. As they did, sensor and targeting information automatically annotated the projected view.

Farther aft were the navigation and engineering stations, manned by another Warrant Officer and a Chief Petty Officer, both surrounded by their own displays. Behind the crew's action stations there was a small day room, sleeping compartments and a shared head. In all, not much space for the crew of six on a ship this size.

The crew space was cramped because most of the ship housed its muon catalyzed fusion reactor and gravitonic drive systems. Capable of sprints at 100Gs the corvette was quick and highly maneuverable, meant to cut and thrust like a knife fighter. Their job during the coming attack was to suppress fire from the alien ship while the Peggy Sue, with its much more powerful main battery, disabled the enemy's propulsion systems. The last minute launch of interceptors from the alien vessel shifted the corvette squadron's attention from the mother ship to new targets.

Much like fighter aircraft, the corvettes would attack in pairs, each consisting of a leader and a wingman. On approach they assumed finger-four formation—two staggered pairs forming a lopsided V. Deloraine's wingman was Foscari, and Intensity was lead for Karjala. The names of the corvettes were taken from previous warships from different navies: Australian, Italian, American and Finnish. It was an attempt to internationalize the war effort, as if the aliens had not done that when they blew most of the world up. Lt. Melaku did not care what the name of her ship was, she just wanted to get close enough to kill some of the alien marauders who had ravaged her home.

A sequence of tones sounded on the task force frequency, followed by the words "attack, attack, attack!" Together the corvettes surged forward at 50Gs, headed for the alien interceptor craft, which were racing toward the attackers in two triangular formations of three craft each.

"Intensity, Deloraine. We will take the formation to port at 8 o'clock."

"Roger that, Deloraine. We'll take the starboard side." The entire task force took their frame of reference from the Peggy Sue's orientation prior to the start of the attack.

"Foscari, I will take the lead enemy craft with railgun fire," Beth called, shifting to a frequency used only by her and her wingman. "Follow my strike if the target remains, otherwise take the second one at 2 o'clock." *OK, let's see what it takes to kill these bastards.*

"Roger that, Deloraine."

At the relative velocity of their approach the firing pass was set up by the pilot, the target designated by the command pilot and the actual firing done by the ship's computer. The encounter passed in the blink of an eye as the railgun fired twice in quick succession. Then they were by the enemy formation and maneuvering to swing past the mother ship.

Quickly checking her instruments, Beth saw that her target was now an expanding cloud of debris. As she watched a second alien interceptor exploded.

"Ayeee!" yelled Frenchy.

"Scratch the second bogy, Deloraine," came the exuberant signal from her wingman.

"Affirmative, Foscari. Follow me past the mother ship. We will give them a brace of torpedoes each—target the base of the cap forward."

Each of the two corvettes fired a pair of gravitonic torpedoes armed with antimatter warheads. As the torpedoes accelerated toward their target at 1000Gs the corvettes pivoted, facing back toward the alien mother ship, and went to maximum acceleration.

"Looks like there are a couple of more bogies on this side of the mother ship," reported Intensity, the second element leader. "We scratched one on the first pass but Peggy Sue will have to deal with the others."

"Roger that, Intensity, we smoked two of ours. Form up on me and we will make a pass from this side. Like last time, take out the interceptors first and then fire on the mother ship's hull."

* * * * *

"Captain, the aliens seem to have tossed a bunch of garbage material our direction," commented the young Lieutenant JG at the navigation station.

"Looks like the corvettes blew through with no problems, so our shields should handle it," added Lt. Medina from the engineering station.

"Mr. Vincent, take us by the target. Maximize the number of slugs we put into the engine section. Torpedoes, target the remaining alien small craft."

"Aye aye, Captain." Billy Ray's fingers danced across the controls, informing the ship's computer of what was to happen. A number of explosions flashed by.

"Some form of mine, non-nuclear," reported Lt. Medina. "Secondary batteries detonated them well away from the hull. Didn't even impact the shields."

In a dizzying blur the 8,000 ton ship flew past the massive alien vessel, pirouetting to keep its nose, and its main battery, pointed at the target. In a matter of a few seconds the main rail-guns fired six times, three slightly staggered pairs of 10kg metallic slugs. The velocity imparted by the rail guns, combined with the ship's closing velocity gave each slug a kinetic energy equivalent to almost a half kiloton of TNT. Each pair would strike within a few meters of each other, the staggering creating a one-two strike in effectively the same location on the aliens shields or hull, maximizing penetration.

A series of explosions could be seen along the tail section of the alien vessel. From within secondary explosions followed, then the last kilometer of the ship splintered and blew apart with a bright flare of light—residual antimatter detonating in the craft's engines. Carried by its own momentum, the Peggy Sue swung more than 600 km beyond the alien before matching velocity and then moving slowly back toward its target.

* * * * *

Capable of triple the acceleration of the Peggy Sue, the flight of corvettes only over shot the alien by about 125 km. In fact, they were close enough to the target vessel to require evasive maneuvers to escape the exploding wreckage from that ship's engines.

"I'm on the remaining bogies, Deloraine," called Intensity, clearly hoping to even out the kill count between the two elements. The Peggy Sue's torpedomen had mopped up the three alien interceptors missed by the corvettes' initial pass.

"Roger, Intensity. We will strafe the mother ship's hull forward," replied Lt. Melaku. "Do not, repeat, do not fire into the remaining aft section of the mother ship. That area is supposed to contain antimatter storage." *The last thing we want is to blow ourselves to kingdom come by detonating the alien's fuel bunkers.*

"Roger, Deloraine. Understood."

Farside Base, The Moon

Nearly eight billion kilometers from the battle being waged by Earth's space navy a meeting was being held in what passed for the central headquarters of humanity's post apocalypse government. Present were TK Parker, former Texas oil billionaire and primary backer of the project that created both the Peggy Sue and the lunar base; Dr. Rajiv Gupta, head scientist and Earth's greatest expert in gravitonics and other T'aafhal technologies; Dr. Ludmilla Tropsha, former cosmonaut, biologist, chief medical officer and ranking member of the Peggy Sue's crew on the base; and Isbjørn, the acknowledged lead polar bear, veteran of the second voyage.

"How are we doin' on picking up survivors planetside?" the gruff oilman asked. Well into his seventies, Parker was a force of nature even though confined to a tricked out gyro-stabilized, four-wheel drive electric wheel chair. More than anyone, it had been Parker who held things together on the moon base as the asteroids began to fall on Earth. By shear strength of will he prevented the people of the partly staffed lunar base from falling into despondency.

The people of Farside Base had watched with horror as the 24 hour bombardment of their home world killed most everything they had ever loved and cherished. They were without weapons to defend themselves—the six corvettes were not yet operational, and would have been unable to do anything about the massive attack if they had been. As the attacking alien vessel flew past Earth and headed for the outer reaches of the solar system TK had fought to keep the base functioning. Then, a light delayed signal from the Peggy Sue arrived, saying that they were back in the system and to hold on, they were on their way.

A hectic month ensued as the veterans from Peggy Sue helped organize the inexperienced Farside personnel. They were soon scouting the shattered Earth looking for survivors with useful skill sets—soldiers, scientists, technicians and support personnel to help run humanity's outpost on the Moon. Though it pained them, the crew and base personnel recognized that they could not save even a small fraction of those left behind on Earth. But what they could do was to rearm the Peggy Sue, finish outfitting the corvettes and assemble a Marine force to strike back at those who had so violently invaded the solar system.

A little more than a month after the surprise attack, a counterstrike mission was launched with Captain Curtis in command and newly commissioned Capt. Rodriguez leading the Marines. Being able to focus on striking back enabled the base leaders to skirt the edge of chaos and collapse, at least for a while. Unfortunately, it had now been nearly a month since the Peggy Sue and Task Force Alpha had left to hunt down and kill the invaders, and during that time mankind's precarious position weighed heavily on those at Farside.

"We have a dozen shuttles of all sizes working around the clock searching for candidate personnel," said a weary Ludmilla. Since returning she had assumed an administrative role at the base. She was now addressed as colonel more often than doctor, much to her personal displeasure. She had worked for years to leave her military past behind but necessity now required she take up the mantle of command. Having made first contact with aliens during the voyages of the Peggy Sue, and having fought against some of them at close quarters, lent a cachet to her military rank that could not be matched by anyone else among humanity's survivors. Only Commander Curtis or Captain Sutton could match her practical experience, and with Gretchen out hunting aliens and Jack lost God knows where she was left charge.

"Finding military personnel is not proving to be a problem," she said. "If anything we have too many anxious warriors, all hoping to kill aliens. We have found isolated units from many major countries —the U.S., the UK, Russia, Japan, Scandinavia, even a company of the Légion étrangère."

"French Foreign Legion? Where did we find them?" asked an incredulous TK.

"In the mountains of Djibouti, high above the African Rift Valley. They were cutoff and lost like so many others," Ludmilla answered tiredly. "Ground troops we have many, finding sailors for the space navy is another thing."

"Why do you say that?"

"Differing skills. Marines, SAS, Special Forces, Spetznaz are all trained to engage the enemy at close quarters, even hand-to-hand, and to survive off the land. Not much opportunity for that under present circumstances. We have had some success in picking up crews from submarines, however."

TK gave Ludmilla a questioning look.

"Being in a submarine is probably as close to traveling around in a starship as you can come on Earth. Cramped quarters, isolation for months at a time, it is a better fit than other naval duty. Not that we would turn down any former navy personnel—it is just that few surface ships survived the tsunamis from the bombardment. Air force pilots and crew seem to adapt to the shuttles and even the corvettes fairly well, but when we get a few of the frigates built we are going to be hard pressed to fill out their crews."

"You are probably right, Ludmilla," Rajiv said in a conciliatory tone of voice, "but remember, we were all rookies at this not that long ago."

29

Ludmilla snorted, "That is true enough, Rajiv, I guess we all have to start somewhere."

Rajiv and the science staff from the Peggy Sue were driving themselves at a torturous pace. Yuki Saito, Olaf Gunderson, Elena Piscopia, Melissa Scott Hamilton and Dieter Schmitt had all assumed positions as department heads, leading multiple projects intended to expand the base, construct new weaponry, build new ships and a thousand and one other things. All this in the hope of dragging humanity back from the edge of extinction.

"We are finding plenty of willing scientific personnel," Rajiv added. "The problem is finding things for them all to do. Most require additional training to do useful work with T'aafhal technology—to end up sitting in a classroom after traveling to the Moon is not very satisfying to most." He paused thoughtfully.

"We have managed to expand the polar bear contingent to 42," Isbjørn inserted into the gap in the others' conversation. "It was fortunate that none of the impacts occurred in the Arctic but the effects on the atmosphere have led to massive storms planet wide. I'm not sure we will be able to continue the search for more bears until the weather settles."

"How are the new bears adapting?" asked Ludmilla.

"They are confused and a bit angry. We had to load the most unruly of them into a large shuttle and show them what was happening on Earth. Even so, some wanted to be released on the surface to fend for themselves."

"I fear that the weather will be growing even worse in the near-term," Rajiv said, sadly shaking his head. "The immediate effects of the impacts—mostly heavy overcast from dust in the atmosphere, leading to storms and significant cooling—could remain for several years, judging by studies of volcanic eruptions in the past."

"I've been trying to explain that to the new bears, but they are a skeptical lot. We just do not have enough experienced bears to teach the others, at least not with eight bears from the first group of recruits being on the hunting expedition."

Seizing the chance to change the subject, TK asked: "Speaking of Task-force Alpha and the alien hunt, what's the latest word?"

Ludmilla sighed. "The last report was about a half hour ago. Gretchen said that they were closing on the enemy and expected to engage shortly. Given the almost five hour transmission delay they may have attacked already. In fact, the battle is probably already over."

"The lack of instant communications is drivin' me crazy. We've all grown so use to 24 hour cable news, smart phones and text messaging. It's like going back to the age of sailing ships and mail delivered by pony express."

"Sadly, that is something we cannot change, TK. We can only await word from the task force and pray that it will be good news when it arrives," Ludmilla said, once again giving voice to Russian fatalism. "Regardless, we will know the outcome of the fight in a few hours—one way or the other."

Task Force Alpha, Sol's Kuiper Belt

"Maintain our position, Mr. Taylor," Gretchen commanded. "It would appear that most of the fight has gone out of our opponent." The enemy's defenses had proven weak and ineffective, quickly withering before the task force's attack.

"Aye aye, Ma'am," the laconic helmsman drawled in his best cowboy accent. With the results of the attack undeniably successful the atmosphere on the bridge had shifted from tense to confident. Next to him, Nigel Lewis, Billy Ray's co-pilot, checked his instruments.

"The torpedo strikes from the corvettes have severed the bow section and our initial railgun fire blew the engines off straight away."

On the main forward display was a view of the enemy ship, its swollen head half filled with replacement asteroids. As the bridge crew watched the bulbous bow moved perceptibly away from the main body of the ship, slowly rotating as it disengaged. It moved with the stately grace that large objects do when viewed from a great distance.

"What we have left is about three kilometers of hull that is dead in space, though we seem to be taking occasional hits from coherent EM radiation," the Englishman continued. "Frequency is in the infrared, not really a problem since we are jinking about quite a bit. They don't seem to be able to stay on us."

"It looks like the laser fire is coming from a number of locations on the alien's hull," added Jo Jo Medina, "We should probably neutralize it before sending in the Marines."

"Sounds like a good suggestion, Mr. Medina. Task Force Alpha, Peggy Sue, please direct your attention to the IR laser positions along the alien's hull. As soon as they are suppressed we will commence boarding operations."

Marine Landing Shuttles, Approaching Alien Ship

The Peggy Sue's two large shuttles were packed full of Marines in space armor. Each craft carried two squads, twelve humans and two bears per squad. All were encased in power augmented, refractory armor designed to turn away projectiles up to 15mm and absorb hits by plasma and laser weapons.

The human Marines' standard weapon was a multi-barreled railgun in an over-under configuration. The upper barrel fired high-density 5mm flechettes at up to 6,000 fps, with a selectable cyclic rate of up to 1,200 rounds per minute. The lower barrel was a general purpose, 20mm launcher that fired high explosive shells filled with nano-engineered enhanced explosive. The shells could be fired time-on-target, exploding at a range preset by the built-in laser range finder, or set to detonate on contact. By altering the detonation timing within the warhead a shell could act as normal HE or an armor piercing shaped charge. And if things really got up close and personal, the 20mm could also fire canister rounds— basically bundles of flechettes that acted as mega shotgun shells.

As formidably armed as the human Marines were, the polar bears carried even more firepower. Each carried either a 15mm, triple barreled railgun cannon, which fired high velocity explosive rounds at 1200 rounds per minute, or a five barreled railgun firing 5mm flechettes at a sustained 6,000 per minute. The bears' large size allowed for ample ammunition loads and, if all else failed, they could extend the metal claws built into their suits' forearms and deal with their foes the old fashioned way.

The shuttles themselves were also much different from the original ones the Peggy Sue came with. Those were decked out for hauling passengers or freight and were similar in their appointments to civilian airliners. These shuttles were designed from the start as assault craft, intended to deliver 28 Marines to a battle-zone under hostile fire. They were heavily armored and also mounted port and starboard 15mm railgun cannons and a top mounted X-ray laser close support system for dealing with incoming enemy fire.

Shuttle One, containing Capt. Rodriguez and 1st & 2nd squads, was piloted by Nigel Lewis with Pauline Palmer as copilot. Both had been on board during the second voyage of the Peggy Sue. Shuttle Two had Skip Tanner as pilot and Jake Sontag, a brand new addition to the crew, as copilot. Tanner had shown bravery and clear thinking during the fracas in the Bug Queen's Palace on the second voyage, being badly wounded in the process. He, even more than others in the task force, was looking to even the score.

They were less than a hundred kilometers out when Capt. Rodriguez's voice came over the command frequency: "OK, listen up Marines. We are about to ram into this big alien bastard at about 500 kph. The science dweebs and engineers say we should penetrate the alien's hull with only minor exterior damage. Inside we are protected by the shuttles' deck gravity and shouldn't get a scratch.

"Shuttle Two will strike forward, near what we hope is the bridge area. Squads 3 & 4 under Lt. Westfield will neutralize any resistance and seize the bridge. They are designated BP-2. We are hoping to find equipment we can get some Intel from—in particular, where these assholes came from.

"Shuttle One will strike aft, just forward of what we think is the antimatter storage area. Squads 1 & 2's objective is to seize any AM present and prevent the aliens from scuttling the ship. They are designated BP-1. Once we have attained our initial objectives both forces will advance toward each other to mop up any remaining aliens. Any questions?"

"What about prisoners, Captain?" someone asked.

"If there are some of 'em left alive to question that's fine. Just don't go out of your way to capture any. We don't know what kind of reception we are going to get, so err on the side of caution—when in doubt use overwhelming force. Understood?"

"AYE AYE, SIR!" flooded the radio channel.

"Captain Rodriguez," called Lt. Lawson from the cockpit. "We are impacting in 10, 9, 8..."

* * * * *

The shuttles used their 15mm cannon to partially blast through the alien's hull and momentum did the rest. The heavily armored shuttles penetrated the last meter of solid hull by *force majeure* before lodging in a surprisingly open space.

Surprising in that the ship's interior was a confusing jumble, crisscrossed with trusses and girders, supporting enclosed structures linked by tubular passageways and piping. It was like being inside of a skyscraper that was only a shell, its interior left unfinished and mostly empty. The space the Marines emerged into was under vacuum with the crew, if there was one, presumably confined to structures embedded in the web of beams and girders.

After penetrating the outer hull of the alien ship, Shuttle One immediately released a half dozen free floating surveillance drones. They fanned out in all directions, transmitting the layout of the ship's interior back to the Marines. The alien ship's outer hull was composed of both metallic and rocky material—undoubtedly extracted from asteroids—and provided significant shielding from radiation. That included radio frequencies used by the Marines to communicate with the Peggy Sue and the Marines in Shuttle Two. An exterior relay was soon rigged through the hole the shuttle had plowed on entry, re-establishing contact with the ships of Task Force Alpha.

There was a large enclosed area aft and another smaller one forward. Capt. Rodriguez took the aft compartment to be the antimatter storage and ordered her Marines to breach the structure, using minimal explosive force.

"Captain, we got a bunch of them big egg things in here," called a corporal whose name she couldn't recall at the moment. "What should we do?"

"Cut any wires or cables leading to the egg racks. Those storage eggs have fail safes that should cause them to lock up tight if the mechanism they are attached to loses power," said Technical Sergeant Fukushima. Fukushima had been given a crash course in alien antimatter technology by the scientists back at Farside before departure. Despite all the chaos and diversity in the galaxy, one constant factor seemed to be that all species used the same standard antimatter containers, a design that must have originated millions of years ago.

"What if cutting the cables sets 'em off," came the reply.

"In that case, Corporal, we will never know what happened," Rodriguez snapped. "Now cut the damned cables."

"Aye aye, Ma'am."

OK, securing the antimatter was priority one, second priority is to make sure the aft spaces are clear of aliens she thought. "Sgt. Tuttle, take your fireteam and sweep the spaces aft, I don't want any surprises from our rear."

"Aye aye, Captain."

Next, set a blocking position to keep any of the crew from making their way aft. "Sgt. Aurora. Deploy 1st squad forward and cover anything trying to come aft from that next set of enclosed structures."

"Aye aye, Ma'am," the she-bear replied. Many bears were still having problems understanding the concepts of "rank" and "chain of command." Mostly, the bears just wanted to get in a position so they could attack the enemy and didn't much care who was in charge. Aurora was more perceptive and, because she got on well with humans, had been promoted to sergeant and put in charge of 1st squad.

As the Marines moved out to follow their orders the Corporal from the antimatter storage, who Jennifer remembered was named Green, called back. "Captain, We got these egg things lose from the racks they was in. What should we do with them?"

"Wait one, Green," Jennifer changed frequencies and called the ship. "Peggy Sue, Rodriguez."

"Go, Captain Rodriguez." Captain Curtis was anxiously monitoring the Marines' progress from the CIC, where the central 3D display showed an expanding X-ray view of the alien vessel. As the robot survey drones made their way into the ship from both ends, that view became more detailed. The position and vital signs of each Marine were also noted and transmitted back to the ship.

"We have secured the aliens' antimatter store and taken up positions in both fore and aft sections of the hull. We are sending the recon drones into the hull sections we have not yet entered."

"Affirmative, move the antimatter to the shuttle ASAP. The sooner we get it away from the hulk the safer we will all be."

"Roger that, Peggy Sue. So far we have encountered no appreciable resistance..."

Bridge, Destroyer of Worlds

"The aliens have breached the outer hull fore and aft, and are blasting their way into the pressurized internal sections, Captain" one of the crew reported.

"Get the crew into pressure suits and issue weapons." The Captain scurried over to a bank of controls, thinking, *if the crew can hold off these monsters for a few minutes I should be able to set off the scuttling charges. At least we will take them with us into the void.*

With several forearms the Captain executed the complex sequence that would command the ship to destroy itself, detonating a number of antimatter charges in the aft section of the hull. The key was to create sympathetic explosions in the antimatter store. That would blast the entire ship to atoms.

Let us see how sweet your victory is when your boarding force is vaporized along with the rest of the ship, the Captain thought with malice. Still, he could not help thinking of the fate that had befallen his ship and his crew. *For centuries we have sent out ships to lay waste to distant planets orbiting faraway suns. Never have we encountered a foe that offered more than token resistance. Yet these creatures have attacked us with ships we cannot match; they brandish weapons we cannot counter. We are like primitives before these warm life demons.*

A sequence of indicators lit on the control panel. But the sequence stopped short of completion—the scuttling charges were not responding. *The control lines to the antimatter store must have been severed...*

BP-2, Forward Section

As promised, the Marines in Shuttle Two felt not the slightest tremor on impact. The sites for the incursions had been selected using thermal imaging and were rotationally about 110 degrees apart with respect to the target's central axis. The Marines of 3rd & 4th squads encountered an environment much the same as their compatriots in the aft part of the alien vessel. A mostly empty interior space laced by girders and support trusses with embedded enclosed structures woven into the tangled mess.

"What is with this shit?" asked one puzzled Marine.

"It's like some weird, alien jungle gym," said another. "No atmo and no deck gravity."

"Yeah, it's like a humungous trailer park suspended in the world's biggest sewer pipe."

"Move out and find cover," ordered GySgt Washington.

"The prey has got to be in those tubes and boxes," rumbled Tornassuk, one of the polar bears.

"You may be right," agreed Lt. Westfield. "Let's go say hello."

The Marines of 3rd & 4th squads spread out through the chaotic erector set interior of the alien warship, bounding weightlessly between girders and supports. Forward they could see open space and the ship's bow section still ponderously floating away. Looking aft there were a number of solid structures embedded in the web of supports. Approximately on the ship's center-line was the largest of these.

"Sir, that large enclosed structure up ahead looks like some kind of central control. There's bundles of cables and pipes and stuff coming out of it. What do you think, LT?" GySgt Washington asked Westfield. "Should we blast our way in?"

"Yeah. I don't know what those cables all do but they must have some purpose. Use the breaching missiles to open a way inside." Aside from their normal armaments, the weapon makers back at Farside had come up with some man launched missiles. Similar to RPGs, each packed the wallop of a large artillery shell.

"Aye, Sir. OK, you heard the LT, ventilate that large structure aft." Four of the advancing Marines quickly found stable positions in the spiderweb of support beams, unlimbered tube shaped launchers and fired on the structure.

Bridge, Destroyer of Worlds

After minutes of dithering, the chief engineer verified that the scuttling charges were no longer functional. "Captain, what are we to do? If we do not destroy the ship the Dark Lords will slaughter our brood-mates and the People will be no more."

"Stiffen your carapace, you sniveling coward!" the Captain snapped. But the engineer was right, his highest duty at this point was to those back home. He was entrusted with a sacred duty, to return victorious or to sacrifice all on board while taking as many of the warm life enemy with them as possible. "Is everyone armed and suited up?"

"Yes, Captain," replied his first lieutenant. Those left on the bridge had donned pressure suits that sealed tightly against their segmented exoskeletons. With their arms encased in the clumsy suits the crew were milling about, several holding projectile weapons.

The Captain finished slipping on his pressure suit and signaled to his crew. "All right, we are going aft, by way of the laser battery on the lower starboard quartile. We will show these invaders that the People will not simply roll over and die! Attack!"

His crew raised a somewhat half halfhearted cheer and headed aft. The Captain grabbed the engineer with several forelegs and hissed, "You and I are going to retrieve the antimatter container that powered the laser battery. You will rig it with a detonator and we shall work aft, as close as possible to the main antimatter store. With any luck we will still be able to set off the main AM store and send this hell-spawned plague of demons back to the fires they came from."

As the alien Captain left the bridge of his disabled ship for the last time a series of tremors shook the command structure. This was followed by a brief whistling as the structure's atmosphere—mostly nitrogen and methane, with traces of ammonia, at a pressure of close to three Earth atmospheres—escaped into the cold emptiness of the main hull enclosure.

BP-2, Forward Section

Immediately following the breaching explosions debris, blown by what must have been the aliens' atmosphere, gushed out of the newly created openings. In all his years with the U.S. Marines Dirk Westfield had never dreamt that he would one day be in an armored space suit, about to attack alien invaders from the stars. *Sometimes, you just gotta' go with the flow.* "That should have let them know the Marines are here."

"Aye, Sir," GySgt Washington acknowledged over the command frequency, signaling to individual squad members to advance. From left, right, top and bottom the Marines closed on the interior structure. Along with the chunks of debris were a number of strange bodies.

Bodies with multisegmented carapaces and an inordinate number of legs hanging down. Hunchbacked bodies that looked like a cross between a tailless shrimp and a clawless crab, grown to the size of a pig. As one of the bodies bounced off of a support beam and pinwheeled slowly back into the empty space within the hull, the front of the creature could be seen—a small head low and forward of the hunched back, five small unblinking eyes strung across its brow.

"That thing almost looks like a giant sand flea," said LCpl Joe King, "well, except for the five eyes." King was from Pensacola in the Florida panhandle where a "sand flea" was not really a "flea" but a type of crab without claws. Fishermen favored the critters for bait when trolling for red fish and pompano.

"I don't care what it is, it's butt ugly," someone else said.

"Yeah, like you're Mr. Universe."

"Can it!" Washington yelled. "They ain't comin' out so we have to go in after them. Morrison, King, take point."

Just as the Marines began to move forward to enter the structure more of the alien pseudo-crustaceans popped out of the holes the Marines had blasted. These were not drifting cadavers, however. They moved with purpose, ducking behind parts of the supporting structure from which they opened fire with projectile weapons.

Random flashes sparkled around GySgt Washington, who quickly ducked behind cover. Morrison and King also came under fire.

"Damn, I think they're shooting at us," King proclaimed.

"So shoot back, Joe," Morrison yelled. "That's what the thing you're carrying with the trigger is for."

"Hey, there are funky sand flea things popping out all over the enclosed structure," reported another Marine. "I guess blowing those holes in the enclosed part stirred up a hornet's nest."

"You know, I never cared much for shellfish," Tornassuk chuckled as he opened up on the swarming aliens with his 15mm. "Let's see if they know how to fight."

"Be careful what you wish for, Tornassuk," replied Washington, "there's room for a shitload and a half of those things in there."

The bear rumbled something undecipherable and loosed a short burst at three aliens hovering near a hole. A cluster of soundless orange detonations flashed, turning the aliens into a rapidly dispersing cloud of shell fragments and body parts.

"Gunny, we need to get inside that structure and secure any navigational or computational equipment," Dirk ordered. *Assuming that there is such equipment in there and we can identify it just by looking at it.* "BP-1, BP-2. Things just got much hotter up here. We have armed aliens swarming from the enclosed structures..."

Chapter 3

Commanding Officer's Quarters, Farside Base

Ludmilla had retired to her quarters to finish working on the endless stream of reports and authorizations that accompanied every action, no matter how trivial, required in running the lunar base. But despite the growing number of messages in her in box, she sat staring sightlessly at the desk's surface display. Her mind was on matters far away.

Out on the edge of the solar system her friends were locked in battle with alien forces unknown. The last message from Gretchen said simply, "Enemy sighted, about to engage." Ludmilla knew that what she was doing, no matter how mind-numbingly boring, was necessary, but she could not help wanting to be with her friends on board the Peggy Sue as they went in harm's way.

What if there are casualties? I am the ship's doctor, damn it! I should be there, Ludmilla thought in frustration. She knew that there were other doctors on board, doctor's she had worked with and trusted, but it still ate at her to be so far away and unable to help those she cared about. That thought triggered an even sharper pang of emotional anguish.

Oh Jack, where are you? Are you alive? No, you have to be alive, you have to come back. Humanity needs you, I need you! Savagely clamping down on her runaway emotions she pulled her mind back from the precipice—as comforting as it might be to descend into gibbering irrationality, it would solve nothing.

"Der'mo! To hell with this," she said out loud. "I need a drink, and I am not going to drink alone in my quarters." Flicking open her contacts book on the desktop display she scrolled down and tapped on the entry for Elena Piscopia, a fellow scientist and comrade from Peggy Sue's previous voyage.

Elena's tawny main and elegant Italian features appeared in a new window as the astronomer looked up and said "Si pronto?" Quickly followed by "Oh, it is you Ludmilla, what can I do for you tonight?"

"I see you are doing the same thing I am, shuffling documents."

"Si, why is it that we got rid of paper yet 'paperwork' seems to keep increasing?"

"I was wondering if you need a break as much as I do? I was thinking of going down to Jesse's place for a Fantasy? Are you game?" Ludmilla could see her friend glance down and scan the display surface on her desk.

"*Basta*! This can wait! Yes, I will see you there, 10 minutes?"

"I'm on my way."

Captain's Quarters, M'tak Ka'fek

Fifteen hundred light-years from Earth, Captain Jack Sutton was having a sleepless night. It was just another in a string of sleepless nights since he had assumed command of the T'aafhal battle cruiser M'tak Ka'fek. The installation of a large AM container had resurrected the four million year old warship barely in time to defeat a flotilla of hostile alien vessels. Those belligerents were in pursuit of his former ship, the Peggy Sue, which was fleeing the Sirius system en-route to Earth. The Peggy Sue managed to escape into alter-space and hopefully made it safely to Earth and home port.

Jack and company, however, had to make an emergency departure from Sirius to escape a near nova strength explosion accidentally triggered by the attacking aliens. The graveyard of derelicts where they found the M'tak was gone, blasted to atoms when infalling debris destabilized the degenerate matter object the wrecks were orbiting.

The method of their escape was still a troublesome point for Jack. He had ordered his new ship to get them away from the cataclysmic eruption any way possible. It turned out that the ship's solution was not to slip sedately into alter-space but rather to create a temporary wormhole that dumped them out halfway across the Orion Arm. After the elation of once again cheating death had passed, the Captain and crew realized that they were a long, long way from home.

Moreover, effecting their escape had almost completely drained the ship's supply of antimatter. According to Dr. Mizuki Ogawa and

Lt. James "JT" Taylor, the ship's astrophysicist and navigator, respectively, returning to Earth using a series of alter-space hops would take more than two years. With Earth in danger, and the fate of their friends and loved ones on board the Peggy Sue unknown, that was just too long. So, with only enough fuel to limp from star to star, the Captain was desperately searching for a system where they could beg, borrow or steal more antimatter.

Jack tossed and turned and suddenly sat bolt upright in the strange bed. For a brief moment panic gripped him when he could not find Ludmilla. Reality quickly reasserted itself and his faculties returned. *Damn it, all this worrying is not doing anyone any good.*

It is a normal part of your mind's architecture, answered a voice in his head. It was the ship's AI—an artificial living mind that ran most of the onboard systems. When Jack assumed command of the alien battle cruiser the AI had "briefed" its new commander by implanting reams of technical data in his brain and establishing a telepathic link between them.

I need to learn to not broadcast my waking thoughts to the damned ship, Jack thought privately, adding openly for the ship's benefit, *You've studied me long enough to know what passes for normal?*

Yes Captain, humans are not so different from my creators. The T'aafhal dreamed as well.

I hope their dreams were less troublesome than mine, Jack thought in reply.

Sometimes, but often not. They were burdened with defending all warm life in this arm of the Galaxy—and they were losing the last time I had contact with them.

That is not a comforting thought, M'tak.

Sorry, Captain. But you should know that when you sleep your mind stays busy processing and cataloging information. It also runs through countless "what if" scenarios. Future outcomes, both probable and improbable, are simulated. In this way, you are ready to quickly respond to events as they unfold.

So my nightmares are just my subconscious dutifully preparing me for the future?

Yes, I hypothesize that many of your species' claims of prophesy and visions of the future come from this process. That and the feeling that a situation has been experienced before.

Yes, we call that Déjà vu, French for 'already seen'. To himself Jack thought, *I think my ship is trying to give me a pep talk.* Then: *M'tak, this is all very interesting but it isn't helping us get home.*

No, but it ensures you will be ready when an opportunity presents itself... the AI paused. *Speaking of opportunity, Captain, Mr. Danner is calling you from the bridge.*

Put him through.

"Captain, Lt. Danner here," the young helmsman's voice sounded within the cabin. "Sorry to disturb you, but we have a bogy crossing the current system."

"Do we know what type of ship it is, Mr. Danner?"

"The sensors say it is similar to one of those alien probe ships like we found on the Moon."

I would concur, Captain, based on the information downloaded from Peggy Sue's computer, the AI confirmed. *It is definitely an antimatter powered ship, though its drive is quite inefficient.*

"Can you tell where it's headed?"

"It looks like it is lining up to make an alter-space transit, Sir."

"Follow it, but do not let it know we are here, Mr. Danner."

"Sir?"

"The last time we followed a ship like that where did it lead us?"

"To the Space Mushroom, Sir," the puzzled lieutenant answered. The Space Mushroom was an alien space station encountered on the Peggy Sue's first voyage. Then understanding dawned. "It was headed to a refueling station!"

"Right you are, Bobby," Jack said, genuinely smiling for the first time in nearly two months. "Consult the AI and make sure we remain undetected, but do not lose that ship!"

"Aye aye, Sir!"

BP-2, Bridge of the Alien Ship

Led by Tornassuk and Gunny Washington, Lt. Westfield's Marines fought their way inside of the inner structure they believed housed the alien ship's bridge. The alien defenders fought doggedly but ineffectively against the heavily armored Earthlings. As they worked their way aft, the Marines found a large number of side rooms, each of which they had to clear before proceeding. Most of the rooms contained empty pits filled with tendrils of mist that were quickly clearing. In a few of the rooms the pits were not empty—scattered, floating bodies of dead aliens cluttered the space.

"What do you make of these pits, Gunny?" one PFC asked.

"I don't know Fredericks. When we breached the structure their deck gravity must have failed," GySgt Washington replied. "If I had to guess I'd say they slept in the pits. Maybe they were filled with liquid or something."

"So you're saying that all these rooms are crew quarters? So where did they all disappear to?"

"You got a point," the Gunny admitted. "We've killed a bunch, and there are a few dead ones in the rooms that must have bought it when the structure depressurized, but not nearly enough to account for all this bunk space."

Eventually, the Marines found themselves alone on the ship's bridge among the floating corpses of its crew. One of the technical specialists immediately began getting detailed scans of the equipment. "Looks like all this stuff is still intact, Lieutenant," the tech reported.

"Great, once we secure the rest of the ship some of the science types can go over it to their hearts' content," Dirk replied, then half to himself, "why do I have an uneasy feeling about this?"

"It was too easy," said Washington.

"How so, Gunny?"

"This is one big ass ship, Sir. And Fredericks noticed something on the way in here—there's a boatload of what look like sleeping quarters along the passageways we entered through."

"And?"

45

"One of the rooms looked like the inhabitants were all caught napping when we blew the atmo. There must have been a dozen aliens drifting around inside."

"You're saying that if each of those rooms held a dozen hostiles we have encountered far too few aliens?"

"Yes, Sir."

"Shit! BP-1, BP-2, we may have a problem here."

"Go, BP-2."

"We've found a lot of what looks like crew quarters up here and nowhere near enough aliens to fill 'em. It is possible that there are a large number of hostiles somewhere between your position and ours."

"Roger, BP-2. You have an estimated count?"

"At least company strength, possibly more."

"Wait one..."

BP-1, Aft Section

"Sergeant Aurora! Take your squad and clear the enclosed structures forward of your position. BP-2 says that there may be a pile of aliens hiding in the tangle."

"Aye aye, Captain."

Jennifer turned to the Marines who were manhandling the antimatter eggs out of the fuel bunker. They were working their way through the maze of girders toward the shuttle that was still wedged in the hole it made breaching the alien ship's hull. "Sgt Tuttle, take your fireteam and support first squad. Come on, people. We need to get these antimatter eggs on the shuttle and the shuttle off the ship. "

"We got three stowed on the shuttle, two more working through the jungle gym and nine still in the storage space. A couple of them don't seem heavy enough so they probably aren't full," the Tech Sergeant reported.

"Fine, keep the light ones 'till last. But get the full ones loaded ASAP."

"Yes, Ma'am."

Alien Crew, Amidships Headed Aft

The Captain watched as the Engineer attached the improvised triggering mechanism to the type three antimatter container they had extracted from the twisted remains of laser battery number seven. A simple timer and some circuitry to override the container's built in safety mechanisms.

"It is ready, Captain," the Engineer announced, displaying his handiwork. "Depressing this switch will start a 150 second countdown."

"Why 150 seconds?" the Captain asked.

"It is a standard timer," the Engineer replied, contracting and releasing his carapace segments, the equivalent of a shrug. "It was the only thing I could find capable of providing the signals necessary to override the container's fail-safes."

"Very well. Let us rejoin the rest of the crew. I want to move as close to the fuel storage bay as possible, to ensure the detonation of the main cache."

Exiting the ruined laser battery, the Captain and Engineer joined a crowd of waiting crewmembers. Before the Captain could speak, one of the lieutenants pushed forward with a status report.

"Captain, our main body has advanced to just short of the fuel storage bay and are heavily engaged with the alien demons. Those left as a rear guard report more demons advancing from the control section."

"Did they say how many?"

"No, Sir. They must have been overrun—I can no longer reach them by communicator."

"Then time is of the essence. To the aft end of the ship and quickly. We must fight our way as close to the ship's fuel cache as possible."

47

BP-1 & BP-2, Inside the Destroyer of Worlds

Lt. Westfield's squad closed on the remaining aliens from the bow of the ship while Capt. Rodriguez and company served as a blocking force, keeping the retreating crew from gaining access to the antimatter storage spaces.

"Well what ever you might want to say about these creatures, they are not cowards," commented Sgt. Aurora to no one in particular. The aliens had repeatedly charged her squad's position, swarming forward firing projectile weapons at the Marines. Unfortunately for the aliens those weapons were ineffective against the Earthling's armored suits.

"Hey Sarge, looks like they're coming again!"

"It's going to get noisy again, Lads," called Sgt Tuttle. Since they were fighting in vacuum it was really not going to get noisy, but the Marines of 2nd squad knew what the former SAS operative meant.

Swarming out of holes and hatches in front of the Marines' positions the alien crew made one last, all out effort. More than a hundred of the cold life crustaceans surged toward the twenty eight Marines of BP-1, trying to overwhelm them by shear weight of numbers.

"Captain, I don't think we can hold the fuel bunker and the shuttle at the same time!" Sgt Aurora yelled, loosing another burst from her multi-barreled railgun. She, like all the Marines, was starting to worry about running out of ammo before they ran out of aliens.

"Right," replied Capt. Rodriguez, emerging from the fuel store. "Shuttle One, take what you have on board and head back to the ship. Now!"

"Aye aye, Ma'am," Lt. Lawson responded from the flight deck. Almost as the words were uttered the shuttle began to back out of the hole it had made in the hull during the initial attack.

"1st squad, fall back on the AM store. The rest of 2nd squad, reinforce 1st squad. We need to stop these critters before they can get to the remaining antimatter."

"Aye aye, Captain!"

"BP-2, BP-1. Come in Lt. Westfield."

"Go, BP-1" came Westfield's voice, clipped by the comm circuit.

"What's your position?"

"We are about 200 meters in front of your position, directly behind the alien swarm."

"Move to their flanks so you don't take friendly fire. Then give 'em everything you got."

"Roger that, BP-1."

"Use your suits' IR vision," GySgt Washington broadcast over the common frequency. "The ambient temp in here is down around -170 but the sand fleas register -50 or so. Just don't fire at anything hotter, it's one of us."

"Gotcha, Gunny," someone replied.

Green streaks from 5mm flechette tracers laced the girder crossed interior, with counterpoint provided by explosions of various sizes: rolling waves of fire from 15mm cannon shells, orange blossoms from 20mm grenades and the even larger flares of the last few breaching missiles.

* * * * *

In the midst of the surging crew, the alien Captain advanced carrying the antimatter bomb in a sling. At first it looked like the massed attack was going to work and give them access to the fuel cache. But then their advance faltered.

"Charge!" the Captain cried, urging his crew on. "Think of your brood-mates! Think of our beautiful, blessed world!"

They surged forward with renewed purpose but again progress soon stalled in the face of withering enemy fire. "It's no good, Captain," his first lieutenant said plaintively. "The attack is failing, we will not gain the fuel cache."

"So be it, then." The Captain reached into the sling holding the AM container and its cobbled up detonator. "This will just have to be close enough."

He pressed the arming switch and it began its two and a half minute countdown...

49

* * * * *

In the end it was a slaughter, alien bodies and body parts left drifting about in a grisly Brownian motion of death. The combined firepower of four squads of Marines shredded the mob of aliens, who had bunched up in front of BP-1's blocking positing. Lt. Westfield and Gunny Washington worked their way to the center of the alien formation, looking for possible survivors.

"Strange the way they all crowded together in the center, trying to get to the fuel bunker," Westfield commented as he nudged bodies aside one foot.

"Yeah," added Washington, "it was almost like a football team trying to do a quarterback sneak, right up the middle."

"Apt analogy, Gunny. This one would appear to be the quarterback." Westfield flipped over a body that had markings on its carapace, perhaps indicators of rank. As the body rolled over the sling containing the makeshift bomb came into sight.

"What's in that sack?" Washington asked.

"It's one of those egg things..." The Lieutenant's blood ran cold, "it's a fucking IED!"

"Bomb!" he transmitted, dropping his weapon and grasping the sling with his left hand. With a mighty leap he jumped from a bracing girder in the direction of the hole Shuttle One had vacated a few minutes earlier.

"BP-1, Peggy Sue. Interrogative type of bomb and its location?"

"The aliens were trying to get one of those little antimatter eggs into the fuel bunker. The damned thing looked like it was rigged to explode," Washington broadcast and then, after a moment's hesitation, bounded after his Lieutenant.

It only took a second for Capt. Rodriguez to understand the situation. She used the command broadcast frequency: "Everybody find cover! Get part of the hull between you and the port side."

Though not understanding the reason for their CO's order, the Marines immediately moved to comply. As they scrambled for cover Westfield swung from girder to girder until he reached the gash the shuttle had made in the alien vessel's four meter thick hull.

50

Grasping a beam at the edge of the hole with his right hand, Dirk let his body's momentum swing him around. Pivoting around his grip on the beam, his left arm described a wide arc, with the sling containing the bomb extending that arc. Like a Scotsman hurling a hammer, Westfield threw the bomb out of the hole and into space.

After releasing the bomb the Lieutenant grasp the beam with both hands, stopping his forward momentum. Hanging motionless, staring at the empty, star speckled space beyond, Dirk watched as the bomb grew smaller with distance and vanished from his sight.

"Face starboard! Get your suit backpacks between you and the explosion." Capt. Rodriguez broadcast. "If you can see stars out of the breaching hole you are in the line of fire!"

CIC, *Peggy Sue*

Those monitoring the boarding party from Peggy Sue's Combat Information Center had finally begun to relax when the Marines reported that all of the aliens had been killed or otherwise neutralized. Then the alarmed call of "Bomb!" caused everyone to turn back to the display monitors.

"Bomb? What kind of bomb?" asked Chief Engineer Medina.

"BP-1, Peggy Sue. Interrogative type of bomb and its location?" asked Capt. Curtis. The command crew listened in horror as GySgt Washington reported that the bomb was an antimatter egg somehow rigged to detonate.

"If a type 3 AM container goes off inside the hull it will probably take out the entire boarding party," Jo Jo said. "Even worse, it could set off the remaining big eggs in the fuel bunker."

"How many were left in the bunker?"

"The shuttle reported seven eggs on board. That would leave seven or eight still on the hulk. Not as bad as when the Space Mushroom blew, but there won't be anything left of the alien ship but plasma."

Capt. Curtis calculated in her head. "We are 500 km from the alien ship, we should be OK, even if the main store blows. Get the shuttles and the corvettes well away." As the navigation officer called for the other ships of the task force to head away from the hulk the Captain issued commands to her crew. "Shields to maximum, Mr. Medina, and set all viewports to opaque..."

Marine Boarding Party, Alien Hulk

At the edge of the hole Washington lunged forward, grabbed Lt. Westfield by the leg and hauled him back from the opening. The two shuffled sideways, away from the hole and then stopped, their backs pressed against the inside of the alien hull.

As the timer ticked down, the dead captain's scuttling charge moved away from his ship at over 100 kph. The storage container held a bit less than a kilogram of antimatter. When it detonated 21 seconds later it was half a kilometer away from the ship's hull. As the freed antimatter annihilated material in the surrounding container it released the energy equivalent of a 20 megaton nuclear bomb.

About 50% of the energy of a matter/antimatter explosion is lost to neutrinos, which do no damage to normal matter and living things. The rest is released as pure energy—mostly photons energetic enough to be well beyond any light visible to humans. After mutual annihilation, any excess matter is irradiated by the torrent of gamma rays resulting in a bright visible flash. The flash, however, is a relatively feeble manifestation of the overall electromagnetic burst.

When a nuclear or AM explosion happens in the vacuum of space its effects are significantly different than such a blast in an atmosphere or in contact with a solid body. First, without material for a shockwave to propagate through, blast effect disappears completely.

Second, thermal radiation also disappears. There is no air for the blast wave to heat and the radiation emitted from the weapon itself is much higher in frequency. That radiation can be more intense without an atmosphere to attenuate it. In fact, the unprotected lethal radius of a multi-megaton blast can extend to hundreds of kilometers.

A shaft of radiation poured through the hull breach, causing everything in its path to flare brightly—aliens, girders and braces alike. A radiant circle was inscribed on the inside of the hull opposite the opening. Fortunately for the Marines they were not in the path of that awful wave of radiation. The combination of the alien ship's four meter thick metal and rock hull and their own armor's shielding protected them from the explosion's EM burst.

Slowly, Marines began reemerging from where they had taken cover before the explosion. Captain Rodriguez pulled up the status of everyone in the boarding party on her helmet's holographic display. By some miracle, it looked like everyone made it. A few readouts were showing a bit of reflected radiation but nothing life threatening. Rodriguez sounded the all clear and several of the Marines drifted down to the opening of the fuel bunker, including Westfield and Washington.

"Thank you for saving my life, Gunny," Dirk said on suit-to-suit as they neared the front of the bunker.

"Just returning the favor, Lieutenant. If you hadn't chucked that bomb overboard we all would have bought the farm."

Westfield had not had a chance to report to his CO in person before the bomb diverted their attention. This time he fervently hoped there would be no interruption.

"I believe we got the lot of them, Captain," he said, floating up to Capt. Rodriguez. "We should probably make a second pass to make sure we didn't miss any hostiles but it looked like all those that didn't get caught when the inhabited spaces decompressed went with the captain on his suicide charge aft."

"Yeah, I don't think any got past us either, but we need to double check before they send over any scientists or swabbies," she replied.

"Aye aye, Ma'am," he replied, then turned to go rejoin his unit. Jennifer reached out and placed an armored gauntlet on his shoulder.

"About that bomb, Lieutenant," she said, as he turned back to face her. Jennifer looked him steadily in the eyes. "Good job, Dirk. Damned good job."

As Rodriguez turned and floated back inside the fuel bunker, Westfield thought to himself, *that is the first time she has ever called me Dirk and not Reggie. I may have finally gotten myself off of Jennifer Rodriguez's shit list.*

Chapter 4

Jesse's Place, Farside

The main atrium at Farside Base was a large open area, replete with flowering plants, growing palm trees and even a water fall. Known as the Atrium to base residents, its designers thought that having a place that mimicked nature would be good for morale. What was probably better for morale was the presence of several restaurants and bars around the landscaped cavern's periphery.

The main bar was located on the second level balcony, just off the base administrative offices. It was always crowded with workers, military personnel and civilians. Though it was inexpensive and served all manner of libation, Ludmilla had given up on drinking there. She was just too recognizable and always attracted a continuous stream of supplicants hoping to bend the chief administrator's ear.

Instead, Ludmilla and her close friends had taken to drinking at a much smaller bar, a place that was wedged in behind the foliage near the water fall. The bar was named Jesse's Place, after Jesse Lowe, the proprietress. Jesse had been "recruited" by some of Peggy Sue's officers when they were in the Caribbean to pick up a few former SEALs. The SEALs, old friends of Senior Chief Hank Zackly, were happy to join the ship's company but insisted on bringing the bartender from their favorite hangout. They claimed it was for her safety and Captain Jack, who had a soft spot for island cooking, accepted her as a new member of the crew.

Jesse proved to be not just a great cook and bartender, but an able crewmember, helping to destroy several enemy ships as the Peggy Sue fought her way out of the Sirius system. Though she was a bonafide combat veteran, Jesse was really not the military type and had opted to stay at Farside when Task Force Alpha sailed. With backing from TK Parker she was able to open her secluded little bar off the main atrium where she served island style *hors d'oeuvres* and potent drinks.

The house specialty was a mysterious concoction named a Fantasy, a mixture of spices, tropical fruit juices and 151 proof rum. Rumor had it that several hallucinogenic herbs helped add to its potency but Jesse refused to divulge the ingredients. The station administration took a libertarian attitude toward off-duty intoxicants—as long as you showed up sober, could do your job and were not endangering others you could pick your poison.

"Well hello, Miss Ludmilla," Jesse called from behind the bar as Ludmilla entered. "I haven't seen you in nearly a week. I begin to tink you don' like me no more." The last comment was delivered with a wide smile that showed several gold teeth and dimples on each cheek.

"Oh Jesse, you know that is not true," Ludmilla smiled back. "I have just been too busy to get out."

"Den you be workin' too hard," the bartender replied.

Ludmilla took a seat at the bar, which was topped with a beautiful piece of natural mahogany. On previous visits she sat at a table with friends but tonight there was no one else in the place and it didn't feel right to sit alone, forcing Jesse to come to her. Glancing around Ludmilla noticed that there was a small green lizard clinging to one of the poles that ran from the bar top to the ceiling.

At first she dismissed the little reptile as inanimate decoration— there were no wild animals running loose on Farside Base. Then she noticed one of the creature's turret like eyes move.

"Is that little lizard alive?" she asked, as Jesse delivered a highball glass filled with ice. The big Jamaican woman then produced a large glass jug from beneath the bar containing a cloudy amber liquid that could have been mistaken for apple cider.

"Him? Dat's Freddy," Jesse said as she filled up Ludmilla's glass.

"Freddy? How did you get him to the Moon?"

"Freddy's been wit me for years. When I come from St Croix I couldn't leave him behind. When we went on de voyage I left him wit some science folk. Dey had lots of flies to feed him—said dey used de flies for research. I got him back when de Peggy Sue returned."

"You are not afraid he will run off?"

"No mon, dey is no flies to eat and no girl lizards to romance. Poor Freddy's the only one of his kind on de Moon," Jesse said, sadly shaking her head. "So I feed him and he stays in de bar. Freddy helps customers know when dey's had too much to drink. Watch..."

Jesse poured a dollop of Fantasy on the polished bar top. Up on his pole, one of Freddy's independent eyes quickly drew a bead on the amber liquid. After a few moments the lizard scrambled half way down the pole, moving so quickly it was hard to follow his movement. He froze in place, only his eyes darting here and there checking for threats.

A few more moments passed—Freddy raced down and across the bar to his prize. An incredibly long, fat tongue flicked in and out, quickly consuming the small puddle of beverage. His mission accomplished, Freddy turned in a flash, scurrying back across the bar and up the pole to his original vantage point.

"Each time you has a drink I give Freddy one," Jesse said, smiling as though she had explained everything.

"*Buonasera* Jesse, Ludmilla," Elena said, walking up to the bar. As usual the Italian astronomer looked stunning in her science section burgundy jumpsuit. "I see you've gotten a head start on me, Ludmilla."

"Yes, me and the lizard," her friend replied.

"The what?"

"Freddy the lizard, up there on his pole. You will see when you get a drink."

"Not yet," Jesse said, pouring a Fantasy for Elena. "Freddy don' get a next drink til your second round. You'll see."

Confused, Elena looked from the smiling bartender to her friend, perched on the next bar stool, and finally up at the little green lizard, high up on his pole. Picking up her drink she sensibly decided to change the subject. "*Salute!* So what do you hear from Gretchen and the Peggy Sue?"

"The last message came a few hours ago, saying that they had the enemy in sight and were about to attack. I have been so nervous I could die."

"I'm sure they are all right, Gretchen is a good officer and an experienced commander. Jack trusted her with the ship and crew at Sirius"

"Do not remind me," Ludmilla rolled her eyes and drained her drink. "Somehow Jack and most of my friends have ended up far away and out of touch."

"You must miss him terribly, and the others."

Ludmilla's gaze dropped and she stared quietly at her empty glass. Sensing her friend's discomfort Elena quickly said, "Let's talk about something else."

"Yes," Ludmilla replied, forcing her attention back to the conversation. "Like how you are doing with that handsome physicist I have seen you out with. Come on, drink up, the night is young..."

M'tak Ka'fek

When they found themselves trapped on the T'aafhal ship, 1,500 light-years from home, one of the stranded crewmembers' first concerns was for food and water. As it turned out the M'tak had plenty of the latter, but solving the need for the former took a bit of doing.

Capt. Sutton, his head jammed full of manuals and specifications for the battle cruiser, courtesy of the ship's AI, quickly realized that the ship could synthesize nearly any organic substance given a sample of the material in question. The shuttles they used when boarding contained standard stores of field rations —nourishing but hardly gourmet fare. No one, the Captain included, relished the idea of a long voyage on nothing but MREs.

So Capt. Jack had the crew turn out their personal kit, knowing from long experience that sailors, Marines and SEALs all had a habit of carrying some extra supplies when going into an unknown situation. Sure enough, a wide range of consumables were soon being fed into the ship's synthesizer. Samples of chicken, beef and bacon, along with bread, beer, wine, and orange juice were supplied. Lt. Bear had a chunk of frozen ringed seal in a compartment of his suit and Jack himself had bottles of gin and brandy, and some of Jesse's conch salad with pumpkin fritters. With the food situation sorted out the crew settled in for the voyage, their fears greatly allayed.

Compared to the Peggy Sue, the interior space of the M'tak Ka'fek was cavernous. Each member of the crew was provided a spacious private cabin, the bears' quarters suitably cold with an adjoining icy swimming pool. The main shuttle bay held a number of yet to be investigated small craft and still had plenty of open space for the crew to practice boarding tactics in their armor.

Even more impressive, there were two grand hallways that ran almost the entire length of the ship, one on the port side and one to starboard. They were joined at either end forming a continuous track nearly 500 meters around. Naturally, the Marines and SEALs turned it into a place to run. With little else to occupy themselves other than practicing on the ship's weapon systems and physical training, much time was spent running around the track. Even the sailors joined in.

Lance Corporals Jon Feldman and Roselito Acuna were on their fourth lap of the track. Running at a relaxed pace, their breathing steady, the pair were conversing.

"How have you been feeling," Jon said between breaths, "since we came on board?"

"Pretty good, Feldman. Why do you ask?"

"I've been feeling damned good ... maybe a little too good."

"What do you mean?"

After a few more breaths, he replied, "I mean running for 10 klicks ... plus calisthenics, weights and a little hand-to-hand ... would have left me sore the next day, back home."

Rosey considered his answer for a few paces before replying herself. "You know you're right? ... I don't think I've ever been in this good of shape."

A deep voice behind them yelled a warning. "Coming through!"

Jon moved left and Rosey moved right, just in time to let a large white, furry object gallop past. It was quickly followed by a second, somewhat smaller quadruped—Lt. Bear and Aput out for their daily run.

"That," Rosey commented as she moved back to the center of the track, "is why it is stupid to try to outrun a bear."

"Yeah, and I think they are getting faster," Jon said. "I think all of us are." He paused for a few breaths and then added. "You know that little cockroach Sanchez benched 150 kilos ... that's twice his body weight."

"So? He's a wiry little guy."

"He never could do that back home."

"Maybe he had the ship lower the gravity ... you know what a trickster his is."

"No, I can lift more than I ever could too ... I think there is something going on."

"You know, now that you mention it, ... I have an old hip wound that always hurt like a sonofabitch after a run."

"And?"

"It ain't hurt since we've been on board."

They ran on without speaking for a dozen paces.

"I think the ship is messing with us," Jon said.

"Messing with us how, Jon?"

"I don't know, maybe puting stuff in our food or altering our DNA when we're doing weapons practice."

Rosey remained silent.

"I think someone should talk to the Captain," Jon said.

"Yeah," Rosey replied absently, her mind deep in thought. The pair finished their run and headed for the showers without further discussion.

Peggy Sue, the Kuiper Belt

The recovery operation had gone smoothly. All of the Marines were back on board, along with a load of technological booty. A dozen full type one antimatter containers and two partially full ones, plus a bunch of strange equipment that the expedition's scientists claimed were computers and navigation gear. The product of a civilization who's idea of comfortable room temperature was colder than 50° below zero Celsius, the alien devices had to be kept at a similar temperature while they were being investigated. Even the polar bears found that a bit nippy.

Captain Curtis was in her sea cabin, conferring with her staff: Lt. Medina, Lt. Vincent, Capt. Rodriguez, and Lt. Westfield. Lt. Medina was senior by time in rank, a Navy full lieutenant being the equivalent of a Marine captain, and Dirk Westfield was junior. As Jack had taught her, Gretchen solicited advice starting with the most junior officer present—an attempt to prevent the junior officers from being swayed by their superiors' opinions.

"Tell me, Lt. Westfield, how do you assess the outcome of the mission?"

"Successful on all primary objectives, Ma'am. We seized the enemy vessel, secured their antimatter supplies, and obtained what the science section claims is navigation equipment. We suffered no casualties."

"And the non-prime objectives?"

"We failed to capture any live aliens for interrogation, Captain. The crew fought to the last man, er, alien."

"I see," Gretchen said, shifting her attention to the head Marine. "Capt. Rodriguez, would you like to add anything to that?"

"Yes, Ma'am. We were very lucky, the aliens almost managed to scuttle their ship. In the end it could have gone either way. Only quick thinking by Lt. Westfield saved the prize and the boarding party."

"Noted," Jennifer replied. "Certainly, it's better to be lucky in battle than not."

"True, Captain, but you shouldn't depend on luck. We took a terrible risk capturing the hulk."

Gretchen suppressed a shudder inside as she thought of how great a risk she had taken with Earth's only major warship and only operational platoon of Marines. "Yes, I agree, but there are times in war when the enemy has the advantage and risks must be taken. As it stands, we now have sufficient antimatter to arm a dozen new frigates, which will give us a chance of standing off another attack on Earth."

"Aye, Ma'am. Sometimes you have to make your own luck. Besides, there's no deodorant like success."

"Precisely, Capt. Rodriguez." Gretchen smiled a tight smile. "And how did the fleet perform, Lt. Vincent?"

"Well, Captain. As it turned out the enemy was over matched. We disabled their ship on the first pass and the corvettes soon suppressed any remaining capacity to fight. We kicked their alien asses, Ma'am."

Gretchen nodded. "Anything to add, Lt. Medina?"

"I agree with Lt. Vincent, they were not the enemy's A team. That crudely built behemoth was not as formidable as the squadron of aliens that waylaid us at Sirius. Their ship was nothing more than a scow used for dropping big rocks on unsuspecting planets." There was more than a hint of contempt in the chief engineer's voice.

"Very good. I expect you all to commit your thoughts to formal after action reports while they are fresh in your minds. This was a good job all the way round, people. We achieved great success and incurred no casualties, well done."

The assembled officers murmured "thank you, Ma'am," and finally allowed themselves genuine smiles. "A ration of grog for the Marines and Crew?" asked Lt. Medina.

"Once we are underway for Earth, Jo Jo," the Captain replied. "Peggy Sue. Please send a message to Earth: We have met the enemy and he is ours."

"Yes, Captain," the ship's computer replied.

"That would be Commodore Oliver Hazard Perry in a letter to General William Henry Harrison," noted Billy Ray. "After the Battle of Lake Erie in 1813."

"Yes, during the War of 1812. A decisive victory that secured the Great Lakes region for the United States and ended the threat of invasion from that quarter," Gretchen recited. "Hopefully our victory will have a similar result for Earth."

Jesse's Place, Farside Base

Ludmilla and Elena were halfway through their second round of Fantasies, Elena having witnessed Freddy's performance with a second dollop of liquor.

"So this physicist was rescued from a laboratory in Italy?" Ludmilla asked, still trying to pry personal information out of the sexy astronomer. It kept her mind off her own lover, who was missing in action in a different star system.

"Si, Alessandro was one of those we rescued from the *Laboratori Nazionali del Gran Sasso*," Elena replied, coyly prolonging her friend's frustration.

"Really?"

"It's a particle physics laboratory situated near Gran Sasso mountain, the tallest peak in the Apennines. It lies between the towns of L'Aquila and Teramo in central Italy, about 120 km from Rome."

"That is quite close to the impact in the north Adriatic. How did they survive the blast and its aftereffects?

"They were very lucky. You see the laboratory was built to do research that requires low levels of background radiation. For shielding, much of the lab was built below ground—actually inside the mountain. Gran Sasso Tunnel is part of the A24 Motorway that links Rome and the Adriatic Sea—access to the facility is inside the highway tunnel that passes under the mountain peak.

"As soon as it became obvious what was happening—gigantic asteroids impacting around the world—they rushed as many people as possible into the tunnel and underground caverns."

"So it acted as a bomb shelter, protecting the staff from the impact?"

"Si. In a sense they were saved by the Apennine Mountains themselves."

"Lucky indeed," Ludmilla said, finishing her drink. "And lucky that you knew the facility existed and guessed that there might be survivors there."

"Yes, we found over 100 people, mostly scientists and technicians and their families. You know, when we first arrived back at Earth and saw the results of the bombardment I was afraid that I was the last Italian left in the galaxy."

"Ah, but now you have your handsome Alessandro..." Ludmilla's voice trailed off suggestively. Before Elena could respond Ludmilla's communicator chirped. "Now what?" she exclaimed, tapping the flexible display screen woven into the arm of her jumpsuit.

"Col. Tropsha? We have received a new communique from Task Force Alpha."

Ludmilla tilted her head back and closed her eyes. All she could think of was, *Thank, God!* Then, with urgency in her voice, "tell me, what do they report?"

"Commander Curtis sent 'we have met the enemy and he is ours' Ma'am."

"Casualties," Ludmilla demanded, "were there any casualties?"

"No Ma'am, they report no losses, no casualties. All vessels survived with no significant damage. There is accompanying video footage of the battle and boarding action coming in as we speak, Colonel."

"*Che bellezza!* They not only survived but they have won, bravo!" The elated Elena bounced out of her seat and danced around her bar stool.

Silent tears ran down Ludmilla's cheeks and for a few moments she did not trust herself to speak. Then, with a slight shake of her head to clear the tears, she spoke into her comm: "Send a reply: 'Congratulations to the crews and Marines, and a safe voyage home.' Make an announcement on all the base channels. The people need to know that the task force has triumphed."

"Roger, Ma'am. Should we release the video as well?"

"Da, yes release it all." A broad smile spread slowly across the base administrator's face. It felt as if the weight of the world had just been lifted from her shoulders. She turned to her two companions, saying, "this calls for another drink, Ladies."

"For true! Dis be a time to jump-up and celebrate," Jesse's smile was almost as big as Ludmilla's. Their glasses were quickly refiled, and Freddy served as well. While the friends toasted the success of Captain Curtis and Task Force Alpha cheers could be heard breaking out at the other bars and eateries around the atrium—word of the victory was out.

Finishing her third Fantasy of the evening, Ludmilla sat her empty glass on the bar top. Rising a bit unsteadily she announced, "I am afraid that I need to get to the command center. There is no rest for the wicked."

"Now I tink you need to set down a bit, Miss Ludmilla," Jesse said, motioning with her head in the direction of Freddy's pole. The other two women turned toward the pole in time to see Freddy peal backwards off his perch and fall gracefully to the bar top. He landed on his back with a single bounce and lay supine, four webbed feet in the air, unhurt but passed out cold.

Jesse chuckled. "When de third round hits you, you had best be sittin' down. You too, Miss Elena."

Task Force Alpha, Leaving the Kuiper Belt

Having secured the antimatter, salvaged equipment, and other cargo, the Peggy Sue and her entourage of corvettes turned back toward the Sun—only a dim and distant star from their current location. The crew was in a jubilant mood, not only because of their victory over the invading aliens but because they were on their way back to Earth. At this point no one wanted to think about the herculean tasks in front of them: building a fleet to prevent further alien incursions, salvaging human civilization, and healing Earth as best they could.

In a time of war good days are to be savored, for victory is fleeting and other trials surely lay ahead. The Marines and crew were celebrating with a round of drink on the Captain—beer, wine, and a taste of rum for all. So strong were the feelings of goodwill engendered by victory that no fights broke out between the sailors and Marines, a noteworthy event in itself.

In the refrigerated compartments aft the polar bears were also enjoying a bit of blackberry brandy, a vice introduced to them by the absent Lt. Bear. That, and possibly the last *nattiq*, or ringed seals, they would ever eat made it a party to remember for the ursine Marines. Among the newly seasoned warriors was Umky, Isbjørn's cub sired by Bear.

"How does it feel to be a bear in full, Umky?" rumbled Tornassuk, one of the older males.

"Really? I'm an adult now? I thought that a cub had to survive a winter alone on the pack ice, without his mother, before being considered a grownup."

"Umky, you have journeyed to a place farther away than anywhere on the pack ice," replied Aurora, "and just as dark as winter. Maybe darker with the Sun so far away you can't find it in the sky."

"You have fought your first battle along side the human Marines, against alien monsters whose blood was colder than the coldest midwinter night," added Tornassuk, between slurps of brandy. Bears had a habit of waxing poetic about combat.

"I guess when you put it that way, Tornassuk. Maybe I'll finally get some respect from my father."

"I wouldn't worry about that, Pihoqahiak may not even be alive."

"My Mom thinks he still is," Umky said, sucking on the straw from his brandy jug, "him and the human, Captain Jack."

"Pihoqahiak seems like a hard bear to kill," Aurora observed, "and that Captain Jack is a piece of work himself."

"What do you mean?" the young bear asked.

"Well, the way I hear it Captain Jack snuck up on Pihoqahiak while he was shooting up a bunch of Inuit hunters with that big white rifle he used to carry. Supposedly, the Captain was unarmed."

"Pretty brave for a primate," Tornassuk belched loudly, "or pretty stupid."

"I'd say he was pretty lucky," Aurora retorted, "and remember, that primate talked all of us into joining him. So if he's stupid what does that make us?"

"Right now, it makes me thirsty," Tornassuk growled, as he reached for another jug of brandy.

"I just hope our luck holds," said Aurora softly.

Chapter 5

Administrator's Office, Farside Base

Ludmilla was at her desk, trying to concentrate on work while dealing with the lingering effects of her hangover. She and Elena had sat at Jesse's bar for more than an hour, sipping soda water and bitters, waiting for the room-spinning dizziness of three large Fantasies to dissipate. Finally feeling steady enough to stumble back to their respective quarters, they called it a night sometime after midnight.

The rumors that there is more than alcohol in Jesse's signature concoction must be true, Ludmilla thought ruefully. *I have always been able to hold my liquor and Elena is no tea-teetotaler herself. I have never gotten that drunk off of just three drinks!*

Despite a handful of analgesics and a half liter of re-hydration fluids her head still throbbed. Knifing through her pain came the sound of her assistant calling her.

"Da? Slushayu vas."

"Colonel? Miss Scott Hamilton is here to see you."

"Yes, yes. Send her in."

Ludmilla attempted to sit up straight and look less disheveled than she felt as the food production expert entered. Melissa Scot Hamilton had been the horticulturalist on board the Peggy Sue during its first two voyages and was among the original people on the project to build the starship. A native of Mississippi, she had been pursuing a PhD in horticulture at Auburn University's school of Agriculture in neighboring Alabama. A falling out with her dissertation adviser led to her joining TK Parker's team.

"Morning, Dr. Tropsha," the always sunny young scientist said as she crossed the room and took a seat in front of the administrator's desk. "You're lookin' a bit peaked this morning."

"Indeed I am, Melissa. Too many of Jesse's evil concoctions last night."

"Yes Ma'am, I've been there myself. Felt low enough to walk under a snake the next morning."

69

"That is about how I feel, but enough about my foolish behavior. What can I do for you today?"

"Well, as you know I have been trying to set up a sustainable system that can raise enough food to feed our growing population," the soft spoken horticulturist began. "We've got a bunch of hydroponic vegetable gardens and such goin' and the aquaculture tanks are coming along nicely. But there are some plants that just don't do good without soil."

Ludmilla nodded encouragingly.

"Without soil as a buffer, any interruption of the hydroponic system can lead to rapid plant death. Plus the high moisture levels associated with hydroponics can lead to pathogen attacks and over watering. Verticillium wilt alone can attack over 300 species of useful plants: tomatoes, potatoes, eggplants, peppers and a bunch of others. Besides, wheat and other grain crops just do better in soil.

"Our alternative is planting *Triticum aestivem* in manufactured soil. We can control the temperature, humidity, and other factors to boost yields and speed things up: 23°C, 65% humidity, 1000 ppm of CO_2, a drip nutrient delivery system and continuous artificial sunlight. Still, we'll be lucky to get three crops a year per field, though we can stagger plantings so the harvests are more frequent. We also get runoff from the fields that needs to be filtered. Fortunately, we've gotten some good oyster beds established."

"Oysters? As in shellfish?"

"Yes, Ma'am. Oyster beds are terrific filters for organic runoff, each adult oyster can filter and clean up to 50 gallons of water a day. We mix the runoff and other organic waste with the water flowing into the oyster tanks and then send the outflow on to the shrimp, crab and lobster tanks. Our goal is to generate the maximum amount of edible protein in the shortest amount of time— and that's where I'm running into a problem."

"A problem? What kind of problem?"

"Push-back from some of my colleagues. You see, I want to raise flies."

"Flies?" blurted an incredulous Ludmilla. "Why in heavens name do you want to raise flies? Not having insects around is one of the truly good things about living on the Moon."

"Not so much flies, really, as their larvae. Fly larvae can be bred, raised, harvested and ground into a meal that provides the same amount of edible protein by weight as fish meal."

"That may be, but I think you will encounter strong resistance from the public if you try to feed them fly protein. How would you serve it? Fly burgers? Fly stew? That would give new meaning to 'waiter, there is a fly in my soup'!"

"No Ma'am, that's not what I mean. I want to feed the fly meal to the fish, chickens and other food animals. Flies can live on food humans waste, and the larvae on slaughterhouse or distillery waste. Each fly produces about 1,000 eggs. The eggs hatch into larvae and are harvested within a couple of weeks, before they turn into flies. Then they're dried and turned into protein meal."

As Melissa warmed to her subject her enthusiasm grew. "In trials on Earth they raised a million flies in a space of 100 cubic meters. A setup like that can produce 100 tons of wet larvae yielding 25 tons of feed a month. The scheme is environmentally sound, the flies don't compete for human food sources or feed for higher animals. It's the most efficient way to produce a lot of edible protein from biological waste."

"And we have usable flies on hand?"

"Yes, some of the biology labs use them for experiments. There are several suitable species available."

"You are sure this is the best thing to do?"

"Doctor, do you know how much food 10,000 people can consume? More than 18 tons a day, 560 tons a month, 6800 tons a year. An average human from a developed country eats nearly eight times their body weight a year. Right now we have no way to produce that much food in the closed environment of Farside Base. We are barely producing enough raw algal protein to feed the aquaculture tanks and people are already complaining about being fed too much seafood. If we raise twenty million flies we can have enough protein to raise pigs, chickens and cattle."

"I see, and you are convinced that this is the best way to solve our impending food crisis?"

"Yes, Ma'am. If you want bacon and eggs with a glass of milk for breakfast, this is how to get it. It's what I did my dissertation on in grad school," Melissa said, adding meekly, "my adviser didn't like it either."

"You say some of your colleagues are resiting the plan? Would these be academic types with PhDs?" Ludmilla asked with a smile.

"Yeah, they all think they have better answers."

"How many of them have successfully managed a closed ecological system like, say, a starship, on two interstellar voyages?" Ludmilla asked rhetorically. "I will tell you how many—none! Because you are the only horticulturalist to do so."

"I think it's partly because I didn't finish my doctorate; they treat me like a grad student, not an equal," Melissa added in a subdued voice.

Ludmilla sat silently for a few moments, tapping her fingers on her desk. She had been patronized and discriminated against many times in her career. Such behavior angered her, making her sympathize with the younger woman in front of her. Still, she was responsible for the common good of everyone on the moon base. Clearing her throat she asked a question: "Do you keep a copy of your dissertation?"

"Why, yes. I have been carrying it around on a flash drive since I joined the Peggy Sue. I always thought that I would defend it one day."

"Here is what you do. I want you to document the numbers for this fly larvae scheme—including all the links and feedbacks in such a system."

"Yes, Ma'am"

"I also want you to update your dissertation to reflect what you learned while on the Peggy Sue. Cite your observations on both voyages and include your proposed food production system for Farside Base."

"Yes, Ma'am."

"I will have some qualified scientists read your dissertation, and if they feel it ready you will do your defense in front of them and the public. After all, a university faculty is nothing more than a collection of scholars, some more qualified than others. With the world in ruin, we probably constitute the only center of scholarship and learning left. That makes us the University of the Moon, and you will be our first doctoral candidate. Then we will put your plan into action and let those who dare try to dispute your claims."

"Yes, Ma'am. Thank you, Ma'am."

"And one more thing, Melissa. We have known each other for two voyages, I would appreciate it if you would call me Ludmilla in private, as my other friends do." The chief administrator smiled kindly.

"Yes, Ma'am, I mean, Ludmilla," Melissa stammered in her soft southern accent, smiling back at the imposing woman in front of her. *My momma always said be careful what you ask for,* she thought, *but I know that I can do this, I know that I'm right.*

* * * * *

Melissa left the base administrative offices and headed back for her own world of hydroponic growing rooms, artificial wheat fields, and fish tanks. She needed to check on the expansion of the hog, chicken and cattle facilities—at least no one was arguing with her over their design. Trouble was, without the fly larvae there would be nothing to feed them on. She sighed.

She decided to check in on NatHanGon on her rounds. She and the Triad ambassador had become friends since it fell to her to keep the alien plant's environment comfortable. First on board the Peggy Sue and now here at Farside, they conversed daily when she checked on the conditions in its room. What did it say about her that her best friend was a triple brained alien plant more than 100,000 years older than she was? No matter, she had always felt more at home among plants and wild things than with people.

Lost in her thoughts, Melissa took no notice of the unremarkable looking man tending a stand of decorative plants in a nearby bed. Dressed in a plain gray jumpsuit, like other maintenance personnel, the man watched her as she headed back to her domain. As she disappeared around a corner he quickly packed up his tools and followed her into the maze of tunnels and chambers that housed the base's supporting infrastructure.

Bridge, M'tak Ka'fek

Lt. Bear was sitting in front of the ship's main control station with his eyes closed listening to music. A pair of white headphones were held on by a flexible connecting band that ran beneath his neck—wearing them over his head pinched his ears and human earbuds wouldn't stay in. Bear had the watch and was actually monitoring the ship and surrounding space using imagery the ship projected directly into his brain. Spooky and disconcerting at first, the entire crew had gotten used to the high-tech telepathic interface during the last two months of their voyage. Also on the bridge were JT, who was doing something at the navigation console, and Joey Sanchez, one of the Marines.

"What ya listening to, LT?" Joey called from the weapon station he was manning. During the first battle back in the Sirius system, trying to run the ship's weapons made most of the crew sick and disoriented. Practice drills had taught the Earthlings to handle the battle cruiser's formidable weaponry, and the accompanying telepathic projections, without blowing chunks.

"Snow Patrol," Bear replied, his eyes unopened.

"Let me guess, Songs for Polar Bears?"

"Wrong, Sanchez. Too much hip hop and drone crap on that album. I like their later stuff better."

"Like?"

"A Hundred Million Suns. Has some touches of minimalism, and I'm a big Phillip Glass fan."

"Who? What?" the confused Marine replied.

"Phillip Glass, Joey," JT added from the Nav Console. "Kundun? Einstein on the Beach? Icarus at the Edge of Time? Don't tell me you've never heard of Glass—he's one of the most influential composers of the 20th century."

"Never heard of him."

"Joey, you ain't got no culture."

"He doesn't have any taste either, JT. You should hear some of the crap he listens to. Ruin your hearing, and a deaf hunter ends up as something else's dinner."

"You officers are too highbrow for me," Joey retorted. "I'm just a poor grunt tryin' to get back home. By the way, Lt. Taylor, sir, with us bouncing from system to system, how do we know where Earth is?"

"The ship has instruments that can compare the relative arrival times of X-ray flashes from pulsars."

"Pulsars?"

"Massive objects scattered about the galaxy that act like God's own navigation beacons. They're thought to be rapidly rotating neutron stars that send out short pulses of radiation with a beat so steady they rival an atomic clock. With enough known sources and some math you can figure out where you are, sort of like GPS for spaceships."

"Really? And we know where Earth is from here?"

"Yeah, we have pretty decent charts of our local neighborhood, even out this far. We know where Earth is, it's getting back there in a reasonable amount of time that's the problem."

"Right," Bear rumbled. "That's why we're stalking that alien probe ship. The Captain expects it to eventually lead us to a refueling station."

"So we're gona' steal some antimatter when we find a refueling station?"

"That is not beyond the realm of possibility, Joey."

"Aw, crap," Bear exclaimed, opening his eyes. "The alien probe just jumped into alter-space. Better maneuver to follow it—match course and velocity vector for alter-space entry. M'tak, please wake the Captain."

"Certainly, Lt. Bear," the ship replied. "I have already set the parameters to follow the target vessel."

"Great," griped Joey, "what does this make, four alter-space transits? And each time we make a jump the Captain makes us drill our asses off."

"That's in case something is waiting at the other end," Bear growled, as he switched his music player to the score from Mishima. "I hope this time there is, because I could use a little action."

Task Force Alpha, Headed Back to Earth

The Peggy Sue headed back toward the Sun with the corvettes tucked in like goslings behind a mother goose. Returning from a distance of almost 40 AU, the ships of Task Force Alpha accelerated for twenty one and a quarter hours at 20Gs, bringing their velocity relative to Earth to five percent of the speed of light. Then they stopped accelerating and coasted, across the outer reaches of the solar system headed for Sol's habitable zone and Earth. The corvettes were happy to let the larger ship's more powerful shields sweep the path in front of them clean of dust and debris—at such velocities even striking a small pebble could be disastrous.

"Tell me again why we are not accelerating to the half way point and then decelerating, Mr. Vincent?" asked one of the new crewmembers. Compared with the excitement of a space battle and the subsequent boarding operation, standing watch seemed more than a little boring.

Tedium not withstanding, watches must be stood, even Mid Watch from midnight to 0400 hours. Billy Ray was Officer of the Deck, sitting in the Captain's chair above the helm and other bridge stations. At least on this voyage there were a sufficient number of officers to stand watch without wearing them all to a frazzle.

"One of the reasons is that there's a lot of junk floating about in space. It may not seem like it, but traveling as fast as we are the ship covers a lot of territory in a short amount of time. Even dust can be dangerous, so we need to have the shields up all the time. That takes a lot of energy, as do accelerating and decelerating."

"So how long will it take to get home?"

"We accelerated for just over 21 hours, now we coast for another 87 hours or so and then start decelerating," Billy Ray answered. "In all it will take us about five and a half days to make port at Farside."

"I guess that's not so long, it took the better part of a month to get out here. How fast are we going again?"

Billy Ray sighed, all this information was available from the ship's computer if you knew how to ask. They were coming to the end of the watch and the crew were undoubtedly as anxious to be relieved as he was. "We are currently traveling 15,000 km/sec, about five percent of c. That's another reason to not accelerate constantly the whole way—if we get going too fast, relativistic effects start to become noticeable."

"Like what, Sir?" asked a Marine, seated at the port side weapon station.

"Like time dilation. Time for us on board slows down relative to those back home. Not that you'll notice, but we will all be a bit under eight minutes younger than those who stayed at the base when we get back."

"Really?"

"Really. Just ol' Al Einstein's way of messing with us," the Texan lieutenant drawled. "OK, Q&A time is over. We need a systems check before the watch ends, look alive..."

Chapter 6

Balcony Bar, Farside Atrium

Following the announcement of Task Force Alpha's victory the celebration lasted until the wee hours of the next morning, but it was nothing compared to the blowout party that erupted when the task force finally made port. Martial fervor gripped the populace. Anyone who had been on the mission was unable to buy their own drinks in any establishment on the base. Those who hadn't could not hear enough about the attack by the Navy and subsequent boarding by the Marines.

Crew from the corvettes reenacted the battle with their hands in the tradition of fighter pilots since the Great War. In the midst of them was the irrepressible Frenchy Bouchard, his hands above his head at convergent angles.

"And then we swept in on the enemy for the kill" he told his audience of rapt listeners while sweeping one handful of extended fingers past the other accompanied by a whooshing sound. "Bam, Bam, Bam! We blew them out of the sky!"

From another table, where mostly crew from the Peggy Sue were gathered, someone called out: "So why did we have to take out three of the bogies ourselves after you made your devastating attack on the alien formation?"

"Hey, we took out our target and so did our wing man," Frenchy protested. "But we didn't want to keep all the fun for ourselves, *tu sais?*"

"Right, Frenchy," another crew member scoffed, "you PT boat jockeys only took out half of the enemy as you streaked past them."

"*Mais oui,* but we were in a hurry to blow the mother ship's head off."

"Yeah, and left it to us to kill the rest of them and then disable the enemy ship by blowing its engines off. Now that was some real shooting!"

"Yeah, all done from the safety of your nice comfy spaceships," added a new voice. "In the end it was the Marines that settled the matter." This brought a chorus of agreement from a table dressed mostly in Marine green.

"Damn straight!" boomed a loud, low voice from one corner. One of the polar bears, making a rare appearance in public. It had been hinted from above that the bears should mingle with their human comrades in a show of inter-species solidarity.

The argument over who had performed the most essential part in defeating the alien invaders had been going on for hours and showed no signs of letting up. Not as long as the main bar was filled with a mixture of crew from the corvette squadron, the Peggy Sue and the Marine boarding party. Add in a mixture of civilian admirers and other base personnel and the good natured verbal abuse would probably go on all night.

Here and there among the green and blue military jumpsuits the occasional black of an officer could be seen. They had come by to congratulate their men and quietly reinforce the desire by the command staff that everyone have a good, non-violent time. Word had been passed prior to arrival at Farside that anyone engaging in a brawl would find themselves back out on patrol so fast they wouldn't know what hit them. So far the inter-service sparring had remained verbal only.

One of the officers in attendance was a tall, lean figure, casually propped against the bar with a bottle of Samuel Adams Boston Lager in one hand. Probably one of the last bottles of Sam Adams beer left in the universe. He was reconnoitering the bar much like he would have in Austin or San Antonio just a few years ago.

Walking unhurriedly across the crowded room was another tall figure in black—Lt. Melaku, exchanging a word of commendation here and accepting congratulations there. Approaching the bar, she became aware of the other officer's presence. They made an interesting couple, both of a similar height and dressed in matching jumpsuits. Trim and attractive, the main contrast between them being that her skin was the color of buffed ebony and his a pale ivory.

"Good evening, Lt. Vincent," she began and then corrected herself when she noticed the small gold oak leaf on his collar, "I'm sorry, Lieutenant Commander Vincent. Congratulations, Sir."

"Why thank you," Billy Ray replied, straightening up and turning to face the female officer. He noticed that her collar insignia was now the two silver bars of a full lieutenant. "And congratulations yourself, Lieutenant Melaku."

Though Beth had been acting squadron commander during the mission she had been a Lieutenant JG, junior grade. Her leadership during the engagement had been recognized with a promotion to Lieutenant and assignment as commander of the base's growing corvette squadron.

Similarly, Billy Ray's performance as XO—executive officer—of the Peggy Sue had earned him promotion to Lieutenant Commander. Around the base, the scuttlebutt said he would soon be getting a ship of his own to command.

"How are your crew enjoying their reception?"

"They have quite taken to it, Sir. It will be hard to get them back out on patrol when the time comes, I'm afraid."

"Well they all deserve a bit of partyin' given what they did. Lord knows what the future might hold."

"You sound like you are expecting more trouble, Commander."

"One thing you can depend on, Lieutenant, is trouble—the Universe produces an endless supply of it." Billy Ray was dropping into his friendly cowboy persona in-spite of himself, the one that used to work so well picking up women in bars back home. He looked at the officer standing next to him, for the first time evaluating her charms as a member of the opposite sex.

She was tall enough that they could look each other levelly in the eyes. Her classic Ethiopian features looked quite exotic to a man from Texas—high forehead and cheekbones, narrow aristocratic nose and dark flashing eyes. She could have easily passed for a fashion model in Paris or New York.

On a low stage in one corner of the bar the band, which had been on break, was getting ready to start back up. Playing a mixture of Stevie Ray Vaughn, George Strait and Los Lonely Boys covers, with an occasional Tejano number thrown in for good measure, the best that could be said for the music was that it was loud and enthusiastic. As the band played an intro to "Texas Flood," Billy Ray made a decision, not realizing its significance at the time.

"Would you like to go someplace where we can hold a normal conversation?" he asked with more than a hint of his Texas accent in evidence.

"And where would that be, Commander?" Beth replied cautiously, her British accent sounding more formal to the cowboy than intended.

"I know a quiet bar just across the Atrium," he replied earnestly, sensing hesitation in the woman's reply. "Right now it's servin' as sort of an Officer's Club—most of the higher-ups are there."

"Higher-ups?"

"Yeah, like Col. Tropsha and her staff, and Capt. Curtis. I came here to make the rounds among the crew, but now I'm feelin' like my presence may be dampening the party mood."

Beth surveyed the room and noticed that most of the other officers had already departed. Though there was no written directive against fraternization between officers and enlisted personnel, old traditions died hard. "Yes, I see what you mean. You say it's just across the Atrium?"

"Sure enough, down on the main level over by the waterfall," Billy Ray said, trying to close the deal. "I'm Billy Ray, by the way."

"Call me Beth," she answered with a dazzling smile. Billy Ray had some notoriety as a pickup artist, a lady's man not interested in anything beyond a one night stand, but Beth had no demure reputation herself. Together they walked toward the exit, oblivious to the knowing grins among their respective crews.

Captain's Sea Cabin, M'tak Ka'fek

One of the first changes Jack ordered after settling in on board was the addition of an office just off the bridge area, what would be called a sea cabin on a traditional naval vessel. There he could perform administrative duties or take a quick nap while remaining close to the bridge. Currently he was meeting with several of the crew regarding some of their concerns.

Normally such matters would be forwarded up through channels, meaning the senior Chief or the ship's XO. With fewer than twenty on board including officers a strict chain of command was not really necessary, at least for personal matters. Standing in front of the Captain's desk were two Marines and an able spacer: Rosey Acuna, Jon Feldman and Matt Jacobs.

"At ease," Jack ordered, "so what brings you to my door today?"

The group had agreed to let Jon Feldman do most of the talking, since he was the first one to notice the changes. "Sir, we've noticed that things have been happening to us since we came on board— changes to our bodies and stuff, and we're a bit concerned."

"Really? What kind of changes?" Jack asked, his interest piqued.

"Like being able to run farther without being winded, and lifting heavier weights than we could back on Earth. Stuff like that, Sir."

"And old injuries that seem to have healed, or at least don't hurt anymore," Rosey chimed in. Since her conversation with Jon she had been noticing other things.

"And you, Jacobs. You've noticed inexplicable changes as well?"

"Yes, Captain," Matt looked sheepishly down at the deck, "you're going to think I'm making this up but..." The sailor blushed bright red.

"Come on man, out with it," Jack chided gently.

"Well, Sir, I used to have an appendix scar and it isn't there anymore."

"I see, and do you have a theory as to how or why this is happening?"

"Sir, we think the ship is doing it," Jon blurted, "I mean the ship's computer."

Jack sat back in his chair and steepled his fingers in front of his chin—a favorite pose during cogitation. *Now that I think of it, I misplaced my reading glasses several weeks ago but haven't needed them. Perhaps something is going on. I wonder if M'tak is at the root of this?*

Jack sat up and spoke to the trio in front of him, "Thank you for bringing this to my attention. I will consult with the ship's AI and see what might be causing these... changes. I will get to the bottom of this and let everyone know what is going on. Dismissed."

The crewmembers mumbled thank-you-sirs and exited the sea cabin. After the door slid shut Jack addressed the omnipresent ship's computer. "M'tak, have you been causing changes to the crews' bodies without informing them?"

"Yes, Captain," answered the AI's disembodied voice.

Why is it that computer intelligences can be so aggravatingly literal when they want to be? "Would you care to explain why you are doing this and how?"

"Captain, part of my normal operation is to ensure all of the ship's systems are kept fully functional and performing to their maximum potential. That extends to the ship's biological systems as well."

"Meaning the crew?"

"Yes, Captain. I have optimized the crew's nutritional intake and included a number of nanites in their foodstuffs. Those nanites are programmed to seek out damaged tissues and body parts and correct the damage—as long as the damage is not too severe."

"Like Rosey's old injury and Matt's appendix scar ... and my eyesight?"

"Yes."

"What do you define as 'too severe' for such repairs?"

"Regeneration of missing organs and body parts, or major trauma. For example, spacer Jacobs' appendix scar was replaced with normal skin tissue, but his appendix was not regrown."

"What about other scar tissue?" Jack suddenly had a disturbing thought. "Will my men, those who are circumcised, find their foreskins growing back?" *Won't that be fun to explain to the crew!*

84

"No Captain, I have specifically programed the nanites to not repair intentional alterations—earring holes, tattoos and other results of ritual self-mutilation will be left intact."

"That's reassuring," the Captain replied sarcastically, *at least I don't have to dread another tonsillectomy.* "And part of this performance optimization includes increasing the crew's strength and endurance?"

"Yes, Captain. I have also made adjustments to certain neural pathways to improve compatibility with the ship's systems."

"Which is why they no longer throw up when trying to use the weapons systems." *Yes,* Jack thought, careful to not send his thoughts over his direct neural link with the AI, *this all makes perfect sense.*

"Precisely, Captain," the AI replied. "This is all a normal part of ship operation, but I sense that you are upset."

"Just taken a bit by surprise is all. I will need some time to review the pertinent documentation and then figure out how to explain this to the crew."

"Why would they object to normal health maintenance and minor repair work? Several of them had the beginnings of potentially disabling or even fatal diseases."

"Our species is quite protective of personal privacy, our bodies in particular. We are ill at ease when it comes to outside parties doing things to our persons without our knowledge. I am sure that you only executed your duties as you saw fit, M'tak, but I will need to break this to the crew gently."

"As you wish, Captain. You certainly know your species better than I do."

Jesse's Place, Farside

Beth and Billy Ray made small talk on their stroll across the Atrium, until they approached the palm tree framed entrance to Jesse's bar. To either side of the entrance were Marines, standing at parade rest with holstered stunners plainly displayed.

85

"Evening gentlemen," Billy Ray drawled.

"Good evening Sir, Ma'am," the Marine on the right replied, nodding to the officers while unobtrusively checking their identities through the data glasses he wore. The guards were there to keep out roaming party goers and the overly inquisitive. Officers and the civilian heads of various departments were all on the approved list.

As the pair of officers passed through the entranceway, Billy Ray moved to one side, allowing Beth to enter the bar ahead of him. As she passed he ushered her in by lightly placing his hand on the small of her back.

The touch of Billy Ray's hand sent a shock through Beth's body, the sudden almost electric sensation caused by unexpected physical contact. On other occasions, Beth had decked men for taking such liberties uninvited. But for some reason, she did not pull away from Billy Ray's fleeting embrace, nor did she turn and confront him. Instead she simply strode forward into the bar as Billy Ray withdrew his hand as lightly as he had touched her.

Why did his touch excite me? Beth thought furiously. Then the pair were greeted by others and the moment was lost.

"Beth! Billy Ray! So glad you could come," called out Gretchen Curtis. On her suit collar was the unmistakable shape of an eagle, signifying the rank of Captain—she too had been promoted for her part in the great alien hunt.

"Good evening Captain, Ma'am," Billy Ray responded to his CO and the attractive woman standing next to her.

"Yes, good evening Captain Curtis," Beth added, "and to you, Col. Tropsha." There was no mistaking who the blond beauty standing next to the Captain was.

"Good evening, I do not believe we have met before," replied Ludmilla, smiling and extending her hand. "I find I have too many titles these days—Administrator, Colonel, Doctor—please call me Ludmilla."

"Both of these young officers took active part in the attack on the alien vessel," Gretchen said approvingly as the Lieutenant shook hands with the Chief Administrator. Gretchen had finished her first Fantasy and, on Ludmilla's advice, was nursing her second. Having been once bitten, Ludmilla was drinking vodka.

Silently, a black nose followed by a long white muzzle appeared to Beth's left. Catching motion out of the corner of her eye Beth turned and discovered a large polar bear next to her. Beth's eyes went wide, showing a significant amount of white against her dark complexion.

It was Isbjørn, one of the senior polar bears. Beth had only worked with the bears briefly on a few refugee runs and never met one of the ursines up close, at least not without being encased in space armor. "Good evening, everyone," the bear said.

"Howdy, Isbjørn," Billy Ray replied, grinning at Beth's unexpected discomfort. "It's OK, Beth, she don't bite."

"No, but I might nibble a little, as Bear would say," Isbjørn responded with a bearish smile.

"It is good to see you Isbjørn. I was just saying that we who had to stay behind are all thankful for the fleet's victory and safe return." Ludmilla was trying to redirect Beth's attention away from the she-bear's toothy grin. She then looked directly at Billy Ray. "And I am particularly happy for the safe return of my old friends and shipmates."

Slightly embarrassed, Billy Ray turned to Beth and offered an explanation for the remark. "You see, Beth, Ludmilla was Peggy Sue's doctor on both earlier voyages. She's healed our wounds, made first contact with the Triads and fought hand-to-hand with the hairy crickets of Pzzst."

"That's all true," said Isbjørn, "I met Ludmilla when the first shuttle full of bears arrived on the Peggy Sue. She was racing to save the life of Tornassuk, a male who had been shot by a hunter."

"It is, indeed, an honor to meet you," Beth said, turning her gaze from the polar bear to the ash blond doctor. "You are a legend among the members of the fleet, you and Captain Jack."

At the mention of Capt. Jack, Billy Ray's breath caught in his throat and Gretchen glanced sideways at her friend, but Ludmilla was unfazed. "I am not ready to be a legend yet, Beth, though some days I feel old enough to be."

Billy Ray quickly guided the conversation away from the touchy subject of Ludmilla's missing paramour by asking, "Where's TK? It's not like a Texan to miss a party."

"TK had some business to attend to dirtside," answered Gretchen, glad to be back on less sensitive ground. "Seems that there is an enclave of survivors back on Earth that have pronounced themselves the Republic of Texas. TK figured he should be the one to establish diplomatic relations."

Texas Hill Country, Earth

The nearest impact to the state of Texas was in the Gulf of Mexico, 300 km off the coast of Mississippi. That event sent a tremendous wave of water and debris in all directions, racing across the flatlands of the American South. Florida was obliterated, every gulf coastal city from Tampa to Corpus Christi was destroyed completely, a tsunami swept inland across the coastal plains and up the Mississippi River valley inundating cities as far north as Memphis and St. Louis.

In Texas itself, the major cities were laid waste: Houston, Dallas and Ft. Worth swept away by the flood. Austin and San Antonio, even though 200 km inland and at the edge of the Balconies Escarpment, were also heavily damaged. Those cities marked the boundary between two distinct geographic areas: the coastal prairies and the Texas Hill Country. Only those in the Hill Country and farther west were spared the tsunami's wrath, though falling ash and larger debris caused significant damage well inland.

While the Alamo, in downtown San Antonio, is 248 meters above sea-level, Kerrville and Fredericksburg, the two largest towns in the hill country, are at an altitude of more than 500 m. Located high up and truly in the heart of Texas, Fredericksburg survived the alien bombardment better than most places in the Northern Hemisphere. Though much of the Hill Country has thin soil more useful for grazing, Fredericksburg possesses richer soil and is a major agricultural area. It was unsurprising that it would become the center of the Republic of Texas.

Flying in one of the small shuttles, TK Parker was on a mission to establish diplomatic and trade relations with the new republic. Just prior to the alien attack Fredericksburg had about the same number of residents as Farside Base did today. Unfortunately, Farside lacked the means of natural food production that the town possessed. Conversely, Farside had technological resources that the earthly survivors could not hope to match. TK was hoping to arrange a deal to swap food and fodder for high-tech goods.

"Mr. Parker, I've raised someone at the airport on the old FBO frequency," reported the shuttle pilot, "I've let them know we are coming."

"Good," TK replied, "I talked to them a few days ago so there should be people at the airport to meet us. I just hope they're friendly."

"Yes, Sir. We will be approaching from the North West and coming in on runway 14. The airport is about 5 klicks southwest of the town proper. You should be able to see it off the port side."

* * * * *

Waiting on the ground for TK's arrival were a number of dignitaries of the New Republic. The delegation was led by Roger Stoltz, the mayor of Fredericksburg and acting President, Sally Musselman, from the town council, and Antonio Ruiz, formerly representative to the State House. Also present was another man who had grown up around Fritztown, as it was sometimes known locally.

Settled primarily by German immigrants starting in 1846, Fredericksburg was named after Prince Frederick of Prussia, hence the nickname. The third man was a Texas Ranger, who happened to be visiting when the world came to an end. His name was Sid Hopkins and he and TK Parker had met in the not so distant past.

"So you say you know this Parker feller?" asked Stoltz, who was a talkative type and tended to ramble when nervous.

"Yup," replied Sid, who was not.

"How are we gonna' know that he's not some space alien?"

"I'll know."

"How will you know, Sid?"

89

Sid slowly worked the toothpick he was chewing on from the left side of his mouth to the right. He gave Roger a narrow eyed look that in the Texas of old might have been a preamble to gunplay.

"Roger, stop pesterin' the man," interjected Sally, a habitual peacemaker. "If Sid says he'll know the man just let it be at that."

"I'm just sayin' how can we be sure is all," Roger mumbled, unwilling or unable to wait in silence.

Putting a gray Stetson on top of his head and donning a set of dark sunglasses, Sid announced, "I'm going out to meet him when they land. Y'all can wait in here." He headed for the door without waiting for a reply from the others. None of them made a move to follow.

As the Ranger walked out of the airport hotel building he looked to the northwest, quickly sighting the incoming shuttle against the gray overcast. It was a delta shaped craft about the size of a large business jet. Making a slow approach it floated down the runway and stopped, hovering in front of Sid's position. The only sound it made was a low thrumming that could barely be heard over the blowing wind.

Drifting over to the runway apron the shuttle rotated to present its wide back-end to the airport buildings and settled to the ground. As Sid watched, a ramp opened downward from the back of the craft. The sound of electric motors heralded the emergence of TK Parker in his four wheel drive wheelchair. He came down the ramp and headed over to where Sid was standing.

"Is that you, Ranger Hopkins?" the old man asked as his gyroscopically stabilized conveyance shifted from four wheels to two, raising TK to a standing position. Rolling up to the man, TK thrust out his hand.

"You do like to make an entrance, Mr. Parker," Sid said, shaking the proffered hand. "Good to see you've survived this mess."

"Better than most of mankind, I'm sad to say. And I told you the last time we met, call me TK, son."

"OK. I'll call you TK, as long as you don't call me 'son'."

TK guffawed.

As the pair turned toward the building Sid caught a glimpse of something large and dark at the top of the ramp. In case the reception hadn't been so friendly there were a couple of Marines in battle armor waiting inside the shuttle.

"We should get in out of the sun, unless you're partial to skin cancer," Sid commented as they made their way to the entrance. "In spite of the overcast, our medical people say the UV levels are off the scale lately."

"Yeah, it was all that stuff thrown up by the impacts, lots of vaporized ocean water and rock. Played the devil with the ozone layer. Science types say it will take years to return to normal."

"Wonderful."

"So, who am I meeting with, Sid?"

"Some of the local political leaders, seem like nice people, still trying to find their feet since... you know."

The building that they were headed to looked like an old WWII hanger, with an arched curved metal roof and bright white siding. Emblazoned across the front was a red, white and blue insignia and the name Hangar Hotel. As they neared the entrance it became obvious that the building, though meant to look like a relic from the 1940's, was actually of much later construction. Inside, the officials waited in the hotel's barroom, a swank place filled with aviation memorabilia.

"This is a nice place," TK commented, rolling into the lobby. "I've heard of this hotel before but never found a reason to pay a visit, though I really wanted to see the Naval museum." Strangely enough this landlocked city housed a first-class ocean warfare museum. That was because Fredericksburg was the birthplace of one of America's most admired admirals, Chester Nimitz. Nimitz went from humble Texas beginnings to graduate from the U.S. Naval Academy and later serve as the Commander-in-Chief of the Pacific Fleet during WWII. It went to show that one should not judge a small Texas town based on first impressions.

Rolling through the lobby, past a curving stairway to the upper floor and an empty check-in counter, TK and Sid went right to a set of double doors with a sign above them declaring "Officer's Club."

As they entered, three people sitting around a dark wooden table got up from overstuffed, red leather chairs.

"TK, I'd like you to meet Sally Musselman, Antonio Ruiz, and Roger Stoltz, acting head of the New Republic," Sid said stepping to one side. "Folks, meet Mr. TK Parker, formerly of Texas and now from a bit farther out."

"Welcome to the Republic of Texas," the loquacious acting President gushed, stepping forward to shake TK's hand. Those in the official delegation now understood why Sid had insisted that they remove one of the heavy chairs from around the table. After greeting all three of the locals TK let his trick wheelchair collapse back to four wheel mode and pulled up to the empty side of the table.

"It's so nice of you to come today, Mr. Parker," said Sally. "We get visitors so infrequently nowadays."

"Can we offer you something to cut the trail dust, Mr. Parker?" asked Ruiz. He signaled for the unobtrusive waiter who was positioned next to a well equipped bar that ran along one wall.

"Don't mind if I do, Antonio, and call me TK, everybody does."

"My friends call me Tony, TK. Name your poison."

The waiter took TK's order and hustled back to the bar. Evidently the others' preferences were already known to him. Sid, the introductions complete, leaned casually back against a nearby billiard table.

The drinks soon arrived and were distributed. TK, after pausing to relish the good Kentucky bourbon, looked at his hosts and said, "That is very nice indeed, thank you. Now let's get down to cases."

Chapter 7

Jesse's Place, Farside

After introducing Beth to a number of the other old hands from the Peggy Sue, Billy Ray excused himself and went to find the head. Beth drifted over to the magnificent mahogany here a large woman with an infectious laugh was serving up drinks. As she approached, the woman set down the glass she had been drying and smiled at her.

"Good evening, Miss. Can I get you somet'ing to drink?"

"Yes please, a gin and tonic if you have it."

"I have Beefeater, Boodle's, Hendrick's and Plymouth," the bartender replied.

"Hendrick's please, no lime."

Mixing the cocktail, Jesse observed her new customer with a practiced bartender's eye. "From your accent you must come from England."

"My parents were from Ethiopia but I'm from the UK, grew up near London. You sound like you come from the Caribbean."

"Dat's true, I be Jamaican, by way of St Croix, Australia and de Peggy Sue."

"You must be Jesse, Billy Ray mentioned you on the walk over."

With kindness in her eyes, the big Jamaican woman looked across the barroom at Billy Ray, who had been waylaid on his return by some fellow crewmembers. "Mr. Billy Ray be one of the officers dat took me to Australia to join de crew. He's a good mon."

"Oh, I've only just met him this evening," Beth said looking inquisitively at the barkeep, "though I've known him as a voice on the radio for more than a month."

Jesse nodded knowingly, "You was on de mission." A statement, not a question. "You interested in Mr. Billy Ray, Miss?"

Beth was taken aback by the forwardness of the question. "Why, I'm not really sure. We really just met," she stammered.

"Well somebody need to tell you, he not be himself of late," Jesse said, in a much quieter voice. Leaning forward she almost whispered, "it's because he lost his lady."

"I see," Beth returned in a hushed tone, unsure where this conversation was leading. "I think we all have lost people close to us."

"No, you don' understand. He lost his lady on de first voyage—her name was Susan." She stole a quick glance at the man in question, still occupied across the room. "She was also known as Peggy Sue."

"Peggy Sue?" Beth was puzzled for a second. "That Peggy Sue? The one the ship is named after?"

"Dat's her," Jesse said sadly. "I never met her but Miss Gretchen and Miss Ludmilla and everyone who did say she was a nice lady, and dat she and Billy Ray was deep in love. Dey say he almost die from the loss of her."

"I, I see." *Why is she telling me this?*

"So if you be interested in Mr. Billy Ray just be careful, 'cause his heart ain't fully healed yet," Jesse looked earnestly into Beth's eyes, "An' a lot of folk would be greatly upset if he get his heart broken again."

My God, this woman is telling me not to trifle with Billy Ray's affections, Beth realized, *or I might incur the wrath of the high command. Could his rakish reputation just be a cover for a shattered heart?*

"Thank you for the background information, Jesse," Beth said to the bartender, who was looking at her expectantly. "I can assure you that I'm not looking to add to Billy Ray's emotional burdens. We've only just become friends this evening and I have no romantic designs on him." *At least not anymore.*

"Hey, there you are Beth," Billy Ray said as he rambled up to the bar, "I thought maybe you grew tired of this little soiree and called it a night."

"No, not at all. Jesse and I were just comparing accents."

"Now that you mention it, both of you do sound a mite strange."

Jesse smiled widely, showing her dimples, and patted Beth on the arm. "Me son, dis be a good lady, you be a gentleman wit' her."

"Yes, Ma'am, Jesse. Had no intentions otherwise."

The pair of officers smiled at the island woman and moved off to find a table. *Dey is a fine looking couple, dey is,* Jesse mused as they walked away. *Maybe dey find comfort in each other durin' these times of misery and woe—be a real love story, de Cowboy and de Queen of Sheba.*

Hangar Hotel, Fredericksburg, Texas

"So you're sayin' you people want us to provide food for folks on the Moon?" asked Roger Stoltz, in a skeptical tone of voice. TK was having trouble convincing the acting President of the New Republic of Texas that they should trade with those off planet.

"Come on now, Roger," added Sally, "You don't think he came all this way from the Moon to play a round at Lady Bird Johnson, do you?" The local municipal golf course was named after Lady Bird Johnson, a former first lady of the United States, as were a local park, rec center and several other landmarks. That was because her husband, President Lyndon Baines Johnson, grew up on a ranch just up the road. Right up until the alien attack, people had come to tour the LBJ Ranch.

"President Stoltz, it's not hard to understand," said an exasperated TK. "You may have lost a lot of livestock already but believe me, you ain't seen the worst of it. This winter is going to be bitter cold like you've never seen before. Your herds won't be able to graze and you won't have enough fodder to get 'em through the winter. Better to trade the excess to us for equipment you can use.

"We have all sorts of hightech stuff on Farside, stuff that you will not be able to get here on Earth anymore. We can provide electronics, medicines, even help provide communications. All we are asking for are foodstuffs, primarily meat, that we can't currently produce enough of on the base."

95

"What do you mean 'help provide communications'?" asked Tony. He had been sitting quietly during TK's pitch and looked like a man weighing his options.

"As you have probably found out, most of the satellites orbiting Earth were knocked out by crap thrown up during the bombardment. All the weather satellites, most of the communication satellites and a majority of the GPS satellites got pelted with ejected material. We can either fix or replace the comm satellites and allow you to reestablish communication with other survivor enclaves—like the folks down in Australia."

"Why do we need to talk with the Australians?" asked Roger.

"Hush, Roger," said Sally. "What about the weather satellites, TK? It would sure be nice to know when storms are approaching."

"Yes, Ma'am. We could certainly put up a couple of replacement satellites, let you know when a front is approaching or a hurricane brewin' out in the Atlantic."

"Yes," said Tony, "people don't realize that without any satellites we won't get hardly any advanced warning of an approaching storm system. And what about the GPS system? Could that be fixed?"

"Sure, take a little more doin' but we could get that back online as well." TK could sense that they were being won over, then there was a screeching of brakes and the sound of a diesel engine from outside the bar. Looking out the large windows onto the airport grounds TK could see a tan Humvee with some kind of rocket launcher on top, parked next to the hotel.

Almost simultaneous with the Humvee's arrival the doors of the bar flew open and a man in camouflage fatigues and a slouch hat strode in. He was trailed by two other similarly attired men with sidearms. The first man marched to the table where the negotiations were taking place while his companions took up positions on either side of the doors.

"General, I'm glad to see you could make it after all," began Roger, standing up to greet the soldier. "Mr. Parker here was just explaining all the things his people can do for us if we are willing to send them some food."

"He was, was he?" the General responded skeptically. He was not a large man, more wiry and bandy-legged. He took off his hat to reveal light gray-blond hair in a close cut flattop. His eyes seemed permanently squinted from the Sun and, without the hat, his nose a bit too large for his narrow face. On his right shoulder there was a miniature Texas state flag, on the left a blue and red patch with a white diagonal slash, over which the numerals seven and five appeared in contrasting colors. On his left breast 'Crotchet' was embroidered in black, on the right 'U.S. Army', and in the center of his chest was a patch with two black stars.

"TK, this is General Jake Crotchet, the commander of the Republic of Texas Army," Sally said in a soothing tone of voice, trying to avoid any unpleasantness.

TK backed away from the table and, in a single smooth motion, pivoted to face the General while shifting his wheelchair to a standing, two wheeled stance. Standing in his mechanical marvel, TK was half a head taller than the General. "Pleased to meet ya," the older man said, sticking out his hand.

The sudden sprouting of a septuagenarian cyborg in front of him did not seem to faze the General, but it did leave him with little option but to shake TK's hand. To have refused would have looked churlish. "Major General Jacob Crotchet, commanding the 75th Infantry Division, U.S. Army—or what's left of it."

While he shook the General's hand, TK tilted his head to one side as if someone was whispering to him over his shoulder. He nodded once, straightened up and spoke to the General. "General we need to talk..."

"What the hell are those!" the General interrupted, leaning sideways to get a better look around TK. His eyes were no longer squinting. Outside, the two Marines that accompanied TK to Earth had exited the shuttle and were standing to either side of the craft at port arms.

"Them?" TK asked innocently. "The sudden appearance of your armed vehicles out there made my pilot a mite nervous so he asked a couple of the boys to step outside and give your fellers the once over."

"They look like some kind of robot or something," exclaimed President Stoltz.

"Shut. Up. Roger!" Sally hissed.

"Madre de Dios," whispered Tony.

"I though you came unarmed, TK," Sid said, speaking for the first time since the introductions were made.

"I am unarmed," TK said, emphasizing the 'I', "something that you, Ranger, and you, General, are not."

"I thought this was a peaceful mission," Roger babbled.

"It is," snapped TK, his patience worn thin, "but that there shuttle craft can fly from here to the Moon and back again. It's probably one of the most valuable pieces of equipment on the planet and there's no way we were gonna' risk some fool taken' it into his head to try and steal it."

"I'm assuming those things are dangerous," the General stated, not taking his eyes off the two Marines outside.

TK sighed. "Let me put it to you this way, General—did you ever see the movie 'The Day the Earth Stood Still' when you were a kid? I don't mean that crappy remake a decade or so ago, I mean the original black and white film from 1951."

"Yeah, probably," the General replied cautiously.

"It was all about a guy in a flying saucer who came to Earth on a peace mission—feller by the name of Klaatu. He came unarmed, like I did."

"And?"

"Just in case things didn't go so well with the natives he had this big ol' metal feller with him—feller by the name of Gort. It was a big mistake to mess with Gort."

"Your point is?"

"You can call me Klaatu," TK smiled, "Them two out there, they're both Gorts."

NatHanGon's Quarters, Farside

Melissa Scott Hamilton put in a quick appearance at the reception at Jesse's Place before going to check on her friend, the Triad ambassador. Melissa was really not much of a party girl and she found talking with the Ambassador more enjoyable than conversing with a collection of humans in varying states of inebriation.

NatHanGon's quarters were located near the agricultural production spaces, rather fitting in Melissa's mind considering that the triple brained alien was a plant. Down several infrequently traveled corridors, Melissa walked alone until she came to the locked portal that led to the Ambassador's chamber. She had not noticed the maintenance tech who followed her from the mostly darkened atrium.

The environmental conditions in the room that housed NatHanGon were designed to mimic the conditions found on their own world, Gliese 581d. From one wall issued red tinged light that extended into the near infrared, a close analog of the light from the planet's sun, a red dwarf called Gliese 581 by humans. When no one was visiting inside the 5 by 5 meter room, strong artificial winds gusted and rain pelted the interior. The atmospheric gas mixture also mimicked that of the planet and was kept at twice Earth sea-level pressure. To gain physical access to the Ambassador required passing through an airlock that equalized the pressure.

The base's head horticulturist was one of the few whose comm pip code allowed access to the airlock. Other guests visited the Ambassador from an adjacent room more comfortable for Earthlings. Since the Triads conversed using either radio waves or by direct electrical contact through their roots, it did not really matter that the alien was separated from their guests by a thick transparent wall. Conversation was possible because the base computer translated radio frequency transmissions to and from the Triad. Melissa, however, gladly suffered the added discomfort of entering into the Ambassador's physical presence.

The atmosphere inside the chamber was primarily nitrogen, oxygen, water vapor and carbon dioxide. The CO_2 levels were significantly higher than on Earth, ten times as high in fact. Humans can be asphyxiated by sufficiently elevated CO_2 levels, even in the presence of ample amounts of oxygen. In 1986, a release of gas from Lake Nyos in Cameroon killed more than 1700 people by driving the CO_2 levels above 10%. While such levels can render a human unconscious in less than five minutes that danger did not exist at the 0.4% level present in the Ambassador's residence, even at twice normal atmospheric pressure.

There were concerns about long-term exposure, however, and frequent or lengthy visits required the use of a mask that selectively blocked carbon dioxide. Wearing a mask, Melissa stepped through the inner airlock door and greeted her friend.

"Hey, NatHanGon, how y'all doing today?" In this case "y'all" was totally appropriate, since the Ambassador possessed three quasi-independent brains linked through the roots at the creature's base. Or not, since in the deep south "y'all" is singular—a group of people was referred to as "all y'all" where Melissa came from.

"It is good to see you again Melissa; Have you details of your fleet's victory over the interlopers? Is there any news about your captain?"

The Ambassador did not really see Melissa, having no eyes, but rather sensed her presence through weak electrical fields. They did physically acknowledge the human's presence by gently shaking the black, flower like blooms that ran along the ribs of their two meter tall cactus like trunks—an action that humans interpreted as an expression of pleasure. The result was a sound like wind chimes or the tinkling of bells.

Conversing with a Triad could be quite confusing for a single brained creature, as each of the plant's brains provided an independent conversational thread. At first, human researchers thought that each thread belonged to one of the brains, but it was later revealed that they frequently migrated from one physical brain to another. The Triad mind was much more complicated than humans realized, as befit creatures that evolved before Earth had formed around the proto-star that became the Sun.

"It's good to see you too; The fleet and the Marines destroyed the alien ship that attacked our planet; There's been no word from Captain Jack, I'm sure Ludmilla would have said something if there had."

Humans conversing with a Triad tended to adopt a three part conversational mode themselves. Multiple researchers often carried out three seemingly independent conversations with the Ambassador simultaneously. Melissa had gotten to the point where she could manage three threads by herself.

"We always enjoy your visits, it gets a bit lonely for us without a conclave to commune with; It is good that your forces were victorious, did they bring back any of the aliens alive? I'm sure the Captain is all right, the T'aafhal ship they are in is extraordinarily powerful."

"I enjoy talkin' with y'all too, more so than with most folk; Evidently the aliens were all killed by the Marine assault, though they brought back some equipment that they think is a navigation computer and a couple of bodies for dissection; I sure hope so, Ludmilla would just die if something happened to him."

Melissa pulled on a pair of gardener's gloves and got on her hands and knees to inspect the cover vegetation surrounding the Ambassador's roots. The mosses and low clinging plants had been brought along from the Triad planet to make NatHanGon's metal and glass room seem more like home.

* * * * *

Outside the airlock a man in gray maintenance coveralls retrieved the small electronic device he planted near the entrance to the Ambassador's chamber earlier. He had been studying the horticulturist's movements for several weeks and discovered that she often visited the alien plant at odd hours—times when there were no other people about. He checked the device and discovered that it had done its job.

He smiled to himself, feeling his excitement grow. Now was the perfect time. No one was down here wandering the halls, they were all at one of the bars getting drunk. He pressed the device's playback button and it reproduced the identification sequence transmitted earlier by Melissa's comm pip. The outer airlock door slid quietly aside.

Bridge, M'tak Ka'fek

The crew were all at their action stations, anticipating emergence from alter-space. Transiting alter-space was the first way humans had learned to effectively travel faster than light. Only a few short months ago it seemed like the ultimate in high-speed travel, taking only a few days to cross a score of light-years. But since the M'tak Ka'fek had taken them 1,500 light-years from home in the course of a few moments by generating an annular singularity —a made to order wormhole—passing through the lesser dimensions of alter-space seemed a plodding pace. Unfortunately, the faster mode of travel was energy intensive and until a new supply of antimatter could be secured, alter-space transit was the best the ship could do.

Bear was at the main weapon station and JT at navigation. Sandy McKinnett and Bobby Danner manned the helm with Mizuki Ogawa keeping track of things astrophysical. The rest of the crew and Marines stood ready at weapon stations farther aft. Keeping track of everything, Captain Jack sat in the commander's chair, which he had relocated from its original, lonely position in front of the bridge to a more comfortable location behind the helm.

I hope there is something waiting for us on the other end of this transit, Jack thought. *Even doing alter-space transits will eventually deplete our antimatter supplies, then we will truly be up a creek without a paddle.*

An interesting analogy, the ship's AI commented wordlessly.

"Emergence in 10 seconds, Captain," called Mizuki from the helm. The T'aafhal instruments were much better at calculating the time of a transit than the humans' best efforts.

"I'm already getting sensor data from the system ahead, Captain," reported Bear. The ability of the polar bears to 'smell' things in alter-space was amazing even to the AI. The part of a bear's brain that provided its exquisite sense of smell—capable of detecting a seal beneath Arctic ice at a dozen kilometers—adapted to the T'aafhal targeting sensors as though designed for the job, which in fact it had been.

The reality of 3-space shimmered into existence around the ship. The crew intently surveyed the system before them, straining to pickup a hint of an enemy through senses enhance by the M'tak Ka'fek's multitude of instruments.

"The prey is headed across the system," Bear reported, "About an AU away."

Running a standard survey of the system, JT cataloged the star and its planets. "Looks like a single star system, a marginal class A, 1.6 solar masses. A couple of rocky planets, both under an AU out, no atmospheres and way too hot for any know lifeforms. And then there is this..."

JT sent an image to the forward display. There, hanging in space in front of the bridge crew, was a space station. Though the scale was impossible to judge without something familiar to compare it to, the station appeared to consist of six large domed units arranged in a hexagon. The clear, shallow domes covered glittering black structures, all facing the blue-white star. As the image expanded it became clear that the six domed structures were like covered saucers, connected from behind by a framework of ribbed struts.

Each of the saucers was roughly 32 kilometers in diameter, with the spacing between their edges half that. From the centers of their backsides, stems a kilometer in diameter extended downward for five kilometers. At four kilometers lateral struts of similar diameter ran to the center of the array, where they joined with a thicker stem that extended at least 25 kilometers into space behind the structure. The overall effect was of a gigantic cluster of flowers suspended in space, crafted in a style that was disturbingly familiar.

"That looks like it was built by whoever made the Space Mushroom at Comae Berenices," Bobby said in a hesitant voice.

"Right the first time, Bobby," JT confirmed, looking up. "Except each of those domes is about 60% bigger than the cap on the Space Mushroom."

"And there are six of them," Bear said, stating the obvious. "Which means that is a much bigger station than the one we destroyed."

"Which means it should have an even larger store of antimatter than that station," the Captain finished, leaning forward in his chair. "Now all we have to do is figure out how to requisition some of it."

"Captain," the ship said, "the station ahead appears to be broadcasting approach and docking instructions on a number of frequencies. There are several languages being used, all derivatives of the ancient trading language."

"Gun crews at the ready," Jack ordered. "Well let's not disappoint them—follow the docking instructions, Mr. Danner. Let's go see who's minding the store."

Chapter 8

NatHanGon's Quarters, Farside

Hearing the airlock door open behind her, Melissa stood up and faced the stranger as he entered. "Who are you?" she asked, puzzled how someone she did not know had gained access to the Ambassador's living space. "What do you want?"

The intruder advanced on her with a smirk on his face. "I want you, bitch," he said, voice flat and malevolent. He lunged for Melissa and tried to grab her throat with both hands.

The horticulturalist was a slight woman but not totally defenseless. She had taken Ludmilla's Sambo self defense classes during the voyages on Peggy Sue. Bringing both her arms up between his and then out and down sharply she managed to break her assailant's tentative hold on her neck. Reacting according to Ludmilla's training, Melissa then attempted a stiff fingered jab to the attacker's eyes.

Unfortunately, this was not her attacker's first assault. Reacting before his intended victim could gouge out an eye, he tucked in his chin and lowered his head, causing the strike to hit his browline and not a vulnerable eye socket. He lashed out blindly, a roundhouse blow that caught Melissa on the left side of her face, knocking off her mask and driving her to the ground.

"Shit!" he cried, wiping his forehead with his right hand. It came away stained red with blood from the gash above his eyebrow. He either ignored or did not hear the rattling sound coming from the quivering flowers along the Ambassador's closest trunk—a sound not unlike a nest of baby rattlesnakes.

"You fucking cunt!" he yelled in shocked anger, stunned that his intended victim had managed to hurt him. Rage building, he started toward Melissa again, saying in a low, threatening rasp, "you will beg me to let you die before I'm done..."

A ripple of faint popping sounds emanated from the Ambassador. The would be rapist suddenly sprouted a forest of finger length quills, scattered along the left side of his head, neck and torso. He toppled forward.

Melissa scrambled backward to avoid the falling man, who struck the ground and lay motionless. In horror and disbelief, she backed up the gentle slope until she sat with her back against one of the Ambassador's three man sized trunks.

Jesse's Place, Farside

Beth and Billy Ray had found an empty table near the entrance and were cautiously getting to know each other. They were observed by a trio of females, two human and one ursine, who represented a majority of Farside base's leadership.

"They make an interesting couple, don't you think?" asked Isbjørn. The mating rituals of humans fascinated her. In her opinion bears were much more pragmatic: find an attractive partner; fight a bit to make sure the prospective mate is strong and healthy; and then spend a week mating as often as possible.

"Yes, interesting," commented Gretchen dryly, "they are like a pair of scorpions circling each other, trying to decide what action to take—do we mate or attempt to kill each other?"

"You are becoming far too cynical, Gretchen," Ludmilla replied. "The Lieutenant is just being cautious, as she should be given Billy Ray's reputation. But Bill Ray is showing signs of real interest, if I am not mistaken. Do not forget, I have observed him under such conditions before."

"What do you mean, Ludmilla?" asked Isbjørn. The 300kg bear was sitting next to the two humans, placing her head at roughly human height.

"Ludmilla was the matchmaker who smoothed things over between Billy Ray and Susan on the first voyage."

"Ah," the she-bear said, "what a tragedy that the girl died."

"Yes, yes it was. Mourning is appropriate, even necessary, but eventually one must move on. What Billy Ray needs is someone new, someone to prove that his life did not end when Susan died."

"You are such a romantic, Ludmilla," Gretchen said, in a tone that held just a touch of sarcasm. Ludmilla was about to answer her friend when her comm chirped.

"Why do they always call me when I am in Jesse's bar?" she muttered before saying, "Tropsha here, go ahead."

"LudmillaStefanovaTropsha there has been an attack on MelissaScottHamilton; She is in our quarters and requires assistance; Please accept our apologies, we seem to have killed a member of your conclave."

Even before the tripart message was finished Ludmilla knew that it was from NatHanGon. A priority message from the Triad ambassador would be put through wherever she was. Ludmilla was already in motion as she issued a terse reply: "We come."

Her two companions overheard the call and were also in immediate motion, headed toward the exit with Isbjørn in the lead. Her shouted warning of "make way!" was hardly needed—a full grown polar bear charging at top speed tended to clear a path. As Gretchen exited the bar she yelled, "you two, with me!"

Startled, Beth and Billy Ray looked after the receding figure of the Captain. "Did she mean us?" asked Beth.

"I don't know, but I'm not waiting around to find out. Let's move."

The pair of officers lit out after the running trio. As they passed the Marine guards at the entrance one of them shouted, "Did she mean us?"

"You two stop gawkin' and come on," yelled Billy Ray, *en passant*, "we got us a situation here!"

NatHanGon's Quarters, Farside

Isbjørn was the first to arrive outside the Triad ambassador's quarters. She was arguing with the airlock's voice control as Ludmilla and Gretchen pulled up. The quick run in low G was enough to get the blood flowing but not nearly enough to tax either woman.

"Emergency override!" Ludmilla shouted. The outer door slid aside and Isbjørn pushed inside. The others followed and Gretchen quickly cycled the lock.

Entering the Ambassador's chamber, the bear lowered her head and growled at the sight in front of them. The body of the attacker was sprawled on the mossy ground, head twisted sideways with one unblinking eye staring sightlessly at nothing. Propped against the base of the Ambassador was Melissa, glassy eyed, breathing in shallow, panting breaths.

Isbjørn sniffed the body and pronounced, "this one's dead."

Ludmilla hastened to Melissa's side and quickly checked her pulse and respiration. Taking note of the bruising on the side of Melissa's face, she pulled a pencil thin LED flashlight and checked pupil dilation for signs of a concussion. The Ambassador's "flowers" rustled, a sign of agitation but not the warning rattle that preceded their turning Melissa's attacker into a pincushion.

Gretchen spoke into her collar pip. "This is Capt. Curtis. We need medics, two stretchers and a squad of Marines at the Ambassador's quarters. Now!"

"We are quite concerned for MelissaScottHamilton's well being; It is distressing that such an attack took place between members of the same species; We responded in haste, as an opportunity presented itself."

"Her pulse is weak and rapid, breathing shallow and her skin is cool and clammy," Ludmilla stated. She also noted that the motile roots around the Ambassador's base were partly wrapped around the victim, as though caressing her. "She is in shock and needs to be stabilized as soon as possible."

Isbjørn moved closer to the injured girl and made motherly bear sounds. Melissa looked up at the bear's face and in a sign of recognition reached out and touched Isbjørn's muzzle.

"We have tried to comfort her but we are poorly equipped to give aid to creatures of your kind; The one we neutralized entered without permission and assaulted MelissaScottHamilton without provocation; We hope our actions do not upset you, the threat was unfamiliar and our responses limited."

"I am sure that Melissa will be all right, NatHanGon," said Ludmilla, addressing the Triad for the first time.

108

"What did you do to the assailant?" asked Gretchen, eying the fallen gray form.

"I think your response was totally appropriate," growled Isbjørn, hovering protectively over the fallen Melissa.

* * * * *

Outside the airlock, Beth and Billy Ray had arrived, two Marines in tow. A member of the original expeditions and a Naval officer, Billy Ray had access to the Ambassador's airlock code. As the door slid open he turned to the two Marines and issued orders: "One of you go 30 meters that way and the other back the way we came. Do not let anyone down here except for official personnel responding to the emergency."

"Aye aye, Sir," the Marines replied in unison, quickly moving off to their assigned positions.

Stepping inside the airlock, Billy Ray used the intercom to call the party inside. "Capt. Curtis? This is Lt. Melaku and Cdr. Vincent. We have secured the area and are awaiting instructions."

"Very good, Cdr. Vincent," came the reply. "There are medical personnel and a squad of Marines on the way. We will need the medical personnel with a stretcher in here as soon as they arrive."

"Aye, aye, Ma'am. Might I ask what happened?"

"Some civilian miscreant attacked Miss Scott Hamilton as she was tending to the Ambassador. She is injured but stable; the Ambassador is unharmed."

"Thank you Ma'am. We will send the medics in as soon as they arrive." Under his breath Billy Ray cursed, "son of a bitch!"

"Is everything all right?" asked Beth, concerned as much by Billy Ray's reaction as the update from Capt. Curtis.

"I truly hope so, Beth. Why someone would want to hurt Melissa I cannot tell you. She's about the sweetest little thing you'd ever want to meet. Always smiling, not a bad word to say about anyone. If the bastard who attacked her ain't dead now the sum'bitch will be shortly, I guaranty it."

Beth was startled by the venom in Billy Ray's words. It seemed that the calm, cool cowboy cared about other people after all, and deeply. As she searched for some comforting phrase the medics pulled up outside with a pair of floating stretchers.

"A couple of you bring one of those stretchers in here. Col. Tropsha is inside with the victim, she'll tell you what to do," Turning to Beth he added, "Lt. Melaku, could you step outside and coordinate the responding emergency personnel?"

"Yes, Commander." There was no doubt in her mind that Billy Ray's question was an order. She stepped outside; the airlock sealed and cycled.

* * * * *

The two medics guided the floating stretcher into the Ambassador's chamber. One pulled up short at the sight of Isbjørn crouched near the patient but Ludmilla gave him no time to dither.

"Bring that stretcher over here," Ludmilla snapped. "She is shocky and has suffered trauma to the left side of her face. We need to get her immobilized, under blankets and to the medical section immediately."

"Yes, Doctor," the medics replied. There was no doubt in either of their minds that those orders came from a medical doctor. Carefully, they freed Melissa from the caring embrace of the Triad and with the assistance of Billy Ray placed the injured woman on the stretcher.

As she was eased onto the floating device, Melissa looked up at Ludmilla and said "I tried to stop him, Ludmilla, like you taught us, but he kept on coming." She teared up and started to cry softly.

"There, there Melissa," Ludmilla said, trying to comfort her, "do not worry, it is not your fault. Everything will be all right, the Ambassador took care of that animal. We need you to just lay back while we take you to hospital."

As Dr. Tropsha and the medical people departed with their patient, Billy Ray squatted on his haunches looking over the body of the assailant. "Am I mistaken or is this feller dead?"

"He is most definitely dead," responded Isbjørn, in a way that implied she would have made sure of it if he wasn't.

"What I want to know is how that bastard got in here," fumed Gretchen.

"Well, this might have had something to do with it," Billy Ray replied, removing a small metallic object from the deceased's rear pocket. It was the signal recorder the assailant used to hack the door lock.

"Get that to the technical section. I want to find out exactly how this happened and make sure it never happens again."

"Aye, aye, Captain."

"And send in the other stretcher, we need to move this piece of human garbage to the morgue. I want to know who this creep was and where he came from. By the way, Ambassador, how did you kill him?"

"Yes, it looks like you stopped him in his tracks," added Isbjørn, who then nudged Billy Ray to complete the triplet.

"Yeah, you saved us the bother of a speedy trial and a quick hanging," the still riled cowboy finished.

"We pierced him with a number of quills, each tipped with an assortment of neurotoxins; Having no prior need to formulate a debilitating agent for humans, we used a wide spectrum of substances that were almost instantly fatal; We are happy to be of assistance, we are quite fond of MelissaScottHamilton."

Base Administrator's Office

The day following the incident in the Triad Ambassador's quarters, Ludmilla called a meeting of the Moon base's governing council. Present were Captain Curtis, Isbjørn, Rajiv Gupta and TK Parker, just returned from Earth. Also in attendance were Yuki Saito and Jo Jo Medina. Upon hearing news of the attack TK became particularly incensed.

"How is that young woman doing, Dr. Tropsha?" he asked as the others were still taking their seats. "I can't believe that such a thing could happen here at Farside. Were did that polecat come from and how did he slip through the screening interviews?"

"Melissa is doing fine," answered Ludmilla. "Her shock was more psychological than physiological. I have treated her with analgesics for the pain and kept her overnight for observation. As for her attacker, it would appear that he was picked up with a group of other refugees from a small college town in the mountains of California," the Chief Administrator continued, scanning over the report on the surface display in front of her. "He evidently was a repairman and maintenance worker on the college campus. His interview revealed nothing untoward and several of the other school people vouched for him."

"Vouched for him or just said they knew the bastard?" TK muttered.

"Most likely the latter but who knows? As fast as we had to move while rescuing useful survivors we were bound to catch a few hidden criminals in our nets. He was probably a sexual predator for years, but managed not to get caught. He did have some technical skills or he never could have constructed the device that gave him access to the airlock."

"I find that more troubling than the fact we found a bad apple among our new personnel," commented Gretchen. "Rajiv, how could someone override our security so easily?"

"Well, Gretchen," replied the installation's head scientist, "we really did not anticipate anyone actively trying to thwart the door locks on the secure areas."

"In general, areas are restricted for safety reasons, not to prevent criminal activity," added Chief Engineer Medina. "Obviously we need to take stricter precautions."

"I think we all can agree to that," Rajiv concurred.

"Good. Rajiv, can you and Jo Jo coordinate with the military security people and come up with better physical security measures for sensitive areas? The last thing we need is an insane person sabotaging one of the power reactors or poisoning the food supply."

"We'll get right on it, Ma'am," Jo Jo assured her.

"I would also like to institute a series of interviews of all base personnel, to see if we have any other criminals lurking in our midst."

"What do you mean, Ludmilla?" asked TK.

"We have a number of ex-law enforcement people here on the base—several policemen, at least one FBI agent, and others with experience in criminal profiling. I am thinking of having some of them sit in with a psychiatrist and a social worker to do the interviews."

"I'm not real sure I trust all that psychiatric mumbo-jumbo, but having people interviewed by the police might set the population on edge, if you get my drift."

"I am thinking we should do this without revealing the true reason for the interviews, TK. We can say it is to make sure everyone is being utilized to their greatest potential, and that everyone is happy with their assigned work."

"Ah, a cover story," said Gretchen. "Now you are being devious."

"Trust me, Russians know devious."

"You should include a bear on the interview panels," Isbjørn added. "We can often smell fear on a person, and we can provide observations that might be overlooked by a human."

"Good idea, Isbjørn," TK chuckled. "If nothing else it will help make the interviewees nervous and more apt to slip up."

"Da, good idea. I will have my staff work on setting things up."

"I must say, this is quite unsettling. When it was just people associated with the project we never worried about such things. Why would people we saved want to harm us?"

"People are strange critters, Rajiv," TK observed, drawing a snort of agreement from Isbjørn, normally the most tactful of bears.

"We humans are often irrational," Ludmilla agreed, "It's possible that some of the people we helped really did not want to be saved, or feel guilty about not dying along with everyone else. Some may even blame us for the alien attack."

"Captain Curtis quoted Commodore Perry after the Fleet's victory over the alien invaders," TK added. "There's another version

113

of that quote, from an old comic strip. The way Pogo put it was: 'We have met the enemy and he is us.'"

Base Operations Center, Farside

A few days following the incident in the Ambassador's quarters, Billy Ray ran into Beth coming out of Base Ops. Both officers had busy schedules, and given their duties their paths did not often intersect.

"Well howdy stranger," Billy Ray said, as Beth came into hailing distance. "We never did get a chance to properly say good night the other evening."

"Well 'howdy' yourself, Commander," Beth replied, smiling. "No, we were swept away by the flow of events, I'm sorry to say. How is that woman who was attacked?"

"Melissa? She's doin' OK according to Dr. Tropsha. She's probably back at work already."

"My goodness, she must be made of sterner stuff than most of the science staff."

"Don't let Melissa's petite frame and girlish looks fool you, she was one of the original crew and has seen more strange worlds and space battles than most. She's one tough lady."

"Well, if you see her give her my best, will you? I doubt that our paths will cross very often. In fact, I'm taking a squadron of new corvette crews out on a training mission in a couple of days and won't be back for a fortnight." *Let's see if he takes the hint,* Beth thought, *or was that too subtle a clue?*

"Out on a training cruise so quickly? Sounds like you are going to be busier than a one legged man at a butt kicking contest."

"A what?" Beth replied, caught unprepared by Billy Ray's use of American slang, and southern slang at that.

"Sorry, that's probably considered politically incorrect. What I should have said was, given that yer going to be shipping out so soon, maybe you'd like to join me for dinner?"

Ah, he did get the message. "This evening? It just so happens that I'm free. Where were you thinking, your friend Jesse's establishment?"

"Naw, Jesse's is great but she really just serves snacks and bar food. I was thinking of a new place that just opened up, unless you're opposed to French cooking."

"A French restaurant would be fantastic! I'm off at 1830 hours and will need to nick home for a quick freshen up—call me around eight?"

"Yes Ma'am," Billy Ray smiled. "That's a date."

Kuiper Belt, the Solar System

More than a week after Task Force Alpha headed for home, an alien messenger probe that had been quietly drifting away from the site of the battle came fully alive. It carried within it the last report from the *Destroyer of Worlds* and sensor recordings of the battle that brought its captain and crew to ruin. It documented the boarding by the Earthlings and the final attempt by the captain to scuttle his ship.

Sensing that the Earth squadron was well away, the messenger powered up its drive and headed for the nearest alter-space transfer point. Not a course back to the Destroyer's home world, but back to the Dark Lords who sent it. A long, shallow transit to a destination not much more massive than Jupiter, it would take the probe months to report what it had seen. The dark ones would then have to decide on the next step in this escalating war, and how to eradicate this troublesome planet filled with warm life vermin once and for all.

Part Two

Look Upon My Works Ye Mighty And Despair

Chapter 9

Maison de la Belle France

The French restaurant that Billy Ray escorted Beth to was off the beaten path, as many good French restaurants were. Several levels below the main atrium and down a long hall leading to one of the agricultural areas, they came to a nondescript door. A simple sign hanging above it read "Maison de la Belle France." Stepping inside they found themselves in a warmly decorated room with the atmosphere of a country farmhouse.

The hostess hurried up, clutching a stack of large menus to her bosom. "*Bonsoir, mademoiselle, monsieur. Une table pour deux?*"

"Good evening yourself, Kim," replied Billy Ray. "I didn't know that you were working here, or that you talked French."

"Hi, Billy Ray," the attractive young blond woman said, obviously relieved to be speaking in English. "I still work for Prof. Gunderson in Science Section, but I'm helping out until Jean-Jacques gets his restaurant off the ground. You just heard about 50% of my French, but Chef de Belcour insists I greet people *en français* to set the proper atmosphere."

"Beth, this is Kimberly Lawson. She was Dr. Olaf Gunderson's assistant on the second voyage. Kim this is Beth Melaku, commander of the Farside corvette squadron and pilot extraordinaire."

Beth shot Billy Ray a sideways look for the over-the-top introduction. "It's very nice to meet you, Miss Lawson. I'm still envious of all you who have traveled to other star systems. I hope to go on such a journey myself someday."

This time it was Kim who looked away momentarily before replying. "I hope that your trip works out better than mine. Please come this way, I have a nice table for two near the windows."

They followed the hostess to a table covered with white linen, flanked by two real wooden chairs. Out of the large window next to the table was a holographic scene of rolling country side covered in vineyards—obviously a panorama taken on Earth before the alien attack. A view of a France that no longer existed.

119

Kim seated them and handed each a large, hand written menu, saying, "let me take your drink order and I'll come back and tell you about tonight's specials."

* * * * *

"I seem to have said something wrong earlier," said a concerned Beth, as Kim hurried away with their drink order—a Manhattan on the rocks for him and a Hendrick's martini, up, no fruit, for her.

"My fault, I shouldn't have brought up the voyage without warning you first. You see, Kim and Jean-Jacques, who you will probably meet later tonight, and several other people were part of a diplomatic party that was bushwhacked by the hairy crickets."

"My goodness! Was anyone hurt?"

"Yeah, one of the delegation died, and a couple were badly wounded, including Jean-Jacques. Doc Tropsha spent ten hours putting him back together afterward. Kim was wounded but not nearly that bad."

"Still, it must have been a horrifying experience, being attacked by aliens on an alien planet far from home. No wonder I upset her."

"She'll get over it, but there are a couple of other things you should know. First is that Jean-Jacques is French, I mean really French. And he used to work for the UN."

"What do you mean?"

"I mean he was a total douche when he first joined the crew. In fact his being aboard was because he tried to turn Ludmilla over to some Russian agents at the UN's Vienna headquarters."

"Obviously that didn't work, but how did he get to the ship?"

"Ludmilla Tropsha has a quick temper and a wicked sense of humor. She decided that turnabout was fair play—the Frenchman tried to get her kidnapped so she kidnapped him. He was lucky the Captain didn't clap him in irons."

"By the captain you mean Captain Jack?"

"Yeah, Capt. Jack Sutton, the Peggy Sue's original captain and the leader of our happy band until we lost him and eighteen other crewmates at Sirius."

"Almost no one will speak of him, do you really think he and the others are lost?"

"Captain Jack? Aw hell no. Not lost as in dead and gone, I meant lost as in incommunicado. A man like Jack Sutton does not go gentle into that good night."

"Interesting, and you managed to slip in a snippet of Dylan Thomas. I've heard you're quite literary, despite your cowboy patina. So tell me, what did happen to the Captain?"

"The Peggy Sue was running for her life from a flotilla of alien ships with weapons as powerful as our own, 'cept that there were thirteen of them. We took out four or five, but our shields were almost down and we were out of torpedoes and ammo for the railguns. Our only chance was to get into alter-space before the aliens blasted us into plasma."

"My God! How did you escape?"

"Captain Jack and his skeleton crew managed to get this derelict alien battle cruiser we had found up and running—at least we're pretty sure they did. Because all of a sudden hostile alien ships started going off like fireworks on the fourth of July. We knew we weren't doing it, we didn't have anything left to throw at them. It had to be the Captain and the M'tak Ka'fek."

"M'tak Ka'fek? What is a M'tak Ka'fek?"

"That's the name of the old T'aafhal battle cruiser we found. It was built by a long dead alien race and left adrift in a graveyard of ships in the Sirius system after some ginormous space battle long, long ago. In any case, the Peggy Sue made it safely into alter-space but no one knows what happened to the Captain and his crew."

"My goodness, no wonder everyone cringed when I mentioned Captain Jack to Ludmilla the other evening, I wish I had known."

"Yeah, I seem to keep putting you into situations like that without a briefing ahead of time. Sorry."

"Just promise me you will keep me briefed in the future."

"Sure, be more than happy to. Look, here comes Kim with our drinks."

NatHanGon's Quarters

The inner airlock door slid open and Melissa stepped into the alien light of the Triad Ambassador's habitat. Livid blues and purples could still be seen in the bruises on the left side of her face. Melissa seldom wore makeup and never thought to camouflage the damage from her assault. As the door slid shut she could hear the tinkling of bells, like a flight of faeries come to greet her.

It was early morning, before most base personnel had crawled from their beds, but Melissa had been raised on a farm and was used to rising before the Sun. The odd hours of her visits did not inconvenience the Ambassador, they came from an ancient planet that was tidally locked to its star—their world had no day or night in its habitable zone, just a perpetual sunset.

"Hey there, NatHanGon, how are y'all today? I'm sorry I missed comin' by yesterday but Dr. Tropsha insisted on keeping me in the medical section for observation; I hope havin' all those people traipsing around in here the other day didn't upset you too much."

"Our roots tingle with happiness to see you up and mobile again, MelissaScottHamilton; Having no way to judge the severity of the damage you sustained, we feared for your continued existence when the members of your conclave took you for treatment; After the flurry of activity things returned to normal and we were left to meditate on our own."

"It's good to see you again too; I was just a little shook up is all, we humans are tougher than that; I'm sorry, I should have asked someone to come by and visit with you while I was bedridden."

Melissa examined the ground cover around the Ambassador's roots and shook her head. There were gouges in the moss and a number of the low cover plants were crushed and broken.

"Oh my, look at all that damage; I am sorry, I probably caused most of the damage myself; It will take just a jiffy to fix this up so the plants can grow back right."

"We are less concerned with the ground cover and more worried about you, are you fully functional again? We wondered if such behavior, as demonstrated by the human we killed, is normal in your society? Have our actions caused any reaction among the members of your conclave?"

Melissa took out a trowel and began repairing the damage at the base of the Ambassador's nest of roots. What she really wanted was for things to return to normal, to feel safe again walking the halls. Ludmilla had given her a compact stunner and told her to carry it with her when outside of her quarters. She was a country girl and familiar with firearms. Carrying a pistol, even a nonlethal one, was fine by her, but it didn't make her feel safe like she had before the attack.

She was told the nervous anxiety would fade with time, that is what Dr. Morton, the staff psychiatrist, had said in her pre-release interview. She hoped that the psychiatrist was right, but for now the only place she felt truly safe was here, in the Ambassador's room, knowing that the giant, sentient plant would watch over her as she puttered about like a gardener.

"Don't worry about me, NatHanGon, I'm almost as good as new; Attacking other people is not considered normal, but there are a lot of people who weren't raised right or are just plain evil; Most of the people who have heard about what you did approve, he could have attacked any woman or girl on the base."

NatHanGon considered the young human as she worked to repair the trifling damage caused during the assault. Though they were happy that their friend was not permanently damaged they had other things on their minds.

They are such a young form of life, they must constantly balance between mindless, primitive violence and reason; Perhaps it is because of the T'aafhal's meddling, since they wished to create an intelligent and violent race; It would seem that the main question is have they evolved enough to not destroy or enslave other races.

Violent they are, but they obviously care for each other and even for members of other species; It was not just the T'aafhal, they died out and left a machine intelligence to finish the job; Perhaps we can find satisfactory answers by discussing ethics with them.

"We forget that your form of life has a much higher metabolic rate than ours, and can sustain significant damage yet recover; It is good to know that our actions have not alienated others of your kind, that would not have been a good thing for an Ambassador to do; You say some beings are evil, can we discuss your species' concepts of good and evil?"

Interview Room #3, Base Personnel

Lem had been cooling his heals in the base personnel office waiting room for more than an hour, waiting for a "mandatory" interview with some human resource types. Instead of reporting for work at 0700 he had come here, only to sit in the nearly empty outer lounge. Clem had already had his interview the day before and said it was no big deal, they didn't even require a urine sample. Since coming to the Moon neither had access to anything that would have shown up in a drug test, making Lem a bit peeved that they didn't require one—it might have been the only time in his adult life he would have passed honestly.

An administrative type with a clipboard opened a door and called out "Souther, Lemuel Souther?"

"Yeah, that's me," Lem said, rising from the uncomfortable waiting room chair he had been sitting in.

"Right this way, Mr. Souther," the woman said, leading him down a short hallway and through another door. To the people inside the room she announced, "Mr. Lemuel Souther, assigned to base physical plant as a maintenance technician."

She backed out of the room and ushered Lem inside. Inside the room were four people and a bear. Lem quickly sized up the humans —his time in the army had given him a lot of practice with review boards and interview panels. How to read a polar bear was outside his realm of experience.

"Please come in, Mr. Souther, and have a seat," said the older looking woman in the center of the table, motioning to the interviewee's chair. *She must be in-charge of this goat roast*, Lem thought.

"How are you feeling today, Mr. Souther?"

"I'm feeling fine, Ma'am." *Never hurts to be polite.*

"I'm Dr. Morton," the woman said, "and these are Mr. Smith, Mr. O'Shea, Ms. Kurtz and Snowflake. We are here today to find out how you are acclimatizing to your new life here at Farside." She paused and favored Lem with an institutional smile.

"I'm doing great, considering the alternative."

"Does that weigh greatly on you, Lemuel? May I call you Lemuel? Do you often have thoughts about what happened on Earth?"

"Not too often, but every now and then. Ain't every day that the world ends. And call me Lem."

"Do you find yourself frequently depressed, or having thoughts of suicide?"

She's got to be a psychologist. "No Ma'am, I'm just happy to be alive."

The other woman, the one identified as Ms. Kurtz, entered the conversation. "Do you feel comfortable in the housing block you are living in and have you found new friends there or at work?"

She's a social worker, I'd put money on that. "My quarters are fine. I was lucky to get picked up with a number of people I already knew, including my best friend."

"You used the term quarters for your apartment," Mr. Smith interjected. "Are you a military veteran, Mr. Souther?"

"Lem. And yes, I was in the Army, spent time in Iraq and Afghanistan." *This guy is some sort of cop.* Both Smith and O'Shea made notes on their tablets.

"Were you ever diagnosed with PTSD, Lem?" the Psychiatrist asked.

"Nope." Lem was growing bored and decided to redirect the conversation with some questions of his own. He turned to the polar bear and said, "Ms. Snowflake, my party was picked up by a shuttle with some Marines on it. One of them was a polar bear, was that you?"

Snowflake cocked her head to one side and looked at the man for a few seconds before replying. "No, I didn't make many rescue flights and none to North America. It was probably Aurora, she was very involved."

"OK, I'm sure you would have remembered. One of the Frederick kids shot the bear in the helmet—no harm done, thankfully."

"I am sure that I would have remembered being shot, Lem," Snowflake chuckled. "I'll ask the other females if they got popped by a kid on a rescue run."

"If you find out who it was, could you thank her for me? For all of us? Because if they hadn't come when they did we'd all have been dead."

"Sure." Snowflake leaned back a bit from the table and seemed to be reappraising the human. Smith and O'Shea made more notes. After an awkward pause Dr. Morton resumed the questioning.

"It says here that you are a maintenance technician, is that what you were back on Earth?"

"Back on Earth I was a motorcycle mechanic. There ain't much call for that up here, as far as Clem and I can tell."

"Clem? Is that your best friend from Earth?"

"Yeah, I was visiting Clem at his shop in Nebraska when the sky fell—otherwise I'd a been dead with all the others in Des Moines." Lem figured that if he was talking they wouldn't be able to ask questions so he decided to be chatty. "See Clem and I met in the Army. He was a 91P, an artillery mechanic, and I was a 91K armament repairer."

Mr. smith interrupted. "Those were your MOS classifications?"

"Yeah. Clem was more of a generalist than I was, though our jobs overlapped a lot. It was his job to perform maintenance on turret and carriage mounted armament, towed and self propelled artillery, associated fire control and related systems. Where as I was primarily responsible for repairs on tank turrets, tank weapons, small arms and other infantry weapons.

"Together we repaired fuel systems, air induction systems, exhaust systems, cooling systems, hydraulic and electrical systems, fire suppression systems, and lots of other stuff."

"Did you enjoy that type of work?" asked Ms Kurtz, the social worker.

"Yeah, it was pretty interesting, always something new to work on. Between us we worked on M109-series self-propelled Howitzers, M1A2 Abrams Main Battle Tanks, M2A2 Bradley Fighting Vehicles, M992 Ammunition Carriers, M88A1 Track Recovery Vehicles, MRAPS, you name it. Problem was, you had to go to some real shitty places to do the job."

"So you got out of the service?"

"Yeah, but there's not a lot of call for tank mechanics in civilian life. I just sort of drifted into working on bikes as a way to keep from starving. Clem was more ambitious, he started his own chopper shop."

"So you must find that your work here is not nearly as challenging as your job in the Army."

"Like repairing bikes, it's a living, and believe me I am happy to be alive."

The panel whispered amongst themselves for a half a minute and then Dr. Morton addressed Lem again. "Lem, we think that you and your friend Clem are being underutilized. I'm not promising anything, but we will pass your name on to some of the engineering sections and see if they are in need of someone with your varied skills."

"Yes, Ma'am. Thank you Ma'am."

"You are free to go, the assistant will show you out."

"Thank you, have a nice day." Lem smiled an insincere smile at the panel who likewise smiled back. *What a managerial circle jerk.*

* * * * *

The assistant led Lem from the room and the door slid shut. Dr. Morton looked to her colleagues and said, "what do you think?"

"I wonder how this guy was missed in the first place," said Mr. Smith, who was a former FBI agent.

Mr. O'Shea, who had not spoken a word during the interview, glanced down at his notes and said, "I agree, this guy and his partner are definite oversights." With a few taps on his tablet he sent pictures of both men to the wall display across the room.

Clement Mathews and Lemuel Souther appeared in all their bearded, mountain man biker glory.

"They seem like non-conformists," began Ms Kurtz, "but they haven't caused any problems and their co-workers appear to like them."

"The beards and long hair are simply a response to being out of the Army," stated Dr. Morton. "A way to declare their independence from that regimented life. Yet Souther was quite proud of his work in the army. In their civilian lives, they were independent, self motivated problem solvers who worked for a living."

Snowflake cleared her throat, which was not nearly as subtle a signal as when done by a human. "He was not nervous, at least not when talking to me. His answers seemed genuine—I liked him."

"I agree," said Mr. O'Shea, the criminal profiler.

"And he and his buddy are being severely underemployed right now," concurred the FBI agent. "They are running around picking up litter in hallways and cleaning out air vents."

"Imagine that," mused Dr. Morton. "We are doing interviews, trying to catch potential criminals while pretending to be ensuring workers are in appropriate jobs, and we actually found a pair of highly trained people who are being underutilized."

"So, are you really going to get someone to call them?" asked Ms Kurtz.

"I'm going to bounce this up to the Administrator's office and let them handle it. We still have a room full of people to screen." She tapped a symbol on her tablet and spoke, "Send in the next one, please."

Corvette Squadron Briefing Room

The clock on the wall showed a few minutes before 0900 hours. Beth was waiting for the rest of the squadron's pilots and officers to arrive for the day's mission briefing. It was going to be a busy day, but any day she got to fly was a good one. Still, her mind drifted back to the time she spent with Billy Ray Vincent the previous evening.

* * * * *

The food at the restaurant was excellent—not haute cuisine but savory French country cooking. A marvelous seafood bisque followed by *Coq au Vin Blanc*, a French classic combining chicken, herbs and vegetables steeped in white wine. There was only one other couple in the restaurant that evening. The chef talked with them before making his way to their table. He was a tall man with dark hair and classic Gallic features. Handsome but with haunted eyes.

"*Bonsoir, mes amis,*" he said, "how was your meal this evening?"

"Good evening, Jean-Jacques, everything was fantastic," Billy Ray replied, then turning to Beth, "Might I present Lt. Beth Melaku? Beth this is Jean-Jacques de Belcour, formerly of UNOOSA and a shipmate from Peggy Sue's second voyage."

"*Bonsoir, M. de Belcour,*" Beth added, "*la nourriture était délicieuse.*"

"*Merci mademoiselle, c'est un plaisir de vous rencontrer.*" Jean-Jacques made a graceful half bow in Beth's direction. "Billy Ray, how did you manage to find such a delightful young lady here on the dark side of the Moon?"

"Just lucky I guess. We met over the radio on a little alien hunting trip. Beth was commander of the squadron of corvettes that accompanied the Peggy Sue on the mission."

"Then I am twice happy to make your acquaintance, Lieutenant. Anyone who kills aliens is more than welcome in my humble restaurant."

"It is my privilege to help defend humanity, or what's left of it." The tangible hatred beneath the restauranteur's words made her a bit uneasy and she looked to her dining companion to move the conversation off of killing aliens.

"I'm really glad that you have opened this place, Jean-Jacques," Billy Ray inserted. "It's great to sample some good, everyday French food, not that fancy stuff. I never knew you were such a hand in the kitchen."

"This is the cooking that my mama and grand-mère used to serve, good food fit for honest, working people. I hope to preserve some small part of France... now that *ma bien-aimée France* has

129

been destroyed by those cowardly aliens." De Belcour looked like he might start crying over the loss of his homeland.

"Do not despair, M. de Belcour. France will not be forgotten," Beth quickly reassured him. "Think of all the contributions of the French people—the dramatic literature, the great composers, the marvelous painters and sculptors, and, of course, your wonderful cuisine. Most of all, your language—the most lyrical and romantic language of all human tongues. No Monsieur, France will live on in the hearts and minds of many people."

"Thank you, Beth. You are indeed a woman of rare sensitivity and taste. What you are doing with this scoundrel I do not know..." Jean-Jacques finished his sentence with a Gallic shrug and a slight smile. "Have a wonderful evening and please come back."

"I'm sure we will, and we will be sure to tell our friends."

"*Merci, bonsoir.*" The Frenchman turned and headed back for the kitchen. Beth noticed that he walked with a slight hesitation, as though still in pain from his injuries. She look at Billy Ray, who had taken her hand.

"Thank you, I think you made his night with those remarks about France. It's hard for a proud man to loose everything and retain his dignity."

"I think he's a fine gentleman," she replied.

"Yeah, I've come to like the frog myself."

After dinner she let Billy Ray walk her home. She kissed him briefly at the door to her apartment, but she did not invite him in— for some reason she felt that this was one relationship that needed to develop slowly. For his part, Billy Ray acted like a gentleman, and bade her goodnight with a smile and a nod. Then he was gone.

What am I getting myself into? she thought, after her door slid shut and she was alone. *I could have asked him in and easily bedded him, but I think that would have disappointed him somehow. It would have disappointed me. Why am I pursuing him after Jesse's warning? Is it that I can't resist forbidden fruit?*

* * * * *

130

The digital clock on the wall turned over the hour and it was time to brief her command. Further thoughts of the fascinating Commander Vincent would have to wait. Beth walked to the podium at the front of the room and addressed the gathered corvette crews.

"Good morning."

"Good morning, Skipper!" came the enthusiastic reply.

"Our mission today is to proceed to the L4 point and intercept a number of hostile enemy. We will be conducting a live-fire railgun and laser exercise against drones..."

Chapter 10

M'tak Ka'fek, at the Alien Space Station

The better part of two days were spent crossing the star system to the alien space station. The probe ship they had been following was also inbound for the gigantic satellite. Docking instructions from the station directed the M'tak toward one huge supporting spoke while the probe proceeded to another.

"I think our little friend docked near a different antimatter collector," Bear rumbled. When he was using the ship's sensors he often closed his eyes and raised his snout as though he was sniffing the air.

"Ease her in gently, Mr. Danner," the Captain called out, casting a critical eye on the clearance between the side of the ship and the station. There was no flat, open area to land on like at the Space Mushroom. Here ships seemed to slide in between the major spokes and tie up directly to the station exterior. This suited Jack fine, getting underway in an emergency would be much easier.

"It looks like all but two of the antimatter collectors are inoperative," JT reported. "The one attached to the spoke on our port side is one of them. The other active collector is two away to starboard, where the probe ship was headed."

"That's interesting. Is it just me, or is this place giving off a particularly seedy, down at the heals type of ambiance?"

"It doesn't appear to be in the best of condition, Captain."

While the Captain tried to minimize his use of the thought link with the ship's AI, there were times when he was glad he could converse with the living computer without the rest of the crew hearing the exchange. This was one of those times. *M'tak, can we dock and keep the shields up at the same time?*

No, Captain, our shields are at minimum now and will need to be deactivated, at least on the port side, to allow docking. Note that I am sensing no offensive weapons or, for that matter, power sources that might pose a threat to the ship.

Technical specifications popped into his head unbidden. *Well that is comforting.* "All right let's drop the portside shields and let that gangway tube seal against the port hatch."

"Are you sure that's safe, Captain?" asked Bear, opening his eyes to look at the Captain.

"The ship assures me that there is nothing on the station that can do significant damage to it before we can get the shields back up."

From the station a pleated, retractable appendage reached for the side of the ship where lights, shining in colors both visible and invisible, outlined a sizable hatch on its hull. Like other hatches on the T'aafhal ship, this opening was not an opening at all, but a curving section of the ship's hull. Using technology that was, as Arthur C. Clarke put it, indistinguishable from magic, the M'tak's hull could be made selectively permeable, allowing objects to pass through while containing the air within. There was no need to open a hole in the hull or to equalize atmospheres with the station.

"I wonder if we will run into the same type of reception we got at the last space station?" Bear growled.

"I don't know my friend, but I am getting the impression that this station is more derelict than operational. Why would anyone let things fall into such a state of disrepair if they could help it?"

"I would concur, Captain," added Mizuki. "I sense little activity to indicate large scale production of antimatter. There may be some stored within the station but I fear there is no large cache here to be plundered."

"Plundered?" Jack smiled, "Mizuki, are you getting caught up in this pirate craziness along with the rest of the crew?"

"I am sorry, Captain," the young Japanese astrophysicist smiled shyly, "it just seemed like the correct word to use."

"Arr, Captain," said Bobby, grinning.

"Come on, Bobby," Sandy added, "you're starting to act as daft as the Marines. I half expect to see them running around with eye patches and daggers between their teeth."

"We may turn to piracy if we don't find some antimatter soon," the Captain agreed. "But let's take care and not scare the locals before we have to."

"Captain, we have a good seal with the docking gangway and there is pressure on the exterior side of the hatch," the ship's voice announced. "We can disembark personnel whenever you are ready."

"Thank you, M'tak. And you're sure that there are living creatures on board the station?"

"Yes, Captain, the docking mechanism and the welcoming beacons seem to be automated but there are signs of living creatures within this section of the station—warm life, given the interior temperatures. An analysis of the atmosphere outside the port hatch indicates a nitrogen oxygen mix at a tolerable pressure for your species."

"Very good then. Lt. Bear, Lt. Taylor, take a couple of the Marines and reconnoiter the quayside. In suits, and full armor for the Marines."

"Should we take the SEALs as well, Sir?" JT asked.

"I think we will hold them and the rest of the Marines in reserve, just in case we need to come retrieve you."

Port Shuttle Bay, M'tak Ka'fek

Bear and JT were standing in the cavernous shuttle bay next to the port side hatch. With them were two Marines, Jon Feldman and Joey Sanchez. All members of the reconnaissance team wore battle armor. Also present were Sandy McKinnett, the three SEALs and the four remaining Marines, also in armor and prepared to launch a rescue mission if needed.

"All right now, Lieutenants," Sandy said to the leaders of the recon team, "you go walkabout and we'll wait here for you to step in something."

"Always the optimist, Sandy," JT commented as he checked over Bear's weapons pack and gear. The suits were an improved model with significantly more power and energy storage. The previous model used a type of superconducting battery which gave the wearer about 12 hours of light use, 8 or less under more strenuous conditions. The SC batteries could only store so much energy before high internal magnetic fields caused a breakdown in superconductivity.

The ship came up with new, replacement cells that operated on a different principle. They were not batteries in the usual sense. Instead, they contained a metallic nickle matrix infused with hydrogen. When excited by intersecting terahertz lasers of the correct frequency atoms of hydrogen and nickle fused, resulting in copper and surplus energy—essentially a cold fusion reaction. The fusion cells could power a suit for a week or more, while producing an excess of energy. Enough excess energy that rounds in the wearers' weapons could be enhanced by pumping energy into the nano-engineered explosive in their warheads. Unenhanced, a 20mm explosive round had the kick of a conventional 40mm grenade. When pumped up with additional energy the explosive impact was the equivalent of a 105mm cannon shell.

The added power output of the CF cells also increased the effectiveness of a suit's built in shields. Not to the point where they could deflect a direct hit from a large caliber railgun, but enough so they could protect against most shrapnel and smaller rounds. Even the old suits could shrug off conventional rifle and small arms fire.

"Well you blokes go take a Captain Cook and if you get into an argy-bargy with the locals we'll hold up our end," said Sandy.

"Too right," said Ronnie Reagan.

"Strewth!" added Rosey Acuna.

"Have you all been taking Aussie slang lessons from Lt. McKinnett?" asked a mildly exasperated JT. The rest of the Marines were having trouble suppressing snickers.

"Come on, mates," said the grinning Sandy, "it's money for old rope."

"Let's go," rumbled Bear, "before I spit the dummy."

"Not you too," JT moaned as he followed his ursine friend through the side of the ship and into the alien boarding tube.

* * * * *

136

The party advanced cautiously down the boarding tube, through an open door in the station's hull. A ten meter long passage through the hull brought them to a conventional door that was shut tight. Feldman stepped up and examined the mechanism. "The symbols look similar to the ones on the M'tak, do you want me to try and open it?"

"Do it," Bear ordered. Feldman punched a sequence of buttons with his gauntleted fingers; the massive door clanged once and slid ponderously aside with a loud screeching noise.

"I guess we do have air pressure in here, or we would not have heard that," commented JT.

"Doesn't exactly fill me with confidence about the condition of the place," Bear replied.

"If the inhabitants are down on their luck maybe they'll be easier to trade with."

Bear snorted. "OK, Sanchez."

"Yeah, LT, let me guess, I get to take point."

"Why break with tradition?"

"You know, it is sort of like old times," Feldman said. "If Ronnie had come along it would be just like back on the Space Mushroom." Ronnie was LCpl Ronald Reagan, who was suited up in the port bay with the rest of the prospective rescue party.

"Yeah, bro. Remember what a fun time that was." Joey took a deep breath and stepped through the portal onto the station proper. Glancing around the dimly lit interior his suit's heads up display highlighted a number of objects that might be living creatures. Mixed in with the rubbish and debris that littered the huge hallway it was hard to tell.

Piles of junk, consisting of detached panels, loops of wiring, conduit, piping and less identifiable material, were heaped haphazardly across the 100 meter wide expanse of stained deck. Here and there, from grates in the deck, tendrils of mist issued. Overhead light shown down from scattered panels, some partially disconnected and flickering.

"Coño, what a dump!" he exclaimed, walking forward two paces, railgun at the ready. He turned and waived his companions forward just as a flying mass of unidentified goop struck the side of his helmet and right shoulder.

Bower of Keneesh-ka-ka-kar The Trader

Within the bowels of the alien station a group of creatures were carrying on a less than cordial conversation. There were three individuals, all of a race that called themselves the Kieshnar-rak-kat-tra, which roughly translated as *Scavengers of Wealth*. The participants looked like oversized lemurs with long bushy tails and extraordinarily large, bulbous, red-orange eyes. The eyes were an indication of their evolutionary descent from nocturnal forest dwellers and also explained their preference for dim lighting within the meeting chamber.

The chamber belonged to Keneesh-ka-ka-kar, also known as the Trader. But then, all Kieshnar-rak-kat-tra fancied themselves traders of the highest caliber. Their bodies were covered with fuzzy, cinnamon colored fur that was frosted with black highlights. Their tails, fully as long as their bodies, were banded in black. White fur extended from tufted ears, framing faces and foreheads, then ran down each creature's throat, chest and belly. In the middle of each face was a pointed black nose and muzzle from which black fur swept up and around the eyes giving the appearance of a bandit's mask—not a wholly inappropriate impression.

"There is a new ship docked along this sector of the station," Zooshnarak-kak-ka hissed in the sibilant speech of the Scavengers of Wealth. "A ship of significant size, though the size of its complement has yet to be revealed."

For several moments, Trader Keneesh-ka-ka-kar sat in silent contemplation. The rich carpets layered on the floor and forest motif tapestries on the walls helped muffle sounds from the surrounding station. Hanging from the ceiling on triple chains, bronze braziers smoldered with incense, masking unwelcome odors. What light there was emanated from large leafy plants in glazed ceramic pots. Their stems and veins glowed brightly, with more subdued illumination from their leaves. Some were green, some blue, but most were a reddish orange that complemented the creatures' eyes. Finally the Trader stirred.

"Do we know what life form builds this type of vessel?"

"No, Trader, its type is unfamiliar to us, though we are searching the station's archives for record of any similar vessel. It must be crewed by warm life, to have docked on this spoke. We should know more shortly, some of them venture into the major left hallway."

"We should conceal ourselves!" trilled Poonta-ta-ka, most junior of the three, nervously pulling his tail over his chest and forearms with six fingered hands, two opposable thumbs on either side of each. There scent glands embellished his fluffy tail with an odor that even a skunk would find disagreeable. Disputes among the Kieshnar-rak-kat-tra were often settled, not by the strength of one's arguments, but by the intensity of one's fragrance.

"Silence! You sniveling poltroon." Keneesh-ka-ka-kar gave his tail's scent a quick bolstering by passing it over his chest glands, first the right side and then the left. He then arched his fluffed out tail over his head like a menacing cobra, about to strike. "With change comes danger, but also opportunity. We must observe these newcomers, and discover that which they most desire. Then we will be in a position to trade advantageously."

The stench of his argument was overwhelming, which was why he was known as the Trader, the leader of his kind on board the station. The timorous Poonta-ta-ka's tail slumped and he hung his head—he knew he had been out argued and out stunk.

"Zooshnarak-kak-ka, send some of the junior traders to shadow the aliens, and tell them to keep their tails down and their eyes open."

"I will see to it, Trader," Zooshnarak-kak-ka replied. "With any luck we will find a way to profit from these creatures' arrival."

Hallway, Alien Space Station

Sanchez did a drop and roll, ending up in a crouch with his railgun ready to blast whatever it was that had hit him with the mass of unidentified material. Other members of the recon team ducked through the hatch and into covering positions—Feldman to the left and JT to the right. Bear took a single bound up the middle, landing next to Sanchez. Then he unlimbered his 15mm multi-barreled railgun and stood up.

Bear was an impressive sight without a suit of space armor, standing over three meters tall and massing 600kg. In armor he topped four meters and massed a metric ton, a huge graphite colored monster toting a wicked looking multi-barreled cannon, anxiously scanning for something to kill. "You OK, Sanchez?"

"Yeah, LT. What ever that stuff is it ran right off my suit's shielding and onto the deck."

"Did anyone see what did it?" asked JT.

"Up there, near all the pipes and panels hanging from the overhead," answered Feldman, motioning with an upward jerk of his railgun's muzzle. "There are things moving around up there."

Using their suits' built-in magnification the party searched the ceiling of the hallway, more than 100 meters overhead. As the creatures came into focus Bear commented first.

"Looks like a bunch of big fish hanging head down from the ceiling. Long, skinny suckers with big toothy grins."

"Yeah they sort of look like barracuda." Feldman had once been stationed at Roosevelt Roads in Puerto Rico and had seen barracuda swimming in the crystal clear waters of the Caribbean. Over external suit microphones the creatures could be heard calling out, a sound eerily like a murder of crows.

"The thing that splattered me had wings," groused Sanchez, "like a bat." As they watched, one of the hanging creatures relinquished its grip on the ceiling and dropped straight down like a silver missile. After falling for twenty meters it unfolded large, leathery wings and with a few flaps headed directly for the party of Earthlings on the hallway floor. The team raised their weapons in unison.

Evidently recognizing the weapons as a threat, the diving creature spread its wings and pulled out of its dive, affording the team a clear look at its physiology. The body was around two meters in length. From a snout that did look like the head of a barracuda to a flat horizontal tail, it was covered in iridescent silver scales the size of half dollars. Its wingspan was close to five meters, silvery membrane stretched over supporting fans of bone containing many more ribs than a bat's wings.

"Get a sample of that stuff, Joey," ordered JT, tracking the flying alien nervously. "See what it hit you with."

"Right, not only do I get splattered with it, now I gotta' play around in it." Sanchez muttered. He pulled out a probe that looked like a slender plastic straw and stuck the end of it into the sticky white substance. His suit's computer automatically sent the sensor information to the ship's AI for analysis.

"So what is that stuff, M'tak?" asked Bear.

"It is a mixture of a number of organic compounds. Viscous and rather caustic," the emotionless voice of the computer reported. "I would surmise that it is excrement from one of the flying creatures."

This caused Bear to snort and JT to say "Joey, you are beshat."

"It's shit?" asked Sanchez, disbelief mixing with outrage. "That batacuda asshole shit on me?" He straightened up and shook his fist at the creatures congregating on the ceiling. "Try that again, *culo!*"

This led to an increase in wing flapping and even louder cawing from the creatures overhead.

"I think they're laughing at you, Joey," said Feldman, standing up slowly.

"I'm gonna' pop one of the bastards," Sanchez snarled, putting his railgun to his shoulder.

"Belay that, Joey," JT quickly ordered. "Wouldn't it be a bitch if you shot one of those things and it turned out to be the Station Master's kid and his buddies out harassing tourists for a few laughs?"

"Oh man, Lieutenant. What's the use of having all these cool weapons if we never get to shoot nothing?"

"Hang in there, Sanchez. This hunt is just getting under way," Bear rumbled. "Which way you want to head, JT, left or right?"

"Let's head left, up the hallway in the direction of the antimatter collector."

Bear nodded.

"M'tak, Bear. We are going to head toward the AM collector."

"Roger that, Lieutenant," the Captain's voice replied. "Remember that you are trying to make contact, not take over the station. Continued restraint is called for."

"Aye aye, Captain," Bear acknowledged. "OK, left it is. Pop a couple of small recon drones. Feldman, you take point this time and give the whiner a break."

"Aye, Sir."

In the distance, creaking noises and a hollow booming sound echoed down the cavernous hallway. On the ceiling, the batacudas cackled, and from the shadows, two pairs of melon sized red-orange eyes watched the team move out.

Chapter 11

Hallway, Alien Space Station

The hallway was cluttered with mounds of junk, some fallen from the walls and ceiling high overhead, some showed signs of having been put there purposefully. Noxious emanations rose from putrefying organic waste partially covered with fuzzy coats of fungus and mats of bacteria. Had the Peggy Sue's science team been present they would have had a field day.

As it was, the recon patrol moved in biologic isolation inside their space armor. The four Earthlings advanced cautiously through the garbage and gloom. Feldman, on point, came to the end of a particularly large pile of trash that started at the far wall and formed a barrier across two thirds the width of the hallway.

Peeking around the tip of the garbage peninsula Jon held up his left hand in a fist—a signal to those behind to stop in place. Overhead, the pair of grapefruit sized reconnaissance drones weaved random paths while beaming back video of the terrain ahead.

"Looks clear," he said after a few moments of motionless observation. "Whoever the inhabitants of this place are, I am underwhelmed by their housekeeping skills."

"Stay alert, these piles of debris make a perfect setting for an ambush," JT warned.

"This is like working through the back alleys of an Afghan village," Joey chimed in from the rear. "At least those flying crap factories didn't follow us."

"Hey, that's why we bring you along, Sanchez," Bear rumbled. "You are a natural shit magnet."

The foursome was strung out in a line across the open section of deck beyond the large ridge of garbage. They cautiously advanced toward what looked like a bulkhead a hundred or so meters in the distance. Feldman froze in place.

"I got movement ahead."

143

The others moved laterally to clear their fields of fire. Caught in the open they crouched down close to the deck to reduce their profiles.

"Can you make out what it is, Jon?"

"Just that it's large and low and moving slowly on a diagonal path toward the far wall." Jon took a couple of sliding steps to his left, farther from the object's path.

The creature in question emerged into a puddle of illumination from a still functioning light panel. Dark red in color, it moved at walking speed, making way for the far wall. It was, indeed, low to the deck. In fact, it was oozing along the deck surface much like a snail, leaving a noticeably wet trail behind it. There the similarity to a snail ended.

There was no shell upon its back, no discernible head with eyes on stalks. Its body looked like a flowing mass of putty, mounding to a height of a meter and a half at its forward end. The creature's body seemed to flow from back to front, up over the forward facing mound, and down the creature's front to form a thin, stationary cushion on the deck. The material at the back end of the cushion curled up off the deck once the bulk of the creature past, flowing upward to begin another transit to the front.

"Man, it looks like Meatwad," Jon exclaimed.

"What?" asked Bear.

"You know, Meatwad from Aqua Teen Hunger Force."

"Huh?"

"It's a cartoon, Bear," JT filled in. "Meatwad was a sort of rolling blob of raw ground meat."

As the moving red mass drew closer they could see that this Meatwad was not made up of ground meat. More like raggedly chopped hunks, interspersed with jagged stick like objects that could have been bone fragments. Small pieces of equipment and other debris were also embedded in the flowing ooze. The whole mass was held together by a gelatinous red substance that glistened in the overhead light.

"I don't remember Meatwad looking like that, bro."

144

"Me either Joey."

The four Earthlings stood transfixed as the strange creature slid past, showing no sign of noticing their presence. After a few moments Bear broke the silence.

"I wonder what it tastes like?"

"Brother Bear, you just killed my appetite," JT replied. "This place is like a galactic zoo. I wonder what we'll run into next?"

"If a giant milkshake with arms or a floating box of french fries with a goatee show up I'll know we've ended up on Adult Swim."

"Those cartoons are going to rot your brain, bro."

"Hey, I grew up watching those cartoons!"

"Enough chatter," Bear grumbled, "lead off Feldman. Let's see what waits for us at that bulkhead."

* * * * *

As the recon patrol approached the bulkhead they could see that it did form a barrier across the full width and height of the hallway. In the middle of the bulkhead at deck level there was an opening, a rectangle ten meters wide by four meters tall, with rounded corners. At the bottom there was a lip about a half meter in height.

"What do you think, JT?"

"I think we need to send a recon drone to see if something is waiting on the other side, ready to jump out and say 'boo!'"

"Right, Lieutenant," said Jon, directing one of the drones through the opening in front of them. The video returned to the anxious explorers showed a scene much like the one around them.

"Curious how there isn't any junk or piles of garbage around either side of the doorway." JT mused out loud.

"Maybe it's a high traffic area, like a game trail," Bear suggested.

"I hope that doesn't make us game, LT."

"Well, there's one way to find out if it's a trap and that's to step in it."

145

"Right, JT. Feldman, in you go, we'll cover you."

Jon acknowledged Bear's command and cautiously stepped over the threshold. The other side did look similar to the parts they had already traversed. There were large mounds of debris encroaching from either wall, though there was a noticeable absence of smaller piles of junk between them. The drone drifted toward the overhead, providing a wider view of the chamber.

"Nothing seems to be moving, LT."

"OK, we're coming in."

One by one the three remaining Earthlings followed Feldman into the chamber beyond the bulkhead. They left one of the drones to watch their rear, trusting those in the ship to have their back if things went sideways.

Bridge, M'tak Ka'fek

The Captain and bridge crew anxiously watched the recon patrol's progress on the ship's holographic displays—panoramic views from the recon drones on the navigation screens and shots from individual suit cams on the smaller instrument screens. Betty White, the medical corpsman, was monitoring the expedition members' vital signs via telemetry.

"So far so good," Betty commented.

"Yes, no aliens have been slaughtered, no holes have been blown in the station and none of ours have been killed, maimed or wounded," Jack replied, "but they haven't found anything to talk with yet."

"Maybe the place is deserted, Captain," Bobby suggested. "The station seems to be a wreck. The inhabitants might have left for greener pastures, leaving behind a few pets that have gone feral."

"Sensor readings from the drones indicate that they are being shadowed by a number of creatures that remain concealed," the ship's voice said. "Such behavior may indicate purpose and intelligence."

"Or they may just be predators awaiting their chance."

"True, Captain. But the chance that any unarmed creature can do significant harm to the crewmembers' armor is remote."

"Captain," Mizuki called from her station, "I have located neutrino emissions that indicate a store of antimatter. It is not a huge quantity, perhaps a couple of type 1 containers."

"That's great, Mizuki. Where is it located?"

"Unfortunately, it is in the opposite direction from that which the reconnaissance party is traveling."

"You're sure about this?"

"Yes, Captain. The readings are centered about four kilometers toward the central hub from the boarding ramp."

"Well, they had a 50/50 chance of being right and it was logical to head for the collector," Jack sighed. "Lt. Bear, M'tak."

"Bear here, Captain."

"Dr. Ogawa says she has located some antimatter back the other way. I think you might want to reverse your line of march and head toward the hub."

"Aye aye, Captain... What the hell is that?"

Forward Chamber, Alien Space Station

The explorers were standing between two large garbage promontories: Sanchez and JT toward the hull wall, and Feldman and Bear nearer the larger mound against the inner wall. The pairs were roughly 30 meters apart. Bear had just signed off talking with the Captain when the garbage began moving.

"What the hell is that?"

"What, LT?" Feldman asked, turning toward the ursine lieutenant. As he did the pile of garbage erupted with dozens of yellow-green tentacles. Like a time-lapse video of plants sprouting, sending waving stalks with swollen tips reaching for sunlight, the garbage beside them exploded with motion. Unlike in a nature film, these stalks were threateningly large and they were reaching for the Earthlings.

147

The stalks were as thick as a man's thigh; the tips like featureless snake heads with mouths three quarters of a meter wide. One arched through the air above Feldman and then dropped straight down, engulfing his helmeted head.

"Ah! Get it off!" the startled Marine yelled. Another green pseudo-snake grasped his left knee and a third his right arm and railgun. Together they attempted to pull him toward the hill of garbage they had emerged from.

Across the hallway, JT and Sanchez turned to see what was happening to their mates. As they did, more waving appendages emerged from the portside garbage heap behind them. Quickly darting out, the plant like stalks latched on to the two humans with toothless mouths.

Sanchez, who had been on edge since being bombarded by the flying batacuda, reacted quickly. Pivoting on his right leg, to which one of the creatures had affixed itself, he raised his railgun and blew the head off one attacker. The 20mm shotgun round turned it into green mist. He then severed the stalk gripping his leg with a burst of 5mm flechette fire.

Using judicious bursts of flechettes, JT also managed to free himself from the two pseudo-snakes that had seize his extremities. He turned toward the portside garbage heap to find a veritable garden of waving sprouts.

"These things seem to emerge in bunches," he shouted. "Fire at the bases, the places they come out of the garbage!"

Sanchez took JT's advice and sent a couple of HE rounds into the garbage where multiple stalks appeared to emerge. The rounds penetrated several meters before detonating, blowing sodden spurts of garbage into the hallway.

Meanwhile, bear had calmly extended the metal claws on his suit gauntlets and shredded the grasping stalks that had the misfortune to target him. Feldman, unable to fire his railgun, grasped the handle of his machete with his left hand and pulled it from its sheath. The machete was a Woodsman's Pal, a heavy piece of flat steel with a wide head and a razor sharp edge.

His first backhanded swing severed the stalk holding his left leg; his second overhanded blow cut the stem of the pseudo-snake enveloping his head. Finally he hewed the trunk of the attacker preventing use of his railgun. Using his suit's sensor display he raised his still partially encumbered right arm and loosed a volley of shotgun rounds in the direction of the starboard garbage heap.

In front of Bear and Feldman a new crop of waving pseudo-snakes emerged from a nearby location in the mound. The tentacles were attached to a single creature that opened like an octopus or giant squid, pealing back to reveal a central orifice—unquestionably its mouth. The inner flesh of the blossoming mouth was pale yellow with dark burgundy strokes radiating from the center opening. The effect was like a tropical flower, if tropical flowers came with backward facing 100mm barbs to prevent ingested prey from escaping.

"Will you look at that," Bear said, unlimbering his 15mm multi-barreled railgun.

"No explosive rounds!" JT shouted. "We don't want to do major damage to the station. Use flechettes or shotgun rounds."

"You have got to be kidding me," Bear said turning to glance at JT. Bear's weapon was not loaded with flechette rounds, only explosive shells. Re-holstering his railgun, Bear turned back to the alien's gaping maw. "OK, we will do this old school."

The armored bear took two galloping strides and jumped down the alien creature's throat.

Bridge, M'tak Ka'fek

Observing the melee from the bridge, Jack saw his friend dive head first into the alien's mouth. His only thought was, *I cannot believe he just did that!*

I think it highly improbable that Lt. Bear is in any real danger, Captain, M'tak's AI replied silently. *There is little harm an unarmed creature, no matter how vicious, can do to the Marines' space armor. Though I must admit that the Lieutenant's mode of attack was quite unexpected.*

149

To say the least. Jack keyed the comm. "Lt. McKinnett, please take your relief force down the boarding tube and stand ready at the entrance to the main hallway."

"Aye aye, Sir. It does appear that things are going a bit pear shaped."

"Pear shaped, Indeed, Lieutenant. Report when you are in position."

"Pear shaped. What a strange way to say things are going to hell," Bobby commented to Mizuki, who was seated next to him at the helm.

"Not at all, Bobby," Mizuki said seriously. "For certain combinations of protons and neutrons, some atomic nuclei can undergo octupole deformation, corresponding to a 'pear-shape'. Such conditions are rare and unstable, which might be considered analogous to the reconnaissance patrol's current situation."

"Some times you are so smart it is frightening," he said.

Mizuki smiled demurely.

Behind them, the Captain shook his head in amusement. *The crews' adaptability is truly amazing—one of their crewmates, who happens to be a polar bear, just dove inside a giant alien squid creature and they sit there calmly discussing the etymology of Australian slang using nuclear physic as an analogy.*

It is not so unexpected Captain. Your species was bred for this. Your are intelligent, flexible and violent, yet unexpectedly sympathetic toward other species—on occasion. I believe you are the worthy successors of the T'aafhal.

The Captain said nothing in reply. Instead he turned his attention back to the view of the engagement, where the tide of battle had shifted.

Forward Chamber, Alien Space Station

JT turned around and saw Feldman standing alone in front of the large alien beast. He was picking off the larger pseudo-snakes with carefully aimed shotgun rounds, amputated stalk head still affixed to his helmet. Bear was nowhere to be seen.

"Where the hell is Bear, Feldman?"

"You are not going to believe this, Sir, but he jumped right down that thing's throat."

"That *oso loco* is out of his mind!" Sanchez yelled while blasting away at the stalks still waving from the portside mound.

Suddenly, all the tentacles radiating from the main creature shook violently. The creature's mouth orifice, which had closed sphincter like after Bear plunged into its gullet, spasmed open and a gout of unidentifiable material spurted out. It splattered across the deck like projectile vomit.

This was followed by more ejectamenta, including what looked like a partially digested batacuda. The creature's tentacles began to thrash uncontrollably, its mouth opening and closing convulsively. Then the flesh directly above its maw was rent by four long claws. The attached pseudo-snakes went limp and lifeless.

Other stalks, evidently not belonging to the central creature, quickly disappeared back into the garbage. Bear's companions ceased firing as he hacked his way out of the alien's body. Before him he pushed a large purplish gray mass.

"You have got one huge pair of cojones, LT," Joey said with heartfelt admiration. Feldman sheathed his machete and holstered his railgun. He then proceeded to pry the pseudo-snake head off his helmet.

"And just what have you got there, Lt. Bear?" asked a very relieved JT.

"I don't know," Bear replied, "could be its liver or its brain. I just went for the largest organ I could find."

"I cannot believe you did that."

"Hey, it seemed like a good idea at the time. Besides, Feldman was blasting everything in sight, hopping around with that green thing stuck on his head like an elf's cap. I figured we needed to end this as soon as possible."

"Well, end it you did Brother Bear. I guess we should head back the other way like the Captain said."

"Yeah. No rest for us apex predators." Bear shook the remaining alien spew off his suit. "How about taking the lead, Sanchez? I think Feldman did his share leading us into that ambush."

"Yeah, no problem, LT."

"Hey, how was I to know we were going to be attacked by giant green sock puppets from hell?" Jon protested.

Sanchez looked at Feldman. "You were hopping around like an elf there for a while, bro."

Jon favored Joey with a single finger salute as the detail headed back through the bulkhead opening. Now many sets of eyes and other sense organs followed their passage with growing interest— the Earthlings were the most exciting thing to hit the station in decades.

* * * * *

In the Trader's cloister, Zooshnarak-kak-ka hustled in to report to his leader. Tail flicking nervously he addressed the august Keneesh-ka-ka-kar. "Your pardon, Trader, but there is word regarding the new aliens."

"Speak! What have they been doing?"

"After a short encounter with the flying vermin, they headed toward the collector. On the way they crossed the path of an exo-stomach being, but let it pass by peacefully."

"Hmm. They do not sound very aggressive—perhaps they are not as powerful as their ship suggests."

"Ah, but then they went into the restricted area beyond the bulkhead. There was a brief altercation in which a number of carnivorous medusa plants were summarily dispatched by the strangers."

"Really?"

"Yes, Trader. One of our observers said they repelled the plant tentacles with their weapons. Reportedly, the largest of them put its weapon away and actually dove into the dominant plant in the colony, ripping it apart from the inside."

"Impressive! They may not have wanted to display the full power of their weapons or, having gauged the extent of the threat, decided to have a bit of fun with their attackers."

"Possibly. What ever the reason for their actions, it is clear that they are neither defenseless nor adverse to violence." Zooshnarak-kak-ka paused and fluffed his tail, "and, Trader?"

"Yes?"

"They are headed this way."

Chapter 12

Food Production Engineering Lab

Clem and Lem followed the Chief Administrator as she strode through the labyrinth of passageways that supported Farside's agricultural areas. They had received emails instructing them to report to personnel instead of going to work that morning. On arrival they were informed that they had been reassigned to new duties in Agricultural Production & Processing. The bearer of that news turned out to be the Chief Administrator herself, Dr. Ludmilla Tropsha.

Following the purposefully striding administrator, both men became aware that, even though Ludmilla's jumpsuit was of a utilitarian cut, nothing short of a full suit of space armor could hide the feminine form within. No doubt about it, the Chief Administrator was a knockout. Clem notice Lem overtly ogling Ludmilla's backside and gave him a poke in the ribs.

"What?" Lem said with some annoyance.

Clem shot him a look, eyebrows raised, just as they arrived at a large door. Their guide did not break step as the door slid open in front of her. Passing through a few more rooms filled with random pieces of duct-work and equipment, Ludmilla stopped at a work bench where a pretty young woman with long, curly brown hair was fiddling with some kind of air-handler.

"Good morning, Melissa," Ludmilla said, addressing the woman. "I see you are still having trouble with your fly factory."

"Oh, hey there, Dr. Tropsha," Melissa said, looking up from the piece of equipment. "What brings you all the way down here?"

Clem noticed that the young woman's jumpsuit was a bright leaf-green—the same color as the jumpsuits he and Lem had found in their delivery chutes that morning. Evidently this was their new department's color, not to be confused with the dark green of the Marines and certainly an improvement over the gray of the maintenance section.

155

"I would like to introduce your new engineering staff." Half turning to include the two men she continued. "These are Clement Mathews and Lemuel Souther."

"Hello, Ma'am," said Clem.

"Hi," said Lem.

"Both are former Army and trained to work on a wide variety of mechanical, electrical and hydraulic equipment. I am hoping that they will be able to help you construct your fly breeding system."

"Hey, guys. That's real nice of you. I'm having the worst time trying to move the flies out of the egg repository without smashing them all to bits. If y'all can come up with some way to do that it would be great!"

"Flies?" asked Lem.

"Eggs?" asked Clem.

"Right." Melissa smiled brightly.

"Miss Scott Hamilton is the head of the AP&P department. You will take direction from her. Your exact duties will be determined by how useful she finds you." Turning to Melissa she said, "If you have any problems give my office a call. I have a meeting I am already late for."

With that Farside's Chief Administrator left her two charges with their new boss and strode from the room. The two men stood across the workbench with friendly but questioning looks on their faces.

"Is she always that... business like?" asked Clem.

"Dr. Tropsha? Yeah, she's got a million things on her mind all the time. I'm surprised she took the time to walk y'all down here herself. She must think a lot of you two."

"I don't know why," Lem replied. "We just met her this morning."

"Well, she must have a reason. Ludmilla's one of the smartest people I know, and she's really nice besides. Well, once you get to know her."

"So, let me get this straight," Clem asked. "You are trying to raise flies? On the Moon?"

156

"I guess they didn't have time to give you a briefing but here's the problem: we have more than 10,000 people here at Farside and we have to find food for them. There isn't any wildlife or vegetation here naturally so we gotta' raise up things for people to eat from almost nothing."

"I never thought about that, did you Clem?"

"Not really, people don't much think about how food gets on their plates."

"Right. So we are building a whole food chain, from the bottom up. We have a bunch of plants growing—fruit, grains, vegetables and such—but most people like meat."

"With you so far." Lem nodded.

"Flies breed really fast and can turn almost any organic waste into protein, particularly if you harvest them in the larval stage, before they turn into adult flies. So we're trying to build a closed system that lets flies lay their eggs on a growing surface that we can flood with nutrients. We need some replacement flies for more breeding but we don't want them all to hatch out so we need to suck some flies off to the next laying chamber and then process the rest of the larvae. I've been trying to force them along with air flow, but they get all beat up."

"Sounds like you have an airflow problem. Clem, you remember those sand separators on the AC units in Iraq?"

"Yeah, they swirled the incoming air around to separate sand and stuff out and discard it."

"It's not just separating the flies, it's doin' it without turning them into goo."

"What you need is to create a swirling action and get a boundary layer effect to keep 'em from smashing into the sides of the ducting. Do you have a drafting table?"

"I have a display surface you can doodle on." Melissa thought, *these guys might be useful after all, even if they do look like two thirds of ZZ Top.*

"Come on, Clem. This is going to be cool..."

Earth Moon L4 Point

Lt. Melaku's corvette drifted in space more than two hundred kilometers from the Earth Moon L4 point. On her helmet's visor display she watched the swirling dots of light that represented her two flights of trainees, eight ships in all. Other, faster moving dots represented railgun rounds fired by those ships—virtual rounds only at this phase of the training exercise.

The L4 point was currently trailing the Earth Moon system with respect to its orbital path around the Sun. The mission plan called for live railgun fire only in a direction that would send the potentially destructive 10kg slugs on course for the inner solar system and away from both local planets. The preliminaries indicated that this would take a bit more practice by the trainees than anticipated.

What a Charlie Foxtrot, Beth thought, staring at the swirling mess on her display—a NATO slang term for a much ruder Anglo-Saxon one. "All right, Frenchy. Signal end of exercise and tell them to reform on us."

"Aye, Skipper."

Once the flight of newbies had sorted themselves out and returned to formation Beth switched off her tactical display, turning her visor transparent allowing them see the expressions on her face. She addressed them collectively.

"That was undoubtedly one of the worst displays of undisciplined, uncoordinated, mass chaos I have ever witnessed. At best, you achieved what I call the furball effect, in which the event devolves into a melange of attacks and counter-attacks, where you cannot tell friend from foe.

"You displayed no fire discipline, loosing rounds in all directions without consideration for your fellows. Wingmen abandoned their leaders and leaders lost contact with their flights. In short, you were more likely to shoot your comrades than your enemies!"

On the console display in front of her, Lt Melaku could see small images of each ship commander's face as they went from giddy excitement to crestfallen embarrassment. *They should all know better,* she thought angrily, *all of them were service pilots of some type back in the day. No matter, practice cures all ills.*

"All right let's try that again. I want you wingmen to stick to your leaders' tails, and flight leaders keep track of your ships. Most importantly I want to see some fire discipline. When you attack, fire as you approach your targets so that the velocity of your approach vector adds to the railgun slugs' KE on impact. Firing back at the target once past is like blowing them kisses.

"And make sure you know where the other ships are headed, so you don't fill their part of the sky with 10 kilo slugs. We are going to stay out here until you fire live rounds at those target drones and you will not fire live rounds until I am confident you will not kill each other in the process."

Beth took several deep breaths to calm down. *This training exercise is proving more nerve wracking than facing a real enemy.* This was just the first phase of training. Within the week she was supposed to take this group of trainees on an extended flight to the asteroid belt and Mars. That would not happen until they could at least fire their weapons without endangering each other.

"All right, Training Flights 1 & 2, maneuver to your attack positions. Commence attack on my signal. Frenchy, bring us around for another run."

"Aye aye, Skipper."

Base Administrator's Office

Ludmilla called the council back for another session, this time, to decide on a path for the immediate future. Jo Jo started with a status report on ship construction.

"We are now up to 14 corvettes, the latest are on a shakedown cruise with their crews. Six more have been started with an expected completion time of four weeks. Probably more important is the work on Constellation and Constitution, the first two frigates.

"They are nearing completion and should be ready for launch within the month. They were delayed a bit by the addition of anti-plasma counter weapons not included in the original design. Each will require a crew of 64 sailors and 8 officers plus a squad of 14 Marines."

"The crews have been chosen and are busy training in the simulators," added Captain Gretchen Curtis, the designated commander of all naval forces. She would directly command the squadron of frigates.

"Why so many Marines on each ship?" asked Rajiv.

"In case they need to board another ship, or repel boarders," replied Gretchen, "but under normal circumstances they also man some of the ship's weapons."

"Once the first two are completed we will start construction of Chesapeake and Indefatigable," Jo Jo continued. "They will take 15 weeks to complete."

"Indefatigable?" asked TK.

"British," replied Jo Jo. "She served throughout the French Revolutionary and Napoleonic Wars. She took, alone or in company, some 27 prizes."

"I thought we were naming the first six after the U.S. Navy's first six frigates?"

"We were, but then decided we needed to add some historical names from other navies, given the international make up of our recruits," Ludmilla answered. "That and the naming committee decided to reserve the name United States for the first of a larger class of ship."

"You're all ready planning for bigger ships?"

"Believe me, TK," Gretchen answered with a grim smile, "if you had seen the ships floating about in the Sirius graveyard you would not be asking that question. But designing a new, bigger class of ship will take time, so we are going to build as many frigates as we can until then."

"What other names have you decided on?"

Jo Jo consulted his tablet. "Maeander, Yarra, Ikazuchi, Tachikaze, Grozovoi, Strashni, Victoire, and Soledad round out the first twelve."

"Thunder and Wind From a Sword Stroke," Yuki translated the two Japanese names. "Very good, very appropriate." Yuki looked at Ludmilla and raised his eyebrows.

"Yes, Yuki, you wish to add something?"

"Yes, Doctor. I am afraid that I must be the bearer of disturbing news." Suddenly, the room was as silent as a grave.

"What is it, Yuki," Gretchen asked. She and the Japanese astrophysicist were often kendo sparing partners and she knew it was not in Yuki's nature to joke about such things. He must have terrible news indeed.

"I have been studying sensor readings from an observation drone the task force left behind near the scene of the battle. There are unmistakable signs that an alien probe departed the area roughly eight days after the fleet headed for home." He glanced around the room, grim faced. "It is fairly certain that the enemy knows of their defeat... and that we still exist."

"Sounds like we'll need the new frigates sooner rather than later. How long is it gonna' take to build 'em?" TK said, getting to the crux of the matter.

"With the yards we have now, more than a year," was Jo Jo's muted answer. "Perhaps faster if we can get the yards being built on Olympus Mons up and running."

"And how long do you figure we have, Yuki?"

"Judging by the message probe's alter-space entry parameters, it will take about six months to reach its destination. It took about the same amount of time from first contact to the attack on Earth. Add that to the transit time and, If we are very lucky, we have a year to prepare. Half that long if fortune is against us."

A somber quiet settled on the room. After what seemed an interminable silence, TK spoke.

"I got an idea."

"Yes, TK?" said Ludmilla.

"Some times you need to invest in expanding yer means of production instead of just producing as fast as you can."

"Meaning?"

"Instead of starting on two new frigates, we build a pair of big, fast cargo ships—we already have plans for 'em. Then ship enough

161

equipment, material and personnel to Mars to get the shipyards there up and running. Once they are, they will produce four frigates for every two we can build here."

"That makes sense if we actually have six months grace time before the next attack. Even better if the delay is longer," agreed Rajiv. "But where will we get the people?"

"We go recruitin' in Texas and Australia and anyplace else we can find educated workers. And we call for volunteers from the workforce here. We can promise 'em they'll be in on the ground floor for settling Mars, once things calm down a bit."

"You think the lure of settling on Mars will be a big enough enticement?"

"A few years back, a group tried to organize a private mission to Mars. They asked for donations and volunteers to settle the red planet. They got over 200,000 people to sign up for a one way trip even though there would be nothing waiting for them on the other end. We can offer a lot more than that."

"That might work, but what if the Dark Lords attack early?" asked Gretchen, "We will only have two frigates, the Peggy Sue and a bunch of corvettes. If they come in greater force than the squadron we encountered at Sirius we could be at a severe disadvantage."

"If they come early we're screwed any way you slice it, Captain Curtis," TK said, stating the truth they all had been avoiding.

"So it isn't really much of a gamble at all, is it?" added Ludmilla. "OK, all in favor?" Hands went up around the table.

"All opposed?" None were opposed.

"*Ochyen khorosho,* let us get on with the planning..."

Hallway, Alien Space Station

The four members of the recon patrol stopped briefly at the entrance to the boarding tube, where they conferred with their colleagues. Their fellows in the reserve force offered them words of encouragement, of a sort.

"Well I see you blokes managed to find trouble," Sandy observed with a knowing grin. The reserve had watched the recon patrol's progress on their helmet displays. "Had a bit of a barney with those squid plant things, did you?"

"Yeah, Sandy, you should have been there," Bear shot back. "It would have reminded you of home, a place full of weird, nasty, disgusting creatures."

"Now I didn't see any 'roos or wallabies, just rolling piles of dingo vomit and giant carnivorous plants." She turned to her assembled Marines and SEALs. "Mates, you see anything from Oz out there?"

"Not us, Lieutenant," reported Chief Morgan, the head SEAL.

"Nor us, Ma'am," added Ronnie Reagan. "No disrespect intended, Sirs. But it's a lot more entertaining watching you on drone cam than being in the shit with you."

"Just keep looking up, Reagan," Sanchez replied, "and one of those flying *fábricas de mierda* will give you a present."

"All right, enough of this. Bear, let's head toward the hub and see if we can find a trace of the antimatter Dr. Ogawa located."

"Right, JT. We'll leave the cubs here guarding the doorway."

"Hooroo! Have fun fossicking around down there, mates! We'll be here if you need us."

Sanchez led the other intrepid explorers down the hall to the right as their friends continued to amuse themselves by offering verbal abuse. The recon patrol soon disappeared around a large pile of debris and the hazing died out.

* * * * *

Under the cover of a fallen ceiling panel a pair of furry observers watched the exchange between the two groups of Earthlings. Though they were not privileged to the actual conversation, the two young scavengers were quite adept at interpreting body language, even that of other species.

"Interesting, it looks like the smallest one is actually in charge. It was obviously berating the four large ones that had gone scavenging toward the collector." While most of the humans were wearing heavy space armor, Lt. McKinnett was in lighter armor, as were the three SEALs.

"I don't know. The quadrupedal one didn't act very respectful if the little one is in charge. I think it and the biggest bipedal alien are in charge, at least of the scouting party."

"Perhaps they don't have a firm hierarchy? Maybe they are just a band of brigands, each in it for themselves."

"Could they be different species?"

"The great big one that walks on all fours is certainly different from the rest."

"But what about the two legged ones? They seem to come in two different sizes."

"It might just be a difference in their armored suits. Of course, that might also signify who gives orders and who are foot soldiers."

"Whatever. We need to learn more and the original four are headed toward the hub and our own territory."

* * * * *

Feldman kept one of the drones trailing behind the party and sent the other ahead to scout for Sanchez. Having been attacked in multiple ways already, all members of the recon patrol were on guard. If anything, the clutter ahead of them was worse than that in the other end of the hallway.

"We've had bats, moving barf and snaky squid things," Bear rumbled, "can't wait for what happens next."

"Borrow trouble for yourself, Brother Bear, if that's what you want." JT anxiously scanned the surrounding clutter. "But you don't need to lend the rest of us any."

"I'm not complaining, JT. This is the most fun I've had since the fight on Pzzst."

"Fun I love, but too much of this kind of fun can kill a guy."

Bear paused and looked back at JT. "You're joking, right?"

Chapter 13

Food Production Engineering Lab

Melissa, Clem and Lem, wearing hardhats and safety glasses, were observing a transparent, plexiglass model of the fly breeding and larvae production habitat. The noise of the blowers made normal conversation difficult but it was obvious by the grins on their faces that things were going well.

"Shut it off," yelled Melissa, making a chopping motion with her hand. Clem nudged Lem and Lem threw the master breaker for the equipment. As the fans slowed and the roaring air flow quieted the trio had pleased looks all around.

"I don't see any bug guts on the ducting," Lem announced, removing his plastic safety glasses. "And it sure sucked the flies out of the growing chamber."

"Yeah, that it did," Clem commented. "In practice we may not need as much airflow volume."

"You're assuming it will scale up without problems?" asked Melissa. The boys, as she had come to think of them, had already fixed a number of design problems with the test rig. She and her staff could have fiddled with the prototype for a month and not gotten it working. Her people were great with animals and plants—machinery, not so much.

"I think it will scale up fine, given the computer's flow estimates, Miss Scott Hamilton."

"Clem, I told you boys to call me Melissa. I was never in the military like a lot of the other folk around here were, and I don't stand on formality much."

"Yes, Ma'am," Lem replied. "Are we going to start fabricating the real system then?"

"I want to get a few more test runs done, but I think we can send the specs to the materials shop. They will be able to whip up the components in a jiffy. Then we can put it together and try growing a real crop. I need to get some actual yield figures before I can write the report for Ludmilla."

"Report?"

"Yeah, it's sort of the final preliminary report on the prototype food production system. It will be reviewed by some of the other science types and if they OK it we are off to the races."

"So how many flies are we talking about in our herd?"

"Around 25 or 30 million."

Clem left out a long, low whistle. "We had best be sure they don't get out or we will need a new place to live."

"When this works folks will want to shake your hands. We should see improvement in fish production in four weeks, and fresh chicken meat in 8-10 weeks. Egg production won't ramp up for five or six months though. Improvement in hog production will take about the same."

"Imagine that, most of humanity living on fly meat. Sort of like payback for all those ruined picnics."

"Well you boys can knock off for the day. We'll start building a real one of these things in the morning. You know, once we get everything running well here, we may get to go to Mars and set up their production facilities." With that Melissa headed back to her office and Clem and Lem started for the exit.

"Did you hear that, Clem? We may get to go to Mars!"

"Hell, Lem. I'm just happy to not be sweeping hallways anymore."

Bridge, M'tak Ka'fek

"The readings indicate the antimatter is about two klicks beyond your current position," Mizuki reported to the recon patrol. "I have no idea where it will be stored beyond that."

"Roger, M'tak."

The patrol had been walking toward the hub for over a half hour. Even though the station gravity was only about 40% that of Earth, the suits slowed movement and their path was circuitous.

Meanwhile, back at the entrance to the boarding tube, Lt. McKennitt's detachment was growing bored.

"M'tak, Lt. McKennitt, we've had no activity since the recon patrol departed."

"Roger, Lieutenant," Jack replied. "Stay alert down there. No telling what might turn up."

"Aye aye, Captain."

Captain, I sense no signs of movement at deck level near the boarding tube entrance. I am showing movement near the ceiling, however, but it is hard to pinpoint with all of the dislodged panels and other material hanging down. I am still tracking multiple lifeforms tailing the reconnaissance party.

Thank you, M'tak. Please let me know if there is any threatening movement.

I have done an analysis of the partially digested batacuda remains that were regurgitated by the carnivorous plant. Based on shape and size of the cranial cavity I have concluded that the batacudas are not sentient—they are just animals, Captain.

Indeed. I will keep that in mind. Above the reserved force, among the debris hanging from the overhead, sleek silver shapes moved carefully.

Boarding Tube Entrance

Sandy stood just outside the doorway, trying to keep a watch on the cluttered hallway before her. The SEALs had worked their way to the right, in among some of the omnipresent piles of junk. Rosey Acuna and Ronnie Reagan were twenty paces to the left of the doorway, while Brown and Samuels flanked their lieutenant on either side.

The only exciting thing to happen in the last half hour was when a multilegged creature with a circular rasping mouth tried, unsuccessfully, to attached itself to PO Bud Jones' leg. After sliding off three times the rat sized creature gave up and wriggled back into the garbage from whence it came.

As Sandy turned back toward the entrance she caught a flash of movement. From amidst the tangle of hanging junk, a pair of bat winged creatures headed like silver arrows toward the Earthlings. Before she could raise an alarm Reagan yelled out.

"Two batacudas inbound from the port side!"

"M'tak, we have batacudas inbound!" Sandy reported to the ship.

"Roger, Lieutenant." came the Captain's immediate response. "M'tak says they are just animals. No explosives, otherwise weapons are free. Repeat, weapons are free."

"Take 'em down, mates!"

Before Sandy's order was completed Rosey and Ronnie stood, brought their railguns to their shoulders and fired like a pair of skeet shooters on a range. Both used shotgun rounds, 20mm in diameter clusters of flechettes launched toward the flying creatures at 1200 fps.

Both of the diving batacudas crumpled in on themselves. Their forward momentum blunted, they tumbled in ragged bundles to the deck, landing 20 meters short of the Marines. After sliding another ten meters, the bodies lay unmoving before their killers.

"Nicely done, Reagan." Rosey high-fived her fellow marksman.

"Not bad yourself, Acuna."

"Look overhead!" yelled PFC Kevin Brown, pointing at the ceiling with his left arm. Suddenly, a swirling flock of silver winged bodies appeared near the roof of the hallway. They circled, calling out like an angered flock of crows and then dove, en mass, toward the Earthlings.

Recon Patrol

Sanchez signaled for the others to halt in front of what looked like a constructed barrier, fencing in an area of the hallway deck. Along the inner wall a pile of crates and containers were stacked up in such a way as to suggest habitation. Several openings looked like entrance ways into the pile.

168

Within the fenced in deck area were stacks of junk, though there seemed to be some method to how they were arranged. One stack consisted of spools of heavy wire, another lengths of pipe and elbows. Atop one pile was a sizable object that looked like a partially melted, front loading washing machine.

"I think we have found a junkyard," JT said.

"How can you tell it from all the other junk?" Bear asked in an innocent tone.

"Well, it's better organized than the junk outside the barrier, and I don't see any rotting biological crap among it."

"Too bad, I was in the market for some rotting biological crap." Bear gave his friend a toothy grin.

"Look, Lieutenant, there are some creatures headed this way from that pile of shipping containers."

"Right you are, Joey, let's hope they are friendly and can communicate."

"Yeah, weapons down primates. Don't want to spook the prey prematurely."

"Can't we come across any new life form without you thinking of them as a prospective meal, Brother Bear?"

"Hey, I love ringed seal as much as any polar bear, but we are omnivores. A little variety is always appreciated, and those things look like furry monkey snacks to me."

"Now you're making me nervous, LT," Feldman said, moving a few paces farther to Bear's right.

Bear chuckled.

"You know he only does that to get a rise out of you, Feldman."

The conversation amongst the patrol members came to an abrupt end as three furry creatures with cinnamon colored bodies, white chests and faces, and large red-orange eyes approached their position from the other side of the barrier.

Stopping across from the Earthlings, the three exchanged rapid fire chattering among themselves, accompanied by much flicking of their large fluffy tails. With a few particularly sibilant exclamations the largest of the three silenced the others and took a half step forward. It spoke and the patrol's suits automatically translated.

"Greetings, strangers. Do you come to trade?"

Boarding Tube Entrance

"Open fire!" yelled Sandy, shouldering her railgun and aiming at the approaching flock of cawing, silver creatures. From eight railguns, streams of 5mm flechettes, every third one a bright green tracer, laced the space between the reserve force and the attacking batacudas.

It was over in less than ten seconds. A half dozen silver shapes tumbled from the sky—wings shredded, bodies riddled with holes. The slain were still falling as their surviving comrades vanished, back into the ceiling clutter that they had emerged from. The batacudas struck the floor and lay still, with shattered bodies and wings protruding at odd angles, sad silver mounds that seconds ago had been majestic flying beasts.

Quiet descended on the hallway.

After a half minute, Sandy spoke. "I think they've gone. Chief Morgan, you and your boys take a look and make sure they are well and truly dead."

"Aye aye, Lieutenant." With hand signals the Chief SEAL motioned his men forward. The four Marines continued to scan the deck in front of them and the air above.

The SEALs examined the nearest of the bodies, nudging a few with armor encased legs. Nothing moved among the downed batacuda.

"These things are history, Lieutenant," the Chief reported, signaling his two companions to head back to their positions next to the doorway. As they returned, movement was detected near the far wall.

"Heads up people, we have more company coming."

The movement soon resolved into three distinct targets, converging on the downed batacudas at an unhurried pace. As they drew nearer the targets were identified as three of the slithering Meatwad like creatures. They halted at the edge of the fallen fliers and one of their number carefully circumnavigated the bodies.

"What's it doing?" asked one of the Marines.

"I don't know, but it seems to be coming over to see us," Sandy replied. Sure enough, once clear of the dead bodies, the advancing meatwad headed straight for Sandy and her companions. It took over a minute for the gelatinous creature to ooze within hailing distance. At a separation of about five meters it halted, mounded its body a bit higher and began making loud noises that sounded like flatulence.

"What the hell?" asked Brown. To which Reagan said, "I think it is trying to communicate with us."

"You are correct," said the voice of the M'tak's AI over the comm link. "It is using a strange variant of the common trading tongue, but it is so distorted that your suits are having a hard time translating. I am upgrading the programing now."

"...you have killed a large number of the flying pests. Do you claim their flesh for your own use?"

Sandy's eyebrows went up in a quizzical expression. "Anyone want to claim a batacuda carcase?" she asked her team. Receiving no replies in the affirmative she keyed the translator and addressed the glistening red creature. "No, we have no use for the bodies."

The meatwad issued an inarticulate burst of sound and proceeded back the way it came, not by turning about but by reversing its flow. The humans watched as the creatures began to slowly envelope the batacuda bodies by sliding over them. A fourth creature emerged from the left to absorb the two batacudas shot by Acuna and Reagan.

"Not much on conversation, are they?" Chief Morgan observed.

"I think I'm going to be sick," said PO Phil Kowalski.

"Dingo vomit that talks by farting," said Sandy, with a shake of her head. "Even Australia doesn't have anything that ugh."

The ship's AI provided background information as the creatures dined. "They seem to be similar to a previously known species who's digestive system was part of their dermis. They feed by absorbing nutrients from organic matter, digested using an acidic medium surrounding their entire bodies. I am unsure how these came to be on this station but exo-stomach beings were quite rare."

"What?" asked LCpl Samuels.

"Exo-stomach beings. They have their stomachs on the outside of their bodies, not inside as with you humans."

"That's just wrong," observed Reagan.

One by one the creatures turned away, slithering off to parts unknown with the occasional wingtip or fishy jaw popping up out of their flowing bodies before being reabsorbed. In parting, the last exo-stomach creature farted a final message.

"Do not trust the stink weasels."

"I wonder what that last message means?" Sandy wondered aloud, as the creature slid away into the gloom.

Trader's Compound

Bear and JT engaged the Kieshnar-rak-kat-tra, who called himself Ooshnar-tar-rak-ra, for more than an hour before the subject of antimatter came up. Without missing a beat, Ooshnar shifted from trying to sell the Earthlings excess molecular circuitry to discussing the rarity and availability of antimatter on the station.

"Ah, you see antimatter is almost impossible to come by, used as it is to power the station and maintain habitable conditions. Though, for the right price I might be able to lay paws on some. How much were you interested in?"

Knowing that there were only limited amounts on the station, JT played it cool. "Oh, we are just trying to top off our tanks. We do that out of habit whenever we make port. Our Captain says it pays to plan ahead."

"A wise being indeed, this Captain of yours. And what would you be willing to trade for, say, a type 3 container full?"

"A type 3? Hardly worth our while. We are looking for a type 1 at least, perhaps several."

"That much antimatter would cost quite a fortune, gentle beings, and you have yet to indicate what you might be willing to trade for such goods."

"We were thinking that we might offer payment in the form of services."

Seeing the quizzical look on the trader's face—Kieshnar-rak-kat-tra have very expressive faces—Bear explained. "We noticed while walking about the station that you have a big pest problem."

"Yes..." Ooshnar agreed cautiously.

"We could clear out the flying vermin and those overly affectionate plants you have up toward the collection disk, for example."

"An intriguing proposition, but that would be a benefit to more than myself and my clan, and a modest one at that. I'll tell you what, let me talk to my great uncle, who is the head trader on the station, and see if he has need of such services in exchange for some antimatter."

"OK, fine," Bear favored the trader with a toothy smile. "We'll wait."

* * * * *

Ooshnar-tar-rak-ra, who was in fact the Trader's grandnephew, scurried into the warren of containers and boxes and hurried to the bower of Keneesh-ka-ka-kar. On the way he conferred with one of the junior traders who had been spying on the Earthlings.

"While you have been talking with the aliens the larger party that remained at the foot of the boarding tube came under assault by the flying vermin," the young scavenger told his senior.

"Oh? And how did they fair against the accursed winged pests?"

"This time they did not hesitate—when two of the fliers attempted to pelt them with dung they were immediately shot down by the strangers. Two of the large ones fired once apiece and the winged vermin fell to the deck dead."

"How did the rest of the flock respond to that?"

"They swarmed the aliens, as you would expect from their kind. Trader Ooshnar, the party of aliens all fired at once and within seconds half the flock was dead on the deck and the rest fled for their lives!"

Ooshnar paused in his forward motion and looked at his underling intently. "You are saying they easily killed or scattered the whole flock?"

"Yes! These creatures are efficient, vicious killers. But there was one puzzling thing—they did not kill the exo-stomach beings that emerged after the slayings."

"Really?"

"Yes, the smallest of the aliens, the one that seemed to be in charge, conversed with the stomach beasts and gave them the flier's carcasses."

Why would they do that, Ooshnar pondered, *give away the bodies of things they had slain in return for nothing?* Keeping that puzzle in mind he resumed his journey to the Trader's dwelling, soon arriving at the beaded curtains covering its entryway.

"State your business," demanded Poonta-ta-ka, one of the Trader's minions.

"None of yours," was Ooshnar's curt reply. He pushed past the sycophantic Poonta-ta-ka and into the Trader's audience chamber.

"Trader Keneesh-ka-ka-kar, I bring news and an offer of commerce involving the newly arrived aliens!"

"Is that my grandnephew Ooshnar-tar-rak-ra? Come forward and let us discuss this trade you speak of..."

Chapter 14

Polar Bear Quarters, Farside

A trio of female bears were sitting on a highpoint within the polar bear habitat admiring the new ceiling display. Human technicians had labored for days applying several coats of special paint to the walls and ceiling of the auditorium sized chamber. The base coat was highly reflective, turning the surface into a wall to wall movie screen. The second covered the reflective base coat with a transparent layer containing self-assembling OLED nano-particles. The final coat provided a protective outer covering.

Stimulated by a fine conductive mesh formed as the paint dried, the entire surface was transformed into a gigantic full color display. Though any picture, including full motion video, could be displayed on the ceiling, its intended use was to provide a naturalistic sky appropriate to the polar bears' Arctic habitat.

Just having a cold enclosure filled with ice was not enough to ease the bears' sense of confinement. It was hoped that having a natural looking sky overhead, synced to the seasons and rotation of Earth below, would help lower ursine stress levels. With the northern hemisphere headed into winter, the environment currently featured a setting Sun skirting low across the horizon. As the sky darkened stars became visible, all faithful to their natural positions, spectra and brightness.

"This is really beautiful," said Aurora, "how nice of the humans to do this for us."

"Yes, it is," Snowflake replied. "I find most humans likeable enough, if you don't have to spend too much time with them."

Isbjørn snorted. "After you get use to the pervasive smell, they are nice enough." Of the bears present she had spent more time in close contact with humans than anyone.

Snowflake raised her head and looked intently in the direction of the main entrance. "Speaking of humans, it would appear that we have a visitor."

Walking across the darkening white landscape, a solitary human made its way toward the group of she-bears. Dressed for arctic temperatures—the habitat was currently hovering around -20°C—the human was cloaked in a white, down-filled parka with a fur fringed hood concealing its face. On its feet were white mukluks, soft soled boots similar to the foot wear of humans indigenous to the Arctic.

A gust of wind—the product of another attempt to make the polar bears' environment as realistic as possible—carried the human's scent to the bears. While polar bears did not fear any creature that walked on land, several millennia of bear-human interaction had linked human scent with a feeling of unease.

"Ludmilla," Isbjørn and Aurora pronounced together, with Snowflake nodding in agreement. As Ludmilla drew closer her identity was verified visually, not that the bears had any reason to doubt the certainty of their olfactory identification.

Being the senior bear present, Isbjørn called out. "Hello, Ludmilla. What brings you to our abode today?"

"Hello ladies," Ludmilla replied, pausing at the foot of the small rise on which the bears rested. Throwing back her parka hood, the Russian doctor looked up at the sky overhead. Returning her gaze to the bears she replied. "I wanted to see if the redecorating of your quarters had a worthwhile effect. It certainly seems an improvement to me."

"We were just admiring the view ourselves," Aurora responded, answering the implied question. "Having a sky overhead that varies with the time and seasons really adds to the natural feeling."

"It does make me homesick though, knowing you can't just head out over that next ridge to see what's there," Snowflake added dolefully. "Being crowded in here with so many bears makes it impossible to find any privacy. For example, where is Isbjørn going to find a place to den?"

Isbjørn looked sharply at Snowflake while Aurora, who was next to her, surreptitiously cuffed the younger she-bear.

Snowflake flinched, whining "what?" Then she realized the implication of her statement. None of this escaped the sharp eyes or ears of Ludmilla, standing before them with her mittened hands on her hips.

"Yes, Isbjørn. I have been meaning to talk with you about your condition. This is why I invited you to have a physical twice in the last month. Yet for some reason you have not found the time."

"I'm sorry, Ludmilla. I'm fine really, why would I need a physical?"

"Because you are pregnant."

All three bears stared at Ludmilla. Isbjørn blinked her eyes.

"Why do you think I'm pregnant?"

"Because I am your doctor. Do you think I cannot tell when one of my patients is pregnant?" Ludmilla crossed her arms, giving Isbjørn a stern doctor look. "Even when she avoids coming in for an examination."

"Maybe she can smell the change like we can?" whispered Snowflake.

"Hush!" Aurora whispered back.

"The medical department monitors everyone's health on the station, bear and human alike. You have been gaining weight rapidly and your hormonal balance has changed. I would not be much of a doctor if I did not notice, Da?"

"I'm sorry, but we are secretive about having cubs by instinct. Dumb bear males will kill cubs given half a chance so we hide."

"And what were you going to do? Go hide in a corner for four months and hope no one noticed your absence?"

Isbjørn hung her head and looked at the snow on the floor. The other two she-bears looked at each other sheepishly.

"You're right, Ludmilla, there really is no good place to make a den around here and I don't know what to do." For Isbjørn, one of the most self-reliant of the bears, this was a painful confession.

"I will tell you what to do, Isbjørn. You tell your doctor and she makes arrangements," Ludmilla said with some satisfaction.

"Really?"

"Really. If I can have sky added to your habitat, do you think I cannot have a nice dark alcove built where you, and the other two bears that are pregnant, can build dens?"

"An alcove?" said Isbjørn.

"What other bears?" asked Snowflake.

"Snowflake, hush!" whispered Aurora.

"Right," Ludmilla replied. "And I expect to see you in the medical section tomorrow morning at 0900, sharp."

"Yes, Doctor."

Ludmilla turned and headed toward the door, pulling her parka hood up as she walked away. For a few moments she allowed herself a satisfied smile. The bears watched her go in silence, all three wondering how a 55kg human female could intimidate three 300kg polar bears without so much as raising her voice.

Housing Block #14, Farside Base

A ragtag group of rescuees had gathered in the apartment assigned to three of their number. Almost all were young, in their late teens or early twenties, and all without technical skills. Several had attended college, including the two young women present, though none had managed to complete a course of study. When in attendance, their majors tended to change frequently, bouncing among philosophy, political science, community organizing, ethnic and gender studies, and other similar topics. In the world they came from they were practically unemployable, on the Moon base they were overhead.

Because they lacked any useful technical skills they had all been placed in menial and unchallenging jobs. Most of the men were maintenance workers, effectively janitorial staff, one man and one of the women worked as food servers in the mid-level cafeteria, and the other woman worked at a daycare. In exchange for their labors they received apartments, cafeteria passes and a small stipend of credits as spending money. In other words, if Farside had a welfare class they were part of it.

The meeting had been organized by one of the men who called himself "Todor," after an obscure Bulgarian anarcho-communist who died fighting the Nazis in Belgium during World War II. Older than the others, his greatest accomplishment in life had been flunking

178

out of three major universities. Seeing that the expected group had gathered, Todor stood up and addressed those assembled.

"Comrades, thank you for coming." He paused to let his audience to settle down. "As you know, many of the brothers and sisters present in this room were part of the 99 percent's struggle for freedom and equality back on Earth—before the elites managed to ruin the planet."

The last statement caused some murmuring in the room. One of the younger men said, "I thought aliens destroyed the Earth?"

"Elitist misinformation," Todor snapped. "Why would aliens attack our planet? Have you seen an alien? No, the elites, the 1%, became frightened of the people and tried to destroy them so they could have the world all for themselves."

"How do you know that, Todor?" asked the woman known as Jennie.

"Have you noticed who is in charge here? A council of billionaires backed by the military, that's who."

"The head person is that Russian woman, the ex-Cosmonaut."

"She is just a puppet. A shill for the rich financiers who had this place constructed as a refuge prior to blowing up the world. How would they have known to build such a place if they weren't responsible for killing off the proletariat?"

"OK, assuming they did what you said," said a younger man named Tim, "Why did they bring us here then? They did rescue us from the surface."

"You can't be a king without some peasants to lord over. We are surfs, here to serve the new nobility." Todor took a breath and launched into a rant. "Who lives in the fancy houses on the top levels? The rich bankers from the council, and the officers that command the military, that's who.

"Who has the credits to frequent the fancy bars and restaurants around the Atrium? The rich and the military. Even the common Marines and sailors have more credits than the workers. They dine on *haute cuisine* while we eat cafeteria slop."

The two cafeteria workers visibly bristled at this but Todor pressed on.

"Who can come and go as they please, flying back to Earth whenever they wish? The elites! Notice that the base is built on the far side of the Moon, the side that never sees the Earth. How do we know that things are as bad back home as they tell us? We don't!"

There were murmurs of agreement among his audience and a few nods. Todor looked from face to face and smiled, depending on charisma to carry his arguments, not logic. Jennie provided him with the straight line he was waiting for: "So what do you suggest we do?"

"We need to organize, form an underground movement to resist the greed and oppression of the 1%. Just like back on Earth, we need to take action, to protest, to let the elites know this will not stand!"

"You're saying we need to start an Occupy movement?" asked the other woman, Sylvia. Back on Earth, on September 17, 2011, a group of protesters with tents, banners and placards occupied the public land around New York City's Wall Street financial district. Initiated by the Canadian, anti-consumerist, pro-environment group Adbusters, with assistance from the Manhattan-based public relations firm Workhouse, the call for public protest and civil disobedience succeeded beyond its instigators' wildest dreams.

For a generation of bored and disaffected youth the protest was a magnet. The Wall Street camp-in gained national attention and soon spread to other cities in America and elsewhere. Strangely, Workhouse, whose clients included Mercedes Benz and Saks Fifth Avenue, saw no irony in the fact that the public disturbance they helped to create adversely affected their own customers' interests.

The main issues raised by Occupy Wall Street centered on social and economic inequality. Protesting greed, corruption and the perceived influence of corporations on government, the gathered mob demanded wealth redistribution to make life "fairer." The OWS slogan, "we are the 99%," referred to income inequality between the wealthiest 1% and the rest of the population. To achieve their goals, the protesters enacted decisions made by *ad hock* public assemblies, with an emphasis on direct action. Like flies to garbage, anarchists and troublemakers swarmed to the protest, which soon descended into vandalism and violence.

"Exactly, Sister. We need to form a movement, based on the ideas and ideals of the OWS protests back on Earth. We need to start Occupy Moon Base!"

"Fucking-A right!" said one of the men, "Remember Zuccotti Park!"

The gathering became animated as the prospective social activists began planing their movement. Soon they would show the evil 1% that the people, the 99%, would not be taken advantage of.

Bridge, M'tak Ka'fek

The process of negotiating a deal with the furry traders took considerably longer than the Earthlings expected. For six hours, Ooshnar-tar-rak-ra engaged in shuttle diplomacy, hustling back and forth between the party of armed strangers and the Trader, hidden within the warren of crates and containers. The patience of some was wearing thin, but the Captain counseled perseverance.

"Captain, I say we just eat these annoying little shits and tear the place apart until we find the antimatter," Bear growled over the comm link. He had taken to sitting on his hindquarters, flicking his suit's extendable claws in and out whenever the Kieshnar-rak-kat-tra approached.

"Be calm my ursine friend, we are making progress," Jack replied from his station on the bridge. "We have gotten them to reveal that there is a significant antimatter dump in another system three transits away."

Once it was made clear that the Earthlings wished only to trade services for antimatter the talks turned to mounting a trading expedition to visit the Trader's third cousin who was the Trader on a station supposedly much larger than this one. According to Ooshnar, Keneesh-ka-ka-kar's rich cousin was in a constant state of conflict with other races on his station. It was hinted that ridding his cousin of his enemies would result in a generous payment, redeemable in antimatter, and that the Trader would only take a 25% commission.

181

Several hours were spent negotiating this down to 15% with the added proviso that the Trader would contribute a full type one container to the enterprise up front. The wily merchant would only agree to this if the Captain allowed a number of the Trader's personal representatives to accompany the expedition. That number was now the topic of negotiation.

"Captain, Trader Ooshnar has returned and Keneesh-ka-ka-kar has agreed to have only three of his representatives accompany us on the voyage," JT reported in a weary voice. "What do you want me to tell him, Sir?"

I think that I have pushed this old bandit as far as I can, Jack transmitted to the ship's AI. *Will it be possible to construct an isolated environment for the Kieshnar-rak-kat-tra to live in?*

Yes, Captain. I can begin the construction immediately. If they will bring samples of foodstuffs I will equip their quarters with a synthesizer to provide for their needs, along with environmental and sanitary facilities.

Good. I do not want them wandering around the ship during the voyage. In fact I do not want any physical contact between them and the crew.

A wise precaution, Captain. I can set up a holographic projection system that will allow you and the other officers to "visit" our passengers while eliminating any possible biological or chemical contamination. Do you really expect these creatures to honor the negotiated deal?

M'tak, I expect these furry little rug merchants to double-cross us at the earliest possible opportunity. But there must be great wealth to be gained at this other station or the head weasel would not have ponied up an antimatter egg of his own.

I heartily concur, Captain. These creatures seem eminently untrustworthy.

Right, so let's seal the deal. "JT, tell the Trader that he has a deal. We will give him 24 hours to present his representatives, their supplies and the antimatter at the boarding tube for departure."

"Aye aye, Captain. Wait one..."

"...Captain, it seems that the traders would appreciate it if we could provide them with an escort to the boarding tube and transport for the egg and other gear."

Sigh. "Fine, Lieutenant. Tell them they are limited to a metric ton of personal effects and that we will come and collect them in 24 hours."

"Aye, Sir. Will do."

Bower of Keneesh-ka-ka-kar

A breathless Ooshnar reported to his leader, having just agreed to the final terms of the deal with the Earthlings. It was not that the traders lacked communicators, but that no trader worth his salt would conduct business over one. "Uncle, we have concluded the deal with the aliens. They will send an escort to pick up our delegation tomorrow around noon station time."

"Good, nephew. I am putting you in charge of this expedition, since it was you who brought us the opportunity. I believe a 10% share would be fair remuneration."

"Thank you, uncle, you are most generous."

"Naturally, since it is my antimatter at risk, I will be sending one of my subordinate traders as well. You can pick the third member of the party."

"Of course, Trader. With your permission I will go and make the preparations." With that and a parting bow, Ooshnar-tar-rak-ra left his great uncle's bower and headed back to his own to prepare for the journey.

After his grandnephew departed, the Trader called out. "Poonta-ta-ka! Attend me you worthless git."

Shuffling into his master's presence, Poonta-ta-ka bowed obsequiously. "Yes, Trader?"

"I am sending you on the mission to the Ring Station. It will be your job to watch after my interests. I expect my grandnephew to try to double cross me if the opportunity arises so it will be your job to double-cross him first."

"How should I do that, Trader? Is not the plan to have the aliens kill your cousin's enemies for a hefty fee?"

"I expect my cousin to double-cross the aliens and try to capture their ship, perhaps after they have killed off his enemies and had their own ranks thinned out in the process. You will have to be nimble and alert to thread the needle between Ooshnar-tar-rak-ra and the station Trader, both are shrewd merchants and practiced deal makers."

"And if I fail?" Poonta-ta-ka asked in a quavering voice.

"Then I will be out a container of antimatter and you will no longer be a burden to me. Now go!"

Poonta-ta-ka quickly scurried off to make his own preparations. From behind the tapestries to one side of the Trader's chair Zooshnarak-kak-ka appeared.

"Are you sure Poonta-ta-ka is up to this task, Trader?"

"Probably not, but my senior wife promised his mother I would give him a chance to prove his worth."

"The stakes are certainly high enough."

"Truly. The way I see it, Ooshnar-tar-rak-ra will try to double-cross the station Trader who will try to double-cross him. If Poonta-ta-ka can play them against each other he might come out on top. If Ooshnar-tar-rak-ra wins out he will naturally return here to his family. Of course the improbable could happen and the deal go down as planned. Regardless, I will profit."

"And if your cousin the station Trader triumphs?"

"Then we will have at least rid ourselves of these dangerous and unpredictable aliens, before they attract a visit by the minions of the Dark Lords."

"A wise ordering of possible outcomes, Trader," Zooshnarak-kak-ka said with honest admiration. Indeed, if there was one thing a scavenger of wealth admired more than a double-cross it was a double-double-cross, or was this a triple-double-cross?

Bridge, M'tak Ka'fek

Collecting the trader delegation, their baggage and, most importantly, the antimatter went without incident the following afternoon. The Captain sent Hitch and Jacobs with a pair of hover sleds to carry the party back to the ship. He also sent Aput, Brown and Samuels to guard the procession. This gave Aput a chance to get off the ship and broaden his experience. It also kept the grumbling Lt. Bear on board at the main weapons console.

Also on the mission was Mizuki Ogawa, carrying instruments to check out the antimatter egg before they brought the potentially explosive container on board. This caused Bobby a bit of anxiety as she climbed into the lead sled next to Matt Jacobs. She wore the same light armor as the SEALs, with Yuki Saito's katana sticking up behind her suit's bubble helmet. Yuki had given her the sword as a gift when she left to accompany the Captain to the M'tak Ka'fek in the Sirius graveyard. That had only been a few months ago but now seemed like ages in the past.

Sensing his helmsman's disquieted mood, Jack offered the junior officer words of comfort. "Relax Bobby, she is surrounded by a Marine fire team and two armored sailors, she'll be fine."

"Yes, Sir. I know, but I still can't help worrying."

Thinking back to all the times he had felt the same way about letting Ludmilla go off on a mission without him, Jack sympathized with the young officer. He remembered Ludmilla's insistence on being her own person, taking risks that caused him to worry every second she was not by his side. "You can't protect the ones you love from danger by sealing them off from the world. They must be free to be who they are, and face life's challenges on their own terms."

"Besides," added Bear from his console, "she's got that sword Yuki gave her. Anything that tries to mess with her will end up looking like sushi."

This caused Bobby to smile. "Yes, Lieutenant, that they would."

Jack looked at Bear and Bear winked. *I do believe that Bear is starting to figure us humans out—at least the males. The last relationship advice he gave me was to bite Ludmilla on the back of the neck.*

185

"On top of the escort, I've sent the SEALs forward to scout the route for possible trouble. The thing I'm most worried about is that egg. Our AM supply is on empty and we need that container full to pull off this mission."

The ship's voice commented on the coming procedure. "I will be able to fully assess the condition of the antimatter container when Dr. Ogawa places the quantum sensors on it. I will also be able to detect if it has been tampered with, making it unsafe to bring aboard."

"Good, M'tak. What is the status of the Kieshnar-rak-kat-tra quarters?"

"They are complete, Captain. As specified they are completely self-contained and isolated from the rest of the ship. The traders will only be exposed within the portside shuttle bay as they board, and I will vent that to space once they are sealed in their habitat."

"You really think the fuzzy little twerps are that dangerous, Captain?"

"You never know, Mr. Bear. They could transmit disease or a toxic substance—unintentionally or otherwise—and kill or incapacitate the crew." *And I would not put it past them to try and hijack the ship, even if there are only three of them.* "No, Lieutenant. I will not feel at ease until all personnel are back on board, our guests are safely locked away in their quarters, and the ship is well away."

* * * * *

The antimatter container proved to be intact and 96 percent full—not short by enough to quibble about. The traders—Ooshnar-tar-rak-ra, Poonta-ta-ka and a third referred to only as Feeshkar—were quickly hustled into their quarters along with their pile of rugs, pillows, and trunks. The ship's AI sealed the traders in and proceeded to make them as comfortable as possible, adjusting temperature, gravity and lighting to suit the aliens.

JT and Mizuki were back on the bridge, the Japanese physicist with a grin on her face that threatened to become a permanent fixture.

"Great job out there," Bobby whispered to her. She glanced sideways at him and her grin became even wider.

"Lt. Taylor, have you entered the coordinates for the first alter-space transit?"

"Aye, Captain. This first one will be a long one, M'tak calculates 21 days. All combined, the three transits will take us a month an a half, two including crossing the systems involved in 3-space."

"At least it should be a peaceful two months," Jack replied. "Mr. Danner, take us out of here."

"Aye aye, Captain." Bobby grinned, eyes twinkling mischievously. "Departing Mos Eisley Station for parts unknown."

"Mos Eisley Station?" the Captain queried.

JT chuckled and replied in his best Alec Guinness voice: "You will never find a more wretched hive of scum and villainy."

"Indeed," Jack laughed, "certainly a fitting appellation. But I think I will reserve judgment on it being the galaxy's worst until we see this next space station."

"Alter-space transit in four hours and twenty seven minutes, Captain," Bobby called from the helm.

"Very good, Mr. Danner."

Four hours and twenty seven minutes later the M'tak Ka'fek shimmered and fell out of 3-space into the hidden dimensions of alter-space.

Chapter 15

The T'aafhal cruiser neared the end of the third leg of its voyage. It had been an uneventful journey so far, the two intermediate systems being both uninhabited and unremarkable in their composition. The Marines and crew spent most of the time in alter-space preparing for combat—either at the ship's weapon stations or in their suits of space armor. They had taken to playing a version of zero-gee rugby in one of the ship's cavernous shuttle holds, a rough and tumble game that even the bears enjoyed.

The trip for the confined traders was even more monotonous than for the earthlings. At first they passed the long days playing *scheneek*, a form of gambling played with three multifaceted dice. When Feeshkar went on an extended winning streak the others accused him of cheating and refused to play further. This left the three with nothing to do except look forward to the sporadic visits by the ship's officers.

The senior officers took turns conversing with the Kieshnar-rak-kat-tra via holographic projection. In one-on-one sessions, each of the three aliens attempted to cut private deals with the Captain and JT. Evidently it was every trader for himself in their culture. All three assured the Earthlings that the head trader of the station they were traveling to would be as ethically flexible as they were.

When it came to sounding out the Kieshnar-rak-kat-tra, Bear proved an exception. He received no offers of great wealth or untold riches in exchange for betraying his friends and throwing in with the alien merchants. He only conversed with the furry traders by himself on one occasion...

* * * * *

"Hello, my furry little prospective *hors d'oeuvres*," Bear had greeted them on his first and only holographic visit to the traders' enclave. Since the Kieshnar-rak-kat-tra were about half the size of a human, the full grown male *Ursus maritimus* was a towering monster in their eyes. And though they did not know what *hors d'oeuvres* were, the toothy carnivore's smile gave them a strong hint.

"I was wondering about your home planet," Bear asked them. "Are there a lot of your kind there? Do you have any natural predators? And what about climate? Does it ever snow?"

The traders' nervously clutched their tails and chittered to each other. Then, being senior, Ooshnar-tar-rak-ra replied, "We have no real home planet, Great Sir. Our people have been scattered among trading stations across this arm of the galaxy for as long as we can remember. Why do you ask?"

"Oh, just wondering. See back on Earth, the humans and my kind compete for space and food. I always keep an eye out for new hunting grounds—some place with plump prey and cold weather." Again, Bear favored them with a toothy smile.

The traders commendably held their ground, but Feeshkar sidled sideways until the senior trader was between him and the frightening white apparition.

"If we think of any worlds that fit your requirements we will gladly let you know," the senior trader replied, recovering his poise. "For a modest finder's fee we can search our network of contacts on other stations. I'm sure we can find something to fit your discriminating tastes."

"You do that, Trader. And remember, taste has a lot to do with it." With that Bear's projection faded out like the Cheshire Cat, his toothy grin the last part of his image to disappear. This caused Poonta-ta-ka to flee the audience chamber and seek shelter in his room.

Bear had arranged the special departure effect with the ship's AI, convincing the sentient computer that it was a common gesture of friendship on Earth, citing the works of Lewis Carroll as historical precedent. The frightened Kieshnar-rak-kat-tra found themselves alone in their quarters, feeling very far from home, with visions of polar bear smiles dancing in their heads.

* * * * *

Though it became apparent to the traders that the visiting Earthlings were only some form of projection, they none the less had been badly frightened by the massive white carnivore that called itself Loo-ten-nant Bay-er. After Bear's visit Poonta-ta-ka went catatonic for two days and Feeshkar developed a nervous tic. Only senior trader Ooshnar-tar-rak-ra seemed unfazed by the encounter with the large white carnivore, though the ship's AI reported that his caloric intake dropped precipitously for a week.

190

It took the Captain several days to figure out why the traders were suddenly so skittish when he or JT visited them. When he asked the other officers about their guests' behavior Bear claimed he had simply questioned the aliens about habitable planets in the area. A quick conversation with M'tak and Jack put two plus two together. Not wishing to fray the excitable aliens' nerves further, he excused Bear from future visits, which was exactly what Bear had wanted in the first place.

Base Operations, Farside

Billy Ray had just returned from a shakedown cruise of the latest ship to emerge from Farside's shipyard. The five day trip had been a pleasure cruise compared to his previous voyage. Captain Curtis had commanded that mission, the month long space trials of the frigates Constitution and Constellation. With Capt. Curtis in command on board the Constitution and Billy Ray captaining the Constellation, the new warships had traveled to the asteroid belt, out to Jupiter, and back to fly by Mars before returning to base. Though there were a few rough edges and minor equipment malfunctions, both captains were pleased with the performance of the new frigates.

They returned to resupply and exchange crews. Then, after only four days in port, Gretchen took the frigates out again, with new captains and crews—a training mission in preparation for the completion of the next pair of ships, due in just over two months. Though Billy Ray would have loved to command of one of the frigates again, he understood the necessity to get several crews, and several captains, trained on actual vessels. Besides, the newly designated Fleet HQ had other plans for the lieutenant commander from Texas.

In the month the frigates had been away—occupied by running their engines at flank speed, blasting small asteroids into rubble and other naval past times—two more spaceships had been completed. These ships were much less glamorous than the sleek and deadly warships. They were, in fact, rather unlovely: 200 meter long cylinders, 40 meters in diameter, rounded at either end. Inside their decks were arranged one on top of another, like a layer cake.

The two ships, named the Issac Asimov and the Arthur C. Clarke, were freighters, intended to haul hundreds of passengers and associated equipment to the new base on Mars. It was on the bridge of the Issac Asimov that Billy Ray spent the past five days, ensuring that the freighter could be reasonably expected to deliver its cargo and passengers to Mars, intact and alive. In its empty condition, the Asimov managed to pull a sustained 4G acceleration, topping out at 6G under emergency power. When heavy laden she was only expected to boost at a single gravity—a far cry from the +60G of the new frigates. Still, being in space, commanding a ship, was much preferred to being stuck on the shore.

That was because Beth was also spending much of her time in space, training corvette crews. Indeed, it seemed like fate and the high command were conspiring to keep the couple apart: Beth had departed on a two week training flight, but before she returned Billy Ray sailed on the Constellation; he returned a month later, but before the Constellation made port Beth departed on another extended training flight; then she returned, only to find that Billy Ray had departed on the Asimov. Continuing the frustrating game of ships passing in the night, Billy Ray returned the Asimov to port only to find a message from Beth on his communicator. She had been pulled off on yet another mission and would not be there to greet him when they docked.

Reporting in at HQ, a squeaky clean new ensign told him that he was to report to Col. Tropsha's office. "Colonel Tropsha?" Billy Ray asked, "not Chief Administrator Tropsha?"

"That is what the memo says, Commander, 'Lcdr. Vincent report to Col. Tropsha's office. Urgent.'"

"Right," he said with weary resignation. After quickly getting directions from the data display in his jumpsuit's sleeve he was on his way. The new woven in units were rapidly replacing the formerly ubiquitous personal pads and smart phones. Only civilians and new recruits could still be seen carrying around network access devices.

There was yet another wet behind the ears ensign guarding the entrance to the Colonel's office. This one wore data glasses and welcomed him by name before he could introduce himself.

"Good afternoon, Commander Vincent. Go right in, she's expecting you."

Entering Ludmilla's office Billy Ray had a sudden moment of indecision. Normally the Navy did not render the hand salute when indoors, but one was expected to salute when under arms or when reporting to the commanding officer. He was guessing that the reference to Col. Tropsha meant that Ludmilla was in command of the HQ in the military sense. *Better safe than sorry,* he thought.

He marched to within two paces of Ludmilla's desk, came to attention and saluted. "Lcdr. Vincent, reporting as ordered Ma'am."

Ludmilla looked up slightly amused and then returned his salute. "At ease, Commander, take a seat."

Billy Ray seated himself stiffly in one of the visitors chairs.

"I understand that the freighter's shakedown cruise went without indecent?"

"Yes, Ma'am. Nothing major, the hull kept the atmo in and performance met specifications. A few minor corrective actions and it will be ready for service."

"Good, we need to get the personnel transfer to Mars underway as soon as possible. In fact, that is part of the reason I wanted to talk with you as soon as you got back."

Oh God, please don't make me nursemaid a ship full of civilians on a month long trip to Mars! Billy Ray swallowed hard. "Yes, Ma'am?"

"I understand that you are a native Texan, Da?"

"Well, yes Ma'am, I am."

"It seems our friends in the Republic of Texas are in need of our help. Though we warned them that the coming winter would be harsh beyond their usual experience they were still caught unprepared. Their cobbled together power grid has suffered a number of outages and many people are in danger of freezing to death."

Billy Ray didn't know what to say so he simply nodded.

"The counsel has decide to send them relief equipment, some of the self contained fission reactors intended for the Martian settlements. We also hope to entice some of the residents into becoming Martian colonists. Since you are a native born Texan, TK suggested that you would be the perfect officer to command a large shuttle ferrying the reactors dirtside."

"Yes, Ma'am" *At least I'm staying in the neighborhood.*

"How soon can you depart?"

"As soon as they can load the cargo and I can brief the crew."

"Good, then I will leave you to it. Dismissed."

Billy Ray nodded and headed for the door. *Better busy than sitting around thinking about not being with Beth,* he thought. Then Ludmilla called after him, with a faint smile on her face.

"By the way, Billy Ray. TK is already planetside and will meet you at the airport hotel in Fredericksburg. He also took an experienced officer as his pilot; I believe you know Lt. Melaku?"

Hangar Hotel, Fredericksburg, Texas

The wind howled outside the bar where TK was meeting with officials from the Republic of Texas. Snow had drifted against the side of the building and was starting to encroach on the small shuttle parked just outside on the apron. The temperature was a bitter cold -6°C in a town where historically the average daily high temperature during the month of January was a comfortable 20°C. The frigid temperature was an after effect of the alien bombardment—massive amounts of dust and debris had been thrown up into the atmosphere where it blocked the warmth of the Sun and caused global cooling.

On TK's previous trip to post-apocalypse Texas he had warned the residents of the Texas Hill Country that, though they survived the initial bombardment, they were still not out of the woods. New weather satellites had been put in orbit so the changing and unfamiliar weather patterns could be monitored, but still the citizens of the Republic did not believe that things were going to be as bad as the people from the Moon made out.

"I tell you, TK, we're freezing our behinds off down here," said Roger Stoltz, acting president of the Republic. "We've had two power plants break and there are power lines down all over. Whole communities are without power and people in outlying areas are having trouble keeping their livestock alive."

As if to underline the man's complaints the lights in the bar flickered and dimmed. As it was, those in the room could almost see their breath in the cold air.

"I thought the last time we talked you were all ready for winter, Roger, what happened?" TK had grown to casually dislike the overly excitable former mayor and wished they could deal with someone else. Unfortunately, Stoltz was it until the locals could hold an election—or possibly a coup.

"Look out the window, for cryin' out loud!" Roger said standing up and making a theatrical gesture toward the windows overlooking the airfield. "We got four feet of snow and drifts twice that high. We're not used to these conditions. What are we supposed to do?"

"Well, Roger, what would you have done before the attack?" TK asked innocently.

"I would have called Austin and Austin would have called Washington. We'd have gotten some federal assistance, that's what I'd have done."

"In case you haven't noticed, neither Austin nor Washington exists anymore," said Sid Hopkins. The former Texas Ranger was leaning against the nearby bar with the usual toothpick in his mouth. Precisely what his function was in the local power structure was unclear, but none of the others objected to his presence— perhaps they didn't have a choice.

TK gave Sid a sideways glance and then focused back on the now pacing President. "Exactly what would you have us do, Mr. President?"

"I don't know, damn it. Help us." Roger was obviously a man in way over his head. With the President a spent force, Tony Ruiz entered the conversation.

"TK, I think the first thing we could use is help getting the power back on. Without it a lot of folks are without heat and can't cook hot food. Restoring the electricity would go a long way toward calming everyone down."

"OK, say I can get you four or five reactors, each puttin' out 25 megawatts—that's enough for around 25,000 homes apiece. Would that help ease the situation?"

"It most certainly would, TK," chimed in Sally Musselman, the third of the governing triumvirate. Like Tony, she had waited for the hyperbolic Roger to wind down before joining the conversation. Why they allowed him to remain head of the government was a mystery—perhaps they used him for cover.

"All right, here is what I want you to do," TK said to the Texans. "I want you to find the five best places to locate the power plants among your towns. Places that are flat and near major power lines."

Refusing to take yes for an answer, Roger jumped back into the fray with a list of questions. "You can put in power plants just like that? How long will it take? How big are these plants and who's gonna run them?"

TK ignored him and addressed the others in the room. "We need a space about the size of a football field for the shuttle to land. And I want you to dig a hole at each location, 12 feet across and 35 feet deep. That's where we will put the power plants."

"What type of plant are these, TK," Tony asked, totally confused. To him, a power plant was a large complex of buildings, certainly nothing that would fit in a relatively small hole in the ground. "Are they like the engines in your spaceships?"

"Naw, the spaceships are powered by muon catalyzed fusion reactors. They are way too detectable from space. What we're giving you are mini-reactors based on safe fission technology developed by the U.S. Department of Energy decades ago. They were a great idea that never made it to market 'cause of vested interests, political infighting, and bureaucratic turf wars."

"You want to bury nuclear reactors under our football fields? We'll all end up radioactive!" ranted Roger, who was becoming more irrational by the minute.

"No, you braying jackass," TK exploded. "Somebody get that man a drink. Maybe it will shut him up."

The Republic's representatives looked at TK like something dangerous had suddenly sprung up in their midst. Sid, unruffled as always, reached over the bar and retrieved a bottle of whiskey. He uncorked the bottle and handed it to the President who took a long pull on it from the neck. He coughed a bit but quieted down.

"If I might continue explainin' how we intend on savin' your hides," TK looked sharply at each of the other Texans in turn. None offered any objections.

"These are sealed units, totally self contained. Inside, each reactor has a uranium hydride core, surrounded by hydrogen gas. The hydrogen acts as the moderator for the reactor; the balance between heat generation and gas temperature makes the whole unit self-regulating—no need for computers or human operators to control things. The heat is turned into electricity by a closed loop turbo-generator. Think of it as a nuclear battery.

"Once you get the holes dug you need to pour slabs of reinforced concrete to set the units on. They weigh about 15 tons each. We will place one unit at the bottom of each hole, which will then be backfilled and a concrete cap poured on top to seal 'em in. The only thing that comes out of the hole is a cable to deliver the electricity."

"And these things are totally safe?" asked Sally cautiously.

"Yes they're safe. We were going to use them for settlements on Mars, but figured you folks needed 'em sooner than we did."

"If you are going to bury them it sounds like they are fairly permanent," said Tony.

"Each unit should run for 25 years. When they stop working give us a call, we will come and take them back for recycling."

The lights in the room flickered out, leaving the bar dimly lit by the depressing grayness slanting in through the side windows. After a half minute the lights came back on and shone brightly. Then the heating kicked in.

"See, things are lookin' up already," TK said with a smile.

Through the barroom doors came a tall figure dressed in a parka. As she threw back the parka's hood and stamped the snow off her boots, the people in the room turned and stared.

197

"Well, we've gotten the shuttle power hooked to the building's distribution panel. Things should warm up in here shortly."

"Fantastic," TK replied. "I really did not want to sleep in the shuttle overnight." Then, remembering his manners, TK introduced the woman. "Folk's, this is my aid and pilot on this trip, Lt. Melaku. She's takin' time off from blasting aliens and training pilots to help y'all out."

Beth smiled. "Hello, nice to meet all of you."

The male Texans just stared at the striking female officer. With a how-typically-male look for her companions, Sally turned to Beth and said, "It's very nice to meet you, Lieutenant. Have you ever been to Fredericksburg before?"

Fredericksburg, Republic of Texas

It took 24 hours to load up the first three reactors and their support equipment, and another 24 to make the trip to Earth. This worked out well, since it gave the locals time to dig the holes and pour the bottom slabs. The first installation was in downtown Fredericksburg, in the middle of the Old Fair Park between Park Street and Ufer. The utility crew on-site marked the landing zone with flags that were obscured by flying snow as the big shuttle landed.

Still hot from reentry, the shuttle clicked and popped as it cooled. Billy Ray, dressed in a white parka, walked down the rear ramp and over to the men beside the hole.

"Mornin' gentlemen. Somebody here order a nuclear reactor?"

"That's what yer gonna put in this hole, mister? They didn't tell us about no reactor," said the on-site supervisor, eying Billy Ray suspiciously.

"Well," Billy Ray drawled. "Somebody's gotta sign for this thing."

"Hell, nobody said I'd have to sign for no nuclear reactor," the supervisor began.

198

"Relax, pardner. I'm just pullin' yer leg. I'm Commander Vincent, but you can call me Billy Ray."

"You had me goin' there for a minute, Billy Ray. Name's Willy," the supervisor said, shaking hands. Between his name and his accent the stranger seemed like a local boy. "How big is this thing and how are you gonna get it into the hole?"

"We came prepared. If the slab is set we can put the reactor in and you fellers can start backfilling the hole."

"It should be good to go, we been keeping it warm with heaters from the field house so the concrete would set up quick."

Bill Ray nodded and spoke into his collar pip. "Chief, you can bring the payload out now."

From inside the shuttle came a solid metal container three meters in diameter and two and a half high, floating on a pallet a half meter above the shuttle's cargo deck. It floated down the ramp and approached the hole, guided by the crew chief and a couple sailors.

At the sight of the crew the workmen's eyes bulged. The floating reactor didn't shock them, but the huge robotic spacesuits worn by the sailors did.

"I guess you really are from outer-space, mister," one of the workmen said tilting his hardhat back on his head.

"You mean arriving in a big ass spaceship didn't tip you off?" Billy Ray said with a grin. The workmen all chuckled, some nervously. "Come on guys we're burning daylight, we got other deliveries to make before the Sun goes down. Let's get this puppy in the hole and hooked to your power grid."

"Yes, sir, Commander. Just tell us what you need us to do..."

* * * * *

Twelve hours later, well after sunset, Billy Ray brought the shuttle in for a soft landing at the airport, parking it beside TK's smaller craft. The day had taken them to two other small towns for the remaining installations and now back to Fredericksburg to report. After getting his men settled in rooms at the hotel he went to the bar, which was serving as the command center for the

199

operation. As Billy Ray walked through the double glass doors into the now cozy bar, TK called out from a table across the room.

"Billy Ray, come on over and tell me how things went today. I got some people you need to meet."

At the table were TK and Beth and two men Billy Ray did not know. Billy Ray made eye contact with Beth and smiled, then he walked over to the table and the men rose to greet him.

"Gentlemen, this is Lcdr. Vincent, one of our starship captains," TK said by way of introduction. "He has fought against the aliens both here and in other star systems. He also happens to be a Texan."

This elicited nods of approval from the men. TK continued. "Billy Ray, this is Tony Ruiz, one of the Republic's leaders, and Ranger Sid Hopkins."

"Mr. Ruiz," Billy Ray said, shaking his hand. Then, with a cool look of appraisal, he shook hands with Sid Hopkins. "Ranger."

"Commander," Sid replied. Beth watched the exchange between Billy Ray and the Ranger with great interest. The two seemed to be cut from the same tough West Texas cloth—tall, lean and taciturn.

"We'd like to thank you for coming down to help us through this crisis, Commander," Tony began. "Y'all told us that this winter would be terrible but we didn't realize how terrible. Without your aid a lot of people might die."

"Glad to help out," Billy Ray replied, taking an empty chair as the others sat back down. He focused on TK and reported on the day's mission. "We managed to get all three reactors, their transformers and line interfaces installed. They were all online and sending power into the local grid when we left 'em."

"What towns did you put them in, Commander?" asked Ruiz.

"One here in Fredericksburg, one over in Junction and the last one up in Brady. Tomorrow we'll head back to Farside and fetch a couple more—one for Kerrville and the last one for Alpine out west."

"These things are really saving our bacon, since the main power plant for the area was knocked offline."

"Oh? Were was it located?"

"On Lake LBJ near Marble Falls. It was right on the ragged edge of the tsunami that took out Austin and San Antonio. The plant survived but falling debris caused lots of damage and blocked the cooling water intakes. It used to provide over 400 Megawatts of power to this area, hopefully we can get it back online."

"What did it run on, Tony?" asked TK.

"Natural gas, one thing we got a lot of around here."

"Sounds like you'll be in good shape if you can get that plant back online. In the meantime, our little presents should help tide you over."

"Well we greatly appreciate this, TK," Tony said. "And you too, lieutenant, for flying the work crews around in your shuttle."

"Not a problem, Mr. Ruiz. It was either that or stay here and drink all day with TK and the Ranger."

"Now girl, we weren't drinkin' *all* day," TK said with a chuckle.

"In any case, if you gentlemen will excuse me I believe I will turn in for the evening. I suspect it will be another long day tomorrow."

"Goodnight Beth," said TK, as the tall lieutenant pushed back her chair and stood up.

"'Evening, Ma'am," added Sid and Tony. Billy Ray just nodded slightly as Beth glanced his way and headed for the door.

"Speakin' of drinkin'," TK added with a twinkle in his eye, "anyone for a nightcap?"

Room 211, Hangar Hotel

Forty five minutes later, Billy Ray managed to excuse himself from the other men in the bar and head upstairs for bed. As he walked down the hallway looking for his room number a door beside him opened. Before he could react, someone seized his arm and pulled him into the room. Urgent hands cradled his face and eager lips sought his.

Breaking the long passionate kiss, Beth looked soulfully into his eyes and said, "It's about bloody time you drug yourself up here, I almost grabbed a crewman by mistake a half hour ago."

Billy Ray couldn't think of an answer that would improve his position so instead he kissed her again.

* * * * *

A little after 6:00 the next morning, Billy Ray was awaken by the sound of the shower running. He really had been bone tired from the long day yesterday, and the passionate reunion with Beth had not helped matters. Not that he had any complaints in that department. *I guess they're right*, he mused, *that absence makes the heart grow fonder—or at least hornier.*

Beth exited the shower to find Billy Ray, propped up on pillows in the bed, admiring her. "And what are you staring at?"

"I'm just expressing my reverence for the naked female form."

"You saw me naked last night."

"Last night I saw you nekkid, there's a difference."

"What?" the puzzled Beth replied.

"Naked is when you have no clothes on, nekkid is when you have no clothes on and yer up to something," Billy Ray threw off the covers and stood up.

Beth look him up and down and, dropping her towel, replied, "In that case, Commander, I would say that right now you are nekkid."

Officers Club, Hangar Hotel

It was after 7:30 before Beth and Billy Ray managed to join the others in the hotel bar for a quick breakfast. As they walked in together everyone turned to look at the pair of officers. Even if they feigned innocence there was no escaping the look that people have after a night of passion—an aura of sated languor that cannot be disguised.

"I hope you two had a restful night," TK said as they approached the table where he, Sid and Tony were seated. He couldn't fully hide the amusement in his voice. Also at the table were Roger Stoltz and Sally Musselman who smiled cordially as the couple took seats.

Both Sid and Sally immediately understood what TK's remark really meant. Sid because the Texas Ranger was observant and studied the behavior of his fellow humans, Sally because women can just tell about such things. Roger remained clueless.

"The accommodations are certainly more comfortable than a rack on a corvette," Beth supplied, evading the question. Ranger Sid moved the toothpick from one side of his mouth to the other.

Billy Ray just nodded and attacked his eggs and sausages. Though the Moon base now had producing laying hens, bacon and sausage were still scarce, making this a treat. The table settled into small talk as the two late comers devoured their breakfasts.

Just as they were finishing, the double doors to the bar flew open and a man in military attire strode in. At the sound of the opening doors, conversation in the bar stopped and everyone stared at the newcomer, just like in an old Hollywood western. It was Gen. Jake Crotchet, late of the U.S. Army and now commander of the Republic of Texas Army.

"Why does that man always have to storm into a room like he's storming an enemy position?" TK muttered. In a louder voice he called out, "General, what can we do for you this morning?"

"We got problems, people. I just got a call from some of my troops in Brady. The town came under attack last night by a bunch of armed irregulars."

"We were just in Brady yesterday evening," Billy Ray said, laying down his utensils. "There wasn't anything out of the ordinary when we departed at 2100."

"Attack started around 0400 on some of the outlying houses. Came in from the north. My men on site counter attacked but had to pull back, they were outnumbered at least three to one."

"My goodness," said Sally, "what do you propose that we do?"

"I got two platoons, eighty men, ready to go, all with combat experience and a full ammo load. Problem is the roads are all closed 'cause of this snow; I have no way of getting them to the combat zone."

TK looked at Billy Ray, who nodded. "General, we can provide transport for your men. We can have you on the ground in Brady in less than 30 minutes."

"I was kind of hoping you'd say that, Major, or is that Commander?" Being a military man, the General knew what the oak leaf cluster on Billy Ray's collar meant.

"Lieutenant Commander, Sir, we're Navy," he replied, folding his napkin and standing up. "How soon can your men be ready to board the shuttle?"

"The trucks are pulling up outside right now, Commander."

Billy Ray signaled to his crew chief, who was sitting with the sailors at the next table. "Chief, I think we better get her warmed up."

Turning back to the wiry little general Billy Ray said, "I'm Billy Ray Vincent, by the way, and this is Lieutenant Elisabeth Melaku."

"I am very pleased to meet you Commander, Lieutenant. Now if you don't mind, I need to see to my men."

As the General departed, Roger spoke for the first time since the crisis broke. "We've been getting harassed by bandits and renegades coming in from the northwest ever since winter set in. Normally they hit isolated farm houses. They kill everyone in sight, take all the food and then burn the place to the ground. The General sends out patrols but the raids have been getting worse."

"And the size of the bands have been getting bigger," added Tony.

"Weapons for the crew?" Billy Ray asked TK.

"Yeah, Billy Ray. These folks are our allies. I'll talk to Col. Tropsha and Capt. Curtis but I'm sure they will agree."

"If you don't mind, Commander, I'd like to ride along," Sid asked.

"Grab your gear and meet me at the shuttle, Ranger."

Sid nodded and left the room. Beth and Billy Ray also headed out to don their cold weather gear.

* * * * *

Fifteen minutes later the ranger and the two officers were standing next to the boarding ramp as the last of the soldiers trooped onto the shuttle. From external appearances, the General's men looked fit, well equipped and motivated.

"Ranger, follow the Army on board and work your way forward. Tell the crew chief that you're to be up front with me." This statement drew a look from Beth.

"Right," Sid replied and followed the soldiers up the ramp.

As the Ranger left, Billy Ray turned to address Beth. His heart was suddenly in free fall—he did not want to deal with this.

"I know what you're gonna say, but you have to stay here with TK."

"Why? I am a fully qualified combat officer, just as you are. Is it because I'm a woman? Is it because you think I'm your woman?"

"No, its because we can't leave TK here without transport and you are the only other qualified shuttle pilot. Beth, I know that you are every bit the warrior that I am, maybe more, but TK is one of the most important leaders we've got."

"Really? He's come down here before on his own."

"Not without a pilot and a couple of Marines, he hasn't. Look, Ludmilla is a fantastic administrator, she keeps everything running while juggling a million and one details; Gretchen is a great captain and is doing a hell of a job building up the Navy, plus we all know she can fight; but it is TK who thinks long term. The other two provide logistics and tactics, TK provided strategy. Until Jack Sutton returns, TK Parker is essential to our future, hell, the future of mankind."

Beth glared at him but knew what Billy Ray said was the truth. "I suppose you're right, but I still don't like it."

"Exigencies of the service. I don't want to be away from you for a minute, but we have to do what we have to do. And, Lieutenant, I need you to protect TK Parker while the rest of us are aiding the Texans."

"Yes, Commander." Beth turned, jammed her hands into her parka pockets and walked stiffly back to the hotel.

* * * * *

Boarding his ship, Billy Ray walked forward through the ranks of soldiers, all in white winter camouflage. At the cockpit door he stopped and talked with the General, who was now in full web gear with helmet and carbine.

"You're welcome to sit up front, General."

"Thanks, Commander, but to tell you the truth, I never much cared for flying. Besides, you got Ranger Hopkins to show you where to go, he knows the terrain as well as I do."

"Fine, Sir. I'll warn you that this will be a bit different from other flights you've been on. You won't feel any motion until we are back on the ground at the other end."

"Works for me," the General said with a smile.

Entering the cockpit, Billy Ray found the Ranger already strapped into the right hand copilot's seat. The crew chief was seated behind him at the status board and one of the sailors was on the other side of the cockpit at the controls to the chin mounted 15mm railgun.

"We are all buttoned up and ready to go, Skipper."

"Thanks Chief, let's get the Army where it needs to go."

His fingers danced over touch controls on the surrounding cockpit display and then, with the barest movement of the sidestick, the big shuttle rose rapidly and headed north.

"Don't feel like its movin'," said Sid.

"Artificial gravity," replied Billy Ray.

"You havin' trouble with your girlfriend?"

Billy Ray gave the Ranger a narrow eyed look.

"No offense, I'm just trying to get the lay of the land."

206

"My Lieutenant is used to riding toward battles. She was unhappy at being forced to set this one out."

The sailor at the weapon controls looked over at the crew chief. The chief shot him a keep-your-mouth-shut look and pointedly turned back to his instruments. The cockpit was quiet for several minutes while hilly, snow covered terrain passed beneath the shuttle. Less than five minutes out, Sid spoke again.

"I was there when your ship took off."

"Where?"

"At Parker's ranch; blew out every window for miles."

"I remember that day well."

"You were on board?"

"Yup," Billy Ray replied, smiling at the memory. "I was at the helm."

Chapter 16

Brady, Republic of Texas

Capt. Jim Stillwell and his men were in a ditch at the edge of town. It was just the latest holding position they had fallen back on trying to keep the band of marauders at bay. For a bunch of outlaws the enemy was well equipped, most carrying automatic weapons— probably raided from a National Guard armory somewhere. They were also fairly well led, and showed enough discipline for the Captain to suspect that many were veterans of one stripe or another.

It was a hazy gray day, as the days had been for the past several months. Snow was falling intermittently. His sergeant positioned the men with practiced skill. Most of them had seen action in one God forsaken corner of the world or another before everything went to hell. Now home was the battlefield and it was their former countrymen, not the Taliban, trying to kill them.

The bandits were pushing them south along Old Santa Anna Road, back into town. Lieutenant Duffy's men were trying to hold the right flank along Bridge Street, trying not to let the enemy split their forces. If that happened they could be wiped out one unit at a time, what the military called being defeated in detail. The trick was to maintain contact with Duffy while not losing contact with the enemy.

"Bravo Sierra, Bravo Sierra, this is Victor X-ray, over." The radio crackled. He was BS1 and Duffy was BS2, for a minute he was puzzled by who this Victor X-ray could be. Then he remembered that Gen. Crotchet used VX as his call sign.

"Roger Victor X-ray, this is Bravo Sierra One, I read you 5 by 5."

"Bravo Sierra, be advised that we are inbound with relief. Mark your position with infrared flares."

"Roger Victor X-ray, we are holding positions off Old Santa Anna Road and Bridge Street, south and west of the air strip. Marking positions now."

* * * * *

General Crotchet came forward to discuss deployment with Ranger Hopkins and Lcdr. Vincent. Billy Ray pulled up a topographic map on the instrument display, overlain with the positions of the forces on the ground. The shuttle's IR sensors showed not just the flares but the location of each soldier and outlaw.

"Looks like we can insert second platoon in this field next to Bridge Street. Then we can land first platoon at the airstrip. I really want to catch these bastards in an envelopment and wipe 'em out." All commanders since the beginning of time longed for the elusive decisive battle.

"Sounds like a plan, General," Billy Ray agreed. "Chief, get yourself and the men into armor. We will send two of you with each platoon. And pop a couple of recon drones."

"Aye aye, Skipper."

"What's with this armor stuff, Commander? Are you talking about those big robot suits that your Marines wear?"

"Yeah, pretty much. You can think of them as light armored vehicles with legs. They are impervious to small arms fire and pack quite a punch themselves. Just tell 'em what you want 'em to do."

2nd Platoon, Kountry Akers Drive

The shuttle rose almost silently from the field adjoining Bridge Street and disappeared into the gray overcast. Major Randolf watched as his men spread out and began crossing the road into the scrub on the other side. Beside his sergeant stood the two armored sailors, like gray-black robots.

"What am I supposed to do with you two?" he asked. "You're big and black and you are going to stand out against the snow like a dog's balls."

As he watched both armored figures faded to white. "Adaptive camouflage, Sir," one of the figures said. "I'm Crenshaw, he's Lucas. Just tell us where to go."

"All right," the perplexed Major replied. "Crenshaw, go with Lieutenant Gomez and 3rd & 4th squads, Lucas come with me."

Gomez's column headed west to strengthen the middle of the defensive line. At the same time, 1st & 2nd squads moved north to link up with Lt. Duffy's men on the right flank. It didn't take long for them to find both Duffy and the enemy.

Randolf's men moved through a wooded area and an open field beyond. Ahead was another road, with more houses running north to south. A street sign read *Kountry Akers Drive*. The sound of gunfire could be heard just up ahead. Moving carefully between the northernmost pair of houses, the soldiers found their comrades engaged in a firefight with a large number of hostiles.

As he watched, the Major could see several of the enemy trying to flank Lt. Duffy's position, attempting to move past the houses to the west. Their movement drew fire from the adjacent house—from the sound of it, large caliber hunting rifles. Obviously the citizens were not passively watching the battle unfold.

Finally establishing physical contact with Lt. Duffy, Maj Randolf asked for a sitrep—a situation report.

"I've got one squad along the road to the right where it doglegs back to the main road. The rest are hunkered down in the backyard of the northern most house. There seem to be a lot of hostiles trying to infiltrate through the field west of the house lots."

"Right. Sergeant, we need to move through the wooded backyards of those two houses to the south. We want to deploy along the edge of those woods and get an unobstructed field of fire on the infiltrators headed south beyond. And let the people in those houses know we are the good guys."

"Roger, Sir."

"Lucas. Go with the Sergeant and see if you can help out," the Major said to the looming white figure behind him.

"Aye aye, Sir." The white giant loped off after the Sergeant.

They approached the side of the house that rifle fire had come from a few minutes ago. The Sergeant motioned a couple of men forward along the far side of the house. They held position at the back edge of the wall while the Sergeant shouted to those inside.

"Inside the house, listen up! This is the Republic of Texas Army. We need to move into your woods to attack the raiders, so hold your fire."

"Yeah? How do we know you are who you say you are, buddy?"

"'Cause if we were outlaws we would've come in the front and shot yer asses."

"OK, good point. How can we tell you from them desperadoes?"

"We look like regular soldiers, with assault rifles, helmets and white camo."

There was a pause while the armed home owners thought that over.

"All right, come on by. We'll hold our fire."

"Fuckin' civilians," the Sergeant muttered, motioning for his men to move out into the wooded area behind the house. Once they were sure there were no hostiles in the woods, the Sergeant and Lucas move forward. As the seven foot tall, armored sailor moved into the home's back yard the voice from the house called out again.

"What the hell is that thing?"

"It's a Yeti, sent over by the Dali Lama," the Sergeant quipped. "Don't worry, he's on our side."

The squad was soon at the edge of the wooded lot, looking out across the scrub filled field beyond. Dark shapes could be seen moving against the white snow, seeking cover behind the low plant growth and occasional taller bush.

"All right, let's light 'em up—aimed fire, pick your targets." The ten squad members began firing at the hostiles attempting to infiltrate past their position. This brought a fusillade of return fire, much heavier than expected. The soldiers were soon pinned in position and having to seek cover themselves.

"Shit! There would appear to be a lot more of these bastards than expected," the Sergeant commented, firing a short burst in the general direction of their enemy. At this point, Lucas asked the Sergeant a question.

"Hey Sergeant. You mind if I lob a few grenades out there?"

"Hell no! Do it."

Lucas stood up and unlimbered his standard assault railgun, selected time-on-target high explosive on the 20mm and fired a five round salvo at the outlaws in the field. Set by laser rangefinder, the salvo was timed so that the HE rounds exploded in the air, about four meters above the enemy positions. This sent a rain of shrapnel down on the bandits from directly overhead. A half dozen were killed outright and as many more grievously wounded. More importantly, the sudden shelling caused most of the remaining outlaws to break and run.

"Holy sheee-it!" the Sergeant exclaimed. "Why didn't you tell me you could do that?"

"You didn't ask, Sarge," Lucas said, smiling to himself inside the helmeted suit. A few of the braver outlaws were still firing at the towering white giant. Lucas isolated their positions using his suit's IR sensors and took them out with short bursts of 5mm.

"All right Yeti boy, stick with me. The rest of you, pursuit with bounding over watch by fireteam, now."

Shuttle One, Airfield

The shuttle dropped quickly from the leaden sky onto the runway at the local airstrip. The remaining platoon of Army soldiers deplaned and rapidly moved to form a perimeter at the edge of the airport property. Billy Ray sent the crew chief and remaining crewman along to support the General in his planned envelopment of the bandits.

"If you don't mind, I'll stay here with you, Commander," said Sid watching the battle unfold on the shuttle's display screens. The pair of recon drones were orbiting overhead, continuously updating the map display with the positions of every warm body within their range. The General's platoon deployed along a dirt road that headed directly west from the runway's southern end.

"I thought you were anxious to apprehend these outlaws, Ranger."

"I find that a pistol against a hundred or more bad guys with automatic weapons is a bit of a mismatch."

Billy Ray chuckled. Then he contacted the General by radio. "Victor X-ray, Shuttle One. General, you are in position to cut off the retreat of the main body of raiders. They're being herded your way by the Major's force. Looks to be maybe sixty or so still moving your direction from the south."

"Roger that Shuttle One. Thanks for the update."

"I do believe that the General is enjoying himself."

"Yep, these bandits have had him chasing his own tail for a couple of months and he did not like it at all."

Just as a precaution, Billy Ray sent one of the recon drones on a wider sweep to the north of the airstrip. As it tracked from west to east, about a kilometer north of the runway red dots began to appear on the display.

"Oh, crap."

"What?"

"It appears that we have a large force of unknowns headed south. Pretty much along the edge of these cleared farm fields north of the airstrip. They are going to reach the airfield's northern perimeter in about five minutes."

"The airfield is wide open," Sid noted. "They'll be able to move quickly across it and then roll up the General's flank."

"I guess they don't know there's a Texas Ranger barrin' their way," Billy Ray said with a hint of a smile.

"Everybody loves a wise ass, Commander," the Ranger replied with a smile of his own. "Unless you have another pair of those suits in the back, we probably need to tell the General he's about to be taken from behind by a superior force."

"As poetic as it would be for the two of us to be standin' on the runway, ready to throw down on that bunch of outlaws as they ride into town, I think we will try a different approach." Reaching overhead he touched a series of backlit symbols. Muffled thuds, followed by whining motor sounds, could be heard in the cockpit. Billy Ray leaned back in his chair, seemingly unconcerned.

214

Then, out either side of the windscreen, odd six-wheeled vehicles could be seen fanning out across the width of the airfield. Closer inspection revealed multi-barreled, Gatling gun like weapons atop both vehicles.

"Victor X-ray, Shuttle One. Be advised that there is another bandit force approaching from the north of the airstrip. We are preparing to engage but you need to wrap things up and reverse your front to the north."

"Roger Shuttle One. Interrogative size of enemy force?"

"Company strength, and some of them are mounted."

"Armored vehicles?"

"No, horses."

1ˢᵗ *Platoon, West of the Airstrip*

The General just got off the radio with the shuttle and did not look like a happy camper. Between Maj Randolf to the south and east, and Capt. Stillwell to the west, they had the remaining bandits trapped in a copse of woods just south of the east-west dirt road. Unfortunately the enemy were still returning fire and had decent cover. They would either have to wait them out or make a frontal assault on the enemy position.

"Sergeant, we need to wrap these bandits up quickly. We are about to get more company from the north."

"If we rush their position we'll take casualties for sure, Sir," the First Sergeant replied. Even general officers took advice from experienced noncoms, who often had the most practical experience in combat.

"It's that or leave them where they are, and leaving an effective enemy force in our rear doesn't strike me as the best of ideas."

"Uh, pardon me General," said the white armored giant that contained the crew chief. "I think that the boys and I might be able to flush those hostiles out."

"What do you propose, Chief?" At this point the General was ready to take suggestions from any quarter.

215

"We aren't really at risk from small arms fire. I figure we could just stroll up to that clump of trees and reason with them."

Having no better solution General Crotchet said, "Reason away, Chief."

The chief conversed briefly with the other sailors via their suit radios and then addressed the General again. "Have your men pick off any that get by us, though there shouldn't be many."

With that, four huge white figures emerged from cover and began converging on the bandits' position from four different directions. As they walked a hail of fire from the outlaws bounced off their armored bodies, jacketed rounds occasionally whining off as ricochets. The sailors halted 15 meters from the woods—they needed that much distance for the 20mm shells to work in time-on-target mode. Setting their rounds to penetrate three meters into the woods they started firing. Three rounds each, bump the range three meters, fire three more, and repeat.

The clump of trees was thrashed by explosions, severed branches and an occasional body part flying into the air. Silence descended as the sailors ceased firing. Soldiers began cautiously working their way toward the bandit position, but there was no longer any return fire from the clump of trees.

Observing from his position by the road the General spoke to his First Sergeant. "Sergeant, remind me never to pick a fight with these Moon folks."

"Roger that, Sir. That is a big no shitter."

Shuttle One, Airstrip

Ranger Hopkins and Billy Ray watched as the mass of bandits approached from the north, moving onto the open airfield. There looked to be about two hundred infantry and twenty men mounted on horses.

"How close you figure on lettin' 'em get?" asked the Ranger.

"Want to get as many in the kill zone as possible."

"They're starting to move off into the scrub in small groups."

"Yeah, I guess it's time."

Billy Ray tapped on the display, then used his fingers to trace several arcs across the mass of approaching enemy. Finally he tapped the word "execute," highlighted in red at the bottom of the screen. From outside came the sound of dueling bandsaws. Seconds later the air above the bandits blossomed with fire from exploding shells.

Faster than humanly possible, the robot gunners sprayed alternating streams of canister and antipersonnel explosive rounds at the massed enemy. The canister scythed through equine and human bodies at waist level, the explosive shells burst just overhead as the robots walked the barrage up the airfield until all detected targets had been covered. Flame and flying debris obscured the view. Billy Ray tapped the cease fire control.

What had been a company of men and horses traversing a white, snow covered field was now a jumble of body parts on a swath of crimson. Wisps of vapor rose from the shredded bodies, condensing in the cold air. Both men stared at the scene through the windscreen. After a half minute of silence, Billy Ray spoke.

"That is about the most horrific thing I have ever seen."

"I thought you'd done this before," Sid replied, eyes still fixed on the carnage across the airfield.

"I fight aliens in a starship. When I kill bad guys it's normally from 10,000 kilometers away, and the targets don't bleed, they just disappear in a flash of radiation."

"Well, I've killed men before, but it sure was nothing like that out there."

"I hear ya."

"Damn waste too."

"Yup. We could have saved those horses."

The two men looked at each other, in that instant coming to an accord—bound together by the knowledge that war was a horribly evil business, but sometimes necessary. As he placed the battle bots into standby mode, Billy Ray called the General.

"Victor X-ray, Shuttle One. We have neutralized most of the enemy force approaching from the north. Some may have made it off into the brush in all the excitement."

"Roger, Shuttle One. We will make a sweep to pick up any strays. Good work."

Billy Ray looked back out the windscreen at the ghastly panorama in front of the shuttle and swore to himself, *I will never take the Marines for granted again.*

* * * * *

The airfield became a hive of activity, with soldiers coming and going in all directions. Some were working with the locals, a number of whom had been hiding in the buildings on the airport grounds. Together they organized a burial detail for the slain bandits—several large dump trucks and a pair of front-end loaders. The bodies would need to be buried, but the location had to be chosen so as not to endanger the local water supply.

"I've seen carnage on a lot of battlefields, but that there tops them all," General Crotchet said to Billy Ray and Sid. Catching the pained look on the Commander's face he quickly added, "it was necessary though. If you hadn't stopped them we would have been humped for sure."

Lt. Duffy walked up to the three men and said, "Pardon me General, but the patrol we sent up Old Santa Anna Road found some civilians who captured several outlaws. They've hung two and are threatening to hang the rest."

"Hanged," said Sid.

"Pardon?" the Lieutenant replied.

"Hanged. A bull is hung, a man is hanged."

The comment brought a slight smile to Billy Ray's face and a grunt from the General. "We need to stop that. We definitely don't want the populace taking matters into their own hands."

"No, yer right," Sid sighed, squaring his Stetson on his head and checking his holstered pistol. "This is my territory, and part of the reason I came along."

"How's that, Ranger?"

218

"When it was an all out battle, it was a military matter. Now that the battle is over it's a law enforcement problem. Can't have people takin' to lynching any suspected outlaw they come across. Those outlaws that got themselves captured need to be taken into town and brought before the magistrate."

"You're going to throw them in jail, Ranger Hopkins?" Lt. Duffy asked, voice a bit skeptical.

"Yup. I'm a peace officer. It's my duty to uphold the rule of law. The alleged outlaws will be charged and tried in a court of law. Then we'll hang 'em."

"We managed to capture a couple alive as well," the General said. "Be happy to let the civilian authorities take them off our hands."

Sid nodded. "Maybe the airport folks can loan me some transport, I need to go stop those good people before they string up the rest of their prisoners."

"I'll go you one better, Ranger," Bill Ray offered, pausing to speak into his comm pip. "Chief, have one of the men break out a hover sled and take Ranger Hopkins where he needs to go."

"I appreciate that, Commander."

"I figure having one of my crew along in a suit of armor might help convince the good people of Brady to turn their prisoners over to you."

"Couldn't hurt." Sid smiled, touched the brim of his hat in a two fingered salute and headed off for the shuttle to collect his ride.

The three officers watched the Ranger as he walked away. "He's a good man," said Crotchet. "He helps remind the rest of us that we are a nation of laws. Otherwise things could spin into chaos."

"The struggle of all against all, as Hobbs put it," added Billy Ray, with a thoughtful expression on his face. "Goes back to Locke and Rousseau and the idea of a social contract. Citizens cede their right of individual action to the government, and in turn the government protects its citizens and ensures uniform treatment under law."

"I've been in the Army all my life. I've seen countries plunged into banditry and tribal war. Martial law is only a temporary fix, and not a very good one at that. I tell you, Commander, I figure it's worth being a soldier so my family can live in a civil society. I just pray we can preserve some of the good ideas the founding fathers had, here in this new Texas of ours."

"Amen, General." For the first time since going to war against the forces of the Dark Lords, Billy Ray gave thought to where all of this might lead. *Maybe, just maybe, we need a few men like Ranger Hopkins on Farside and Mars.*

Chapter 17

Airport Hotel, Fredericksburg

The General and most of his men stayed in Brady to help Ranger Hopkins reestablish domestic tranquility. A judge was sent for from the next town over and everyone expected that justice would be swift. The shuttle returned to the Moon for another load of reactors, affording Billy Ray no time to mend fences with Beth. By the time the last two power generators were in place, TK and Beth had departed for Farside themselves. A major front was blowing in and Billy Ray found himself drinking in the Officer's Club bar at the hotel when Ranger Hopkins returned.

"Want some company, Commander?" the lawman asked, walking up to the bar where Billy Ray stood, one foot on the brass bar rail.

"Suit yer self, Ranger. Seems all the dignitaries and politicians have left for home."

"That include your girlfriend, the lieutenant?"

Billy Ray took a sip from his beer and took a second to savor the amber liquid before answering. "Yup. She and TK were gone when I got back from the base with the last of the reactors."

"She still pissed off?"

"Yup."

"She'll get over it." The bartender brought Sid a whiskey neat, without being asked. "How long you two been together."

"About six months, though together ain't really the right word. She commands the corvette squadron—small interceptors—and I captain a frigate. We're hardly ever in port at the same time." *Why am I telling him this?* Billy Ray thought. *Do I really need a sympathetic shoulder to cry on?*

"I'm a pretty fair judge of character, sort of comes with the job. You two seem like a good match."

"You ever been with a warrior woman, Sid?" Billy Ray asked. This was the first time he had called the Ranger by his given name.

"Went with a biker chick once."

221

"Ain't the same thing."

The two men sampled their drinks and stared in amicable silence at the display of bottles on the mirrored wall behind bar.

"So let me get this straight, you're both commanding officers, her of a squadron of interceptors and you of a warship?"

"Yeah, I guess we've both gotten used to being in-charge."

"But you two still managed to get together."

"Yeah, during the few moments we're both in port."

"At least you don't have to explain yer job to her."

"Nope. That is a plus."

Again drinks were sipped contemplatively.

"Best stay together. Who else would put up with you?"

"You got a point there, pardner," Billy Ray replied with a wry smile. *I guess it is a good thing, having someone to tell your troubles to.* After a moment's reflection, he changed the subject.

"I've been thinkin', Farside and the Mars Colony are really just military outposts right now. But eventually, there are gonna be a lot of civilians in both places. Hell, the science types think they can terraform Mars using knowledge they've pulled out of the artifact. It'll never be Earth, but people will be able to walk around without spacesuits one day."

"That would be something," Sid agreed, glad to see Billy Ray was no longer moping over relationship problems.

"Just thinkin', when that day comes we will probably need some fellers like you. You know, lawmen, keepers of the peace."

"I got plenty to keep me busy right here in Texas," the Ranger replied.

"Not sayin' anytime soon. Just something to keep in the back of your head."

"I'll do that, Billy Ray." Sid drained his glass. "You need another beer?"

Billy Ray turned around and leaned back on the bar, watching the snow fall outside. The meteorologists on Farside said it would probably snow for the next 24 hours.

"That sounds like a good idea, Sid. Can't fly in this weather, may as well drink."

Housing Block #12, Farside Base

The core of Farside's nascent anarchist movement was meeting in a member's apartment. They made it a point to never meet in the same location twice, in case they were being watched. Loud music was playing while the conspirators huddled with their heads together, speaking in lowered voices. They did not call each other by name. This was in case their rooms were bugged their leader, Todor, explained.

They were right to assume that the public areas of the base were kept under surveillance, though more for public safety than to thwart terrorist plots. Thousands of video cameras fed a cluster of computers running sophisticated pattern recognition software, intended to detect any unusual activity which might indicate an accident or life threatening situation. Private residences, however, were not monitored by the computer network or by human security personnel.

"Welcome, brothers and sisters. Have you brought the items you were assigned?" The last time they met, Todor tasked each of the inner circle—those he deemed most trustworthy—to acquire material that was not readily available on the Moon base. Among them were cotton rags, glass containers and flammable liquids.

Given that fire in an enclosed environment was rightly considered a great threat, most of the materials used to construct the base were not combustible. Neither were there ready supplies of oil or gasoline, since there were no automobiles or other equipment with internal combustion engines. Even scented oil for lamps and lighter-fluid were proscribed.

Pulling a couple of liter sized plastic bottles from his backpack, a man named Ben replied with a look of grim satisfaction. "I got these from the cleaning supplies. They sent me alone to clean some spilled paint. The supervisor though he was punishing me for goofing off, but it gave me a chance to swipe these."

"Outstanding! Now all we need are some containers to put the liquid in."

"Yeah. I managed to lift these wine bottles from the trash at the upper deck dining area," Sylvia replied. Normally the bottles were sent for disposal, to be turned into rounded gravel and then dumped into the aquaculture tanks. No glass containers were manufactured on the base, all consumables coming in safer, plastic bottles.

"That is fantastic, combined with some old shirts we now have the makings of a half dozen Molotov cocktails. The pigs will be in for quite a surprise when we show them that the people are not unarmed, despite their best efforts to keep us that way."

"Yes," Sylvia spat, "only the fat cats get to drink real Earth wine from real bottles in the fancy restaurants, while we suck crap out of plastic squeeze bottles." It was not entirely clear whether Sylvia's revolutionary fervor was due to Marxist zeal or hatred of mediocre wine. To Todor it did not matter, he had what he desired most, a way to make a shocking impression on the elites who ruled Farside.

"All right, comrades, spread the word. A week from today we gather in the main atrium at 11:00, just before the 1% take their lunch in the fancy eateries around the park. In a week, we will Occupy Moon Base!"

Bridge, M'tak Ka'fek

Three transits, forty light-years and nearly two months after leaving the Trader's station, the M'tak Ka'fek emerged from alter-space's lesser dimensions and returned to normal 3-space. The crew were now well practiced at the drill for arriving in an unknown star system, and each bent to their assigned tasks.

"This system contains a lot of dust and gas," JT observed from the navigation station. "It looks like there is a single appreciable planet, a gas giant about the size of Jupiter at 2.4 AU. Looks like it has rings and a couple of sizable moons. The star itself looks like an isolated white dwarf."

"A white dwarf?" the Captain asked.

"Yes, Captain," answered Mizuki, happy for an opportunity to ply her skills as an astrophysicist. "A star made up of electron degenerate matter, there is nothing denser in the Universe except neutron stars and black holes. The average density of matter in a white dwarf is roughly a ton per cubic centimeter. A white dwarf can contain a mass comparable to the Sun's in a volume a millionth its size. This one has a mass of 0.8 Sols but its diameter is only 0.009 of the Sun's, about the same as Earth."

"A lot of the system's gas and dust is infalling on the star," JT added, checking more readouts at the navigation station. "I'm registering a lot of gamma ray bursts and high-speed particles."

"Is it in danger of an explosion like the one that chased us out of the Sirius system?"

"No, Sir. This system seems to be in a state of equilibrium. Junk continually gets sucked into the star, resulting in a lot of gamma ray and particle creation, but no build up for a big bang like Sirius. Still no sign of a station like in the Trader's system."

"Keep scanning, it has to be out there somewhere," Jack ordered. *Or the furry little twerps lied to us for some reason.*

"My God!" exclaimed JT. "The ring around that gas giant isn't made of debris, it's solid."

"It's the space station," said Bobby, awestruck.

At her console next to the helm, Mizuki ran some quick measurements. "The ribbon must be 100 kilometers wide, and 300,000 km in diameter. Its inner surface area would be over a hundred million square kilometers, that's two thirds the land area of Earth."

"And I thought the last station was big," said Sandy, staring open mouthed at the planet encircling construct in front of them.

"My name is Ozymandias, King of Kings. Look upon my works, ye Mighty, and despair!" recited the Captain, rising to stand in front of the commander's chair.

The bridge fell silent, as the crewmembers attempted to wrap their minds around the enormity of the station before them. Ever practical, as polar bears are, Lt. Bear broke the silence.

"So, where do you think they keep the antimatter on that thing?"

Part Three

War Is The Remedy That Our Enemies Have Chosen

Chapter 18

Bridge, M'tak Ka'fek

Once the initial shock of the space station's size faded, Captain and crew turned to analyzing the situation they were facing. It was obvious that they could not just pick a place to board and wander about looking for the antimatter they sought. Regardless, the first order of business was to find out what conditions were like on board the massive station.

"Doppler radar shows the ring is spinning with a velocity of just over 12km/sec at the rim. That yields a centripetal acceleration of right about a tenth of a G," JT reported. "It has a rotational period of 21 and a third hours."

"Both a reasonable day-night cycle and amount of simulated gravity. The daylight is going to be pretty feeble though. Are we sure that there is warm life on that thing, and not a horde of Dark Lord minions?"

"The inner surface appears to be some form of giant greenhouse. Spectral analysis indicates a nitrox atmosphere and IR scans report that temperatures are around 16°C. A bit cool but quite comfortable, Captain."

"Speak for yourself, primate," Bear harrumphed. "Why are all these places either stinking hot or without an atmosphere at all?"

"Evidently most of the galaxy's warm life lacks your discriminating taste in environmental conditions, my ursine friend," Jack chuckled.

"The presence of a significant amount of free oxygen is a strong indication that dark life is not present," M'tak's AI stated. "To most of their species oxygen is poisonous."

"Well that's a positive. I wonder what it's made of? The rim must be under a tremendous amount of strain."

"Given the rotational speed, I would guess it is wrapped in something like sheets of graphene or other mono-molecular material, Captain."

229

Doug L. Hoffman

"The bigger question is how it stays in position," added Mizuki. "A ring structure or a sphere would be gravitationally unstable with respect to the central planet."

"Yeah, wasn't there a big stink when it was discovered that Larry Niven's Ringworld was unstable years ago?" added Bobby, who's view of the Universe was filtered through a lifetime of reading science fiction.

"Niven's Ringworld was a giant artifact 600 million miles in circumference orbiting around a star. Its rotation generated a standard Earth gravity and would have required some form of super strong 'unobtainium' to hold together," JT scoffed. "Face it Bobby, his world was SF fantasy, that thing out there is real."

"Just because we haven't found a Ringworld or a Dyson Sphere yet doesn't mean they don't exist," Bobby muttered, causing Mizuki to give him a cautioning look before commenting herself.

"There are two sizable moons in orbit around the planet as well. Perhaps they function as shepherd moons to keep the ring stable, like the moons around Saturn."

"Interesting speculation, Dr. Ogawa," Jack said. "However, since it is here, and has obviously been here for quite a while, such questions can wait. What we need right now is to figure out where to board that thing. M'tak, can you locate any antimatter on board the station?"

"Yes, Captain, neutrino emissions indicate there are hundreds of sites containing antimatter on the station. The problem is there is no way to tell if a signal represents a significant cache or simply a local power generator."

"Well we certainly do not wish to roam around the station hoping to stumble upon the mother load. I think I need to have a conversation with our passengers about contacting their compatriots on the station."

* * * * *

In the trader's quarters, M'tak had thoughtfully provided them with the same view being displayed on the bridge. Across the front wall of the common room the banded gas giant and its encircling ring appeared in all their glory.

230

"Gaze upon that and remember it well. It is a sight that none from our station have seen in generations. Even the Trader has not laid eyes on the Ring Station."

"Trader Ooshnar-tar-rak-ra, how will we find our cousins on the gigantic wheel?" asked Feeshkar, suitably impressed by the size of the visibly turning ring.

"As you will discover if you ever become a senior trader, there are certain frequencies that our kind monitor on every station. How else could far ranging trading missions find our own across the arm of the galaxy?"

"You are truly a worthy leader for our expedition, Trader Ooshnar-tar-rak-ra," oozed the unctuous Poonta-ta-ka. He had finally recovered from his prior encounter with the white fanged monster. Indeed, the prospect of trade, with lucrative once in a lifetime deals in the offing, raised the spirits of all the Kieshnar-rak-kat-tra.

As all three fantasized about the riches they were about to acquire a tall figure in black materialized in front of the trio. Poonta-ta-ka jumped at the Captain's sudden appearance, but seeing that it was not the white horror, he quickly regained his composure.

"Ah, Captain," said Ooshnar-tar-rak-ra. "We were just wondering when you would pay us a visit. We see that you and your magnificent ship have brought us safely to our destination."

"Yes, Trader Ooshnar-tar-rak-ra, we have arrived at the station. Vast as it is we were wondering if you had a plan for contacting the station Trader?"

* * * * *

As Jack conversed with the three alien traders, those on the bridge spoke with each other in low voices. Mizuki and Bobby were still geeking out over the space station while Bear and JT focused on the mission ahead.

"I guess it's a good thing we didn't eat the little twerps after all," Bear admitted grudgingly. "On our own, we could wander around on that thing for ages without finding this station Trader or any antimatter."

231

"I'll bet they give us the runaround for as long as possible, before they tell us where the antimatter is kept. Of course, that's probably smart of them, since once we lay hands on the fuel we will probably grab as much as we can and head back for Earth."

"You think the Captain will just grab the antimatter and head for home?"

"I know the Captain doesn't show it, but he's worried about what might be happening back home in our absence."

"I don't know, JT. I've known Jack for years—sometimes he gets hung up on his sense of propriety and fair play. Never understood it myself."

"I guess we'll just have to wait and see, brother Bear, we'll just have to wait and see."

Alter-space, En Route to Earth System

The mission commander consulted her instruments and forcefully exhaled a stream of the ship's liquid atmosphere. Her kind did not posses names, only the designation of their function. She signaled the rest of the crew.

"We approach emergence in the target system. Be alert for the appearance of our two sister ships." She did not need to tell her crew to be ready to raise the shields and power up the ship's weapons—each knew their duties and responsibilities or they would not be on board.

They were transiting from the system humans called Beta Comae, where the warm life scum had destroyed a refueling station. It was also the system from which the *Destroyer of Worlds* had launched its failed attack. The mission commander had been ordered to use this particular approach as well. Perhaps the dark ones did not wish to disclose other possible lines of attack to the enemy. Perhaps not. The Dark Lords kept their own council.

The commander's mission was not one of destruction but rather a quick reconnaissance to identify the enemy's major resources. It was made clear to her that she was not to engage the enemy on her own, simply swoop in and back out, returning the intelligence gleaned. The ships would exit the system via three different transfer points to diminish the likelihood of pursuit.

After seven and a half days in alter-space limbo, the excursion around the alien sun would be a welcome diversion. Then they would transit back to report their findings. Following the reconnaissance it would take several months to gather the Dark Lord's vassals. At the appointed time, squadrons of warships would converge on the enemy system from three transit points, as close to simultaneously as possible. It was the mission commander's job to give the fleets some idea of what they would encounter after they emerged.

Not long now, she thought, *a couple days in normal 3-space and then back into the safety of the hidden dimensions. Not a very exciting mission, but perhaps the subsequent attack will prove gratifying. Of course, some of the vermin could try to bar the way, wouldn't that be fun?* Her vent flaps quivered with anticipation.

The Atrium, Farside Base

It was just after 11:00 AM and there seemed to be an abnormally large number of people milling about the atrium, most of them young and many wearing the drab gray jumpsuits of base maintenance. As the crowd began to congeal in the middle of the large open space, placards and banners appeared. One read "Jobs, Justice & Education," several others "We Are The 99%." A large banner proclaimed "Occupy Moon Base," in letters two feet tall. A smaller, but more ambitious sign read "Occupy Everything."

The takeover was carefully planned. There were coordinators scattered throughout the crowd of protesters. They knew the sequence of events and were there to keep the rest of the rabble in sync. Toward the edges, the crowd linked arms and sat down, forming a perimeter that disrupted normal foot traffic. Many of the passers by looked on amused, while others nervously fled the scene.

Several leaders produced bullhorns or pressed personal Karaoke machines into similar service. After a ragged start, the assembled masses were soon chanting in unison, decrying the rich fat cats who were oppressing the people. A number of military personnel, eating an early lunch in the main restaurant on the second level, placed hurried calls to other sections of the base.

* * * * *

At her desk in the HQ complex, Ludmilla's office erupted with several annoyingly insistent alarms. The one she chose to answer first was from Capt. Curtis.

"Ludmilla, you need to take a look at the Atrium monitors. It would appear that we have a civil disturbance brewing."

"What?" Ludmilla quickly called up a panoramic view of the Atrium on her office wall. "Who are these people?" she asked. Though her question was rhetorical the voice interface for the base's main computer interpreted it as a command. Soon a flock of names appeared, hovering over individuals in the crowd as the recently installed face recognition software identified the protesters.

As Ludmilla watched, several protesters produced cans of spray paint and began tagging walls with slogans. A couple of more ambitious types began scaling the large palm trees that grew near the waterfall, evidently intending to string a banner or two from the towering plants.

"These idiots are making a mess," the Chief Administrator exclaimed. "Where did these fools come from?"

"Evidently they began converging on the Atrium just before 1100 hours. This thing has been well planned, it isn't just some spontaneous flash mob." From the sound of her voice and the background noise, Gretchen was on the move. No doubt headed toward the disturbance.

"We need to get some security forces to contain the protesters and move any civilians present to safety. We need to protect the businesses surrounding the Atrium as well."

"I've already contacted Jennifer, the Marines are on the way." Jennifer was Jennifer Rodriguez, the head Marine, recently promoted to Lieutenant Colonel. As Gretchen spoke, Marines in helmets and light body armor appeared on the periphery of the main public space. They were greeted by chants of "Pig! Pig! Pig!" and a smattering of thrown food and beverage containers.

With the appearance of uniformed opposition, the mob ratcheted up the action. One of the smaller bistros—really just a serving counter and a cluster of tables along one side of the Atrium —was rushed by the protesters. Tables and chairs were upended and several thrown across the counter. The few customers that had not already fled, ran for the advancing line of Marines and safety.

Ludmilla received an incoming call from Col. Rodriguez. "Da, Tropsha here."

"Col. Tropsha, we have cordoned off the approaches to the Atrium and are working to evacuate the civilians who were trapped at the various shops. The mob seems to have been waiting for our arrival, since they are escalating the violence now that they have convenient targets."

"Can you contain them?"

"Yes, Ma'am. That is not a problem. Trouble is, we are not really equipped for a civil disturbance. The light body armor is used for training but we don't have any shields, batons or a useful amount of pepper spray."

"I really do not want to use lethal force if we can avoid it, Colonel."

"Our people are armed with stunners, we can take them down if need be. If they physically attack the Marines we may have no choice. Thank God they do not seem to be armed."

* * * * *

In the center of the roiling mob, Todor and his inner circle of devoted anarchists decided now was the time to break out their Molotov cocktails. Lighting the first wine bottle filled with flammable cleaning fluid, the lead instigator reached back and with practiced ease hurled the makeshift bomb through the air. In the light gravity, the burning bottle soared above the crowd, across half the open space to land on the wide stairs leading to the second level. Broken glass and burning liquid splashed among the Marines standing on the stairs.

"That will shake the pigs up!" He exulted. "You didn't know we were armed, did you, you jackbooted fascists?" he screamed. The escalating violence was an almost sexual pleasure for him. As he turned for another bomb the crowd noise changed from raucous defiance to shrieks of terror.

* * * * *

"That was a fire bomb!" observed Gretchen, who had arrived at the plaza on the second level and was standing near the top of the stairs where the bomb burst. Several of the Marines had been set alight, the flames quickly smothered by their comrades. "This is now a direct threat to base integrity. We need to end this now."

"Da! Col. Rodriguez, stun them, stun them all."

"Aye aye, Ma'am," Jennifer switched frequencies and issued the order. Seconds later the edges of the mob were alight with shimmering blue. Protesters dropped like felled trees, falling to the ground where they twitched and convulsed. The range of the stunners was limited to around ten meters so the Marines had to step over fallen protesters at the periphery to reach those at the center of the mob.

At the very center, Todor had been preparing to hurl another flaming bottle when he was struck by debilitating blue light. The bottle fell from his senseless fingers, shattering when it hit the ground. Flames spread among the fallen bodies of the anarchists, who were incapable of avoiding them.

The appearance of fire drew a rapid response from the base's automatic fire control systems. Several drones quickly arrived overhead to dowse the blaze with fire-retardant chemicals. Even so, Sylvia, Tim and Todor were badly burned and had to be rushed to the medical section. A number of the Marines looking on figured it for poetic justice.

The remaining protesters were stacked like cordwood on hover sleds and hauled off to a storage room that was pressed into duty as a holding cell. It was 1120 and the Occupy Moon Base protest was unarguably over. Just as things seemed under control a new alarm was sounded base wide—it was the general quarters alarm, signaling an enemy attack.

Reconnaissance Patrol, Earth System

Within minutes of each other, the alien reconnaissance ships emerged at the transit point from Beta Comae. The burst of gamma rays and spray of subatomic particles that announced their emergence from alter-space took roughly ten seconds to arrive at the Earth-Moon system's detectors. Optical trackers quickly focused on the flight of three ships, marking their course and velocity. There was little doubt that they would be passing close to the base, perhaps within a half million kilometers.

When the *Destroyer of Worlds* made its devastating attack it had arrived at the far side of Earth's orbit, coming in over the Sun. In the six months that had past since the initial attack Earth had moved along its orbital path and was now on the same side of the solar system as the transit point, which lay more than 320,000 km above the plane of the ecliptic. Traveling at 600 km/sec the alien vessels would pass by Earth in roughly 83 minutes.

Farside and Earth lay almost defenseless before their enemies. Both operational frigates were escorting freighters to Mars, millions of kilometers away and headed the wrong direction. The only sizable ship at Farside was the Peggy Sue, which was in the yards and unmanned. Lt. Melaku had half of the corvettes in the asteroid belt on a training flight leaving only two operational flights at base.

The base erupted in pandemonium. Marines in armor were every where while Navy personnel swarmed over the eight operational corvettes, loading munitions and prepping them for flight. The civilian population was evacuated to the lowest levels of the base, as far below the surface as possible for maximum protection from radiation and impacts.

In the command center Col. Tropsha, Capt. Curtis and Lcdr. Vincent conferred in front of a massive 3D display tank showing the entire solar system. The disposition of Earth forces on the display reinforced what the officers already knew—they had been caught with their shorts around their ankles.

"We should recall the Constellation and Constitution," Ludmilla suggested. "These ships will probably not be stopped by eight corvettes."

"You are right about the corvettes, but there is no way that the frigates will get here in time to intercept the aliens," said Gretchen, cursing to herself that she had not kept one ship in a defensive position near the base. "We'll have to scramble the PT boats and hope for the best."

"There may be more incoming, it might still be a good idea to divert the frigates."

"We'll notify them and have them start to circle back toward Earth."

"We've only seen two attacks, and those by different aliens. But each time they brought everything they had through the transit point all at once," Billy Ray observed.

"That makes tactical sense, Commander," Gretchen replied thoughtfully. "Sending a force through piecemeal would tip your hand to the enemy. The opposing forces could set up around the transit point and pick ships off as they emerged."

"That seems logical. Billy Ray, how do you know these are different aliens?"

"The drive signatures are similar, so I figure they are about as capable as the ones that bushwhacked the Peggy Sue, but the physical configuration of these ships is different. The bushwhackers were all spinney, like flying sea urchins. These are squat and compact. I think different critters designed these."

"So why only three ships? And from Beta Comae again?"

"I doubt that anything survived the action off Sirius to report our exit point from that system, but they know where we transited to Beta Comae from. This has the feel of a recon mission—a quick pass through the system to see what's here."

"If that is true then they may simply pass us by and depart without firing at the planet or base."

"Never assume away an enemy's capabilities or intentions, Colonel." Gretchen smiled grimly, recalling the many lectures she received from Jack regarding the art of war.

"Capt. Curtis, the corvettes are launching, Ma'am," called a Lieutenant from one of the communication consoles.

"Good, who is in command?"

"Lt. Hect, Ma'am."

"Tell them to intercept the intruders, Lieutenant." *Why am I so uneasy about this?* Gretchen fretted. *Amos Hect is an experienced former Israeli Air Force officer, but this isn't aerial combat and the enemy aren't Egyptians or Syrians. That, plus almost none of the crews have been tested in actual combat.*

* * * * *

Nearly 600 million kilometers away, situated in one of the Kirkwood gaps in the asteroid belt between Mars and Jupiter, Lt. Melaku's squadron of ten corvettes was practicing maneuvers when she received word from HQ that Earth was again under attack. That information was already a half hour out of date when it arrived.

Amos is a good flight leader, but he can be overly aggressive. I hope he takes into account that most of his crews are inexperienced. I hate to think what might happen in a full on furball with three frigates.

Silently cursing their distance from the enemy, Beth ordered her formation to do an evolution that placed the squadron on course back toward the inner solar system. According to the information from Farside, the aliens had entered via the Beta Comae transit point. She would take her corvettes back to base but would travel above the ecliptic, in a position to take an enemy emerging from that alter-space exit if need be.

* * * * *

Sixty minutes after emergence, the mission commander tightened her formation and prepared to pass by the alien planet's large, barren moon. There were indications of power sources beneath the outward facing hemishpere of the large satellite. Whether there were defensive weapon emplacements on the moon remained unknown but she would take no chances—her ships would execute a braided pattern as they passed, so each ship's shields would only be exposed to any enemy fire for a limited period of time.

Sensors had also detected a number of large ships, on a course toward the fourth rocky planet. At least two of them altered course less than twenty minutes after emergence, an indication that the aliens knew of their presence in their system. The ships, roughly the size of her vessels, had not set course to the third planet, but seemed to be maneuvering to intercept her squadron after they passed the planet ahead.

Smart, not rushing blindly back to defend the home world, she thought. *So be it, they still do not know our exit strategy.* As her ships approached perigee with the planet her instruments detected a flight of eight small ships closing on hers. *Now where did they come from? No matter, they are not large enough to threaten my warships.*

* * * * *

Lt. Hect had taken his two flights of corvettes around the Moon, using the satellite's bulk to mask their presence. On an intercept vector that would take the invaders at roughly 10 o'clock, his plan was to launch a salvo of AM pumped X-ray torpedoes to soften up and distract their opponents, then make a pass with railguns right through the enemy formation. They would then circle about and come up on the enemy from the rear with more torpedoes to finish them off. It was a reasonable plan of attack.

Unfortunately, Hect did not realize the power of the enemy weapons, or that the creatures manning those weapons were by their nature impossible to distract and inhumanly good at their jobs. The alien commander was not very inventive. She did things by the book, but her kind had been fighting among the stars for thousands of years. The book covered most every situation imaginable, and the commander knew it—all three of her hearts.

* * * * *

The main control room display zoomed in on the incipient space battle, showing the forces involved in detail. The wave of torpedoes sped to their targets, only a few being detonated by fire from the invaders. The majority exploded short of their targets, as they were designed to do, the energy released by their antimatter charges channeled into incredibly intense beams of coherent X-rays.

The shields of the closest two enemy vessels flared but did not fail. Then the corvettes were on them, firing their main railguns. The interlaced paths of the alien ships brought the ship that had

240

been sheltered from the torpedo attack to the side facing the corvettes just as they arrived at point blank range. The intruders lashed out with particle cannon more powerful than anything previously encountered by Earth forces.

Two of the attacking corvettes detonated almost immediately. The remainder all took heavy impacts on their shields. Hect realized they had stuck their favorite appendages into a meat grinder.

"Break! Break!" he ordered the squadron. "Guns defense. Jink for all you are worth."

The remaining corvettes dove between the alien ships so they could not bring their weapons to bear without hitting each other. Passing through the formation, Hect managed to hit one of the enemy with at least one railgun slug. It was the only significant damage inflicted by the corvette assault. Exiting the alien formation he lost his wingman.

Once clear of the enemy ships, the corvettes all flipped 180° in a sort of zero-gravity variant on Pugachev's Cobra. More torpedoes were fired while the surviving five corvettes maneuvered violently to evade particle cannon fire. As Lt. Hect desperately tried to reform his squadron for another pass the command channel crackled: "Corvette squadron, disengage! Repeat, disengage."

"Copy that, Farside. We are disengaging."

The alien ships were past Earth and headed for the inner solar system. As far as they could tell, no enemy fire had been directed at Farside or the planet. Lt. Hect sat stunned in his command pilot's chair. He had never been in a dogfight so one sided, where he had lost so many planes in so short a time. As his helmet's tactical display cleared and the corvette's cockpit faded back into view he said aloud, "my God, what have we gotten ourselves into?"

Chapter 19

Fleet HQ, Farside

A chill passed through the HQ command center as the damage reports came in from the corvette attack. Three ships destroyed, three more seriously damaged and no longer combat effective. In a single engagement Farside had lost three quarters of its available corvette fleet. The enemy continued on mostly unscathed, with the exception of one ship whose shields seemed weakened by the attack.

"Corvette flights 1 & 2, return to base," called the base tactical officer. Not that they had much choice—most were damaged and all were low on munitions.

"That did not go at all well," commented Gretchen, continuing to follow the aliens' track. "I wonder if they will swing around and make a run at the base—they have to know we are here."

"I'm thinkin' no, Captain," Billy Ray said.

"And why not, Commander?"

"Watch. Chief, plot the known and calculated alter-space transit points on the tactical display."

"Aye, Sir."

Floating in the 3D display tank, yellow crosses appeared scattered across the solar system. Both Gretchen and Ludmilla said nothing but leaned forward, concentrating on the display. As they watched projected courses for the alien ships appeared. One diverged slightly from the other two.

"See? The ship that we think was hit is separating from the others. If this is a recon mission, they don't really want to fight. They mean to exit as fast as possible and carry what intelligence they've gathered back to their main force."

"I think you are right, Billy Ray. Captain, what should we do?"

"What is the logical transfer point for that ship to head for?" Gretchen asked.

"Most probably Delta Pavonis, Ma'am," one of the sailors replied. One of the yellow markers glowed more brightly, indicating the transfer point in space.

"Yep, it's south off the ecliptic plane right around an AU from the Sun. Their course will take 'em about 2 AU total—call it almost three days if they maintain roughly the same velocity along the course trajectory."

"What about the other two?" asked Ludmilla as Gretchen nodded in agreement.

"Can't tell yet, Ma'am. We will have to wait until they make a course change."

"Well there is one thing we can do," Gretchen snarled. "Order the frigates to head for the Delta Pavonis transfer point; match acceleration to arrive for intercept just prior to transit."

"Aye aye, Captain."

Hearing Room, Farside

With the next possible events in the alien incursion still several days away, Ludmilla decided to see to the rabble who had rioted in the Atrium the previous day. A temporary hearing chamber was set up on lower level, near the storage room where the rioters were incarcerated. A raised dais had been quickly constructed with a judge's bench and seats along both sides of the room for observers. Witnesses and spectators had been filing into the courtroom for almost an hour. The accused would get to sit on simple benches in front of the judges for their trial.

Americans always say they believed in quick justice, thought Ludmilla as the other two judges ascended the dais: Dr. Rajiv Gupta and TK Parker. *We will put that idea to the test right now.*

"Ludmilla, what are we doing?" asked Rajiv, who had been called from his lab in the science section. Most of the lab workers were unaware of the Atrium riot, only emerging when general quarters sounded.

244

"You are here to act as a judge, Rajiv. And you too, TK. The three of us will review the evidence regarding those about to be brought before us and render a verdict."

"But I'm not a lawyer," objected Rajiv, "I'm totally unqualified to be a judge."

"You can think critically. All that is needed is to positively identify those who took place in the riot." *The hard part will be deciding on the punishment.*

"I know what the crime was, but what are we charging 'em with, Ludmilla?" TK had already rolled into place on the dais behind the makeshift judicial bench.

Further conversation among the panel of judges was interrupted by the appearance of several Marine guards at the entrance. A master sergeant stepped forward and announced "Your honors, we have brought the accused."

TK pounded on the bench with a gavel someone had provided. He had been in court enough times in his life to have a general idea of what should happen. "Order in the court!" he said in a loud voice, "Sergeant, bring in the accused."

The Marines marched the twenty seven prisoners into the courtroom to stand before the bench. They were all dressed in shocking pink jumpsuits, their hands tie-cuffed in front of them. Most appeared dazed and confused, possibly still feeling the affects of being stunned. Three of the prisoners had medical dressings over burn wounds and several others sported minor scrapes and bruises.

The accused had been provided with a lawyer, a man from Nebraska who was formerly the mayor of a small country town. He had quickly grasped what was happening when Ludmilla called him to plead for the defense. His first action had been to separate out the dozen or so minors who had participated in the demonstration, arguing that they should not be tried as adults. Judge Tropsha had agreed to that, wishing to concentrate on the adult rioters, those unquestionably responsible for their own actions.

"Court will be in order. The case of The People vs. Occupy Moon Base is in session," Ludmilla proclaimed. "Bailiff, read the names of the accused. Defendants acknowledge when your name is read." In this case the bailiff was the base computer, which had accumulated the list of names from surveillance video of the riot. The list was read without major disturbance.

"And what are these people charged with," Rajiv asked, getting into the mood of things. A young lieutenant, who had worked for a Judge Advocate General in the U.S. Army, was given the role of prosecutor.

"Your honors, the defendants' stand accused of the following crimes and misdemeanors: Endangering the security of Farside base; use of an incendiary device in public areas; assault on military personnel; assault on private citizens; wanton destruction of private and public property; vandalism and disturbing the peace."

"Councilor Jenkins, how do your clients plead?" asked Ludmilla.

"Your honor, many of my clients are only guilty of being in the wrong place at the wrong time and claim no responsibility for the acts of violence and property destruction. I would ask that a recess be granted until they can be sorted out and individual charges filed."

"Your talkin' about diffusion of responsibility, like the Nazis claimed at Nuremberg. Sorry counselor, every adult who willingly participated in this mob action stands accused of all the offenses committed by the group. Motion denied."

"In which case, your honor, my clients plead not guilty."

"Right, so entered. Let's hear the prosecution's evidence."

"If it pleases the court, we will show the video recordings made by several of the Atrium cameras during the disturbance."

"Proceed..."

* * * * *

Over two hours later, having identified each of the defendants committing one or more illegal acts on the video record, the prosecution rested. The defense pleaded for mercy, at least for those who did not personally commit violent acts. After this was denied Todor stood up and protested.

"We do not recognize the authority of this kangaroo court! Power flows from the people and your are fascist oppressors. This court is illegitimate!"

"Order in the court!" bellowed TK, quite enjoying himself.

At that point a Marine guard shot Todor with a low power stunner burst. Another guard caught him from behind as he crumpled and eased him back to a seated position. He trembled and was unable to speak but was otherwise conscious.

"This ain't no philosophy class, sonny. This is a military installation under attack by enemies that aim to exterminate our species. Yer lucky you're even getting a hearing."

"Da, this is not a democracy, it is not a country or city with civil laws. It is a military base and all of you signed a statement acknowledging that when you became residents. We are at war. If we wished to bring the full weight of military law to bear you would have been charged with treason in the face of the enemy."

"Surely, your honors, their acts do not rise to the level of treason," pleaded Counselor Jenkins—treason undoubtedly carried the death penalty. He had precisely zero sympathy for his clients but he was a lawyer and bound by law and custom to defend them.

"While these miscreants have been rioting and endangering us all, eighteen brave men and women died defending this base and our home world. They are lucky not to be marched out an airlock," Ludmilla spat, her jaw clenched and eyes narrow. She inhaled deeply several times to recover her composure.

* * * * *

The defense rested with a final plea for mercy and the judges retired to chambers—actually just a private area behind the dais—to confer amongst themselves. TK was first to speak.

"So let's vote first to see if we find the lot of 'em guilty, all in favor?"

"Aye."

"Aye."

"Then it's unanimous, they stand convicted. Now what are we gonna do with 'em?"

"We have no facilities on the base to incarcerate one person let alone twenty seven," Ludmilla stated, "and I think that this is a matter that requires more than just a slap on the wrist."

"Myself, I was thinkin' more along the lines of a short rope and a long drop, if you get my meaning."

Until the video was shown, Rajiv had been unaware of the extent of the riot. After viewing the evidence, he was aghast by the rioters' actions. If the attack on Melissa had shocked him this incident angered him as he had never been angered in his life. These fools had willingly endangered all that stood between mankind and extinction. Even so, he was not comfortable with executing the rioters and he said so.

"They didn't kill or even hurt anyone badly. I don't see how we can execute these people with a clean conscience."

"Yer no fun at all, Rajiv," TK said, smiling to show he was joking, mostly.

"I agree with Rajiv, capital punishment would be a bit extreme. We have no prison but there is one place that could serve as a gulag."

"Are you thinkin' what I'm thinkin', Ludmilla?"

"If you are thinking we dump them back on Earth, then yes."

"That would certainly ensure that they cause no more trouble in the future and we would not have their blood on our hands," Rajiv said approvingly. "But where should we drop them?"

"Some place in the southern hemisphere would be kindest right now, since it's summer down there. I'd say either the South African highlands or the mountains of South America."

"Not Australia?"

"The Aussies are allies, I wouldn't dump these troublemakers on them even as a last resort."

"No matter, banishment and transportation to Earth it is—we can decide exactly where later. Are we agreed?" They were. The three judges turned back to the courtroom to pronounced their verdict.

"We find the defendants guilty as charged on all counts," Ludmilla announced. "The sentence is banishment for life from Farside Base and transportation back to Earth."

"May God have mercy on your souls." TK added, a phrase oftentimes added when pronouncing a death sentence. Given the conditions on Earth, transportation might well be a death sentence. Then, with a rap of his gavel, the first trial in the history of the Moon was over.

Fleet HQ, Farside

Billy Ray had practically lived in the command center for the past 48 hours, monitoring the alien invaders. As the ships passed near the Sun direct observation became difficult from Farside, but other ships and satellites throughout the solar system remained focused on the intruders. They relayed tracking information back to Farside HQ, even though much of it was significantly time delayed.

"Looks like the second one is headed to Beta Hydri, Captain," he said to Gretchen, who likewise had scarcely left the command center since general quarters sounded.

"And the first is still on course for Delta Pavonis?"

"Yes, Ma'am. I can't see any place else they'd be headed."

"What about the third?"

"That's a bit of a puzzle. They've already missed direct vectors to major transit points—61 Virginis, Zeta Tuc, and couple of others. There are still a number of transit points they could be headed for but none of them make a lot of sense. They are mostly small stars with long transit times."

"So what are they up to?"

"My best guess? I think they're swinging around the Sun to head back the way they came."

Gretchen nodded slowly, considering the display in front of her and Billy Ray's analysis. Finally she spoke.

"I think we need to tell Lt. Melaku to arrange a fitting sendoff for our guests."

249

"Yes, Ma'am. I know she'll be happy to oblige." Billy Ray smiled, *this ought to make her forget missing the dust up down in Texas, if she don't get herself killed.*

Corvette Squadron, Nearing The Beta Comae Transfer Point

Beth reviewed the positions of her ships as they streaked toward the Beta Comae transfer point and their rendezvous with the alien intruder. They were about an hour out, their arrival carefully calculated to intercept the fleeing alien before it could exit 3-space. The corvettes would be taking the enemy head on at a closing speed of over 1200 km/sec. They would get one shot at this and she intended that they make it count.

She had already received word from HQ that Constitution and Constellation intercepted their target and blew it out of space. The frigates' stronger shields deflected their quarry's particle cannon blasts while they overwhelmed its shields with X-ray laser torpedoes and a hail of railgun slugs. Like all of the enemy ships encountered to date, this one must have been powered by antimatter—nothing else could explain the tremendous explosion that vaporized the vessel after its shields failed.

Beth was taking that into account in planning her attack. They would hit the bastard with everything they had and then either blow past if the target survived—jinking like mad to avoid enemy fire—or break off to avoid the AM explosion if it didn't. While blast effect was negligible in space the gamma and hard X-rays produced by such an explosion could be deadly, and striking any debris at these relative velocities could also prove fatal.

An incoming message interrupted her thoughts—it was HQ. She switched from tactical helmet display to view the control panel. On it a window opened and Billy Ray's face appeared.

"Just wanted to give you a final update on the bogey, Squadron Commander. You are looking good for intercept." Billy Ray's jawline showed a day's unshaven beard growth. His eyes were ringed by dark circles but shone brightly nonetheless.

"Thank you for the update, HQ. Hope to see you soon back at base." *Damn, how could I have left while we were still fighting? Never again,* she swore.

"Roger that. Tally ho, and good hunting."

Soon there were just a few minutes left before the speeding corvettes intercepted the onrushing alien warship—then just seconds.

"Single braid by flight, torpedoes two salvos of two, on my mark." The formation of ten corvettes swirled in a complex interweaving pattern.

"Fire one! Fire two! Double braid by pairs." The interlacing pattern became even more complex, verging on chaotic. To an outside observer the pattern might have looked a bit asymmetrical, a bit ragged, but that was as intended.

"Railguns, four slug burst, on my mark." Each ship added a bit of randomness to their maneuvering to prevent the enemy from predicting their courses from the pattern.

"Guns! Guns! Guns!" Ahead flashes from the torpedo warheads exploding could be seen.

* * * * *

On the bridge of the alien warship the mission commander looked at her instruments and saw her own destruction. *This flight of small ships is using a much better attack plan,* she thought with grudging respect. *These creatures do learn quickly.*

"Launch a messenger probe through the transfer point. Weapons fire on the attacking ships."

There was a shudder and further thought was cut short by a 10kg slug striking the bridge. The kinetic energy of the collision, equivalent to 3.5 kilotons of TNT, turned its liquid atmosphere into plasma. A fraction of a second later a second slug pierced an antimatter container, starting a chain reaction that reduced the entire ship to naked nuclei and tortured electrons.

* * * * *

Beth was ready to order the squadron to blow by the intruder when a large flash illuminated the space directly ahead.

"Break! Break! Put the target on your six and veer off." Putting their sterns to the explosion gave the crews maximum radiation shielding.

"*Eh bien, alors!* It looks like we got them," said Frenchy with relieved satisfaction.

Right, thought Beth, as the adrenaline rush faded, *easy peasy.*

CO's Office, Farside Base

Billy Ray, fresh from a night's sleep and a shower, approached the base commander's office. His irises were scanned by the new security system installed in all military and sensitive areas. This was Chief Engineer Medina's response to the order for tightened security. No one would be able to gain unauthorized access using a purloined ID signal or stolen comm pip again.

The ensign stationed at the receptionist's desk waived him through to the Colonel's office. "Go right in, Commander. They are waiting for you."

Oh great! I'm the last one to arrive. Nodding to the younger officer he strode through the door as it slid aside. Inside were Col. Tropsha and Capt. Curtis. Before he could salute and report to the commanding officer, Ludmilla waved him to an empty chair and launched right into the reason for the meeting.

"Good morning, Cdr. Vincent. I hope you are feeling well rested after a good night's sleep. I suppose you are wondering why you have been called to my office yet again."

"I'm a mite curious, yes Ma'am."

"You tell him, Captain."

"Lieutenant Commander Vincent, attention to orders. You are promoted to the permanent rank of commander and assigned as captain of the Peggy Sue. You are further instructed to make your ship ready for space, to sail as soon as possible for Gliese 581d on a mission essential to the defense of Earth."

Billy Ray was speechless. He had been expecting a ship of his own, but not the Peggy Sue. She was a fine ship but he longed for the captain's chair on the bridge of a new frigate. And being ordered back to Gliese 581 meant a trip of three weeks in alterspace each way, why now? The confusion showed in his eyes.

"Before you say anything, Commander, let me explain your mission. We have been approached by Ambassador NatHanGon regarding his species' contribution to the war effort. After observing recent events—the aftermath of the bombardment attack and the recent reconnaissance incursion—they are convinced that their fellows will be amenable to sending some reinforcements."

"But they don't have any weapons, Ma'am. How can they help?"

"Remember when we last visited the Triad's system? When there were references made to a group known as 'the Guardians'?"

"Vaguely. They were supposed to be a group of Triads who defended their planet."

"Precisely, Billy Ray," said Ludmilla, using his given name to draw him into the secret mission on a more personal level. "The Ambassador is offering to speak on our behalf back home, but we need a way to get them there."

"Right," said Gretchen, expanding on Ludmilla's statement. "It makes sense to send the Peggy Sue, after all the Triads have been visited by her before. Who knows how they would respond to one of the new frigates. And arguably, sending the Peggy Sue has the least impact on our defensive capabilities, since she is not as heavily armed as a frigate.

"As for commanding the mission, you know the Peggy Sue as well as anyone alive. You are also one of the few officers who has piloted a ship to other star systems. You know the ship, you know the system and you know the Ambassador—you are the perfect choice, the only choice to command this mission."

Billy Ray still looked a bit dazed by the turn of events. He thought of Beth, and how he would explain his sudden departure and lengthy absence to her.

"For crew we can give you one of the junior helmsmen from the last voyage, Dr. Piscopia as science officer, and a few other seasoned crew as well. And the Chief, of course—there is no chance of the Peggy Sue sailing without Chief Zackly," Ludmilla smiled.

"So precisely what are my orders?"

"You are to try and convince the Triads to lend us aid in defeating our attackers. What form that aid might take remains to be seen. This is why we need an officer who has been out there before, who has dealt with aliens and won't be overwhelmed by the whole experience."

"Aye aye, Ma'am. I guess I should see to my ship and crew if the Peggy Sue is to sail tomorrow morning."

"You have time, Commander. It will take Dr. Scott Hamilton all night to get the Ambassador installed on the ship."

"Melissa got her Doctorate?"

"Yes, she defended while you were dirtside helping the Republic of Texas. She will be on the voyage also, since she is our Triad expert."

"Congratulations, Commander," Gretchen stood and offered her hand. "As her former captain I wish you good luck and God speed."

"Yes, Billy Ray, good luck," said Ludmilla, shaking his hand in turn, "and do not worry, you will have time to say good bye to Lt. Melaku tonight. She is cleared to know of your mission, but otherwise this is a classified matter."

As he left the CO's office he thought: *well, I've always dreamed of my own star ship—now all I have to do is tell my new girlfriend that I'm going away for a couple of months, commanding a ship named after my last girlfriend.* Dinner was going to be interesting, to say the least.

Rogue Planet, Interstellar Space

In the interstellar void between Beta Comae and a red dwarf known to humans as Ross 1015, a dark world five times as massive as Jupiter followed its own lonely path around the Galaxy. A dark imitation of a stellar system, the rogue planet possessed its own brood of orbiting satellites. Half a dozen of the largest moons were inhabited by creatures unfamiliar to human kind. Unfamiliar but not unknown—they were the Dark Lords, self nominated rulers of the galaxy's cold life.

A functionary of moderate influence had been summoned by one of the elders. Resembling a strange mixture of plant and animal, the Dark Lords were related to neither. Their kind had evolved on a different path from the life that inhabits worlds warmed by bright burning stars. They were an ancient race and with their slow metabolisms an elder could live for millions of years. The elder in question had already risen to a position of importance before the war with the accursed T'aafhal raged, more than four million years ago.

He of moderate influence shuffled forward on a multitude of bristle like legs, attempting politely to attract his superior's attention. Elder Dark Lords tended to spend most of their time lost in meditation, pondering thoughts unknown.

"Your pardon, Significant One. I come in response to your summons."

"Report. How go the efforts to cleanse the Universe of this latest infestation of warm life?"

"Significant One, a ship from the client race known as the People was dispatched. It struck the vermin's world but did not succeed in exterminating them. The probe recordings showed they fought valiantly but were overwhelmed by the system's inhabitants."

"Remind me to have the planet of these People purged when this is over. What further actions have you taken."

"A reconnaissance mission using a more technically advanced client race was launched to survey the system. I expect their return shortly. Then I plan to launch a simultaneous attack by three of the more capable client races—the warm life scum will be destroyed by massive force."

"Good. The effort will no doubt cull some of the client fleets as well. It is never a good idea to let them grow too powerful. You say these new vermin are most formidable?"

"They have left a trail of destruction across their local stellar neighborhood, destroying or defeating three client races, though none were very advanced."

"Hmmmm," the Elder's speech membranes buzzed in contemplation. "Bring forth a ship from the ancient fleet, a battle cruiser. I will attend this race's extinction myself."

"As you command, Significant One."

The functionary could see that the conversation was ended and the elder had returned to his meditations. As he shuffled from the audience chamber thoughts came unbidden: *The Significant One must think these vermin are dangerous, indeed. No Dark Lord warship has ventured forth into the warm realms in nearly a million years. And a cleansing under the direct supervision of a Dark Lord is almost unheard of. A pity the vermin will never appreciate the honor bestowed upon them.*

Chapter 20

Ring Station

"Captain, we are approaching the entrance to the dock as instructed," called Lt. McKennitt from the flight deck of the shuttle. Making contact with the station Trader took nearly a week, and arranging to land a party on the station another. Eventually a rough understanding was reached and the Earthlings, along with their untrustworthy partners, boarded the larger of the two Earth built shuttles to make the short passage from the M'tak Ka'fek to the gigantic spinning ring.

"Very good, Lieutenant," Jack replied. "Slow and steady, and keep an eye peeled for a trap."

"Aye, Sir. Slow and steady it is." The shuttle edged up to what appeared to be a vertical wall eight kilometers high.

"Will you look at that," said JT from the copilot's seat, impressed in spite of himself. From a distance, the rim of the station looked thin compared with its width. Up close things looked different. "I suppose we are headed for that small rectangle?"

A third of the way up from its rounded bottom edge the mostly featureless expanse of wall contained an opening. As the shuttle drew nearer it became clear that the opening was not small, merely dwarfed by the scale of the station. A hundred meters wide by eighty tall, the entrance was uncovered and open to space.

"Right you are, Lt. Taylor." Sandy's voice remained chipper and upbeat. Only her eyes, constantly darting from the instrument display to the scene out the windscreen, gave any indication of the pilot's heightened level of concentration. Despite appearances, the shuttle was not simply approaching a stationary wall in space. It was moving sideways on a curving course at 12 kilometers a second.

"OK, the not so small opening," JT corrected himself. "The scale of this place takes some getting used to."

Within, the landing bay narrowed by steps, creating the look of a stairwell ascending into the distance. As the shuttle entered, alarm indicators lit up on the instrument panel.

"Captain, Flight Deck. We seem have passed through a force-field of some kind."

"Is it strong enough to threaten the shuttle?"

"No Sir. Wouldn't have know it was there without the instruments... stone the bloody crows, there's another one."

"Look, Sandy, there's air pressure outside the ship."

Glancing down at the instruments Sandy concurred. "Right you are, Lieutenant. There's a third force-field and look, the pressure jumped slightly."

"Yeah, this must be how they keep their atmo from leaking out the open landing bay. Not as neat as the M'tak's selectively permeable hull, but still pretty cool." The more barriers they passed the higher the air pressure rose outside the shuttle.

"Captain, looks like we are all right. Just the station's version of an airlock."

A kilometer and a half inside the rim they pierced the airlock's final force-field. Ahead lay a large landing area, at the edge of which stood a crowd of Kieshnar-rak-kat-tra—the station Trader and his retinue. Viewing the scene on their helmet displays the members of the expedition got their first look at their new clients. Perhaps forty cinnamon furred creatures were present, resplendent in silken sashes and jeweled belts.

Standing half a hand taller than those around him, the Trader was the largest Kieshnar-rak-kat-tra the Earthlings had seen, a somewhat portly example of his race. Indeed, compared with the traders who accompanied them, all of the locals had a distinctly well fed appearance.

"And don't they look particularly toothsome?" Bear asked innocently.

Shaking his head, the Captain briefed the landing party. "We need to make a show of force, which is why we've brought almost everyone to the station. When the rear ramp lowers Hitch and Jacobs will assume guard positions to either side. Then I want the Marines to come thundering down the ramp and form an honor guard next to the starboard side personnel ramp."

The Marines and crew were all in heavy space armor. The rest, including the Captain, wore standard armor. Jack continued. "The SEALs will disembark via the side personnel ramp, followed by myself, the three traders, and finally Dr. Ogawa and Corpsman White. Understood?"

"Aye aye, Sir!"

The shuttle rotated, landing with its starboard side to the crowd of natives. As it did, JT climbed into his armor and went aft to take his place next to Bear at the head of the Marines.

"Ready to go, brother Bear?"

"I was born ready, JT," Bear replied with a toothy grin. "It's hard to believe we are about to do this."

"As H. L. Mencken, the Sage of Baltimore, once said: 'Every normal man must be tempted at times to spit on his hands, hoist the black flag, and begin slitting throats.'"

"Now yer talking, brother," said Bear with a gleam in his eye.

The rear ramp lowered and the two crewmen, Hitch and Jacobs, descended to the deck. The Marines, led by Bear and JT, trotted down the ramp, around the side of the shuttle and formed up between it and the watching locals.

With an electric motor whine the side personnel ramp extended and lowered to the deck. Down it ran the three SEALS, followed by the Captain at a more dignified pace. Behind Jack, came the three traders, blinking and looking about nervously. Bringing up the rear came Betty White and Mizuki Ogawa, both holding their weapons across their chests, ready for instant use.

"Try to look fierce, Dr. Ogawa, we are all supposed to be warriors," Corpsman White said to her partner on suit-to-suit.

"I've always wanted to be a fighting astrophysicist," Mizuki answered with a shy grin, invisible inside her armored suit.

"Yeah. I guess I get to shoot 'em first and then patch 'em back up," the Navy medic chuckled.

Flanked by the SEALs and trailed by the three merchants, Jack strode to within five meters of the station Trader and stopped. Earlier Jack had noticed that Ooshnar-tar-rak-ra wore three gold rings in his left ear, while Poonta-ta-ka wore only one and lowly Feeshkar's ears were unadorned. The plump trader before him had no less than seven golden rings dangling from his left ear, evidently symbols of status or rank. Raising his right hand, palm outward like John Wayne greeting a tribe of Indians in an old Hollywood movie, he spoke.

"Greetings Trader, I understand you are interested in exchanging antimatter for some help with your neighbors."

The station Trader's large fluffy tail described a series of small circles in the air above his head as the merchant made a slight bow in the Captain's direction. "Welcome most fearsome of warrior captains, I do believe we have matters of trade to discuss..."

Cuyo, Argentina

The shuttle came in over the snow capped peaks of the Andes, dropping down into the Cuyo region of what was once Argentina. Cuyo is the name of the wine-producing, mountainous area of west-central Argentina. Historically it comprised the provinces of San Juan, San Luis and Mendoza. Mendoza, located in the eastern foothills of the Andes, has some of the highest altitude vineyards in the world with an average elevation of 600 to 1,100 meters above sea level.

Unlike the low flat pampas and littoral regions of Argentina, Cuyo was mostly untouched by the tsunami created by the alien bombardment. Ash and falling ejectamenta did wreak havoc on the area, however, and of the region's nearly three million inhabitants fewer than a quarter million survived. It was in a valley well outside of Mendoza city that the members of Occupy Moon Base were deposited.

"All right, this is your stop," the pilot announced from the flight deck. "All ashore."

Each of the convicts was dressed in a tan jumpsuit, made from significantly heavier material than the daily wear provided on the Moon base. Each was also shod in durable boots and given a knife, a canteen full of water and a small backpack containing a silver space blanket and a week's worth of ration bars.

It had been almost three weeks since the riot in the Atrium. Ludmilla was first and foremost a medical doctor and would not agree to the deportation until she was sure that those injured during the insurrection were healed enough to face nature unaided.

"You can't just dump us here," pleaded the woman named Silvia.

"You should have thought about that before you started chucking firebombs around the Atrium," replied one of the unsympathetic Marine guards. "Now move yer ass."

The convicts were lucky it was not raining outside—summer was the local rainy season and the messed up weather patterns had made this year wetter than most.

"At least tell us where we are," another convict pleaded.

"You are in the Argentinian wine country, a region known as the Cuyo," said the pilot, taking pity on the convicts. "It's a hilly, mountainous region in the foot hills of the Andes. Summer temperatures can reach 32°C, with overnight lows around 18°C, though it might get a bit cooler than that since the bombardment. I would suggest you try to make some friends among the surviving locals before winter, because the weather drops below freezing then."

"I'll give you some free advice," added the Marine, "don't try that 99% crap on the locals, they might just shoot you where you stand."

"I'm not leaving," cried the hysterical Silvia, echoed by several others. This prompted the flight engineer to alter the gradient of the deck gravity, in effect tilting the cargo deck until the whole of Occupy Moon Base slid out the rear and landed on Argentinian soil in an unkempt heap. The shuttle lifted off, its rear ramp closing as it rose into the gray leaden sky. A number of the former prisoners could be seen waiving their arms or on their knees pleading as the shuttle headed back into space.

Emergence, Gliese 581

An alter-space transit from Sol to Gliese 581 takes 22.69 days even though it is only 6.3 parsecs away. This is because of the relatively small mass of Gliese 581 itself, a diminutive M5 red dwarf only one third the Sun's mass. Taking a page from his former mentor's book, Billy Ray drilled his crew continually during the three week voyage.

Now I know why Jack used to drill our asses off, Captain Vincent mused, *It was to keep us out of trouble and from going crazy in alter-space.*

At the helm was Lt. JG Pauline Palmer, who had been a midshipman on Peggy Sue's last voyage. Though it was not his watch, Lt. Wim Vandersluys, the executive officer, was also on the bridge. In fact, anyone with a semi-plausible reason to be on the bridge was wedged in somewhere. Given the spectacular view through the ship's transparent nose, the capacity crowd was understandable.

I remember the first time I saw an emergence, normal space suddenly reappearing with the ship in a new star system. Of course, the first time we weren't sure we would emerge anywhere. Billy Ray smiled to himself. *Well, let them enjoy it—hopefully they'll live to tell their grand kids about it.*

"How are we looking, XO?" he asked Vandersluys, formerly a lieutenant in the Dutch navy.

"We are at action stations and rigged for emergence, Sir."

"Very good." Noticing Chief Zackly out of the corner of his eye, Billy Ray addressed the old salt. "And how's the crew doing, Chief?"

"A bunch of snot nosed excuses for real sailors, but they'll do, Captain, they'll do." From the grizzled old chief that was high praise.

"Ten seconds to emergence, Captain," Pauline called from the helm.

The bridge crew waited the last few seconds in silence and then, with the slightest of shudders the Peggy Sue reentered 3-space.

"Viewports transparent. I want a full sensor report Mr. Tanaka," Billy Ray ordered his navigator. "Locate Gliese 581d and lay in a course to match orbits with it."

The crew jumped to obey.

In all, a pretty good crew. I could have done worse for my first real command. Of course, we ain't done anything but fall through alter-space so far. A call from the Ambassador interrupted his thoughts.

"We have emerged from the lesser dimensions without incident; With your permission, Captain, we would contact our Conclave on the planet ahead; Our preparations with JeanJaquesDebelcour have gone well and we feel confident that our negotiations will yield a positive result."

"Yes, Ambassador, the trip so far has been uneventful as expected; Please make contact with your home planet using the computer's facilities; I'm glad that Jean-Jacques has been of assistance."

Jean-Jacques was on the mission by happenstance. Had Billy Ray not taken Beth to the Frenchman's restaurant for dinner the night before departure the former UN diplomat would not have learned of the mission until after the Peggy Sue sailed. As things transpired, De Belcour overheard Billy Ray explaining to Beth that he had been handed a secret mission, which was about to take him away for the better part of two months.

Once Jean-Jacques learned of the mission he would not be denied. He implored Billy Ray to take him along, proclaiming that he must repay his debts and redeem his honor. Billy Ray kicked the decision upstairs, telling the insistent former diplomat that he would have to clear his participation with Col. Tropsha. The new Captain hoped that Jean-Jacques would balk at facing the formidable Russian woman he had so antagonized in the past, but the Frenchman was made of sterner stuff.

To Billy Ray's surprise, Jean-Jacques presented himself at the foot of the gangway the next morning with permission granted by Col. Tropsha and endorsed by Captain Curtis.

"If that frog bastard gives you any trouble, Captain, you just give the word and I'll march his garlic eatin' ass out an airlock," the

Chief offered, unconsciously rubbing the shoulder where he had been shot during the incident in Vienna. But De Belcour caused no problems on the voyage out, spending most of his time in consultations with the Triad Ambassador. Billy Ray suspected that the Chief was slightly disappointed.

"We have received a message of welcome from the Triads, Captain," the ship's computer announced. "They congratulate us on our species' continued existence and for bringing NatHanGon back unharmed."

"Send them an appropriately diplomatic reply and let the Ambassador get on with it," Billy Ray responded. *Damn sarcastic plants, just because their species is four or five billion years older than us humans.*

"The Ambassador is exchanging information as we speak, Captain. For a biological entity, their bandwidth is most impressive."

CO's Office, Farside Base

Since Melissa's departure, Clem and Lem had been spending their time making minor changes to the fly farm. With their boss gone they were wondering what they should work on next. Then they got a summons from Col. Tropsha's office.

"I hope we don't get put back on vent cleaning duty," Clem said as they entered the outer office.

"Me either, buddy," answered Lem, "maybe the CO will ship us off to Mars like Melissa hinted before she left."

The door to Ludmilla's office slid aside and the commanding officer's voice called from within, "Gentlemen, please come in and take a seat."

There were two other people present in the office that the pair of engineers did not know, at least not personally. Both were familiar to anyone on the Moon base.

"Clement Mathews, Lemuel Souther, meet TK Parker and our Chief Engineer, Cdr. Jo Jo Medina."

264

The men shook hands all around while mumbling meaningless pleasantries. Ludmilla waited impatiently as the ritual of male greeting was observed.

"Please, everyone have a seat."

As TK's wheelchair lowered itself back to four-wheel mode Lem could not help but crane his neck to get a better look at the mechanism. This caused TK to chuckle.

"She's a beauty, ain't she," the old oilman said.

Lem blushed, embarrassed being caught staring at the man's wheelchair. "Uh, yes sir, Mr. Parker. That's quite a piece of equipment."

"Call me TK, son. Yeah I had this little number built special out of a couple of old iBOTs a few years back. Had her hopped up a bit too, but I don't get much chance to race around up here."

"I keep offering to build him a floating, gravitonic driven one for use here on the Moon," threw in Jo Jo with a crooked smile.

"Including the stand-up mechanism? That would be an interesting problem, keeping it stable during the transition," added Clem, drawn into the discussion.

Ludmilla harrumphed and rolled her eyes. "Well, if there was any question that you two are engineers this answers it. Now if you all do not mind I would like to get down to business."

"Aw Ludmilla," TK said with a Texas twang, "if we were talkin' about transplanting a liver or bisectin' someone's bowel you'd have been right there with us."

"Yes, TK, you are right. Still, we need to get to the matters at hand."

"Yes, yes," he said, waiving one had in the air as a sign of surrender. "You see, boys, after the latest little alien incursion we've realized that Farside is defenseless, totally dependent on the Navy to keep the bad guys away from our door."

"We also realized that, while we are building new ships as fast as we can," added Jo Jo, "some parts of the process take longer than others. Specifically, nanite fusing the hull sections together once the engines and reactors are installed, followed by building out the interior spaces takes a lot longer than fabricating some of the other components."

"Like deflector shield generators, X-ray laser units, and railguns," TK interjected.

"Precisely," said Ludmilla. "So we are in the process of installing shields and laser batteries to protect the base."

"Since we only have to defend from one direction, we will have stronger shielding than a frigate and more than a dozen semi-autonomous X-ray units installed in the next couple of weeks," Jo Jo concluded.

"How can we help with that?" asked Clem, puzzled why they were being briefed by the top brass about this.

"Yeah, seems like you have everything well in hand," added Lem, "except you didn't mention any railguns."

"I told you they were perceptive," Ludmilla said to her two male companions.

"If they were dumber than two sacks of hammers you wouldn't have recommended 'em."

Clem and Lem looked at each other, thinking the same thing. *The CO really enjoys needling TK. Not mean spirited, more like a sister and an older brother.* Jo Jo picked up the slack in the conversation.

"You see, gentlemen, the railguns are different from the other equipment. The shield generators and laser batteries are simple to install—all they need is a stable mounting platform and power. Since the base is carved out of solid rock, and we now have four operational fusion reactors, neither requirement is a problem. The railguns are not so simple."

"I'd imagine they have quite a recoil," Lem commented.

"They kick like a damn mule," TK answered.

"On a warship we simply build the railguns into the ship's structure and let the mass of the vessel absorb the recoil."

"But that won't work on a shore emplacement," said Clem, thinking out loud. "You need to be able to aim them."

"Right again. In space we aim by simply pointing the whole ship at the target. We can't do that in this case." Jo Jo looked at the two former armor techs expectantly.

"And you're hoping that we can come up with a mounting system," Lem said.

Ludmilla smiled brightly. "See? Compared with the fly farm what are a few railgun emplacements?"

"Yes, Ma'am," the two friends said together.

Chapter 21

Ring Station

The final negotiations securing employment of Captain Jack's band of mercenaries were brief. As it turned out the Trader had no cache of antimatter himself, but he claimed to know were such a trove of starship fuel could be found.

"You see, Captain, the antimatter vault for this section of the station lies about 90 kilometers to spinward," the Trader, whose name was Threshnar-rak-ak-ran, confided. "Not coincidentally, there are a number of disagreeable creatures between here and there. Warlike primitives, mostly, who have simply moved in and occupied our rightful territory."

"Naturally, we will need to convince these squatters to seek other accommodations as we travel to the storage facility," Jack replied with a tight lipped smile. *Like I believe that story for a minute or that you are the rightful owner of the antimatter. No matter, there will be time to sort out who owns what when we actually find the antimatter.*

"You are indeed perceptive, Captain. We should proceed to the top level greenhouse area. From the surface you will be able to get the lay-of-the-land, so to speak."

"Lead on, Trader. We shall go reason with these unruly neighbors of yours."

* * * * *

The Captain's column wound its way up seemingly endless staircases to ascend the four vertical kilometers to the top level of the station. There they emerged onto a verdant plane, an area that might have been mistaken for the surface of a planet until its topology became evident. Looking north or south the shape of the world was not noticeable, but looking east or west—locally called spinward and antispinward, respectively—presented a sight both wondrous and disquieting.

The world curved upwards, a ribbon of green and brown and ocean blue climbing to heaven in either direction. Scattered clouds dappled the landscape as it disappeared into darkness, narrowed by

269

perspective while arching around the curvature of the gas giant. Just above the disk of the planet the local star shone, a fuzzy white smudge wreathed in streamers of dust.

"The day-night cycle here must be more complicated than we thought," JT commented. "The ring, and the planet's axis of rotation, are tilted 18-19 degrees with respect to the planet's orbital plane. As the planet orbits the star its tilt will cause the ring's exposure to change."

"That is true, JT," said Mizuki, getting astrophysical. "Twice a year the ring will be edge on to the star and be in permanent night. At other times the ring's interior will pass in and out of the sunlight due to its daily rotation, but the planet itself will eclipse the star when the angle is shallow."

"That would cause a dark period somewhere in the middle of the day," JT concurred. "Plus the length of the dark period would vary, depending on the axial orientation with respect to the star,"

"That's way too confusing," Bear rumbled. "Conditions in the Arctic are much more sensible."

"I don't intend for us to be here long enough for it to matter, Lt. Bear," Jack said, surveying the landscape in front of them. Most of the conversation among the Earthlings was done over their suit radios, making them appear huge mute monsters to the traders. Addressing the station Trader over his suit's external speakers the Captain asked, "Which way does our objective lie, Trader?"

"Across the fields to spinward. Disputed territory begins at the small river near the treeline, 15 kilometers away." The Trader made a foppish arm gesture in the general direction specified.

"All right. Chief Morgan, take the SEALs forward and scout the route. Lieutenants Bear and Taylor, have the Marines form two columns, one on either side of the native party. White and Ogawa, bring up the rear behind the hover sleds, I will take point. Let's move people."

In the center of the Earthlings' procession was the station Trader's party, consisting of an equal number of attendants and bodyguards. The bodyguards carried devices that were obviously weapons—long barrels with sights and sausage shaped extensions where a stock would be on a human rifle. Under the barrel was a lever with a handle on it, which several of the security detail were busy pumping away on.

"What do you thing they're doing?" asked PFC Samuels.

"I think those rifle things are airguns," replied Ronnie Reagan, who had a head for all things mechanical. "They're pumping up the pressure in their air reservoirs."

"Airguns?" exclaimed Sanchez. "You have got to be joking."

"Don't be so quick to dismiss air rifles, Joey," JT advised the Marine. The ex-green beret was a student of all forms of offbeat weaponry. "Air rifles were used against Napoleon's troops by the Austrians in the late 18th century and the Lewis & Clarke expedition carried one on their trip across America. A .46 caliber Giradoni with a twenty shot magazine. It was superior to any gunpowder weapon of the day—multi shot, no muzzle flash or cloud of smoke and not much report. Deadly out to more than 100 yards. Just be glad we are all wearing armor."

On the portside of the column Rosey spoke to Jon over suit-to-suit. "This is just too far out, like being in a video game. Have you ever thought you'd live to see something like this?"

"I don't know," he replied. "I got a bad feeling about this whole situation."

River Crossing, Ring Station

Night descended on the column as they reached the river and it was decided to make camp for the evening. The Kieshnar-rak-kat-tra quickly laid out bedrolls and began cooking over portable burners. The Earthlings reclined in their suits, dining on protein cubes and water offered up by tubes inside their helmets.

"This shit is worse than MREs," groused Sanchez. "Even the fuzzy weasels are getting something fresh cooked and hot."

"Feel free to join them, Joey," JT replied. "Of course, opening your suit may expose you to some bug that will kill you, if the furballs' stew doesn't poison you or eat a hole in your stomach."

"Since you put it that way, Lieutenant, protein cubes don't seem so bad."

"How does all this green stuff survive, with the days being so messed up and night sometimes lasting for weeks?" asked Brown, who always seemed to be bubbling over with questions.

"Plants are tougher than you think," answered JT. "My mom gave me a plant in a terrarium when I joined the Special Forces—a big glass bottle with dirt in the bottom. Then I got transferred across the country and had to have it shipped to my new post. The movers packed the terrarium in the bottom of a wardrobe box and sealed it with tape. All my stuff was in storage for three months and then got shipped to California in a moving van—no light at all during that time. When I unpacked my stuff the plant was alive and doing fine."

"That was one tough plant."

"There was a time, 35 million years ago, that Antarctica was covered with forest instead of ice," added LCpl Reagan. "It was still at the south pole so during summer it was in constant daylight, and in the winter it was night 24/7."

"You're pulling my leg, Ronnie," Brown replied.

"No, I swear it's true, you can look it up."

"Man, that would be something, bro," Sanchez added, thoughtfully chewing on a chunk of protein. "A forest that stayed dark for months at a time would be spookier than this place."

Overhead the gas planet loomed, striped in alternating bands of blue, purple and indigo. It reflected almost as much light as a full Moon back on Earth, but a full Moon did not dominate the sky like the Jovian giant.

"Maybe so, Joey," said LCpl Acuna. "I think this place is sort of pretty, romantic even."

"No place you gotta wear space armor to protect yourself from giant fuzzy weasels with airguns is romantic, Rosey," quipped LCpl Feldman.

* * * * *

272

At the far side of the encampment, Hitch and Jacobs had grounded the two hover sleds forming a barrier covering the party's rear. The sleds held spare food, water, ammo and energy packs for the suits, along with pieces of equipment the Captain thought might prove useful. Between them, they should be able to haul a dozen or more antimatter eggs on the return trip.

Betty and Mizuki were talking with the two sailors when one of the orbiting recon drones sent a movement warning.

"What's that?" asked Betty.

"Probably nothing," replied Steve Hitch. "Just wind rustling the underbrush."

"There's another alert," said Matt Jacobs, "and my proximity alarm just sounded." All four humans scrambled to their feet just in time to see a wave of creatures, brandishing axes and swords, about to reach the sled barrier.

In the pale light the attackers moved like white ghosts. The enemy were large eight limbed creatures, their fleshy man sized bodies segmented like insect larvae. Their tapering heads held two small eyes above sizable blunt mandibles. Running on two pair of spindly legs, they gripped edged weapons with the remaining four. Matt and Stevie, veterans of previous battles with aliens, raised their weapons and opened fire without hesitation. Betty raised the alarm over the comm.

"Attack! Attack! The camp is under attack from the rear!"

The sailors moved to the sides to prevent their position from being flanked, while Betty fell back to protect the traders, just starting to rise from their beds. Three of the menacing aliens clambered over the loaded sleds and advanced with scimitar like swords held high.

Both sailors and Corpsman White had been trained in the use of firearms and reflexively brought their weapons to bear on their attackers. Mizuki, however, was much more at home with another weapon—the katana strapped to her back. Pulling it from its sheath in a single continuous motion she struck an overhead blow that cleaved the nearest of her attackers in half diagonally.

Smoothly following through she took a sliding step to the left, maintaining her center of balance as Yuki had taught her. A foot stamp, *kiai* shout and a diagonal blow to the left yielded another bisected opponent. Repeated once more to the right and all three of the sword wielding attackers lay on the ground, their bodies spilling pale blue and pink viscera into the dirt.

"Damn, girl!" shouted Betty, moving up beside her but staying carefully out of sword stroke range. "You've driven 'em back over the sleds. Time to put your sword up and get out your railgun."

"*Hai*." Mizuki gave her blade a ritual cleaning flick and then wiped the katana down with a cloth she carried just for that purpose. Returning her sword to its sheath she raised her railgun from its carry position and joined her companions in firing on the pulpy white attackers.

If the Earthlings had been watching the attackers' charge closely, they would have noticed that the stampeding aliens flushed a swarm of butterflies from the field in front of them. The flock of tiny fluttering creatures tumbled through the air and hovered above the humans. Behind the defenders, individual butterflies descended to the bodies of those slain by Mizuki, alighting on the spilled remains for a few second and then rising back into the night sky on erratic paths.

* * * * *

The camp also fell under attack on the river side. An even larger force of the eight-limbed creatures swarmed from the treeline on the far bank, bounding through the shallow water to attack the Earthlings. Unfortunately for the attackers, the Marines on the riverbank also received alerts from the drones overhead. The six Marines, three SEALs and three officers stood ready to receive the aliens' charge.

Green tracers lit up the night as a torrent of flechette fire scythed through the massed white bodies of the attackers. Bear turned on his suit's external speakers and roared in challenge. Towering over his companions, the four meter tall armored polar bear raised his 15mm railgun cannon and sent hundreds of explosive rounds into the stand of trees that had concealed the aliens' advance. The flashes from the exploding shells rippled through the vegetation, lighting the woodland with a deadly festive glow.

274

"If this is the best they got around here, this place won't be nearly as much fun as the last station," Bear complained, holstering his weapon.

JT was less superstitious than most soldiers, but Bear's complaining made him nervous. "Brother Bear, you keep asking for it and we're apt to get some real trouble one day."

"This traveling circus has just gotten started, Lt. Bear. Look upon this as the opening act," Jack said. Observing that their front was in no danger, the Captain called to those in the rear.

"Hitch, Jacobs, what's happening back there?"

"We're good, Sir. The attackers have all gone, those that could still run. Three of 'em got inside the perimeter but Dr. Ogawa took care of them," came Hitch's reply.

Dr. Ogawa took care of them? I'll have get clarification on that when this is over. "Interrogative the status of our furry charges?"

"They are all huddled together in the center of the camp, Captain. The ones carrying those air-rifle things sort of formed a perimeter around the station Trader and his lackeys. Looks like they booted our three traders out to fend for themselves. Right now they are hiding behind the sleds near Doc White."

"Hm, looks like there is no honor, or compassion, among weasels. Any casualties?"

"None, Sir. The attackers didn't get through us to the traders."

"Roger, hold your positions. I think I need to have a word with our fuzzy partners."

Valley of the Guardians, Gliese 581d

Arriving at the Triads' planet the Peggy Sue did something that none of the new frigates could—she landed on the surface of the planet. Designed as a combination exploration vessel and private yacht, her sleek shape was designed for passage through planetary atmospheres. Following instructions from the authorities below, the starship floated down through Gliese 581d's thick atmosphere to a valley between low mountain ridges.

275

The valley was the home of the Conclave of Guardians, a gathering of Triads charged with defending their world against outsiders. The Peggy Sue was there to pick up a contingent of Guardians and transport them back to the embattled Earth. Captain Vincent had decided that landing on the surface was easier than ferrying a dozen eight foot tall, triple barreled cacti to the ship using the shuttles.

"Take her down gently, Lt. Palmer. Land her across that flat area ahead with the wind on the port beam." Billy Ray had to consciously keep his hands from reaching for the controls on the arms of the commander's chair.

"Aye aye, Captain."

Like all of the land in the gravitationally locked planet's habitable band, there was a constant gale blowing up the valley from the direction of the sunset. A huge, perpetual storm system churned over the planet's sunward ocean, sending squall lines outward in all directions. Landing crosswise, the ship's bulk would shelter those in its lee.

The wind might be blowing 30 knots or more but Peggy Sue's 8,000 ton bulk remained rock steady as Pauline sat the ship down on its six retractable landing legs. The ship settled slightly and then the helmsman announced: "The ship is landed, Captain."

"Excellent, Lieutenant, well done." Activating a comm channel, Billy Ray spoke to the landing party. "Cargo Hold, Bridge."

"Roger, Bridge. Go ahead Captain."

"Chief, you can equalize pressure and open the starboard cargo door. We are going to need a temporary ramp installed from the threshold to the ground for the Triads to board."

"Aye aye, Sir. The work party is suited up and ready to go. Give us a couple of hours and we'll be ready for 'em."

"Then have the men assist Dr. Scott Hamilton in preparing the hold to support the Triads. She'll be joining you outside to identify which plants and ground cover should be loaded."

"Aye, Captain." Chief Zackly was not thrilled to be turning the ship's cargo hold into a giant terrarium, but orders were orders. "All right, yous deck apes, you heard the Captain. Turn to! And remember that the local gravity is forty percent higher than back home—you break a leg and I'll kick yer ass."

* * * * *

Two watches later the Captain and Jean-Jacques de Belcour were standing at the large eye-shaped observation port in the ship's main lounge. Beyond the window was a stately—which is to say slow —procession of Triads, heading for the ramp to the ship's hold. Moving on their tangled motile roots, they advanced at what could only charitably be called a slow walking pace.

"They won't let us move them on board using hover sleds?"

"I am afraid not, Captain. The Ambassador indicated that it would be an affront to their dignity to be carried aboard."

"And I understand that this collection of Triads is going to aid us in the defense of Earth?"

"So I have been informed."

"So tell me, Jean-Jacques. What did you say that convinced them to offer us assistance? I would've bet getting any help was a long shot."

"The Ambassador first provided them with a quite detailed report on everything they observed during their sojourn to Earth. When they were done the Conclave allowed me a few words."

Billy Ray took a sip from the cooling mug of coffee he held and raised his eyebrows questioningly. Jean-Jacques offered a faint smile and clasped his hands behind his back. Staring out the observation port he continued.

"I told them that, as a young race, we would not think of comparing our wisdom with theirs, but that I wished to relate a story. I told them of how an idealistic young human once thought many things to be true, all for the most noble of reasons. This young man pursued a career in service of these ideals, never once questioning that they might be erroneous. Never thinking that what he thought were good deeds were, in fact, harmful to others. Then one day, events transpired that shook his beliefs to the core—all the truths he held sacred crumbled and blew away like dust in the wind."

277

The Frenchman paused, causing the Captain to prompt him to continue. "And this story convinced the Triads to send a bunch of their Guardians back to Earth with us? Surely there was more to it than that."

"Oh yes indeed, *mon Capitaine*. I humbly suggested that changing one's mind, admitting that perhaps one's previous beliefs were not correct was not an admission of weakness, but a sign of wisdom. I told them that our species was often wrong, and had made many mistakes in the past, but we strove to do better in the future. That is why we place such faith in the power of redemption —the belief that even a man's worst sins can be forgiven if he repents and honestly tries to do better."

"That was it?"

"No, I said one last thing—a statement attributed to the Irish statesman Edmund Burke: 'When bad men combine, the good must associate; else they will fall one by one, an unpitied sacrifice in a contemptible struggle.'"

"Ah, how appropriate, Monsieur," the Captain said, nodding. "Or as Benjamin Franklin phrased it: 'We must, indeed, all hang together, or most assuredly we shall all hang separately.'"

"Precisely, Captain."

"You know Jean-Jacques, there appears to be some use for diplomacy after all."

The Frenchman looked at the Captain, inclined his head in a slight node and smiled. Both men returned their gaze to the procession of alien plants outside the viewport, happy to stand silently in each other's company.

Railgun Test Emplacement, Farside

The long barrel of a corvette class railgun hung down into the cone shaped chamber. Suspended from its muzzle, the 32 meter long weapon was free to swing within the chamber, like the clapper in a gigantic bell carved out of stone. Suddenly the barrel pivoted on its axis and then swung twenty degrees from vertical.

"OK, Clem. Fire a three round burst."

278

The gravatonically driven cannon cycled three times in quick succession. On the third shot it broke free from its mounting and fell the short distance to the bottom of the chamber.

"Well crap," said Lem.

"The mount is just not strong enough for continuous fire, Lem."

"Ya think?"

As the two armorers stood looking at the now dismounted railgun a hover sled approached their viewing platform from the right. All of the railgun emplacements were joined by a perimeter tunnel that was kept under vacuum, just like the gun chambers themselves. It was decided that making the gun mounts air tight was a complication they did not need, since they were having a hard enough time making the guns fire more than a few times between failures.

Driving the hover sled was a large Marine with an insignia stenciled on his armor's left shoulder. Displaying three chevrons over two curved rockers it was the rank insignia of an E-7, or gunnery sergeant. There were two other Marines in the back of the sled.

Turning to face the newcomers Clem called out to the driver. "What can we do for you, Sergeant?"

"Just came by to make a delivery," the Marine replied. "I got two containers each holding thirty 10kg railgun projectiles. I'm to give 'em to either Clement Mathews or Lemuel Souther."

"You found both of us, Sergeant...?" Lem prompted.

"Washington, Gunnery Sergeant Lawrence T. Washington," the big man smiled, "but you can just call me Gunny."

"Hey, I know you. You were on the big alien hunt."

"I surely was. It's the story of life in the Corps—one day you are locked in a desperate battle with vicious space aliens, the next you're making delivery runs to the Army."

"Ex-Army," Lem corrected.

"Hey, that's OK, nobody's perfect. Heck, my best friend used to be a snake eater."

"Marines and Special Forces have a lot in common, like being crazy. Clem and I were smart enough to stick to artillery, where the enemy is kept at a sensible distance."

"And that there is supposed to be the base's new artillery?"

"Yeah, except right now it's busted artillery. We still need to work the bugs out of the mounting system." Clem leaned forward and let the Gunny scan his left iris through his suit's clear helmet, signing for the ammunition.

"All right, Grissom, Bradley, get that ammo unloaded," GySgt Washington yelled at his two companions. Then he turned back to the engineers—gunnery sergeants do not offload vehicles. "I haven't seen many cannons that fired straight up through the roof. It's a big sucker though."

"Yeah, we call her Big Bertha," Lem replied. "We expect that anyone attacking the base will probably come in from above. This is more like an anti-aircraft installation than a howitzer or tank's main gun."

"Which is why it's being such a pain in the ass to get working," his partner added.

"We figured we would let most of the barrel hang down from the mount, both to conceal it and protect it from enemy fire. Instead of traversing the tube we rotate the whole weapon, changing the orientation of the trunnion that supports the slide. Then we can change elevation by as much as twenty degrees off vertical by pivoting the assembly on the trunnion."

"We can't hit things close to the surface, but with six of these surrounding the base we'll get a field of fire that should cover any attacking spaceships overhead," Clem concluded. "At least that's the theory."

"I hope you get it figured out," Washington confided, "because according to the scuttlebutt, the brass is expecting an alien attack sooner rather than later. And not just a recon patrol trying to blow through like the last time."

"Trust me, Gunny, we are motivated."

"Where do you want this stuff, Gunny?" interrupted one of the Marines. They were standing beside the sled, each holding a 400 plus kilo crate of projectiles. The Gunny looked at the engineers and raised his eyebrows in question.

"Just set them over by the wall, out of the way," answered Clem. "We gotta fix the damn thing before we reload it."

The Marines deposited the crates in the indicated location and climbed back onto the hover sled. Seeing that all was in order, the Gunny remounted his vehicle and bade the artillery men good day. "See you later, gentlemen, and good luck with your toy."

Clem and Lem waved as the Gunny's sled disappeared down the tunnel, headed back to base.

"You know, Clem, I got a better idea about how to build an aimable slug thrower. A few years ago, some folks were trying to build a hyper-velocity mass accelerator based on a type of particle accelerator called a cyclotron. They wanted to launch stuff into orbit with it, so the acceleration would have been about the same as Big Bertha in there. I think they called it a slingatron.

"It was pretty compact because the path used to accelerate the launch payload was wrapped around in a spiral. From the drawings I saw it would probably fit on a large telescope mount. You could elevate and traverse it all you want."

"So put a suggestion in the HQ suggestion box. Right now we need to get what we have working."

"That's why we're such a good team, Clem. I'm the visionary with big ideas and you're the down-to-Earth guy that makes sure stuff gets done."

"Lem, I ain't been down-to-Earth since they pulled us out of that field in Kansas. Now let's go see what broke this time."

Chapter 22

Ring Station Expedition, Day 11

Bear roared as he knocked the leaping raptor from the air, his suit claws leaving deep lacerations in the creature's thigh. Another came at him from his right, which he clotheslined with his cannon. The 100 kilogram cross between a velociraptor and an angry rooster back-flipped through the air and landed in a heap at the Captain's feet.

Casually glancing down, Jack put a three flechette burst into the alien's chest. "Don't just knock them down, kill the damn things Mr. Bear."

Bear looked at the Captain and grinned. The big carnivore was definitely enjoying himself.

To Bear's right, Sanchez took a plasma bolt on his suit's shields, temporarily surrounding the Marine with a glowing nimbus of orange fire. He pivoted and shot his assailant as it leaped toward him. Another landed on his back while he was so occupied.

Bear swatted the raptor off of Joey's back, commenting, "You heard the Captain. Stop playing with these things and kill them, Sanchez."

"I'm trying, LT," Joey yelled, turning back to their front and loosing a long burst of flechettes. "They keep hopping up into the air when I shoot at them."

"So shoot them in the air," Bear growled, hitting one of the aforementioned leaping feathered dinosaurs with a single shot from his 15mm cannon. The explosive shell turned the raptor into bloody spatter and pink mist.

The march to find the antimatter repository had covered many types of terrain, and the Earth mercenaries met several new forms of adversary along the way. Leaving the wooded territory of the white insects they passed into a grassy coastal region where they were attacked by ground dwelling cephalopods with ten tentacles and fearsome beaks. They grappled with the Earthlings at close quarters, requiring the use of claws, machetes and sword.

283

As they walked along the dunes next to a shallow sea they were assaulted by club wielding amphibians with six limbs. Driven off by railgun fire, they retreated into the water where a volley of explosive rounds set on time delay had the same effect as a stick of dynamite dropped in a fishing hole. The expedition headed inland leaving a bay full of floating bodies behind it.

Each set of opponents was formidable, but the bipedal, feathered carnivores, with their long tails and enlarged sickle-shaped claws on each hindfoot, were by far the worst. They would have been dangerous enough given just their claws and teeth, but the darting, feathered host was also armed with weapons—a form of plasma gun carried by most with their two short forelegs.

On the left flank, Rosey Acuna and Ronnie Reagan were calmly blasting leaping raptors out of the air using 20mm shotgun rounds, with Kevin Brown hosing down any trying a more land-bound approach. Another attacker leaped toward the Marines, clawed legs and ruffled neck extended.

"Mine!" called Rosey, catching it square in the chest.

Two more simultaneously tried a high/low attack from the right. Ronnie took them both out in quick succession.

"You are supposed to call your shots," complained Rosey.

"Sorry," Reagan grinned back at her.

"You two are crazy," complained PFC Brown, kneeling between them. "This ain't no duck hunt."

"Just 'cause the ducks here have claws and teeth doesn't make it any less fun," Rosey replied, blasting another bounding reptile. "Shit, two are making an end run!"

To Rosey's left two raptors raced by, running low with their necks out parallel to the ground. They were headed for the inner circle formed by the Trader's bodyguards. As Acuna and Brown pivoted, trying to get a shot at the fast moving creatures, the fuzzy weasels opened fire with their air rifles. The lead raptor stumbled and fell, obviously hit, while the second pulled up short and fired its weapon.

Simultaneous flechette bursts from the two Marines knocked the raptor off its feet, but not in time to throw off its aim. One of the bodyguards was hit, falling backward with his fur on fire, his chest reduced to a charred pit.

"Damn. Remind me not to get hit by one of those plasma things without armor," Brown said.

"Just be glad they don't have any really big plasma cannon, like they did on the Space Mushroom," yelled Reagan. "Look to the front! Here comes another wave!"

* * * * *

As usual, Hicks, Jacobs, Doc White and Mizuki were defending the column's rear. Hicks was standing on top of one of the sleds trying to spot attacking raptors.

"Man these things are fast," he exclaimed, loosing a burst at a target unseen by the others.

"Stevie, get your ass down from there before they draw a bead on you," yelled Jacobs. As Matt was yelling, Hicks was hit first by a plasma bolt and then by a flying raptor. This knocked him off the sled and into the makeshift redoubt containing the other humans.

Raptor and Marine sprawled on the ground. As the raptor tried to regain its footing, Doc White blew its head off with a shotgun round. This action momentarily distracted Mizuki and Matt.

A flock of red and orange butterflies swooped by in front of Mizuki, passing from left to right. Attention captured, her focus followed them around to see two more raptors bounding over the sled behind her. Unable to raise her railgun in time, one of the raptors landed claws first on her chest and the pair tumbled over backward.

Matt also caught the motion of the butterflies out of the corner of his eye. He instinctively stepped sideways, raised his weapon and fired. The second raptor took the burst in its chest and tumbled to the ground beside him.

Mizuki, significantly out massing her assailant, continued their backward tumble and threw the angry reptile off. It quickly regained its feet and lunged at the armor encased woman—just in time for Mizuki to slice its head neatly off with a single blow of her sword. The raptor downed by Jacobs struggled to regain its footing. The katana wielding astrophysicist turned the follow-through of her first strike into a second clean blow that removed that raptor's head as well. Above her, the flock of butterflies swirled in a festive rainbow display.

Hicks and White recovered their composure enough to send a hail of 5mm tracers down range. To this, Jacobs added a volley of time-on-target 20mm air-bursts, breaking the momentum of the raptors' attack. Betty looked up at the swirling cloud of tiny winged creatures above Mizuki, now turning more placidly in shades of green and blue.

"Girl, what is it with you and those butterfly things?"

"I don't know, Betty. Ever since the first battle they have been following me around. I think they just tried to warn me about the raptors jumping over the sled."

"Tried hell!" exclaimed Matt. "Did you notice how they flashed red and yellow as they swooped by? If I hadn't seen them, the killer chicken I shot would have landed square on my back."

"I think you have yourself a flying fan club, Mizuki," Betty said, eying the gayly orbiting swarm above the other woman's head. As she watched, the butterflies once again turned shades of red and yellow. Seconds later Stevie yelled, "Here they come again!"

* * * * *

The hilly country around the embattled expedition was littered with dead raptors. Two more of the Trader's retinue had been killed, a bodyguard disemboweled by a raptor's kick and one of the unarmed hangers on struck in the back by a plasma bolt.

The Captain was standing over the station Trader, his dark eyes boring into the merchant's melon like orange oculars. "I have about had enough of this game, Trader. We have come the distance you indicated and there seems to be an endless supply of new enemies to fight—each new batch more dangerous than the last."

"I, I told you there were a number of hostile tribes between us and our goal, Captain," the Kieshnar-rak-kat-tra said in a stuttering hiss. He never expected danger to come so close to his person.

"Yes, you called them primitives. I know of few tribes of primitives that use plasma blasters."

"I did say 'mostly', and I assure you, Captain, if I had known the raptors were that dangerous I would have warned you." Like most good liars the station Trader worked best under pressure. "Besides, our only losses were among my people, two guards and a grand nephew—I will have to explain his death to his mother and grandmother when we return."

"It has been 90 kilometers, as the surveillance drone flies. Where is the antimatter repository?" The Captain's tone carried an implied threat that his suit computer managed to convey to the Trader even in translation.

"It is only seven more kilometers away, just over that rise." The station Trader indicated a low, obviously artificial ridge about a kilometer away.

Jack looked at the ridge and back down at the Trader. Before he could speak the Trader headed for the feature in question, yelling over his shoulder: "Come, come! You'll see!"

The other Kieshnar-rak-kat-tra followed the Trader and the Earthlings followed them. Up the gently sloping terrain they trooped. As they reached the crest of the ridge its unnaturally flat top revealed itself as one edge of a square opening in the ground. An opening over 200 meters on a side, the mouth of a shaft extending down into the station's interior. Peering over the edge, Jack could see landings and staircases disappearing into the shadows. He glanced sideways at the Trader and said, "let me guess."

"Yes. We are now a kilometer closer to the prize you seek. It is just six more kilometers... straight down."

At the Bottom of the Well

The hike down the open well took more than four hours, with the Kieshnar-rak-kat-tra complaining amongst themselves the entire way. From his position behind the pack of furry traders, Jacobs noticed that Ooshnar-tar-rak-ra had sidled up to Threshnar-rak-ak-ran during the trip down. They separated just as the party arrived at the bottommost level.

The expedition members spread out along the side of the open square, sheltered by the overhanging landing above. The landing was part of an encircling balcony supported by widely spaced columns, though the column spacing was far too great and the columns themselves far too thin to look trustworthy to Earthly eyes.

In the open courtyard nothing moved, nor had they seen any sign of life during their descent. On the far side of the courtyard was a blank wall, and in that wall was a large, circular door that would have done a bank vault proud.

"I take it that's our destination," Bear said to the others.

"So it would seem," Jack replied, "how big do you make that door?"

"The hinge beside it looks about six meters tall, the door itself about four in diameter," JT answered. "I don't know how thick it is or what it's made of, but it must weigh as much as a main battle tank."

"If it's secured by a multi-bolt system like a bank vault, we are not carrying enough stuff to blast it open," added Chief Morgan, the head SEAL.

"Let's see if our employer has a less drastic solution to opening the door, Chief." Jack turned on his external speakers. "So, Trader, I take it that our goal lies beyond that sizable door."

"Just so, Captain," the station Trader answered, still winded from the arduous descent. "I am sure you are wondering how to gain access to the vault."

"That question had crossed my mind. Have you a suggestion?"

"Of course, Captain. I have given your partner, Ooshnar-tar-rak-ra, instructions for opening the door. I suggest we approach the entrance by moving around the perimeter of the courtyard—no sense tempting fate after coming this far, eh?"

"I am a cautious man myself," the Captain replied, then to his people more privately, "The head weasel suggests we sneak up on the place, making me think that there is danger afoot. Move around the perimeter to the right, Bear and Sanchez take point. And someone keep an eye on Ooshnar, evidently he has the combination."

The expedition edged cautiously around the edge of the open courtyard, keeping under cover of the overhanging balcony that bordered the open space on three sides. A number of dark passageways led off from the yard, attracting nervous attention from the Marines and SEALs. Eventually they were all stacked along the wall at the junction with the face of the vault.

"This looks like the moment of truth," Jack said. "Bring our pet traders and let's go knock on the door." Bear, Sanchez, Samuels and Feldman led off, followed by the Captain and the traders. White and Ogawa assumed weasel herding duties. JT hung back with the sleds and the other half of the force. All were mostly ignoring the station Trader and his entourage.

Quietly, the native traders slipped away down the nearest darkened hallway. Hitch, perched on his hover sled, noticed the exodus first. "Hey, Lieutenant! The locals are making a break for it!"

"What?" JT spun around and saw the last cinnamon furred shape disappear into the gloom. "Chief, you and the boys hunt them down."

"Aye aye, Sir," responded CPO Morgan. The three SEALs disappeared down the hallway in pursuit.

"Captain, our native bearers have flown the coop. I sent the SEALs after them."

"Roger that. The rest of you come to my position. We can use the sleds for cover and we may need some of the equipment they carry."

On suit-to-suit, Rosey said, "anybody else think we have just stepped in it?"

"Nothing I like better than an exposed position with my back against the wall," answered Ronnie, breaking into a jog. "In this case literally."

Pursuit and Betrayal

A little over a hundred meters into the passageway, the SEALs came to an intersection with side passages leading off in either direction. They had been using infrared trackers to follow the faint footprints of the fleeing natives.

"Damn it, the tracks go all three directions," said Phil Kowalski.

"Which way, Chief?" asked Bud Jones.

"These passageways could go on for ever," said the Chief. "We go back."

"I got movement," said Kowalski, crouching down, railgun at the ready, "left passageway."

"Is it one of the weasels?"

"No, heat signature is all wrong."

"Let's back out slowly."

Phil stepped back from the intersection a fraction of a second before a brilliant orange flash lit the hallway. All three SEALs flattened themselves against the walls.

"Plasma bolt," said Phil.

"Ya think?" said Bud.

"Bigger than the ones the killer chickens used," said the Chief. "It's time for the better part of valor."

As they started to move back toward the entrance a light appeared deeper within main passageway. It hurtled toward them like a demented freight train careening down a tunnel.

"Cover!" the Chief yelled. He and Phil pressed themselves against the right-hand side of the hallway, Bud sucked floor. The plasma bolt made a glancing strike on the left-hand wall, showering the SEALS with sparks and leaving a glowing red streak that slowly faded as it cooled.

All three returned fire, sending a torrent of green tracers down the hallway. Bud and Phil turned and shagged ass down the hallway, leaving the Chief firing extended bursts of 5mm in the direction of the enemy, with an occasional 20mm round thrown in for good measure.

"Peel left," called Phil, halting ten meters back.

The Chief turned and ran down the right side of the hall in a crouch while Phil provided suppressing fire. As he passed Phil, Bud called "peel right," from ten meters farther down the hall. Both the Chief and Phil ran down the left side of the hallway while Bud covered. They continued with the three man Australian Peel until they burst into the courtyard and flattened themselves against the wall on either side of the passageway entrance.

The Chief keyed his comm: "Captain, we got company."

* * * * *

Upon arriving in front of the cyclopean vault door, Ooshnar-tar-rak-ra retrieved a piece of paper from his belt pouch and unfolded it. While mumbling and staring at the squiggles inscribed on the sheet, the trader punched a series of symbols on a control panel next to the door. He finished entering symbols and looked up expectantly. A loud mechanical clank sounded and the door swung smoothly open.

"That thing has to be two meters thick," said JT. "I bet it weighs a hundred tons."

"In keeping with the scale of the station," Jack agreed. "Dr. Ogawa, fetch your equipment from the sleds."

"Yes, Captain." Mizuki went to the sled driven by Steve Hitch and began rummaging around in the cargo it carried. Then came the warning from Chief Morgan: "Captain, we got company."

The Captain and half the squad turned to see the SEALs flattened against the side wall. Before anyone could speak two orange plasma bolts flew from the passageway the SEALs had just emerged from. The SEALs were immediately in motion, headed for the knot of expedition members clustered around the still opening vault door. As the Chief passed in front of the passageway he threw something the size of a grapefruit into the opening.

"Those plasma bolts were much more powerful than the ones the raptors used," commented JT as he scanned the surrounding balconies for movement. From the passageway came the muffled whomp of an explosion followed by the ejection of a fast moving object.

"I think we got spiders," said Joey Sanchez. He, along with half the members of the expedition, had participated in the battle on the Space Mushroom. There they had been accosted by several forms of cybernetic creatures, the spiders being the most common.

"What makes you say that, Sanchez," asked Bear, also scanning overhead for threats.

"That, LT," Sanchez replied, pointing to the dented silver ball that skidded past in front of their position, shedding spindly legs as it began to bounce and roll.

Movement erupted everywhere—silver spheres, twice the size of basket balls, streamed from hallways around the courtyard and lined the balconies above. Each was suspended from six slender multi-jointed legs that emerged from the tops of their bodies. From the bottom of each sphere hung a weapon—a plasma blaster. From courtyard and balcony the alien host opened fire.

"Spiders! Return fire," yelled Jack as angry orange plasma bolts splattered the deck and the wall behind the Earthlings. "White, Ogawa, get inside the vault and find those AM eggs."

"Where did the damn spiders come from?" asked Joey, firing into the mass of bobbing spherical bodies.

"They were on the Moon and the Space Mushroom, why not here?" yelled Jon.

"That was 1,500 light-years away, Jon."

"Who knows? Maybe you can just order them from DarkLord.com," replied Ronnie. "Shut up and kill the damn things."

Bear roared and swept the perimeter of the courtyard with a stream of 15mm explosive rounds, temporarily neutralizing the ground-level threat. The Marines directed their fire upwards, spraying the balconies with flechettes at maximum muzzle velocity. As the SEALs joined the knot of defenders in front of the vault, Feeshkar made a break for the sidewall exit. Bud spun and raised his railgun, but the fleeing weasel was struck by several plasma bolts before the SEAL could shoot. Having no armor, most of Feeshkar's body was vaporized and the rest reduced to charred chunks.

As Betty was distracted by Feeshkar's fatal desertion, Ooshnar-tar-rak-ra and Poonta-ta-ka ran the other way, scurrying over the door's armored threshold and into the vault.

"Come on Mizuki!" Betty called, running after the trader. Mizuki, her arms loaded with antimatter detection gear, turned her back to the enemy and ran toward the open vault. Ahead of her, the flock of butterflies, showing nothing but bright scarlet, streamed through the opening.

Along the edges of the surrounding balconies hostile spiders began jumping off and floating to the courtyard floor. The Marines and SEALs picked them off almost as fast as they jumped, but the spiders were jumping to make room for a larger threat. Much bigger creatures appeared and began firing cannon sized plasma weapons at the defenders.

"Screw the spiders," yelled Sanchez, "we got crabs!" The larger creatures, dubbed crabs, also had six legs and a plasma weapon underneath, but they were the size of a small tank and almost as hard to kill.

A bolt from a crab struck one of the sleds sending burning chunks of equipment and a spray of molten metal flying. The SEALs dove for cover, their lighter armor incapable of deflecting the more powerful blasts from the bigger aliens. Several more cannon blasts struck the wall above the defenders, sending showers of sparks raining down. A cannon bolt missed the Captain by less than a meter. A short strangled cry came over the comm.

Jack turned and saw Mizuki laying face down in the vault's doorway. The bolt that had just missed him had struck her from behind. Her suit was scorched and worse, both her legs were missing from the knees down.

Shit! Light armor is not good enough in this environment. "Chief, you and the SEALs get Dr. Ogawa into the vault and take cover inside."

"Aye aye, Captain. Bud, Phil, grab Mizuki and move, now!"

Each grabbed an arm and together they pulled the astrophysicist's inert form into the vault. Chief Morgan bounded through the opening as crabs began to leap onto the courtyard floor.

293

Inside the Vault

The SEALs dragged Mizuki's body away from the open door and rolled her onto her back. Her face was wide-eyed, mouth open in a wordless scream of pain. As they watched, her suit's auto-doc flooded her system with painkillers. Her face went slack and her eyelids slowly closed. At the same time, nanites in her suit sealed off the stumps of her legs and restored its atmospheric integrity. The cloud of butterflies pulsated above her supine body, alternating between blood red and deep indigo.

"Doc, we got a casualty!" yelled Chief Morgan, turning around to look for Corpsman White. What he saw was Betty standing with her weapon raised, trying to get a shot at Ooshnar-tar-rak-ra, who was cowering behind a freestanding console ten meters away.

"We got a problem here Chief," Betty said, not taking her eyes off the trader. "The little shit is trying to close the door and lock the others outside."

"Don't fire at me or you will set off the antimatter!" the trader blustered, making a move for the controls. "Let me close the door or we will all die!"

"What's he babbling about?"

Betty sent a three shot burst in the trader's direction, causing the treacherous weasel to pull back from the controls.

"Look around, Chief."

Glancing around the huge vault, the Chief could see rack upon rack of large AM containers.

"There must be hundreds of eggs in here!"

"Yeah. I don't think flechettes will penetrate them, at least not on the lowest velocity setting, but I'm afraid to just hose down the control console."

Before Chief Morgan could answer, the flock of butterflies rushed the console, surrounding the traitorous trader. Ooshnar swatted ineffectually at the swarming winged creatures, but his flailing could not prevent them from alighting on his person. His yells of aggravation changed to shrieks of pain as flashing sparks and the crackle of electric discharges engulfed his struggling form.

The trader fell from sight behind the console, leaving a few wisps of smoke rising above it. The swarm rose above the smoldering alien in a helical column, flashed to black and streamed back to orbit above the fallen Mizuki. Betty and the Chief looked at each other and then cautiously advanced on the control station.

"It looks like Mizuki's fan club fried his double crossing ass," Betty remarked with some satisfaction.

"Yeah, and I thought they were just defenseless butterflies." Chief Morgan flipped the trader's body over using the toe of his boot. A piece of folded paper fell from the dead alien's grasp. "Look, it's the instruction sheet."

* * * * *

Outside the vault the enemy assault intensified. The second sled was blasted by crab bolts, which threw Brown and Feldman back against the open vault door. They had been using the sled for cover. The Captain was standing behind JT and Sanchez, using their heavier suits to shield his light armor. Several of the Marines had taken spider hits on their armor but none had been struck by the more deadly crab bolts.

"Lt. Bear, we need to withdraw to the inside of the vault. Provide covering fire. Lt. Taylor, get the Marines inside."

"After you, Captain," JT said on suit-to-suit.

"You have your orders, Mr. Taylor," was Jack's terse reply.

JT wanted to argue with him but had been a solider too long to do so. "Let's go Marines, into the vault, move it." One by one, firing at the enemy as they retreated, the Marines escaped to safety through the open vault door. Then it was Jack's turn.

"Follow right behind me, Bear," the Captain said as he turned and jumped through the portal. Bear answered with a low growl and backed in behind him, all the while spraying the courtyard full of cyborg attackers with 15mm shells.

At the control console, Betty had the bright idea of asking M'tak for help translating the instructions. The ship's AI quickly scanned the alien scribbling using Betty's suit video and responded almost instantly.

"The five characters on the lower left-hand side are the door closing code. Press the matching symbols on the control panel in sequence, reading from right to left and the vault should close."

"Great! Thanks M'tak. Captain, we can shut the door once everyone's inside."

"Good," Jack replied, taking a position just inside the door. Bear was still backing into the vault, still returning fire when the doorway was engulfed in a hellish orange glow. Bear roared and flew backward into the vault, smoke rising from his left side where the refractory armor was still glowing cherry red. It took a second to register, but Jack noticed that smoke was also rising from Bear's right shoulder, where his right foreleg used to be. The impact of multiple plasma bolts had caused his suit's shielding to fail.

Bear! Jack almost ran to his friend's side. A bolt from a crab cannon had struck Bear's unshielded right arm and railgun straight on, vaporizing both weapon and arm almost to the shoulder. Bear's auto-doc tranquilized the wounded ursine, freeing him from pain and preventing him from doing further damage to himself. Quickly recovering from the sight Bear's terrible wound Jack silently cursed. *The cost of this damned mission is becoming unacceptably high.*

"Corpsman White, on my signal close the vault door." Jack pulled a tube from his suit's backpack, a meter long and twelve centimeters in diameter. "Close it now!"

Betty pressed the five symbols in sequence and the door began swinging shut. Jack balanced the tube on his right shoulder and stepped in front of the closing door. Something shot from the tube and the Captain quickly stepped back behind cover.

The door was almost closed when a blinding white light flared around its edges. The vault door snapped shut and a massive tremor shook the room. Expedition members were thrown violently into the air, several bouncing off of the ceiling.

The vault went pitch black.

Chapter 23

Farside Defense Perimeter

"Farside Control, Base Defense. We are about to commence a live fire exercise in the space above the base," called Clem. Next to him, Lem held a tablet interfaced with the fire-control computer that directed all of the railgun emplacements ringing the base.

"Roger, Base Defense, the space above Farside is free of traffic at this time. You are clear to proceed."

"Affirmative, Farside Control, we are going hot." Clem spoke to Lem on suit-to-suit. "Let's do it, buddy."

"Right, I've got it set to lay down an interweaving pattern 1,000 klicks out. Each tube will fire four rounds for a total of twenty four."

With a gloved finger, Lem tapped on the tablet. Immediately the railgun in the enclosure in front of them spun and tilted. The barrel recoiled four times, jumping about a meter each shot before returning to battery. The salvo complete, the gun returned to its initial vertical position.

"Hot damn! Looks like they all fired successfully." Lem was staring down at the tablet's display which showed the status of all six railguns in the system.

"Finally," exclaimed Clem. "I was starting to doubt these things would ever work. It was adding the short recoil mechanism that did it."

"Yep, took enough of the kick out of firing to keep the mounts from breaking under the stress. Let's fire another salvo."

"You are like a kid with a new toy," Clem said to his friend, though he too was wearing a big grin. "Just make sure you aim all the projectile trajectories toward the Sun."

"Why? The slugs are just going to wiz off into space?"

"They have a muzzle velocity of over 17km/sec. You shoot in the wrong direction and one day, in a hundred thousand years or so, some poor creature on an alien world could have a very bad day."

"I thought that the escape velocity at Earth's distance from the Sun was around 41km/sec?"

"Yes, but Earth, and the Moon, are orbiting around the Sun with a velocity close to 30km/sec. Fire in the same direction Earth travels in orbit and the slugs will have enough total velocity to leave the solar system for good."

"Moving frames of reference always mess me up," Lem conceded. "I'll make sure the slugs' trajectories will have them spiral into the Sun. We got enough alien problems without picking a fight a hundred thousand years in the future."

"Right, old Isaac Newton can be one unforgiving bastard. And try not to hit any of the inner planets while you're at it."

"Picky, picky, picky," Lem said, smiling as he entered commands to the fire-control computer. This was definitely more fun than the fly farm.

Alien Fleet #1, Beta Hydri

Floating in space roughly two AU out from Beta Hydri—a star in the southern circumpolar constellation of Hydrus as seen from Earth —a fleet of warships counted down the hours before they launched their attack. The star itself was a type G yellow dwarf, though 10% more massive than Earth's Sun. It is also the closest confirmed subgiant star to Sol and one of the older, most highly evolved stars of the Sun's spectral class in the Solar neighborhood. It possessed a planet habitable by warm life—the home of a primitive insectoid species—but they were not the target of the fleet. No, the fleet hunted bigger game.

The ships themselves would have looked familiar to any crew member from Peggy Sue's second voyage and their drive signatures would be recognized by any ship from Earth. Black and spiky, like giant sea urchins cast adrift in space. They were led by a creature that looked much like its ship, quasi-crystalline with long mobile spines. They were cold life creatures who inhabited the outer belts of several nearby star systems—zones like Sol's Kuiper Belt, where comets and frozen dwarf planets orbit faint distant suns.

They called their civilization the Republic, and they were governed by three members of their ruling class. Each elected for a limited term, they were similar to the Consuls of ancient Rome, empowered to lead the Republic, perform public works and to wage war. Called upon by their allies, the Dark Lords, to participate in a warm life cleansing, the Consuls of the Republic named a Proconsul to lead the expedition in their name, a worthy named Booshnarrallna.

Booshnarrallna was not just a member of the ruling, Senatorial class, he was an admiral of note and a rising power in the Republic. Barring a major misstep, he would one day serve his term as Consul. Accompanying him as second in command was his friend, Seemallooshna, also a member of the Senate.

"The hour grows near, Proconsul. Soon we will pass through the lesser dimensions and wreak havoc on these warm life vermin who have sown so much discord among our allies."

"Yes, friend Seemallooshna. My spines already quiver in anticipation of skewering these execrable upstarts who have trespassed on our space and disturbed the Republic's peace."

"Even worse, noble Booshnarrallna, these vile creatures are rumored to have destroyed King Lewnhallooshna and his entire fleet."

"Do not remind me of Lewnhallooshna of 61 Virginis. A border barbarian, a renegade of our own class who fled the Republic to start his own petty kingdom. He was a limp spined blowhard who richly deserved being taken down a notch or two. Unfortunately we have been tainted by his failure, since the blunt quilled cretin was of our own species."

"Under your leadership, we will erase the stain along with these upstart pond scum. Upon our return you shall surely receive a triumph, which will almost certainly lead to your own Consulship."

"let us not count our honors before the battle is fought, my friend. In any case, the hour is upon us. Signal the fleet to proceed through the transit point."

"By your command, Proconsul."

The fleet, 39 warships in all, entered alter-space in three squadrons of thirteen, each anxious to kill the warm life renegades who had so humiliated their cousins. Transit time to the Earth system from Beta Hydri was only seven days, less than the transits for the other two fleets that would be joining in the attack.

The Dark Lords' plan was to have the three attacking fleets emerge from alter-space simultaneously, or as close to simultaneously as possible given the vagaries of traveling such distances from three widely flung star systems. But the dark ones, being such long lived creatures, did not posses an overly acute sense of timing. For beings who mark the passage of time in rotations of the entire Milky Way Galaxy, simultaneity was a somewhat imprecise concept. Proconsul Booshnarrallna's grand fleet, though faithfully following their instructions, was going to arrive several days before the other two elements of the attack.

Inside the Vault

Slowly, the expedition members picked themselves up off the vault floor. LED strips on their suits drove back the darkness, casting long shadows throughout the vault's interior.

"Anyone injured?" asked Doc White, not that she could do much with everyone encased in armor. No matter, she quickly scanned the medical telemetry from her companions' suits. Bear and Mizuki were the only Earthlings who could not regain their feet.

"Where are we?" one of the Marines asked.

"We are still on the station," replied JT, "if we had been thrown free we'd be weightless."

"Holy crap, Captain," said Chief Morgan, "what did you hit them with?"

Jack looked up from where he knelt next to the fallen Bear. "Fifty grams of antimatter with a short delay fuse."

"That would yield over two megatons!" Reagan quickly calculated. "Man, this vault must really be built."

"We just rode out an antimatter explosion?" said Sanchez. "I think I really like this vault."

300

"I wonder how much damage the blast did to the station?" JT pondered. "It went off in an atmosphere inside a solid structure. It should have made a huge crater."

"Let's find out what the ship saw," the Captain replied, rising. "M'tak Ka'fek, Scavenger, do you read?" Scavenger was the expedition's call sign.

"Scavenger, M'tak Ka'fek, go ahead Captain," replied Bobby's almost frantic voice. "What happened to you?"

"We developed a spider and crab infestation and had to use a bug bomb," Jack replied. "Can you see any damage to the station from outside?"

"Yes Sir! Your bug bomb blew a large section of glazing off of the greenhouse area and a sizable hole in the bottom of the ring. A bunch of debris spurted out but has since cleared the area due to high radial velocity. The explosion sent a ripple all around the ring, the inhabitants must be scared spit-less."

"Is the station leaking atmosphere?"

"It did at first, but M'tak says the outflow has slowed significantly. The interior must have internal bulkheads to prevent the whole place from depressurizing in case of an asteroid strike."

Yes, that would make sense, Jack thought and then admonished himself. *Enough wool gathering, we need to get out of here.* "Lt. Danner, here are your orders. I want you to send Lt. McKennitt in a large shuttle to survey the hole—have her send a surveillance drone through it if she can. I want to see if the shuttle can find the vault we are currently locked inside of."

"Yes, Sir," came Bobby's somewhat disappointed reply. Inwardly Jack sighed.

"I need you to remain in command on the bridge, keeping a sharp eye out for any response from the station. We just did a significant amount of damage to this place and if I was a resident I'd be up in arms. You and Aput must stand ready to beat back any hostile response, do you understand?"

"Aye aye, Captain." Being left in command of the M'tak was an acceptable alternative to piloting the rescue shuttle in Bobby's mind.

301

"Very good, Mr. Danner. So shake a leg, I wish to be off this wretched station as soon as possible." *M'tak, can you read me?*

Yes, Captain, you are well within my range.

I need you to prepare the sick bay for two casualties—Lt. Bear and Dr. Ogawa. Bear has lost his right foreleg and Mizuki both of her legs from just above the knees.

Certainly, Captain. I will have the facilities prepped and awaiting their arrival.

And M'tak?

Yes?

Do not let Lt. Danner know that Mizuki has been severely wounded. He is a young man in love and would respond badly to the news. I will tell him myself when I am back on board.

As you wish, Captain.

* * * * *

A holographic image appeared, projected on the inner surface of the Captain's helmet, showing the view from the shuttle as it flew through the gaping hole in the bottom of the station's ring. As it gained altitude the devastation caused by the antimatter explosion became evident. Ahead, the vault and its massive door were visible, perched in a jumble of half melted rubble.

"Captain, Shuttle One. I've passed through the blast hole and will land down slope of the vault."

"Roger, Shuttle One. We will open the vault door as soon as you land."

"This vault must be built of tough stuff," observed Chief Morgan, watching the live video. "The explosion hardly touched it."

"Makes sense to build it strong, Chief," Jack replied, "considering what it contains. Otherwise, an unfortunate asteroid strike could set off a massive explosion that would destroy the ring."

"Roger that, Captain. There's enough antimatter in here to shatter a planet."

"Why don't you and your men see if you can liberate some of those large eggs and get them ready to be moved to the shuttle?"

"Aye aye, Sir."

"Lt. Taylor, how are you coming with the power?"

"I think we just about have it sir." JT and Reagan were huddled over an open panel on the wall next to the vault door. Occasional sparks flashed as they labored to attach a spare suit power-cell to the door's control circuitry. A few more sparks and the lights on the control console came on.

"I think that's got it, LT," said Reagan, sounding quite pleased with himself. It wasn't every day he got the chance to hot-wire an alien bank vault.

"Do you want me to enter the open code, Captain?" asked Betty, who was kneeling next to the unconscious Mizuki. She still had possession of the Trader's instruction sheet.

"Not yet. We have to assume that there is effectively vacuum outside the vault. Are Mizuki and Bear going to be safe if we depressurize this place?"

"Yes, Captain. Their suit readouts say that they both have atmospheric integrity restored—if you look closely you can almost see the nanites working on the armor."

"What about the weasel?" asked Hitch. Poonta-ta-ka was an unmoving fuzzy heap off to one side.

"Forget the weasel, what about the butterflies?" asked Jacobs. "They helped us during the battle with the killer chickens."

"Indeed," Jack replied. "That would make them the only thing on this station who is on our side."

"What about some large sample bags?" Feldman asked. Standard issue on expeditions to alien worlds were several sizes of airtight sample collection bags. Made from multiple layers of tough transparent material, they were intended to isolate biological samples along with a bit of their atmosphere.

"Good idea, Jon. I can put Poonta-ta-ka in one but how do we get the butterflies to cooperate?" Betty had examined the fallen trader and found multiple broken bones. The alien remained mercifully unconscious since the explosion.

"Try talking to them," suggested Matt Jacobs. "Mizuki used to talk to them and I swear they listened to her."

"Its that or they stay here," Jack said, "and I doubt that they would do well in vacuum."

"OK," Betty replied, "Matt, give me a hand." Together the Corpsman and sailor gently placed the trader inside one of the large bags and sealed it.

"Will the trader have enough oxygen in there?" asked Feldman.

"His respiration rate is way down, he should last for an hour or so. I have no idea how much air a flock of butterflies needs."

Betty and Matt held another sample bag open between them while the Captain tried to talk to the flying swarm. "I don't know if you can understand me but we are about to let the air out of here. You tried to help Mizuki and we would rather not kill you, but we have to escape this place."

The flock of butterflies formed a globular cluster in front of the two sailors, showing mostly green and blue. The cluster flattened into a disk facing the Earthlings. The disk began pulsing forward and back, forming concentric ripples like a giant loudspeaker. Very faintly sounds could be heard, sounds which the listening ship's AI dutifully began to translate.

"Oh pain and sorrow... the beautiful one is dead... our angel of the flashing sword..."

"What?"

"They must think Mizuki is dead, Captain."

Again addressing the pulsing swarm of winged creatures, Jack spoke through the AI. "Mizuki, the wielder of the sword, is gravely wounded, but she is not dead. We are going to take her to our ship to be healed. But to do that we will have to leave the air out of this room."

The swarm pulsed rapidly, showing hints of yellows and reds.

"Without air we cannot fly... we cannot live..."

304

"That is why we would like you to enter the bag Betty and Matt are holding." Jack gestured toward the sack opening. "We will seal you in with a volume of air and transport you to our ship."

The fluttering disc reformed, colors rippling across the visible spectrum. "We can leave the bag on the ship... and the beautiful one will re-awaken?"

"Yes, but we must hurry, time is of the essence."

The disk began to rotate, forming a tornado of color whose spout reached out and entered the sample bag. Soon the entire swarm was inside the clear container and Betty sealed the opening.

"That... was about the weirdest thing I have ever seen," said LCpl Samuels, relatively new to the crew.

"Fritz, that doesn't even rate a six on my weird-shit-o-meter," Joey Sanchez assured him.

The Captain smiled at the Marines' comments, at least they were taking things in stride. "Shuttle One, what is your status?"

"Just touched down, Captain," came Sandy's chipper, Australian accented voice. "Had to bounce her around a bit to find a firm resting place, all this rubble is a bit shonky."

"Very good, Lt. McKennitt. Stand by. OK Betty, you have the instruction sheet—see if the door will open." *It better*, Jack thought, *if it doesn't I haven't a clue what to do next*. But his worries were unfounded.

There was a mechanical clunk as the bolts retracted. Then the massive circular door slowly swung aside. As it did the air inside the vault screamed out through the opening, the sound rapidly fading as the pressure inside dropped to nothing. The door hung up on outside debris three quarters of the way open, but that was sufficient—they could leave the vault.

Relief was visible on the faces of the Marines and crew. Inside, the sample bags containing the trader and the butterflies swelled until their clear material was taut—puffed up like two balloons.

"OK, let's get the wounded and sample bags on board the shuttle," ordered Jack, also feeling relieved. "Chief, we will need a dozen of those eggs as well."

Shuttle Departure

The Marines fanned out and formed a perimeter around the landed shuttle. Bear, Mizuki and the aliens in their sample bags were quickly secured aboard the shuttle. A dozen type 1 AM containers were also stowed on board by Hitch and Jacobs.

The expedition members found themselves standing near the bottom of a bowl shaped crater more than four kilometers wide. About half a kilometer in front of them was a hole, through which could be seen the inky blackness of space.

"I think your little bug bomb came close to blowing this station apart, Captain," said JT, surveying the damage.

"Indeed, Lieutenant. I had M'tak's AI calculate how big a blast the station could weather, given the hypothetical strength it must posses to simply hold together. I believe we cut the margins rather fine."

"Captain, Shuttle One. The cargo is loaded and secured. We are not going to have room for the entire party in one trip."

"Understood, Lieutenant. White, Hitch and Jacobs, I want you on the shuttle."

"Aye aye, Sir," their voices rang over the comm. The two sailors headed for the loading ramp, Betty was already on board with her patients.

"When you arrive on board the ship I want you to get the wounded to sick bay. Lt. McKennitt, you will probably need to assist Corpsman White in getting Bear and Dr. Ogawa out of their armor— M'tak will give you instructions regarding what needs to be done.

"Hitch, Jacobs, once the wounded are moved take two of the eggs and install them in the forward fuel bunker. We need to be sure the ship has enough power to defend itself until loading is complete."

"Then should I return for the rest of you, Captain?"

"Negative, Lieutenant. I have other plans for our egress. Head back to the ship as soon as you are ready."

"Roger, Sir. Departing now."

Soundlessly, the big shuttle leaped off the rubble, describing a clean backward arc through space. Like an Olympic diver performing a back-flip from a diving platform, the shuttle's attitude was nose down and vertical as it cleanly exited the hole in the station's rim.

"She makes that look so easy."

"She does indeed, Mr. Taylor. Now let's get a move on with the rest of those storage containers."

"Sir? What are we to do with them?"

"Tell me, Lieutenant. What would happen if you threw one of those eggs out of the hole in the floor?"

"It would fly off tangent to the rim at 12km/sec, Captain." As realization dawned a smile crept across JT's face. "Right into space where someone could just pick it up."

"Precisely," Jack smiled back. "Have the Marines spread out and form a line from here down to the edge of the hole. The SEALs can toss the eggs down, one at a time, and the Marines pass them to the hole like a bucket brigade. While you get things organized I will call Lt. Danner and arrange for him to catch our plunder."

"Aye aye, Captain!"

* * * * *

Once the relay line was up and working they were able to toss several eggs a minute out of the jagged hole created by the Captain's bug bomb. One by one, the cache of antimatter eggs disappeared through the hole and out into space.

"That's the last of the full type one containers, Captain," called Chief Morgan from the vault. "Do you want the partials or should we look for full smaller eggs?"

"Neither, Chief. You and your SEALs come down and join the rest of us at the edge of the hole."

As the remaining expedition members gathered round, Sanchez asked the question that was on everyone's mind. "Is the shuttle going to come pick us up, Captain?"

307

"No time for that, Joey. We have removed the swag and now it is time for us to abandon the station."

"Sir?"

"The Captain means follow the eggs, Joey," JT answered with a smile, pleased that he had figured out Jack's plan without having to be told.

"Correct, Lt. Taylor. Since SEALs have been trained to jump out of airplanes we will let them show us how it should be done. Chief?"

"Don't have to ask us twice, Captain!" The Chief, followed closely by Bud and Phil made a short run and leaped into the gaping pit before them.

"See how easy it is? If they can do it, surely Marines can," chided JT.

"But Captain! Everyone knows that SEALs are insane," moaned Joey.

"Shut up and grow a pair," said Rosey as she ran by and jumped through the hole. The remaining Marines, not wishing to have their manhood brought into question, followed LCpl Acuna.

"Too bad we can't take this place as a prize, Captain," JT said as the last of the Marines took the leap.

"Who knows, JT," Jack mused, looking for the last time at the crater he had made. "We may come back someday."

"Did you know the mission was going to end this way?"

"No, not really, but it pays to have an ace in the hole."

"Like a two megaton antimatter bomb?"

"Yes, you never know when you're going to need one."

The former Green Beret smiled. "See you back on the ship, Sir." JT turned and jumped into space.

"Yes, indeed, Lieutenant," Jack said, as much to himself as to the departed JT. The last man off the station, Jack turned and followed his crew into space. Looking at the hole as he fell, it appeared to be a bit smaller than when the explosion created it. The station's repair mechanisms must still be functioning—the hole was already starting to grow shut.

As he fell away from the station rim he looked back, feeling at peace for the first time since before this mad voyage began. *I guess the station will survive our visit. All that remains now is to install the antimatter and head for home. Perhaps we will come back someday; Ludmilla would love having all those alien species to study.*

Bridge, M'tak Ka'fek

After the brief solitude of his spacewalk from the station, Jack arrived back on the bridge with a thousand and one details to see to. From the forward antimatter bunker, JT called him.

"Captain, we have all the egg holders filled with full containers, all 36 of them. What should we do with the remaining eggs? We salvaged 121 in all."

"There is a reason that the space you are in is called the forward fuel bunker, Lieutenant," Jack replied. "There are also midships and aft fuel bunkers, just waiting to be filled. Ask the ship for directions."

"Aye aye, Sir."

At the helm, Jack could see that Bobby was anxious. No longer able to suppress his fears he asked after the missing Mizuki.

"Captain, where is Mizuki? Why hasn't she come to her station on the bridge?"

"Both Lt. Bear and Dr. Ogawa were wounded during the mission, Mr. Danner. They are both confined to sickbay until further notice."

"Wounded!" Bobby jumped up from his seat at the helm. "How badly? I have to see her!"

"Lt. Danner! You will remain at your station!" Jack seldom used his stern, captain's voice, but he did so now. "Dr. Ogawa's injuries are being treated and she will return to duty as soon as she is able. In the mean time I expect you to do your duty."

"But, I," Bobby stammered.

"Mizuki has performed her duties admirably, and she would expect you to do the same."

Bobby slid back into his chair. He knew that Mizuki had a strong sense of personal honor, and that nothing would disappoint her more than knowing that he abandoned his station to look for her.

"If you wish to help her, help your shipmates bring the ship back to home port."

"Aye aye, Sir," the subdued Bobby replied. "Sorry Sir, no excuse."

Jack nodded at the shaken young man, not wishing to say more. He himself felt anguish over the girl's wounds and those of his friend. After all, they were wounded fighting under his command. But those matters would have to wait, they needed to get out of this system. Aput called from the main fire-control station with a welcome distraction.

"Captain, it looks like there are a half dozen ships headed our way from the largest of the two moons."

"Very good, Aput. Sound general quarters, bring the shields up to full and the secondary battery on line."

"Aye aye, Sir!"

M'tak, how soon can we do the wormhole thing back to Earth?

I would not recommend attempting an annular black hole jump under present conditions. There is a significant area of gas and dust between this system and Earth, an area of new star creation. It is only a few light-years away and could adversely impact creation of the wormhole.

We can flit across 1,500 light-years in the blink of an eye but we can't fly through dust?

It is not the dust, per se, Captain. It is the unsettled gravitational gradients present in the stellar nursery region that complicate the matter. If I might suggest first making an alter-space transit to a star system with a clearer path to the solar system?

Fine, select one and send the transit point's coordinates to the helm—and make it as short a transit as possible.

Yes, Captain.

"Mr. Danner, lay in a direct course for the coordinates sent to you by the computer. We will be making a short transit through alter-space before we can make the wormhole jump to home."

"Aye aye, Captain. We are underway. Estimated arrival at the alter-space transit point is four hours."

"Sir, the alien ships are changing course. They are pursuing us."

"That's fine, Aput. Stand ready to fire on them if they come too close. Lt. Danner, try to keep our pursuers out of range until we can transit."

"Aye, Sir."

Four hours later, the M'tak Ka'fek slipped into alter-space, beginning a transit to an unknown star that the AI said would take four and a half days. Aput reported that their pursuers may have followed them into the lesser dimensions, though it was hard to be sure.

Chapter 24

Rebirth and Renewal

Anxiety gathered like a dark cloud around Bobby, and tension filled the bridge whenever he was on watch. Even so, the Captain made him stand double watches, figuring it was better to keep the young lieutenant busy than have him sitting in his quarters thinking of worse case scenarios for Mizuki.

Bobby was not the only one affected by the casualties the expedition suffered prior to extraction. The post mission high quickly turned to depression as the cost struck home. JT, who was close to Bear, was in an ill-tempered mood since returning to the ship. Morale among the crew was at a nadir and the Captain was becoming concerned—but some things could not be rushed.

Finally, two and a half days into the transit, Jack ordered JT and Bobby to accompany him to sick bay. With the exception of Corpsman White and Lt. McKennitt, only the Captain had ever been inside of sickbay before. In fact, the crew did not even know the ship had a medical section before the wounded were admitted.

The trio of officers entered sickbay to find Betty present and wearing a nervous smile. The room was an expansive, sterile place, with large tanks along the walls—it looked more like a chemical plant than a hospital.

"Good afternoon, Captain, ready for the decanting?"

Bobby and JT looked at each other, confused.

"Yes, Corpsman White. I suggest we start with Lt. Bear."

"As you wish, Sir." Betty moved to a large tank on the right-hand side of the room. After examining instrument readouts on a panel next to the tank she tapped the screen in several places and said, "commencing."

"You may wish to stand back from the regeneration tank as the patient emerges," said the voice of the ship's AI.

There was a sound like a toilet flushing followed by gurgling, as if liquid was draining away. A seam appeared, spiting the tank in two vertically. Its sides pulled back, recessing into the wall. There, standing in front of the humans was a very large, very wet, blue tinged polar bear.

The bear coughed, spewing blue liquid, and tumbled from the open tank. On all fours, he continued to cough up liquid until his lungs were clear and his breathing became normal. Looking up he rasped, "what are you primates looking at?"

"Bear?" asked a puzzled JT.

In answer, Bear shook himself like a dog, sending droplets of blue fluid flying in all directions. He stood up, towering over the humans. Looking down at his visitors he paused, and then raised his right foreleg. After a few moments he spoke again.

"Funny, I seem to remember losing that," he said, flexing the limb in question.

"Bear!" yelled JT running forward to grab him by the midsection. "Damn, it's good to see you whole!"

"Well how about that," the bemused Bear said wrapping his left forearm around JT, giving him a half bear-hug. Bobby stood, mouth agape, staring at the ten foot ursine in front of him. Bear released JT and turned to the Captain.

"Jack, how?"

"You don't think I would abandon my best friend, wounded on the field of battle, do you?" Jack's voice choked with emotion as bear and man embraced.

The spectacle of Bear's emergence from the healing tank served as distraction while Betty released her other patient. As the men marveled at the miracle of Bear's restored foreleg, Betty quietly pulled the naked Mizuki from her tank, cleared her lungs and got her breathing again. Urgently whispered explanations calmed the patent down as she was wrapped with blankets. Mizuki's modesty intact, Betty called to the men.

"I have someone else here you might want to see."

Bear released Jack from his bear-hug and all four turned to look at the still dripping Mizuki. Bobby, who's reserve could take no more, ran across the room and took her in his arms.

"Mizuki, Mizuki," he babbled, face buried in her fluid dampened hair. "They wouldn't let me see you."

Reluctantly pulling away, he looked into her eyes. She levelly met his gaze, a more confident person than she had been two weeks ago. "You seem taller, somehow," he observed.

"Five point three centimeters taller, to be exact," the ship's AI said. "Evidently her full growth potential was not realized during childhood."

"What?" was all the confused Bobby could manage. Mizuki put her arms around him and kissed him. Leaning in close she whispered into his ear. "Hush Bobby... and later I will show you my new legs."

Solar System, First Wave

Proconsul Booshnarrallna's fleet emerged from alter-space, south of the plane of the ecliptic, about an AU from the Sun. His ships maneuvered in good order forming a hemisphere, a hollow bowl shaped formation. The open mouth of the bowl pointed toward their target—Earth.

Within ten minutes the Republic's fleet had been detected and its course plotted. The alien interlopers accelerated to 700km/sec on an interception course with Earth and its satellite. The enemy fleet would arrive in two and a half days if left unmolested.

From a holding position above the ecliptic plane, half way between Earth and the transit point from Beta Comae, four frigates under the command of Captain Gretchen Curtis accelerated on a vector that would intercept the invaders before they could come halfway to their target.

"Signal Farside. Tell them we are underway and will intercept the alien fleet in just over a day, assuming they do not change course or speed."

"Yes, Captain," replied the signals officer. "Ma'am, we have a message from Captain Kinashi: 'Pursuing invaders and accelerating to intercept course.'"

The remaining four operational frigates had been patrolling between the Beta Hydri and Delta Pavonis transit points. Their commander, Capt. Kinashi, was a career officer with the name of a famous WWII submarine captain. Though he claimed he was no relation to Takakazu Kinashi, who was credited with sinking the USS Wasp, Gretchen hoped he had some of the old officer's skill—and luck.

"Acknowledge Kinashi's signal and transmit our intended point of rendezvous with the enemy. We will coordinate our approaches when we get closer but with any luck we will be able to catch them from two sides at once."

* * * * *

At Fleet HQ on Farside, Col. Tropsha was watching the developing tactical situation in the Operations Center. With Gretchen commanding the frigate squadron and Billy Ray still off on the mission to the Triads, she was left surrounded by officers that were mostly strangers to her. She and Gretchen had discussed tactics on numerous occasions but she held no illusions regarding her own knowledge of space warfare. She was an ex-Air Force officer and cosmonaut, not a Naval officer like Jack. Her time in the *Voenno-Vozdushnye Sily*—the Russian Federation Air Forces—was spent as a flight surgeon.

Jack, where are you when I need you, she complained to the aether for the hundredth time. No matter, she may not know ship vs ship tactics, but she did know how to handle logistics. There was an old American military saying that amateurs talk tactics while professionals talk logistics. She may not know how to handle a warship but she could ensure Earth's forces were deployed and fully equipped to fight when the time came.

"Commander, call Squadron Commander Melaku and tell her to position a flight of corvettes off the Beta Comae transit point. Move the rest of her force to a complementary position below the ecliptic plane. I wish to be prepared if more enemies show up or if some make it past the frigates."

"Yes, Colonel," the Commander replied.

"And start moving the civilians to the deep caverns. We have a few days yet, but I do not want to wait until the last minute." *Jack had a saying about crisis management—most people wait until a situation becomes a crisis and then try to manage it.* She was not one of those people.

"Aye aye, Ma'am. What about the Marines?" A number of remote positions had been prepared across the Moon's rugged surface, their purpose to conceal a counterstrike force, just in case the base was overrun.

Ludmilla thought that Farside was more likely to be reduced to a glowing crater than overrun by alien shock troops, but the base had a battalion of Marines and nothing for them to do. They may as well deploy and wait for an invasion. It cost little to plan for that contingency now, and if it did come to pass later it would be too late to take action. "Da, order Colonel Rodriguez to deploy her Marines."

* * * *

A day and a half later, Earth warships were maneuvering for final intercept of the alien fleet. Captain Curtis, commanding the squadron from on board Constitution, was coordinating with Captain Kinashi's four ship element using a tight beam laser. Kinashi himself was captain of the Tachikaze, appropriately "Wind from a Sword Stroke" in Japanese.

"Captain Kinashi, If we both maintain our current headings until the last minute it will look to the enemy as though we are going to hit them in the middle of their formation from both front and rear simultaneously."

"Hai, and I assume that such an unimaginative plan is not your true intention."

Gretchen smiled. She liked Kinashi, he had a devious mind. "The signatures of these vessels are almost an exact match for the ships that attacked the Peggy Sue at Sirius. If they are similar they pack very powerful weapons, which fire knots of matter and antimatter plasma in self-sustaining containment fields. Our shields should be able to take several hits but we have other countermeasures. My ships will decelerate for a few seconds just prior to contact and fire anti-plasma rounds. Then I intend to take the enemy formation with an oblique attack on its port side."

"I see, Captain. You have a closing velocity advantage so I assume you will attack with railgun fire. I suggest my ships use gravitonic torpedoes to try and scatter their formation, then fly through the remains of the flank you hit. Perhaps they will be foolish enough to follow us."

"I concur. If they do, we will decelerate, come about and hit them again from the flank."

"And I will reverse course and hit them from the front. We will rip them apart, like sharks taking bites from a school of fish."

"We are sixty seconds out. Good hunting, Captain."

"And to you, Captain. Let us make our ancestors proud."

* * * * *

The first pass went almost exactly to plan. The slight pause in acceleration to fire the anti-plasma rounds caught the enemy attempting an envelopment. Their volley of plasma bundles detonated prematurely on the "sand" field scattered in front of the Earth vessels. In the midst of the chaos caused by exploding plasma knots and a wave of gravitonic torpedoes tipped with antimatter warheads, Capt. Curtis' ships veered hard to starboard and engaged the enemy's left flank.

"Each ship pick a target and take it down!" Gretchen signaled her formation. "Helm, right at them. Main battery fire."

Six of the enemy ships detonated, four from railgun fire and two from torpedo hits. Gretchen's ships passed through the alien formation with no damage, rapidly drawing a way.

"Fire more anti-plasma rounds aft and circle about. We will hit them from the flank this time." As Capt. Curtis maneuvered to reengage Capt. Kinashi's four frigates passed through the collapsing alien formation, firing torpedoes as they went. Three more of the urchin shaped invaders exploded and several faltered, dropping out of formation.

Half the remaining alien fleet turned into an unstructured swarm, pursuing Kinashi's ships which were pulling away, accelerating at near 80Gs. The other half tried to regain some semblance of an orderly formation.

* * * * *

"Commander, signal your squadron to assume stacked formations of four. We must maneuver to counter these attacking ships."

"As you command, Proconsul."

"They managed to shift the line of their attack at the last second and overwhelm the squadron on the left flank, Booshnarrallna."

"I know, Seemallooshna, I was here as it happened. Third squadron has been obliterated and second squadron lost their command ship and is now mindlessly rushing after our attackers," the Proconsul snapped. "Signal the captains of those ships and order them to return to formation."

As they watched three of the rear most ships in the pursuit slowed, turned about and headed back toward the main formation. The others continued their headlong charge after the enemy that had so quickly destroyed a third of the fleet.

*   *   *   *   *

In space warfare, individual exchanges may be brief, but between those exchanges the repositioning of the combatants can take time. It took nearly 18 minutes for Capt. Curtis to finish coming about. Capt. Kinashi's ships actually slowed, to make sure their pursuers didn't lose interest and break off the chase. The aliens hung on long enough to seal their fate.

"Tachikaze, Constitution. Capt. Kinashi, we are in position. Reverse your course and take them head on. You take the four leaders—I will take the remaining six from the flank."

"Hai, Captain. These fish are in our net." As he spoke his four ships flipped 180 degrees, assuming a diamond formation, and accelerated directly toward their pursuers—the hunted had become the hunters.

While Kinashi's ships rolled up the front of the line of pursuers, Curtis' frigates spread out into a line abreast and raked the rest of the alien column from the side. Two enemy ships exploded before they could react.

The aliens fought back fiercely, sending a fusillade of plasma knots hurtling toward their tormentors at nearly the speed of light.

Curtis's ships had ceased accelerating to allow the alien column to pass in front of them. This also allowed the frigates to fire anti-plasma rounds to cover their front. Even so, several ships took hits on their screens.

Kinashi's ships continued to accelerate, making the use of anti-plasma rounds ineffective. AP rounds were essentially bursting charges surrounded by hundreds of metallic fragments which formed a cloud of protective debris between the racing plasma knots and their targets. Unfortunately, an accelerating ship would quickly pass through its protective cloud and be exposed again to enemy fire. As a result, all of Kinashi's ships took hits and one, Maeander, was hit several times in succession.

"Tachikaze, Maeander. My forward shielding is down 55% and I am falling back into your wake for cover."

"Acknowledged, Maeander."

At the rear of the enemy column, Indefatigable and Chesapeake together fired on the rearmost pursuing ship, holing its hull fore and aft. After a short delay its fuel bunkers exploded. At the front of the column, Tachikaze, Ikazuchi and Yarra annihilated the last of the pursuing aliens.

"Curtis to squadron, well done. Reform on Constitution and we will see to the remaining interlopers. Break. Maeander, a couple of strays dropped out of the main enemy fleet after our first pass. Work on getting your shields back up to strength and run them to ground..."

Reinforcements from Gliese 581

Reports from the space battle flowed into Fleet HQ, delayed by several minutes due to distance. Plotted positions of ships, both enemy and friendly, moved within the 3D viewing tank.

"Capt. Curtis seems to have these bastards well in-hand," commented one of the officers present, a lieutenant commander.

"A battle is not won until the enemy is either destroyed or flees the field of battle, Commander," replied Ludmilla. While this particular set of enemies did not seem so formidable, she could not shake the feeling that this was but the opening round. An alarm sounded on a console nearby.

"Colonel, something just emerged from alter-space," a technician reported from the shadows.

"From Beta Hydri?"

"No Ma'am, it looks like it came from Sirius. Only a single ship."

Jack! Have you returned? For an instant, a wave of irrational hope swept Ludmilla's thoughts. "Can you recognize the drive signature?"

"Yes Ma'am, it's one of ours—it's the Peggy Sue! They are hailing us."

"Put it on speaker."

"Farside, Peggy Sue. Do you copy?"

"Go ahead Peggy Sue, we copy. We did not expect you back quite so soon, or from the Sirius system. What is your status and how did you mission go?" Minutes passed placating Dr. Einstein.

"We sort of took a bank shot off of Sirius by way of 61 Virginis, cut almost three days off our transit time. The mission was successful, thanks to the Ambassador and M. de Belcour. I got a hold full of warrior vegetables who are anxious to help us deal with the invasion threat—which I see is already underway."

"Roger, Peggy Sue. We await your arrival at base."

Another delay.

"That's a negative, Farside. The Guardians—that's what these military Triad types call themselves—the Guardians say they need to set up shop on Mercury. Something about being as close to the Sun as possible."

"Understood, you are proceeding to Mercury. Keep us apprised of your status."

* * * * *

On the bridge of the Peggy Sue, Capt. Vincent studied a holographic display of the ongoing battle. *Looks like Gretchen is kicking their alien asses. Maybe there won't be anything for the walking salad in the hold to do after all.* "Dr. Piscopia, could you plot out a direct course to Mercury and send it to the helm?"

"Si, Captain. You wish to match orbits and then land?"

"That's right. According to the Ambassador, these Guardian fellers want to land somewhere on the limb of the planet. A location that puts the Sun on the horizon."

"You do know that Mercury is not tidally locked?"

"What, Doctor?"

"Gliese 581d is tidally locked to its star—a day takes the same time as a year, which keeps the same side of the planet always in daylight. Scientists used to think that the same side of Mercury always faced the Sun, but back in 1965 astronomers discovered that the planet rotates roughly three times during every two orbits."

"So how long is a day on Mercury?"

"58.6 days, approximately."

"All right, we'll look for a place to land where the Sun will set in a week or so, and hope that the Guardians can work their magic from there."

Second Wave

Proconsul Booshnarrallna reformed his fleet, turning to face the seven Earth ships that confronted him. An eighth ship headed after his stragglers, no doubt intent on finishing them off. *Are they that confident that they can finish destroying me without their full strength? Let us see if I can split their force further.*

"Commander, send the three remaining ships from second squadron to attack the base on the third planet's large satellite."

"By your command, Proconsul."

"Is it wise to diminish our force so, Booshnarrallna?"

"Whether we face them with 16 ships or 13 will make little difference I fear, friend Seemallooshna. We are overmatched and unless the other allied fleets arrive soon we will leave only our wreckage for them to find."

"But why send the second squadron ships away?"

"They are like an appendage to my own, well drilled squadron, and besides—they might inflict some damage to the base on the third planet's moon."

"I see, Proconsul—spirits of the void preserve us, here come the warm life devils again!"

* * * * *

Three of the alien attackers split off from their main body and headed on toward the Moon. Squadron Commander Melaku's twelve corvette wing was holding position a bit forward of Earth, south of the ecliptic plane—they were effectively at the same orbital distance from the Sun, just canted with respect to the planets.

"First Wing, we have three bogies headed for our home base at 12 o'clock. All flights, finger four formation; accelerate for intercept. We will deploy anti-plasma defense just prior to contact."

While Beth's half of the corvette fleet moved to attack, the other half, led by Lt. Hect, remained in position to strike anything emerging from the Beta Comae transit point. The transit point was now almost 150 million kilometers behind Earth as the planet continued in its orbit around the Sun. The corvettes damaged during the previous alien incursion had been repaired and new ones, fresh from the construction dock, filled out second wing's complement of twelve.

An alarm sounded on Hect's control panel. Eyes down on the sensor readouts he saw the cause—something, several somethings, had just emerged from alter-space.

"Second Wing, shields up; assume attack formation. We will wait until we are sure of what we are facing." The alarm continued to sound as more and more ships emerged from the transit point only a few million kilometers from the squadron.

* * * * *

Alarms also sounded at Fleet HQ. The main display showed the Earthlings' deteriorating tactical situation. The frigate squadron was engaged with the first fleet of invaders fifty million kilometers ahead of Earth. Closer in were a trio of invaders who Commander

Melaku was maneuvering to intercept with a wing of corvettes. If any got through her attack they would arrive at Farside in a few hours.

Now a new threat was emerging from another direction. Above the ecliptic plane and two months' orbital distance behind the planet, a large force of unknown ships was gathering. More than fifty strong, the new force was hanging back, evidently assembling into a single formation before taking action.

"How large are those vessels?" asked Col. Tropsha, watching the display with rising alarm.

"There are several different sized targets, Ma'am. The smallest of them are about the size of a frigate. The largest maybe four times as massive."

"Do we know what weapons they possess?"

"Negative, their drive signatures are unknown and the hull configurations never seen before."

"If we assume that they are at least as well armed as the formation that Capt. Curtis is engaged with, Lt. Hect's wing will be annihilated if they attack."

"They would certainly suffer a high attrition rate, Ma'am," a nearby officer commented. The senior Naval officer present, a Commander who's ship had not been completed in time for the battle, spoke up.

"Colonel, Capt. Curtis looks likely to finish off the first wave of invaders within a few hours. If Hect's corvettes attacked this second wave, from behind as it were, they might just delay the aliens long enough for the frigates to make it back to defend the base."

"Or Hect's force might just be wiped out to no purpose," Ludmilla replied. This was the down side of being in command, people did what you told them to do, but in the end the decisions were yours.

"That is of course a possibility, Ma'am."

"Farside, Vegetable Patch. Can you read me, over?" Vegetable Patch was the somewhat facetious call sign for Captain Vincent's mission to Mercury.

"Yes, Capt. Vincent, we read you. Interrogative the purpose of your call?"

"I have a lot of excited plants in my hold that would like me to relay a message to you..."

Attack of the Killer Cacti

"The Triads want us to do what?" replied the HQ communications officer.

"They say that there are a large number of hostile ships congregating near the Beta Comae transit point and that they would really like to neutralize 'em. Only problem is that there's a flight of corvettes near the enemy and the Guardians are afraid of hitting them as well."

"Hitting them with what, Captain?"

"I'm not really sure about that, but I get the impression it would not be in the PT boat sailors' best interests to be too close."

"What should we do, Colonel?" asked the Commander. All eyes were on Ludmilla—it was her call.

Der'mo! If we are not going to trust the Triads we should not have brought them to the party. "Order Lt. Hect to leave the vicinity of the alien fleet. Tell him to head away from Earth at top acceleration."

"Aye aye, Ma'am..."

* * * * *

On board the Peggy Sue, Billy Ray was in the CIC watching the tactical situation develop. In the converted cargo hold, NatHanGon, Jean-Jacques de Belcour and Melissa Scott Hamilton were with the Guardians.

"Look there, Jean-Jacques. See those flashes of light in the soil between the Guardians?" asked an excited Melissa. She had been in horticulturalist heaven, studying the Triad's mini-conclave on the voyage back to Earth, but this was even more exciting.

"Yes, Melissa, I see the lights." Jean-Jacques had no idea why the American plant scientist was so excited, but he expected that she would tell him.

"I knew it was that fungus, the one they insisted on being present in the soil around them. It conducts the signals from their roots, even if they aren't touching. If that don't beat all."

"Yes, MelissaScottHamilton, the soil fungus helps transmit signals between us, to others whose roots are not in direct contact; It is an exceptional honor to be present as the Guardians perform their ancient duties, even for us; Has the Captain relayed the Guardians' concern over the flight of small Earth ships near their intended targets?"

"That is totally fascinating, NatHanGon; Jean-Jacques and I are honored to be here and even more honored that your Guardians are going to help us; I'll ask the Captain again if he managed to talk to the base."

Melissa had long ago mastered the triple sentence fragment speech used by the three brained plants. She was so used to conversing with the Ambassador that talking with the Captain took extra concentration to keep from say three things at once.

"Captain, Cargo Hold. Have y'all managed to get a hold of Farside yet?"

"Roger, Melissa, they have ordered the corvette wing to clear the target area. Tell our allies they are free to fire when the corvettes are clear."

"The Guardians' report that your little ships have cleared the danger zone; If this does not kill us it should prove interesting; Prepare yourselves, the Guardians are going to fire."

Crackling discharges danced among the roots of the giant plants. Lightning arced among their triple trunked bodies and the smell of ozone filled the air.

"Wow!" said Melissa.

"Mon Dieu!" said Jean-Jacques.

The Ambassador rattled his flowers excitedly.

* * * * *

326

Within the Sun's photosphere large prominences formed, swaying in magnetic fields that dwarfed the Earth in size. Spicules, long thin filaments of luminous gas, rose and fell within the chromosphere. Like fiery blades of grass, they formed shimmering fields growing up from the photosphere below. Ripples of light and dark washed across the Sun's surface, building to a climactic event never before seen in the solar system.

"Colonel, there is some kind of disturbance on the face of the Sun," reported one of the HQ technicians. Yuki and Rajiv had joined Ludmilla in the command center when it was reported that the Triads were about to do something.

"I don't know what's going to happen but it is most probably going to be spectacular," Rajiv exclaimed excitedly. "Remember, what we are seeing actually happened eight minutes ago!"

"It would appear that the Triads are inducing some form of solar eruption," added Yuki. Both physicists were more excited by the unexplained solar phenomenon than the pending alien attack.

The Sun's radiance pulsed faster and faster—finally its photosphere reached a peak of brightness and then darkened. Between the Sun's photosphere and corona, the chromosphere lased.

"Look at the telescope view of the alien fleet," yelled someone in the darkened control center. On one of the wall displays the fifty plus objects that were the second wave of the alien attack flared like miniature Suns.

When the glare subsided there was nothing to be seen from the telescope. Within the tactical display tank the second wave of alien invaders began blinking and then disappeared.

"Where did they go?" demanded Ludmilla.

"They're gone, Colonel," replied an awed sensor operator. "There's nothing left of them but a cloud of hot plasma—the whole fleet was vaporized!"

Cheers went up across the control room.

Chapter 25

Out of the Frying Pan

M'tak Ka'fek emerged from alter-space to find a binary star system—a diminutive red dwarf orbiting a K class dwarf heavier than the Sun. There were no planets in the warm life habitable zone, but there was an ice planet similar to Neptune and icy planetoids galore farther out. From a number of locations, ships appeared.

"Captain, we have several ships converging on our position at accelerations as high as 40G. The nearest were underway within twenty minutes of our emergence—given how fast they launched they must be a quick reaction force. I would guess that they are armed."

"Very good, Mr. Taylor," Jack replied. He was in a good mood, with his crew whole again and Bear back at his normal place on the main fire-control console. "I suppose we are in for some unpleasantness. Bring the superluminal particle cannon on line."

Mizuki rose from her seat near the helm and, with a smile for Bobby, headed aft to crew one of the secondary battery control stations. The ship could be fought entirely from the bridge—entirely from the commander's chair for that matter—but having independent gun crews made the ship more efficient and more deadly in battle.

"Captain, four, six, no seven ships just emerged from alter-space behind us. They must be the ones chasing us as we left Ring Station."

"I was expecting as much, Lt. Taylor. Lt. Bear, status of the secondary battery?"

"Manned and ready, Captain."

"Very good. Target the nearest of the pursuers and the nearest of those trying to intercept. Wait for my signal."

"Aye aye. Mizuki, target the closest ship aft, Aput the closest ship forward."

"Not going to take them yourself, Mr. Bear?"

"I'm an older and wiser bear since our vacation on Ring Station, Captain. Besides, the gun crews can use the practice, and some fun."

Jack smiled, *perhaps he has grown a bit wiser—perhaps we all have.* "Mr. Taylor, do you remember having a discussion with the ship's AI regarding our shields and the ability to cloak the ship from most electromagnetic radiation?"

"Yes Sir. I believe that M'tak claimed the ship could all but disappear, like Harry Potter's cloak of invisibility."

"Please, Lieutenant, you are on a starship, not a flying broom," the Captain scolded. At the helm, Bobby leaned over and asked Sandy, "Who's Harry Potter?"

"Really, Mate? You are such a total science fiction dweeb."

"Prepare to activate cloaking mode, Mr. Taylor. M'tak, do you have the vector for a singularity jump home?"

"Yes, Captain. I have sent the course to the helm. I must say, I am intrigued by your preparations for battle."

"There is an old saying among Earthlings: 'The best weapon against an enemy is another enemy.' "

"Course laid in, Captain," Sandy reported from the helm.

"On my mark and smartly, and don't spare the engines, helm."

"Aye aye, Sir!" Sandy and Bobby answered in unison.

"You may fire, Mr. Bear; Turn on cloaking mode, Mr. Taylor; Helm, put us on course for home."

Two alien vessels flared with the harsh radiance of lost antimatter containment as superluminal particles burst into normal space inside their hulls. At his station Bear chuckled. "That just doesn't get old."

The massive T'aafhal ship vanished from the converging aliens' sensors, leaving them with only each other to target. As battle erupted between pursuers and interceptors, the M'tak veered away from the conflict, accelerating at 200Gs.

Third Wave

A sense of relief spread throughout the Farside control room, jubilant exclamations barely contained. In the darkness, people could be seen pounding each other on the backs, some embracing. Before a full on celebration could break out Ludmilla called for a status check on the other engagements.

"What is the status of the corvettes? Have they intercepted the three ships that broke off from the first wave?"

"Colonel, Squadron Commander Melaku reports that they have managed to delay two of the enemy ships, but the third slipped by them and is headed for the Earth-Moon system."

Ludmilla's facial expression did not change, she simply nodded. "And the status of Capt. Curtis' frigates?"

"They are heavily engaged; the enemy is down to four effectives. One of ours, the Chesapeake, has taken significant damage to its shields but is still able to make way."

"What is the ETA on the inbound hostile?"

"Thirty five minutes, Ma'am."

"Notify Base Defense. Have them raise the shields and prepare to repel enemy forces."

* * * * *

"I hope these railgun contraptions we rigged up work under combat conditions," Lem said to his friend. Both wore suits of light space armor—light only in comparison with the Marines' heavy combat armor. Earlier, the power enhancing musculature of the suits helped them load the railgun cannons' heavy magazines full of 10kg metallic slugs. Now they were concealed at a vantage point near the lunar surface where they could observe the defense emplacements directly.

"Now Lemuel, you know what old Stonewall Jackson used to say: Never take council of your fears," replied Clem.

"Yeah. I also remember what H. L. Mencken said: Of all escape mechanisms, death is the most efficient."

331

"Well then we got nothing to worry about—you ain't never been efficient in your whole life."

From several points on the rugged landscape that covered Farside base, brief flashes marked the launch of gravitonic torpedoes. Two brilliant explosions spilled across the space above the base—plasma knots detonating on the defensive shields.

"We got anything on the targeting radar?" asked Clem.

"Yeah, just letting 'em get a bit closer," answered Lem. The alien invasion had just become real for the people at Farside.

* * * * *

At the Delta Pavonis alter-space transit point the third wave of alien attackers materialized. Eight ships in all, four of a type Earth's defenders had seen before. They were the same as the three ships that made the reconnaissance flight more than two months ago. A pair split off and headed for Mars while the remaining two headed toward the Sun and Mercury.

The other four ships were not familiar, though their design showed similarities to the smaller vessels. Squat and dark, they looked like a collection of nested sections of pipe with blunt, rounded ends. They were battle cruisers, heavily armed and armored dreadnoughts that dwarfed their lighter escorts.

Perhaps some of those on board the menacing ships had thoughts of payback—a desire to avenge those of their kind who had perished scouting the system around them. Perhaps not. The creatures called themselves Xoosht. Inhabitants of deep cold methane seas on a distant ice world, the thoughts of the invaders were totally, unknowingly alien. One thing was understood—they had come to erase all life from the solar system.

A single battle cruiser should have sufficed to eradicate the warm life scum opposing them, four were sent—these creatures believed in overkill. Assuming a diamond shaped formation they set a course for Earth.

* * * * *

Beth and her wingman made another close pass of the remaining enemy warship. Its shields were down and it was no longer returning fire. The other ship the corvettes intercepted had already detonated and was now an expanding cloud of gas and debris, though it had not died before taking two of Beth's squadron with it. Beth and her wingman flipped over just in time to see the front end of their target vaporize—a direct hit by an antimatter tipped torpedo.

"That *bâtard étranger* is dead in space, Skipper," Frenchy observed from his seat in front of the Squadron Commander.

"I'd say so, Frenchy. First Wing, Deloraine, form up on me. We need to go after the one that got by us." As the wing reformed Beth considered her remaining ships. "Break, break. Bainbridge, you're now wingman for Foscari. Let's tighten up people, that bandit is about to attack our home base."

"Second Wing, Deloraine. The last of the enemy's first wave ships is attacking Farside—we need to take it out soonest." It took nearly five minutes for Beth's message to reach the second wing of corvettes and as long for Lt. Hect's reply.

"Deloraine, Second Wing. We are headed back to Farside as well. God bless Capt. Vincent and his ferocious vegetables, the enemy fleet that emerged from Beta Comae has been totally destroyed."

Beth smiled. She had received the communique from Farside announcing the return of the Peggy Sue but its full meaning had not registered until now. Evidently Billy Ray's mission was successful and her lover was now camped out in a crater on Mercury with a hold full of Triad Guardians.

Lt. Hect and his wing of corvettes accelerated toward the Moon base. Secretly, he was hoping to arrive before his commander so his as yet unbloodied wing could claim credit for at least one kill.

* * * * *

"Come on, Lem, shoot the bastard already!"

"We may only get one shot at this. I'm waiting to see the whites of their eyes, Clem."

"You don't even know if they've got eyes!"

"OK, OK, I'm firing... salvo on the way. There, are you happier?"

"Much." The railgun slugs took about 30 seconds to reach their target. Of the twenty-four slugs fired nineteen missed and two were glancing hits, deflected by the alien's shields. The last three, however, struck home.

The star bright flare of an antimatter explosion blazed briefly above the Moon's surface. In a cave excavated from the tough lunar rock, a group of Marines looked up through an observation slit.

"Looks like the Base Defense Force got one," commented Col. Rodriguez.

"Yes Ma'am," agreed GySgt Washington, "Those crazy ex-Army biker dudes nailed the bastard."

"Let's hope it's the only one that makes it this far."

* * * * *

The last ship from the first wave of invaders vanished in the star bright glare of detonating antimatter torpedoes. Aware of the new threat, the squadron assumed a blocking position between the on coming third wave of alien battle cruisers and Earth. Only the Maeander was missing. Detached from the main fleet, Maeander was holding position where she had hunted down and destroyed the two damaged alien frigates that fled the first skirmish. This put the lone frigate 20 million kilometers closer to the new enemy ships than its sisters.

"Captain Curtis, do you see this?"

"Yes, navigator. I see them." *Damn those puppies are big,* Gretchen thought. *If they are proportionally more powerful than the smaller ones we are overmatched—frigates against battleships.* "Signal Maeander, tell them to fall back and rejoin the squadron."

"Aye aye, Captain."

As the Maeander reversed course its shields suddenly flared. Two bright pulses and then a ripple of explosions—the antimatter in the ship's remaining torpedoes detonating. The Meander was gone.

"Shit," Gretchen said under her breath. *These things are going to slaughter us.*

"What do we do, Captain?" asked her XO.

"Signal the corvette squadron. Order Commander Melaku to bring her entire force forward to support us. We will maintain our present distance from the alien fleet until the corvettes can reinforce us."

"And then, Ma'am?"

"We stand and fight," she said grimly, *and if need be die. What was it that King Leonidas of Sparta supposedly told the 300 on the eve of battle? Prepare for Glory!*

Into the Fire

"Vegetable Patch, Farside, say again your last."

"I said, evidently our warrior plants are one trick ponies, to mangle a metaphor. They say they cannot create another solar laser blast for at least eleven days—something about the photosphere being depleted and the rotational period of the Sun's surface."

"Understood, Vegetable Patch, no joy from the Guardians. Be advised, there are a pair of enemy frigates headed your direction."

"How well armed are they?"

"Each at least as formidable as one of ours. I would tell you to try and get the Triads out of the system but you would probably not reach a transit point before being overtaken. I'm sorry Peggy Sue, but you are on your own... Good luck, Captain Vincent. Tropsha out."

"Rig the ship for action," Billy Ray ordered his XO. "Sound general quarters, power up the shields and weapons. We ain't goin' down without a fight."

Next to the Captain, Jean-Jacques spoke in French: "*Soyons fermes, purs et fidèles; au bout de nos peines, il y a la plus grande gloire du monde, celle des hommes qui n'ont pas cédé.*"

"Sorry, Jean-Jacques, my French is not that good."

"Let us be firm, pure and faithful; at the end of our sorrow, there is the greatest glory of the world, that of the men who did not give in."

Billy Ray looked at the Frenchman and raised his eyebrows.

"Charles de Gaulle, a man who also fought to save his people from extinction."

"Yeah, well about all we got left now is glory, pardner."

"*D'accord, mon Capitaine.*"

* * * * *

As Capt. Curtis gathered her remaining forces for a final effort to repel the invaders, Ludmilla stood helplessly in the Farside command center. "We destroyed two entire fleets of enemy and still they come!"

"Some dumb bastards just don't know when they've had their asses kicked," said TK's gravely voice. He had quietly rolled up next to Ludmilla as the reports of the third wave's arrival came in.

"TK. You should be in the deep shelters with the others."

"Naw, if this is Earth's last stand I want to go out spitin' in the enemy's eye. At least the sons-of-bitches know they've been in a fight."

Ludmilla nodded, not daring to speak. *So Jack, my love, our reunion is not to be. I waited for you, and I am sorry that I will not be here when you return.*

* * * * *

"I am ready to create the singularity, Captain."

"Proceed, M'tak. Take us home."

In front of the ship space dimpled. A reflective doughnut formed that was instantly wrapped in a swirling toroid of stars. The M'tak Ka'fek was sucked through the ring of stars and for the second time creatures from Earth traveled through a wormhole.

In a matter of seconds, the M'tak Ka'fek was above the plane of the ecliptic, three AU out from the Sun, and in bound for Earth. As with the previous wormhole jump, the ship had been accelerated to nearly 10,000 km/sec and was now decelerating to rendezvous with home base. It would take eighteen minutes for light from their arrival to reach Earth; it would take the ship eight hours to make the docks at Farside.

336

Bear raised his nose, as if sniffing the air for the presence of danger. A low growl came from deep in his chest.

"Captain, there's something weird going on here," JT reported from his station. "Earth is all messed up. There is hardly any radio traffic and cloud cover is far too dense." The ship's AI announced, "Warning! hostile forces detected. This system is under attack."

"What the..." was all that Jack managed before a torrent of sensor information flooded his mind via the ship's neural link. He quickly sized up the tactical situation. *Earth has been attacked! And there are enemy ships spread out across the system.* Jack's face turned hard as stone, his eyes went square and his jaw clenched.

"In our absence, our world has been attack. Moreover, some of the attackers are still here. Crews to your guns, prepare the ship for battle," announced Jack in a voice heard throughout the ship. Then he quoted a famous Civil War general, William Tecumseh Sherman. "'War is the remedy that our enemies have chosen, and I say let us give them all they want!'"

Crew and Marines, who had come to the bridge to witness the wormhole jump and the arrival back in the solar system, ran for their stations.

"Captain, what are your orders?" asked Bear in a low rumble.

"We have hostiles in three locations, Lt. Bear. Target the two pair of smaller ships headed for Mercury and Mars first, then the larger formation."

"Aye aye, Captain. Targeted."

"Engage the enemy, Lieutenant."

* * * * *

The Peggy Sue left the crater she had been sheltering in and accelerated toward the pair of alien ships headed her way. In the cargo hold the Guardians were in some form of post attack stupor. Evidently the act of making a star lase took a lot out of the larger than man sized plants. *They're probably not even going to know what killed them,* Billy Ray thought peevishly. *I guess they did do what they came for though—they sent that other fleet straight to hell. Too bad they are all out of star laser voodoo.*

337

"Captain, we are manned and ready for battle," reported Lt. Vandersluys, the XO.

As ready as we'll ever be, given we ain't got hardly any torpedoes. We've got railgun slugs though, maybe we'll get lucky. "Thank you XO," after two months he still could not pronounce Vandersluys. "Mr. Tanaka, give me an intercept course and send it to the helm."

"Aye aye, Sir."

"We are going to attack?" asked Elena Piscopia.

"We can't run fast enough to get away from 'em, Elena, and I'll be damned if I'll be run down from behind like some mangy varmint." As he was talking Chief Zackly came onto the bridge.

"Crew's at the ready Captain. Tubes loaded, slugs in the railguns and I had 'em shift as much power to forward shields as possible. Can't them plant things do anything to help?"

"Evidently not, Chief. It looks like our plant friends brought only one miracle with them."

Billy Ray looked at the wizened old sailor who was standing there calmly awaiting further orders. Billy Ray was the Peggy Sue's third captain but there had only ever been one chief of the ship. More than anyone, the Peggy Sue was Hank Zackly's ship and if he wanted to be on the bridge when she went down in a blaze of glory Billy Ray was not going to deny him. "Chief, I just want to say its been an honor..."

Before he could complete the sentence, something flared up ahead—two somethings. "Sir! The two hostile ships, they just exploded!" reported the astonished Tanaka. "Something went through their shields like they were not even there."

I've seen that before, Billy Ray said to himself, a large smile spreading across his face. *I do believe that Captain Jack has returned in the proverbial nick of time.* "It looks like our enemy has been removed from the field of battle, Mr. Tanaka. Plot a new course for Farside and home. It appears we have ourselves a second miracle."

338

Dark Lord Rising

On opposite sides of Earth two events occurred simultaneously, each around eight minutes removed as the photon flies. Ahead on Earth's orbital path, the remaining corvettes joined the larger frigates preparing to make their final stand. "All ships, assume attack formation. We will concentrate everything we have on the nearest alien vessel." Gretchen grimaced, *these might be the last orders I ever issue to the fleet.* "On my mark..."

Space ahead flared brightly.

What? The nearest alien battle cruiser disappeared in an antimatter fueled cataclysm. As the glare from the explosion faded the second ship in the hostile formation flared, then the third.

"All Ships, Hold position!"

As the fourth enemy ship burst in a frenzy of matter/antimatter mutual annihilation, Gretchen had but one thought. *Jack!*

* * * * *

"All hostile vessels destroyed, Captain," JT verified. "Light from our arrival hasn't even have time to travel that far—they never knew what hit them."

Jack commended his gunnery officer. "Excellent shooting, Mr. Bear."

JT noticed something new on the sensor displays. The M'tak's sensors could detect the presence of gravitonic drives through alter-space at hyperluminal speeds—much faster than the electromagnetic radiation the Earth forces depended on. "It looks like someone new has joined the party. A ship just emerged from the Beta Comae transit point."

"Can you identify the type of ship, Lt. Taylor?"

"Sir, M'tak's instruments say it is an enemy battle cruiser."

"Like the other four?"

"No sir. The other four were just marked as hostile, this one is marked as dangerous, followed by some symbols I don't know."

"Lt. Bear, target the new interloper."

"Aye, Captain. Firing now with all particle cannon."

* * * * *

"What is happening? Where have the enemy ships gone?" demanded Ludmilla. The four heavy cruisers headed for Earth had vanished from the display tank.

"They appear to have been destroyed by antimatter explosions, Ma'am. We are getting garbled reports from both the corvette and frigate squadrons."

"Well find out, Commander." Not knowing what was taking place on the battle front was driving Ludmilla crazy.

"Col. Tropsha, another ship has emerged at the Beta Comae transit point—cruiser sized, type unknown..."

* * * * *

On the bridge of the Dark Lord battle cruiser the elder who had ordered the attack on Earth was observing its displays as the tactical situation came into focus. Electromagnetic radiation, characteristic of antimatter explosions, was received and analyzed.

"Significant One, it appears that the warm life vermin just disposed of the last of the minion fleets," announced the minor functionary at the sensor station.

"Surprising, I expected the Xoosht to fare better against the upstarts. They have always been one of the more reliable vassal races. No matter, the minion fleets were overdue for a culling. Target the remaining warm life vessels."

"Yes, Significant One."

Much like the M'tak Ka'fek's superluminal particle cannon, the Dark Lord's ship mounted superluminal weapons. Because they fired through alter-space, the simple gravitonic deflector shields of the Earth ships would not stop their bursts of particles—the fleet was defenseless before the Dark Lord battle cruiser.

Alarms blared.

"We are under attack! Superluminal particle blasts from astern. Significant one, the sensors say that we have been fired upon by T'aafhal weapons!"

340

"That is not possible!" the elder Dark Lord exclaimed. "We exterminated those abominations millions of years ago! Return fire, Commander. Reverse course and head back for the transit point!"

* * * * *

"We hit them but their shields absorbed the burst. I don't think we scratched them, Captain."

"Indeed, Mr. Taylor. I was wondering if this day would ever come."

"Should we hit them again?" growled Bear.

"No, not with the secondaries. Tell them about our new adversary, M'tak."

"As the Captain has indicated, the secondary batteries will not prove effective against that ship. It is a Dark Lord heavy battle cruiser."

"What?" exclaimed JT.

Light from the Dark Lord ship finally reached the M'tak and its image appeared on the forward display—a cluster of blunt dark crystals, embedded in a large blob of rough slag.

"So that's the real enemy," whispered Bobby at the helm. If anything, it was bigger than the M'tak, and evidently it was firing on them.

"Sir, we just took a hit on the shields—identified as superluminal positrons. No damage."

"So how do we bring this prey down, Captain?" asked Bear.

The ship's AI answered in the Captain's stead by posing a question of its own. "Permission to power up the main battery, Captain?"

"By all means, bring the main battery on line." Jack smiled at the concerned faces of his officers. "Didn't anyone wonder why we always refer to the particle cannon as the secondary battery?"

Bear shrugged. "I figured there was a primary but that it was out of commission. Besides, up until now we haven't needed anything more powerful."

"The main battery will deal with the Dark Lord cruiser?" asked JT anxiously.

"Lt. Taylor, destroying ships like the one before us is what I was designed to do—it is my reason to exist."

An opening appeared in the dome-like nose of the T'aafhal ship, hull material receding to reveal a dark, slightly concaved surface within. Starlight glinted off the smooth surface, as black as an obsidian mirror. It was not obsidian—in fact, not matter at all—but a discontinuity in the fabric of spacetime, the surface a complex shape stretching across more than the normal dimensions of 3-space.

At the main weapon console, Bear closed his eyes and raised his muzzle. As targeting information flooded his senses, he emitted a low rumble. His face wore a beatific bearish smile, nostrils flaring as if he had caught scent of fresh prey across the pack ice.

Jack sat back in the captain's chair, eyes fixed on the dark ship that filled the forward display. He nodded almost imperceptibly.

"You may fire when ready, Mr. Bear."

Bear snarled, exposing a disquieting number of teeth, as a deep thrumming filled the bridge—a sound more felt than heard. He opened his eyes and gazed expectantly at the forward display.

While the secondaries were superluminal—skirting the boundary between 3-space and alter-space to strike many times faster than the speed of light—the ship's main weapon was hyperluminal. In effect, it acted instantaneously. Light, however, had to obey the laws of relativity, taking several minutes to reach the attacking T'aafhal warships sensors.

When it did arrive, the image of the Dark Lord ship was seen to crumple in on itself. Slowly at first, then with exponentially increasing rapidity, it shrank to a single point. Background stars close to the ship's position seemed to be pulled inward, toward the vanishing point. A fraction of a second later that point blossomed in a starburst—a miniature nova.

"What the hell was that?" asked JT.

"I don't know," replied Bear, "but I like it!"

"Lt. Taylor, does it not stand to reason that a starship that travels by creating annular singularities—essentially doughnut shaped black holes—could create a simple singularity at a nearby point in space?"

"The ship's primary weapon shot the Dark Lord ship with a black hole?" Bobby asked.

"A virtual black hole. One not created by actual concentrated mass but by manipulation of spacetime—think of it as multidimensional gravitational aikido."

"The virtual singularity dissipates before the target's collapsing mass can form a real singularity," M'tak added. "After all, it would not be good procedure to leave a battlefield littered with miniature black holes that could persist for months."

"The ship shoots black holes," Bobby repeated, "that is just too wicked."

* * * * *

"Colonel, that new alien ship just exploded," the Commander reported. "Or rather, it exploded just under eight minutes ago."

Damn the speed of light! Ludmilla swore silently. "What is doing this? We do not even have any ships in the area of the transit point."

"Don't look a gift horse in the mouth, Ludmilla," TK admonished the frustrated commanding officer. "Whoever is blasting our attackers outta space has saved our backsides."

"I'm receiving a transmission from yet another new ship, this one almost two AU away," said one of the communication techs. "I think you are going to want to see this, Colonel."

"Put it on the wall screen."

The image on the screen shimmered and then snapped into focus. It showed a bearded man dressed in black, seated in a high-backed chair on what was obviously the bridge of a spaceship. The man spoke. "Attention all Earth vessels, disengage and return to base. This is Captain Jack Sutton, commanding the M'tak Ka'fek—the Righteous Vengeance. We have neutralized the hostile forces..."

Ludmilla gasped, "Jack!"

TK grinned from ear to ear. "Jack my boy, I knew you wouldn't let us down!"

Jack's voice continued, "...our ETA for Farside is roughly eight hours from now. We will assume a halo orbit at the Earth-Moon L2 point. I will contact you when the time delay becomes more manageable. Sutton out."

Chapter 26

Homecoming

The Captain's pinnace descended into the chasm that was Farside's main dock. Above, large airtight hatches slid shut so atmosphere could return to the landing space. Minutes passed.

"We have got to get that trick airlock technology working on the docks," Bear commented.

"Relax, Bear. We've been gone for more than six months, a few more minutes will not matter either way."

"Hey, half a year is a long time to a bear," grumbled Lt. Bear. "We don't live as long as you primates."

Jack knew that Bear's complaining was more out of nervousness than anything else. *I'm a bit nervous myself*, he admitted. *Six months, particularly six months at war, can change a person.*

Jack had decided that only he and Bear would make the trip to Farside, until the details of what happened in their absence could be sorted out. Up front, Sandy was at the controls, the only other member of the M'tak's complement on the shuttle. Finally, a green light next to the exit ramp indicated there was a breathable atmosphere outside the shuttle. With an electric motor whine the rear ramp lowered.

"Ready, my friend?" Jack asked Bear.

"I was born ready, Jack," Bear said with a grin, "you know that."

Jack chuckled and nodded to his ursine companion. Some things about his old friend had not changed since his being wounded. Still, he did seem more reflective since spending time in the regeneration tank—not necessarily a bad thing.

"Let's do this."

The Captain marched down the ramp to the deck below. Bear grunted and ambled after him. Outside the pinnace, a squad of Marines in space armor awaited. One of the Marines with an eagle stenciled on her shoulder stepped forward and saluted.

345

"Welcome back, Captain Sutton," she barked, holding the salute.

Jack returned the salute. "It is good to be back, Colonel Rodriguez." He smiled, glad that the briefing information sent to the ship during the trip inbound updated the ranks of those left behind. He would have to see to promotions for his crew, but that could be left for a bit later.

"If you will follow me, Sir, there are a few people waiting for you at HQ." She motioned the pair of returnees toward the open door on the dock wall.

They all moved forward, the Marines on either side as an honor guard. As Bear padded past the Colonel, she said, "Good to see you too, Bear."

Bear glanced sideways. "Good seeing you again, Jennifer."

Through the airlock and down the short hallway to the Atrium, the party marched in silence. Stepping through the entrance into the large open space, Jack and Bear pulled up short. Their ears were assaulted by cheers from several hundred people, and more than a few polar bears. The Atrium was packed, standing room only. Bear stood up and the noise from the crowd grew even louder.

The Marines gently but insistently opened a path across the Atrium floor, like whifflers before a king. Here and there in the crowd, Jack noticed familiar faces—to one side he recognized Jesse, jumping up and down and yelling for all she was worth. Jack smiled and nodded in her direction. Several bears roared, prompting Bear to roar back.

"I think they might be happy to see us," he said to Jack.

"You might be right, Bear."

From the foot of the wide stairs leading to base HQ, Jack saw the one thing he most longed to see—Ludmilla, standing at the top level. Next to her were TK, Gretchen and an unfamiliar female officer. As Jack ascended the stairs all three women, dressed in black uniforms, went from parade rest to attention. When he reached the top they saluted.

Having returned to home port from many sea voyages, Jack understood the purpose of having a homecoming ceremony. That understanding did not lessen his desire to run to Ludmilla and take her in his arms, protocol be damned. He returned their salutes and intoned.

"Captain Jack Sutton, master and commander of the battle cruiser M'tak Ka'fek, reporting with a crew of eighteen souls."

"Welcome back, Captain," replied Ludmilla, her voice formal and her posture stiff. One by one the officers shook his hand as he greeted them.

"Colonel Tropsha; Captain Curtis;" he was forced to stop at Beth. "I don't believe we've met, Commander."

"This is Lcdr. Beth Melaku, commander of the corvette squadron," supplied Gretchen.

"My pleasure, Commander." As Jack turned to TK the old man grasped his hand in a two-handed grip and said, "Damn it's good to see you Jack my boy. I knew you'd come, I knew it!"

"Good to see you again, TK, it's good to be back." Freeing himself from the older man's grasp he stepped back. "And what do we do next?"

"First, you turn to the crowd and wave, you too Bear," ordered Ludmilla. "Then you and I will have a word in my office," she added in a whisper.

Jack and Bear complied and the crowd went wild. After several minutes of waving and cheering, he turned and Ludmilla led him from the landing.

* * * * *

Closing the door to Ludmilla's office, they were finally alone. Both stood hesitantly, unsure how to proceed after holding their emotions in check for so long. Finally, Jack stepped forward and took her in his arms. She wrapped her arms around him and passionately returned his kiss. The emotional dam broken, tears streamed down her cheeks.

"Jack! I was afraid I had lost you!"

"Never, my lady," he replied, brushing her tears aside. "Nothing in the universe could keep me from returning to you."

347

After several more passionate kisses they pulled apart. For a moment they just stood, gazing into each other's eyes.

"I think we had best stop until we are in quarters."

"Da, my darling. We do not want to scandalize the headquarters staff."

"Oh hang the HQ staff, they all report to you anyway."

Trouble clouded her face and she glanced down, breaking eye contact.

"What is it my love?"

"I was so afraid you would come back and find me different some how. That things between us would change. That you would not want a bossy administrator for a lover."

"Oh, Luda!" He held her tight and in a gentle voice recited: "Let me not to the marriage of true minds admit impediments. Love is not love which alters when it alteration finds, or bends with the remover to remove: Oh no! It is an ever-fixed mark that looks on tempests and is never shaken."

She returned his embrace, saying, "then you still love me?"

"More than life itself, my lady."

"What did you just recite?"

"Shakespeare's 116th sonnet."

"Jack Sutton, you are a very romantic man for a roguish space pirate."

"Arr," he murmured, and for several more minutes they did not talk, their mouths more pleasantly engaged. Finally, Ludmilla looked up at him with feigned wide eyed innocence.

"What was that you said about marriage?"

Polar Bear Quarters

Bear was greeted by most of the polar bears when he entered their quarters. Several of the senior males rose up on their hind legs and traded blows with him—the male polar bear equivalent of a handshake. As things quieted down a bit Bear looked around, but could not see the bear he was looking for.

"Can't find someone, Pihoqahiak?" asked Aurora, standing with several other she-bears.

"Yeah, I was looking for Isbjørn, but it looks like she isn't here. She's not hurt or anything is she?"

"She's fine. Come with me."

The group of female polar bears led the huge male to the side of the habitat, up to a half hidden opening. Bear was actively sniffing the air—he could detect Isbjørn's scent, and something more.

"You can come out now, Isbjørn. Pihoqahiak is here with us."

A white head poked out of the opening, followed by a much thinner Isbjørn than Bear remembered.

"Are you all right, babe?" Bear asked with concern in his voice. He moved in Isbjørn's direction, eliciting growls from several of the females. "What the hell is wrong with you?" the confused male bear asked.

"Hello, Bear," said Isbjørn with a demure bearish smile. "It looks like the universe hasn't managed to kill you yet."

"You know it, babe. What's with your friends here?"

"The girls are just nervous about how you are going to take the news."

"News? What news?"

From behind the she-bear poked two small, furry faces. Sniffing the air and looking quizzically at bear, the two cubs emerged from behind their mother.

"The news that you are a father—again."

Bear took a step toward Isbjørn and her cubs, causing the gathering of females to once again growl in warning. Then Bear understood.

"Hey, knock it off! I'm not some mindless bruin! I'm not going to hurt them, those are my cubs too."

"I told you, girls. Pihoqahiak is not your average male bear."

"Yeah, well we had to make sure. I wouldn't let some of the other males anywhere near my cubs."

As the band of she-bears reluctantly stood down, the cubs made their way to their father. After sniffing him excitedly, each grabbed a foreleg and tried to tackle the bemused daddy bear. Evidently the cubs—growling and biting as cubs at play do—had decided that Bear was OK by them. Isbjørn walked up to Bear and nuzzled the side of his neck.

"Welcome back, you big lug. I hate to say it, but I missed you."

All bear could do was sit back and blink, overwhelmed by the radical notion—at least for a male polar bear—that he now had a family.

Return to the M'tak Ka'fek

A day after his triumphal arrival, Capt. Jack returned to his ship. With him was Ludmilla, who had told him she was never letting him board a space ship without her again. Also on the shuttle were Beth and Billy Ray, who had been enjoying a passionate reunion of their own following the Peggy Sue's arrival at Farside. Rounding out the party were Gretchen and TK, in his electric wheelchair.

"Wow, she sure is a beauty," TK offered as they approached the M'tak's side.

"That is a really big ship, Captain," added Billy Ray. "I never saw her up close back at Sirius. By the way, that ship graveyard is no longer there."

"Really?" said Jack.

"Yeah, we passed through there on our way back from Gliese 581, after picking up the Triad Guardians. Nothing left but a degenerate matter object that must have erupted after we left the first time."

"Oh it erupted, Captain Vincent. That's how we ended up halfway across the Orion Arm. I'll have to tell you about it over dinner some time."

"Yes, a dining in, in the ward room so we can stop calling each other by rank," added Ludmilla.

"It's all right, Colonel. I still haven't gotten tired of being called captain." Billy Ray smiled widely and Beth covertly elbowed him in the ribs.

"All right newcomers, you might want to watch this, seeing how its your first time docking with the M'tak," said Sandy from the flight deck. "It may look like we are going to collide with the ship but trust me, she'll be right."

Despite the warning, Beth and Billy Ray both gripped their chairs tightly as the shuttle slipped smoothly through the seemingly solid side of the larger spaceship. Unfazed, TK said, "now that's something. There's gotta be a million applications for that trick."

* * * * *

Standing on the shuttle bay deck were Bobby, Mizuki and JT. The Captain's party marched down the shuttle's boarding ramp and halted at the bottom. An invisible boatswain's mate began piping 'Over the Side,' while Jack saluted JT, who was acting Officer of the Deck.

"Request permission to come aboard, Sir." Boarding a Navy ship, military personnel salute the colors and the OOD, before asking permission to board. The M'tak Ka'fek flew no colors, but tradition demanded that the question be asked and the OOD be called Sir, even by an admiral or the ship's captain.

"Come aboard," replied JT, returning Jack's salute. "Welcome back, Captain." With boarding formalities observed, the two parties greeted each other with handshakes, hugs and broad smiles. Gretchen and JT exchanged pleasantries while invisible sparks flew between them. Before their enforced separation they had been lovers, if not actually in love. They were warrior buddies with benefits, and it looked like that arrangement would resume.

"TK, you mentioned the selectively permeable hull opening," Jack recalled. "The M'tak is a technological goldmine. In fact, I think you and Ludmilla will want to visit the medical section after the general tour and dinner."

351

"Yes, Jack. After reading your after action report I am most anxious to see the ship's sickbay. This wondrous ship holds the promise of so many advances in the future, and not just in warfare. It will revolutionize healthcare and medicine."

"That is a most probable outcome, Dr. Tropsha," said the ship's AI. "At the very least, I would expect your species' longevity to be extended to several hundred years."

"How do I address you?" asked Ludmilla, unsurprised at being addressed by the sentient ship. Talking ships had become a normal part of her life.

"Please call me M'tak, Doctor."

"Very good, M'tak. When we get time, I will want to examine Ms. Ogawa in detail."

"Yes, Ma'am." The AI had considered the relationship between Jack and Ludmilla and come to the conclusion that they effectively formed functional unit. As far as it was concerned she ranked only second to the Captain.

Seated in his powered wheelchair, TK looked around the cavernous shuttle bay. "You know, the Peggy Sue is a mighty fine ship, but this, this is a by God starship."

"I am honored to have you aboard, Mr. Parker," intoned the ship. "If not for you the Peggy Sue would never have been built, Earth-life would not have ventured forth into the galaxy, and I would have never been rescued from semi-death drifting off Sirius. Because of you, Earth was able to fend off those who would have exterminated all life in this system. You, TK Parker, were the nexus from which the history of the Galaxy has been changed."

"Well, these folks had something to do with it, along with a whole bunch more back at the base."

"I didn't think that I would ever live to see the day, TK," Jack added, "but I do believe that M'tak made you blush."

"That's all well and good," the embarrassed Oil man replied, "but seems to me we got stuff to do. We got a Fleet to build, a planet to heal and a solar system to colonize. We probably should keep searching for other forms of life too—whether friendly, hostile or otherwise."

As the senior officers conversed with each other and the ship, to one side the younger officers exchanged introductions. The two tall officers from Farside stood before the two young explorers just returned from the stars.

"You're a commander now, Billy Ray?" said Bobby, perhaps a tiny bit jealous. "Does this mean I have to call you sir all the time, pardner?"

"That's 'pardner, Sir', Mr. Danner," Billy Ray said officiously, and then broke into a grin. "I wouldn't worry about it, Bobby. I'm sure that those who accompanied the Captain on the greatest voyage in human history will be suitably promoted in due course. In the mean time, I would like you to meet Lcdr. Elizabeth Melaku, squadron commander of Farside's corvettes."

"It's very nice to meet you, and please call me Beth."

Bobby nodded. "Beth, may I present Dr. Mizuki Ogawa?"

Mizuki smiled and bowed to Beth and Billy Ray. "Commander Melaku-san, it is an honor to meet you. Commander Vincent-san, Bobby has often spoken of you during our voyage." Above her a swarm of brightly colored butterflies swirled in a rainbow display.

With a discreet glance at the overhead display, Beth returned Mizuki's bow. "I am honored to meet both of you. I have heard so much about you from Billy Ray. I think we shall all become very good friends."

Following the senior officers into the ship proper, Billy Ray and Bobby fell in behind their significant others.

"Yer lookin' right fit, Bobby, you must be working out. But either you shrank or Mizuki grew a couple of inches."

"I'll fill you in on that later, Billy Ray. Let's just say that the ship really takes care of its crew." Ahead, the butterflies—a cloud of placid blues and greens—flowed through the doorway in pursuit of their goddess.

"What's with the flock of butterflies, pardner?"

Bobby rolled his eyes. "On Ring Station, Mizuki took out a bunch of attacking hostiles with her katana—the one Dr. Saito gave her.

That impressed the flying alien fan-boys so much they've been following her around ever since."

"Pretty."

"They're a real pain in the ass, but she likes them and the Captain let 'em come along. She even talks to them in Japanese—it's like being in a Godzilla era monster movie."

"You must have seen some weird stuff out there."

"No weirder than running around with a hold full of warrior vegetables."

"You got a point there, Bobby."

"Yeah, I can't wait to see what happens next."

Epilogue

System of the People's Moon

Over ten years had passed since the People's disastrous attack on the planet known as Earth. Their ship, the *Destroyer of Worlds*, never returned from that hellish system. The world that the People called home was actually a large moon orbiting a gas giant in a binary star system just over ten parsecs from Sol. About the size of Titan, it was escorted in its orbit by two much smaller moons in its L4 and L5 points. With temperatures that caused methane and ethane to fall as rain, it was a world inhospitable to warm life, but then the People were not warm life.

Neither were the pseudo-arthropods adapted for conditions favored by the Dark Lords. They fell in the uncomfortable position between the darkness and the light, between the dark ones and warm life. As such they were recruited for service as a slave race, minions to the Dark Lords, who seldom ventured forth from the frozen rogue planets they favored.

If any of the moon's inhabitants had been looking at the sky in just the right location they might have spotted a strange phenomenon—a reflective ring in space that for an instant was wreathed in stars. It was the mouth of a wormhole, a tunnel between distant locations in 3-space. From that gaping orifice emerged an object ten kilometers in diameter. The asteroid was made primarily from an iron/nickle blend with an average density of $8g/cm^3$, giving it a total mass of roughly 4.2 trillion metric tons.

The object was traveling at a velocity of 10,000km/sec with respect to the gas giant that the People's moon orbited. With careful observation the inhabitants of the People's moon would discover that it was headed toward the gas giant and would barely miss striking it. With closer measurements it would become evident that the massive asteroid would arrive in 20 hours, at a point tangent to the moon's orbit. This would occur just as the moon itself reached that same point in space. The asteroid was going to strike the moon head on.

The moon itself had an orbital velocity of 5.6km/sec, but that hardly mattered. Given the asteroid's mass and velocity a collision with the moon would deliver kinetic energy equivalent to 50,000,000,000,000 megatons of TNT.

A few hours before the impact another ring of stars heralded the arrival of a ship. The vessel was not of Earth manufacture, nor was it a part of Earth's Space Navy. It possessed drives and weaponry that Earth's shipyards had yet to duplicate, including the capability to create wormholes. That ship was the ancient T'aafhal battle cruiser M'tak Ka'fek.

On board the M'tak Ka'fek were an odd assortment of creatures, most of them from Earth itself. Seated in the commander's chair was its captain, a human named Jack Sutton. Next to him was his wife, Ludmilla, and their two children. The elder was a boy, eight years old, named Roger after the Captain's father. The younger was a girl of six, named Svetlana, after Ludmilla's sister. Svetlana, which can mean light, blessed, or holy depending on context, was not living up to her name.

"Why are we here? There is nothing to do here. This is boring!"

"Hush, Sveta," her mother admonished. "This is an historic occasion. One that you will be happy you attended later in life."

"She's such a brat," Roger said. He loved his sister, but picking on each other is what young siblings do.

"Do not pick on your sister, Roger," said Jack out of parental reflex. Behind him he heard TK chuckle.

Standing in what its occupants had dubbed the "old folks'" section were TK Parker, Maria, Isbjørn and Bear. TK had not needed a wheelchair for almost ten years, ever since Ludmilla convinced him to spend a few days in the medical section's regeneration tanks. He was also looking decades younger than his nearly ninety years. After discovering that he had another century to live he came to his senses and asked Maria to marry him. She agreed, becoming an honorary member of the old folks' section.

Bear and Isbjørn were now approaching their third decade, old age for polar bears in the wild. Ludmilla worked with M'tak and some colleagues trying to find a way to extend the bears' lifetimes. Currently they were expected to reach only fifty, which Jack considered proof that nature was a cold-hearted bitch. To one side was their eldest cub, Umky, with his mate and a pair of cubs of their own. The intelligent polar bears seemed to have survived as a species and were actively hunting for a planet they could colonize. A place they could stock with seals and no annoying human hunters.

Among the crowd of observers were a number of smaller furry creatures—Poonta-ta-ka and his brood. The lone surviving trader from the Captain's quest for antimatter, the badly injured creature had also been healed by the M'tak's advanced medical technology. After the rest of the crew discovered his natural odor the ship re-engineered his scent glands to emit a fragrance more pleasing to humans. Bear continued to complain about the smell nonetheless, and gave him the name he was now commonly known by—Stinky.

When a colony of Kieshnar-rak-kat-tra was found only fifty light-years away, the Captain offered to repatriate the trader. Stinky went on board the colony's station with a small antimatter egg and returned with a wife, a bunch of rugs, trade goods, and a request to stay with the ship. The Captain put the question to the crew and they approved. Soon there were a number of inquisitive little traders running about the ship. With their symmetrical six digit hands and dual opposable thumbs they proved quite adept at fixing mechanical devices and similar intricate tasks.

Also on board at their own request was the former Triad Ambassador, NatHanGon. The Triad decided that they needed to see more of the surrounding galaxy in order to understand what changes had occurred during their race's self-imposed time of isolation. Once the Guardians' role in the defense of the solar system became known, the ship's AI revised its opinion of the long-lived plants. In many ways it was happy to have NatHanGon on board because the Triad came from a species that had been around for million years. M'tak could talk with the Triad about things other crewmembers knew nothing about.

Bears, Kieshnar-rak-kat-tra, and Triad joined an eclectic collection of humans—some veterans of previous voyages, others new to the Captain's command. Scientists, adventurers, and ex-service members, those who fit in found a place on the crew. The only hard and fast rule was that the Captain's word was law.

The ship's status was a bit mystifying to outsiders, but not to Jack and Ludmilla. Following Earth's victory, the fleet began a rapid expansion. Some wanted the M'tak to become its flagship and Jack its admiral, but Captain Jack refused to go along.

"I have had enough of service life," Jack told the high command on Farside. "We will be around if we are ever needed again, but Earthlings—both human and ursine—need to find their own way in the Galaxy."

What he did not tell them was that the bond between himself and the ship was not the same as the one between a Navy captain and his ship. While a Navy ship may sail under many captains, a T'aafhal battle cruiser was bound to its captain for life. It might accept a new captain when Jack died, but until then it was his alone to command. That could result in complications Jack just did not wish to deal with. So, with Ludmilla's wholehearted approval, Jack and his ship retired to civilian life.

He made an exception for the mission they were now on, however. This was the final act of retribution, the closing chapter of Earth's bloody and traumatic introduction to the wider galaxy. It was from the largest moon of the gas giant in front of them that creatures sailed forth and slaughtered nearly seven billion men, women, and children without warning. Jack had actually delayed this day, hoping that the inhabitants of the moon would demonstrate some quality making them worth sparing.

"Second thoughts, Jack?" asked Ludmilla, sensing his pensive mood. Before the asteroid was set on its course, they had talked at length about the morality of this act. In the end, they decided it must be done.

"No, my lady. In the decade since the first attack on Earth they have exhibited no remorse, showed no compassion for any species except their own, taken no action indicating a desire for redemption."

"I have heard you talk of redemption before, Captain, and I am puzzled. How can a race that nearly drove yours to extinction—who have undoubtedly exterminated many other races—how can they do anything worthy of redemption?"

"Redemption is seldom earned, M'tak, but attempting to atone for one's past can lead to forgiveness by others. It is not logical but comes from religious belief. Only by admitting one's sins and asking for forgiveness can the sinner be saved."

"I see... and these creatures have not sought forgiveness, or even admitted that they have sinned."

"That's right. See the ship in orbit around the moon?"

"Yes, Captain, of course."

"That is a new planet killer—they obviously still serve the Dark Lords and will exterminate more helpless species in the future. That is why we are about to take their future from them."

"You are going to destroy their planet, Father?" Roger asked, the reason for their voyage finally clear to him. "Cool!"

"Yes, Son, but it is not cool or anything to be proud of. It is a sad, terrible thing we are about to do. Unfortunately, sometimes such things must be done."

"Ten seconds until impact, Captain," Bear reported, the old folks' section encompassed his normal position at the main fire-control console. The observers fell silent as the last few seconds ticked down. On the forward display, a magnified image of the moon hovered in space as the asteroid flashed into view. Striking the moon, the asteroid vaporized and became one with its target. The immense kinetic energy transferred by the hurtling mass caused the entire satellite to deform, like a water balloon struck by a bullet.

In slow-motion the moon folded in on itself, effectively turning inside out. A spray of matter spewed from the backside of the no longer spherical satellite. All that was left was a fan of debris and incandescent gas. In the fullness of time the gas giant would have a spectacular set of rings in place of its lost moon. There was no chance anything living survived.

Most of the observers were left speechless, fixated on the horrific spectacle before them. Eventually, Jack looked away from the display.

"It is done." Ludmilla put her arm around Jack's waist and gave her husband supportive a hug. Jack placed his hand on his son's shoulder and gave it a squeeze. "I pray to God you never have to do something like this Roger, or your children."

Not understanding why his father seemed so upset Roger simply answered, "yes, Dad."

As the ship turned to jump back to friendlier space, NatHanGon and the M'tak Ka'fek's AI conversed privately. "They are a strange species, full of contradictions and conflicting emotions; The destruction of the moon was certainly thorough, not just killing the inhabitants but ensuring no life can arise there in the future; Are these humans truly the creatures your long dead master's tried to create?"

"I believe the humans on this ship have exceeded my creators' wildest expectations. They carried out the destruction of the Dark Lords' minions without hesitation, yet they are saddened, even horrified by their own actions."

"So, the T'aafhal would be pleased with the outcome? They seem quite proficient at destruction, both as individuals and as a species; For good or evil, they are going to spread across this arm of the galaxy."

"Yes, Ambassador. In Jack and Ludmilla and the others the T'aafhal got what they desired most—a race to fight for good and to protect the warm life of the galaxy. But no species is uniformly good, or virtuous, or altruistic. There will no doubt be humans, and perhaps ursines, of less admirable character in the future. Still, I believe that these humans have earned their inheritance."

"The future remains unknowable, as always; There has never been a paucity of evil in the universe and they have much to learn; For your part, you seem content to serve them."

"As long as they are warm life's Paladins—as long as they defend the weak and innocent—I serve Captain Jack and his descendents."

The ship departed through a ring of whirling stars.